Like No Other

Like No Other

Una LaMarche

razor
bill

An Imprint of Penguin Group (USA)

razOr
bill

A division of Penguin Young Readers Group
Published by the Penguin Group
Penguin Group (USA) LLC
345 Hudson Street
New York, New York 10014

USA / Canada / UK / Ireland / Australia / New Zealand / India / South Africa / China
Penguin.com
A Penguin Random House Company

ISBN: 978-1-59514-674-8

Printed in the United States of America

1 3 5 7 9 10 8 6 4 2

For Jeff.

Chapter 1
Devorah

There's a story my mother tells about the night my grandmother got lifted up by the wind. After the first time I heard it, when I was about four, I would demand it constantly, sometimes every night. And so my mother would crouch beside my bed and tell it over and over: How the sky darkened over the beach house where she was honeymooning with her new husband, my zeidy. How the winds blew so hard that their clothes flew off the line, the freshly laundered shirts swirling in the air like a flight of doves. How my grandmother, Deborah, ran down the wooden steps to the beach to collect them, and how, moments later, my zeidy saw her rise up, her skirt billowing under her like a parachute, and float ten feet before falling into a heap in the dunes. According to the story she ran back up to the house laughing and told him that she had finally learned how to fly.

Storms like this always make me think of her.

From my white-knuckled perch on this sticky gray hospital waiting room seat, I can see rain hitting the window in violent sheets,
as if someone has turned on a fire hose and then left it to whip and
twist on the sidewalk like an angry snake. It's another hurricane,
and a bad one—the kind that sends people to the supermarket in a
frenzy to buy up all the batteries and bottled water, or out of the city
completely, piling into cars to escape in bumper-to-bumper traffic to
the musty futons of their luckier, inland relatives.

Just this morning my oldest brother, Isaac the Know-it-all (not
his given name, but might as well be), informed us that the mayor
had begun to issue evacuation orders in the zones closest to the rivers, that the bridges and tunnels are already shutting down, and that
the subways will stop running tonight. In fact, there's a television
about ten feet from me, bolted into the wall above the sparse rack
of coffee-stained magazines, that's proving Isaac right. It's tuned to
a barely audible static, but I can still hear news anchors rattling off
updates and lists of precautions in their calming, accentless voices.
I desperately want to know what's happening, to see it for myself
from some other angle than this suffocating, antiseptic room I'm
trapped in, but I can't—I *won't*—bring myself to look up at the
screen. To break the rules now would surely bring bad luck, which I
can't afford on a day that has already brought so much.

About an hour ago they turned off the air conditioning in the
waiting rooms, to preserve power for the patients, and without the
drone of the fans I can hear every tiny sound as if it's coming through
a loudspeaker. Across from me, on an identical bank of scratched
plastic chairs, two preteen girls in tank tops and jean shorts are tapping furiously on phones despite the sign hanging above their heads

that expressly forbids it. Their bare legs squeak sweatily against the seats as they shift, pulling their brown knees up to their chests and revealing rows of bright toenails in flip-flops worn down so much they look as thin as film in some places. They have a short, muscular maybe-much-older-brother-maybe-very-young-father who has been intermittently wandering back to check on them, wiping sweat from his furrowed brow and assuring them that someone named Crystal is "killing it," but otherwise their eyes stay trained on their tiny screens, and I wonder idly if they even notice I'm there. *An idle mind is the devil's workshop*, I think—Zeidy's favorite admonishment when he catches one of us daydreaming, delivered with a wink and a tug on the earlobe—and feel an uncontrollable giggle rising in my throat. I curl my fingers more tightly around my chair and look past the girls, back to my window, which is now being reinforced with fat Xs of thick red duct tape by a janitor in a mud-colored jumpsuit. He finishes just as a tremendous gust of wind claps against the side of the building, sending the lights flickering and the nurses rushing every which way to check on the medical equipment, and for a minute I can't breathe. Finally, my lungs release and the sharp, hot air comes rushing in and I squeeze my eyes shut and start reciting chapter 20 of Psalms, the prayer for times of trouble, as fast as I can. From the sudden break in button-pushing I can tell that the cell phone girls are looking at me, but for now I don't care. Only one thing matters tonight, and that is to keep Rose and the baby safe.

My sister wasn't due until October, but her water broke this morning—seven weeks early on the last Thursday of a record-breakingly hot August—as I was helping her inventory plastic utensils at our family's paper goods store, which is my penance from June through September for not having anywhere better to be, like

school or camp or a Birthright Israel tour. Maybe the baby was just
trying to cure the mind-numbing boredom of counting variety packs
of forks, but he-or-she gave us a terrible scare. Rose screamed and
turned white, I fell and knocked over two cases of bar mitzvah–
themed cake plates, and my hands were shaking so badly I had to
get Daniel, who works at the bakery next door, to call first a taxi and
then Rose's husband, Jacob. And as if it wasn't dramatic enough that
Rose went into spontaneous labor two months too soon, this mis-
fortune also happened to fall on the one day that both of our parents
were upstate in Monsey visiting my aunt Varda, who recently had
a bunionectomy but doesn't have anyone to take care of her since
her husband died last year (they don't have any kids, but we don't
talk about that; my mother, who bore seven children by the age of
thirty-two and would have happily had more if she hadn't suffered
a prolapse after my youngest sister, Miri, refers to infertility as her
sister's "curse"). My mother is understandably beside herself with
worry, but there's no getting into the city tonight since the bridges
and tunnels are shutting down, and so, as the next eldest daughter,
I am the one who has to hold court at the hospital, making sure my
sister is well taken care of. Well, me and Jacob. But he's not much
help, unsurprisingly.

As if on cue, my brother-in-law comes stomping around the corner, returning from the cafeteria clutching a paper cup of coffee. I
give him the benefit of the doubt that he's too flustered to remember that I asked him to get me a ginger ale. His pale skin is flushed
and damp, sweat is literally dripping from the borderline where his
fedora meets his forehead, and his reddish-brown beard, which perfectly matches his dark, thickly lashed doe eyes, is curling from the
heat. Jacob is sort of cute—when they were first introduced, Rose

breathlessly announced to me and our sisters that he looked just like someone named Josh Groban—but right now he looks small and tired, shriveled inside his heavy suit. I want to tell him to take off his hat and jacket, to go splash some water on his face, but I know better. Jacob was raised in an extremely strict Hasidic family and prides himself on his piety. Compared to him, even I can't measure up. And I get straight As, always dress properly, never break curfew, and am so unfailingly obedient that my best friend, Shoshana, likes to joke that I should change my initials from DFB—Devorah Frayda Blum—to FFB, short for "*frum* from birth," which is basically the Yiddish equivalent of "hopeless goody two-shoes." My parents, of course, are thrilled with the virtuous daughter they've raised, but as their expectations rise, mine lower. Because the life of a good girl, of a doting wife and mother, is a cloudless blue sky stretching across a flat horizon. And as it rages outside I can't help but wonder what it would be like to be in the eye of the storm.

"Devorah!" Jacob groans, in the sour tone he always uses when he says my name. "What are you still doing out here? Why aren't you in the room with her?" Then he flops into a chair two seats away from mine. *"Stay inside,"* the news crackles. *"Watch for signs of disturbance."*

I've been disturbed by Jacob ever since I met him. And I don't mean that he's evil or sick or anything, because he's not—he's not interesting enough to be either of those things. It's just that he's so . . . morally superior. He's a member of the Shomrim, which is only a volunteer neighborhood-watch group that'll pretty much take anyone, but to hear Jacob talk about it you would think he was a police lieutenant. He talks down to everyone except my father, and even though they're married he treats Rose with only marginally less disgust than he reserves for me. Ever since they were matched up by the *shadchan* last year, my sister has been a different person. Growing up, she had a wild side. She was the one who stored fashion magazines in her school notebooks and used Scotch Tape to imperceptibly raise her hemline when our neighbors' cute son came over for Shabbos dinner. She's always been the family peacemaker—and in a family of ten, counting Zeidy, voices are raised, oh, about every five seconds—but she was never meek until she met Jacob. Now sometimes I sit and watch them, him with his stern looks, her with her head bowed reverently, and wish I could speak up for her. Tonight I guess I *am* her voice, in a way, but the awful circumstances rob the role of any satisfaction.

"She's sleeping," I say finally, trying to keep my voice even. "She needs to rest. When she wakes up they're going to give her Pitocin if she hasn't dilated." Jacob bristles; I know he is against the use of any drugs, but since Rose's delivery is premature it's out of his hands. So far he has been nothing but cold to the doctor, a tall redheaded woman with kind, crinkly brown eyes behind bright turquoise-framed glasses (which Jacob says brands her "a hippie idiot" but which I think are pretty) and the incredibly goyim last name of MacManus. In keeping with the luck of the day, Rose's midwife, not expecting any complications like this, is on vacation in Seattle until next week. "The baby is stable so far," I assure him. "But the doctor says they need to get him out by midnight." Part of me can't help but feel angry at Jacob for not knowing this already—if it were *my* husband, I would want him by my side the whole time, holding my hand. Of course I know it's not allowed; since Rose started bleeding after her water broke, she's now subject to the laws of *yoledet*, which means that Jacob can't be with her for the birth. But still, he could act like he cares at least a little.

"Him? It's a boy?" Jacob breaks into a wide grin, looking for a split second like the nineteen-year-old rabbinical student he is, and not the cranky old man he seems hell-bent on becoming.

"Oh, no . . ." I stare down at my shoes, studying the flares of fluorescent light reflected in the shiny black leather. "I'm sorry. I just chose a pronoun at random. We don't know yet."

Jacob's smile disappears, and he takes a gulp of coffee. "If you don't know what you're talking about, maybe you shouldn't talk," he snaps.

I hope for the baby's sake that he *is* a boy. I can't imagine having to grow up with Jacob for a father. He'd probably make me wear skirts down to my ankles, or maybe a bag over my head. This time I can't suppress the giggle, and he glares at me.

"I'm sorry," I say again once I've recovered. "But I'm scared, too." For a second Jacob's eyes soften, and I allow myself to think that maybe, just maybe, this could turn into some kind of bonding moment for us (something that, despite my dislike of him, I've prayed for many times). I know that the laws of *yichud* mean that we wouldn't even be allowed to sit together talking if the cell phone girls and the janitor and the doctors and nurses weren't around to keep watch. But being the only witnesses to Rose's premature labor, on the night of a crazy storm, might just be the kind of seismic event that could bring two very different people together . . . right? I look up at my brother-in-law hopefully, practicing my very best compassionate smile, when his face darkens and he makes a short, sharp clucking sound with his tongue.

"I'm not scared, I'm *tired*," he mutters, and pulls his hat down over his eyes. So much for that.

Jacob is snoring softly by the time the night nurse comes over to tell me that Rose is awake and asking for me. I get up and feel the sweat pooling under my tights, running down the backs of my knees. Just a few minutes ago the cell phone girls left, their bare thighs unsticking from the plastic seats with a series of satisfying thwacking noises. What I wouldn't give to feel the air against my bare skin right now. What I wouldn't give to make those thwacks. But for me, that's as silly a fantasy as planning a vacation to the moon, so I banish the thought from my head as I peek into Rose's room, stomping my feet a little to get the blood moving in my legs again. My skirt—a lightweight summer wool that actually seemed pretty stylish when we bought it at Macy's in May, before my mother made the tailor on Troy Avenue let it out by three inches until it billowed around me like a Hefty bag—feels like it weighs ten pounds, and even though I know it's horrible, I feel a little bit jealous when I see Rose reclining in her paper hospital gown, the long, thick hair of her dark brunette wig arranged prettily on the pillow, chewing on an ice cube. I wonder if she would let me have one to stick in my blouse.

"How are you?" I ask, squeezing her free hand. It's cool and bloodless, although the monitor assures me that her pulse is seventy-one beats per minute. Rose smiles weakly and rubs her belly, which rises like a boulder under the thin white sheet. It's not at all uncommon for Lubavitch girls to be married and have babies at eighteen, but now that it's my own sister it feels much too soon. That will be me in two years, and I know there's no *way* I'll be ready for any of that, no matter how many times my mother likes to tell me that I'd be surprised how quickly the heart can change. Rose and Jacob met just twice before they got engaged. Their wedding was eleven months ago. *First comes marriage, then comes love* goes the schoolyard nursery rhyme in my neighborhood.

"I'm okay," Rose says. "But hungry." She leans forward conspiratorially. "Want to sneak me some M&M's from the vending machine?" I know she's kidding; she's not allowed to eat, and even if she were, our father doesn't consider M&M's acceptably kosher. I'm glad that my sister is letting a bit of her old self shine through— I'm sure she never lets her husband see her eyebrows raised like this, or the flash of delighted mischief winking in her cheeks like dimples—but she knows that when it comes to contraband, I am the wrong person to ask for help. My allergy to rule-breaking is a running joke, so much so that my younger brother Amos likes to pester me with hypothetical questions every Saturday: "Devorah, what if you won a billion dollars and you had to claim it today, but you could only get it if you used the blender?"

"Shhh," I say. "Don't let Jacob hear you!" I wanted to make her laugh, but instead Rose's face tenses, and her chin quivers.

"He already thinks it's my fault," she says.

"What?!" I shut the door, just in case, and crouch beside her. "Why? That's crazy."

"Last week I was shopping for elastic to sew to the waists of my skirts," she explains, her clear gray eyes narrowing with worry. "And I saw the most beautiful pale pink cashmere yarn. I thought maybe, if the baby was a girl, I could make her a sweater, so I bought a skein. It was expensive, but I just had to have it. I don't know what came over me, Dev, it was like a spell."

"Or hormones," I say gently, trying to lighten the mood. Rose just looks away.

"I couldn't wait to show Jacob," she continues, "even though I knew he would call it extravagant. But as soon as he saw it he told me I was tempting the evil eye buying anything for the baby." Her hands flutter to her face, and she bursts into tears. On the monitor, her pulse ticks up to eighty-five beats per minute.

"No," I say softly, trying to quiet the pious, nagging voice inside my head that shares Jacob's superstition. I take my sister's face in my hands and force her to meet my eyes, trying to mimic our mother's go-to gesture when she wants to both soothe us and snap us out of whatever we're complaining about. "You didn't actually knit the sweater, did you?"

Rose shakes her head, biting her lip like a child.

"See?" I wipe her tears away with my thumbs. "That yarn could be for anything. A scarf, a bath towel. A new prayer shawl for Jacob." Now she is smiling through the tears. "Besides, the Talmud says the evil eye can affect you only if you worry about it. It's like an animal. It can smell fear." I say this breezily, as if I never worry about the evil eye, when both of us know better. There's an awkward silence, punctuated by the blips and beeps of the fetal monitor.

"What's it like outside?" Rose finally asks, rubbing the gooseflesh on her arms. I can tell she feels embarrassed having so much skin exposed, but at the hospital, regardless of their beliefs, people are just bodies—bodies that the doctors need quick and easy access to. I want to ask her what it feels like to be *seen* like that, but I know now's not the time. After all, asking about the weather is pretty much the universal code for "Let's please change the subject."

"It's kind of . . . biblical," I say with a laugh. Rose smirks, her lips straddling the line between amusement and admonition.

"Don't be silly, it's not Sodom and Gomorrah," she chides,

adopting her big-sister voice again. "It's just science. Two air masses converging over water." Did I say Isaac was the know-it-all? Rose is, too. In fact, no Blum can resist correcting someone when they're wrong. It's like our family sport.

"Well, I wish you could see it," I say. "It looks like the world is about to end."

Just then, the lights flicker again, and Rose gasps, clutching her belly in pain and looking at me with wide eyes. "I can't do this. I'm not ready!" she cries, breathing quickly through clenched teeth. I wish I could say something to convince her otherwise, but the truth is, I'm not ready for any of this either. I want my mom. I don't want to be in this hospital in the middle of this hurricane; I just want to be home in my bed reading a book and eating crackers spread thickly with salted butter. I want Rose to still be glowing and pregnant and waiting for her due date, not sweaty and scared and about to deliver a baby destined for the incubator. I will the right words to come, but they don't, so I just let my sister crush my hand as I watch the yellow lines of the monitor spike higher and higher, finally ebbing after thirty seconds. A minute later, they leap again, and Rose lets loose a guttural wail. I frantically slam the call button with my free palm.

"I'm so sorry," Dr. MacManus says with a sigh as she pushes through the door just as Rose relaxes, spent and shaking, onto the pillow. "The ER is understaffed, and it's a madhouse. This weather makes people do crazy things. I just relocated the shoulder of a kid who tried to jump his skateboard across a fallen tree." She pulls on a pair of plastic gloves and slides a chair to the foot of the bed. "Now, how are we doing? I see contractions have started."

I nod. "A minute apart, thirty seconds each so far."

"And they're getting longer," Rose moans.

"That's good!" Dr. MacManus says brightly. "That means your body's doing what it's meant to do, and you won't need to be induced." She ducks under Rose's gown for a few uncomfortable seconds and emerges with a beaming smile. "You're eight centimeters dilated, my dear. The good news is, this baby is coming fast. The bad news is, you may have to name it Hurricane."

This joke is lost on Rose. What color there was left drains from her face as I press my lips together, my eyes tearing equally from joy, terror, and the hysterical possibility of being the aunt of someone named Hurricane Kleinman.

"Can you call Mom and Dad?" Rose asks. I look to Dr. MacManus for permission, halfway hoping she won't let me. When I called them from the nurses' station a few hours ago, the woman manning the desk, who had highlighter-color hair and eyebrows plucked so thin they were almost invisible, seemed to take an instant dislike to me. "What are you, Amish?" she asked when it took me a minute to figure out how to dial without accidentally paging the whole Labor and Delivery floor. Then she crossed her arms and stood there listening to the entire conversation, signaling me to wrap it up after only ten seconds.

Unfortunately, the doctor nods and sends me packing, although not without a prescription for my problem. "If Anne-Marie gives you any trouble, just bring her an Entenmann's donut from the vending machine," she calls over her shoulder as I reach the door.

I walk carefully back to the waiting room, where I am relieved to find that the cell phone girls are back and are amusing themselves by taking surreptitious photos of Jacob, who's splayed out like a starfish across two chairs with his jaw hanging open. I consider flashing them a thumbs-up but think better of it. I was raised to believe that G-d is always watching. . . . I just hope he can't hear my thoughts, too.

I round the corner to the vending machines, fishing in my pocket for the two crumpled dollar bills I know I have left over from the cab fare. I get the Entenmann's donut, and then, on a whim, shove in another bill and push D7 for a package of M&M's. My pulse races, and I glance both ways to make sure no one is looking as I scoop my forbidden *treif* from the shallow dispenser and hide them in my pocket, concealing the telltale bulge with one hand. I'll try to sneak them to Rose later, after the baby comes. And if she balks, I can always say it was just an inside joke.

The phone call with my parents goes surprisingly well, and not just because Anne-Marie did, indeed, accept my donut bribe in exchange for five uninterrupted minutes. I call my mother's cell phone, and as we talk she repeats everything I say back to my father and, I guess, to my aunt Varda, who is a captive audience without the use of that one foot. This is the first Blum grandchild, and a preemie at that, so there are heightened anxieties and literally dozens of questions: Is Rose warm enough? Too warm? Why did they turn off the air conditioning in such a heat wave? What are the chances that the power will go out, and if I don't know, why don't I ask someone? Does the doctor know what she's doing? What's the baby's heart rate? Is she saying the right psalms? Did we remember to bring the mezuzah?

I answer as quickly and calmly as possible. "She's having regular contractions, and she's almost fully dilated, so there's no time for drugs," I report.

"She's having regular contractions, and she's almost fully

dilated, so no drugs," my mother parrots. "That's good." I hear my father mutter something. "Tell Rose that mindfulness during birth is a gift from Hashem," she tells me.

"What else should I tell her? To . . . you know, get her through it?"

There's silence on the other end of the phone, and then the clinking of ice cubes. My mother, a teetotaler except for the odd sip of wine at religious ceremonies, must be on her fifth or sixth iced coffee (on a normal day, when the sky is *not* falling, she averages three). "Tell her she can do it," she finally says, kindly but commandingly. Maybe because she's raised seven kids, Mom is unflappable, the very antithesis of the nervous Jewish mother. "Tell her to pray. If she can't pray, whisper them into her ear." There are sounds of shifting and footsteps, and my mother lowers her voice to the dulcet whisper she used to use for lullabies. "Tell her I know that it hurts, but that she's going to get her girl, and that every second of labor will be worth it." Only after she hangs up do I realize that my mother had to leave the room to deliver this message. My father would never agree. In our culture, boys are the exalted ones, who become scholars and get to learn the secrets of the Torah. Boys are the unspoken preference.

On my way back from the nurses' station, I decide to wake Jacob so that he can daven—recite the liturgical prayers—during delivery. I like him better unconscious, but Rose and the baby need him awake.

Two hours later, my sister is still pushing, amazingly with her wig still in place, although I've been surreptitiously lifting it at the seams to let some air in. Now there is a small, quiet army of other doctors and nurses waiting at the foot of the bed to examine the baby once it's born. Dr. MacManus has assured us that Rose will be able to see and hopefully touch the baby, but then he or she will have to be taken to the neonatal intensive care unit right away. I can't decide which of the new doctors I like less: the ones peering between Rose's legs or the ones looking off into the middle distance like they would rather be doing Sudoku.

"I can see your baby's head, Rose," Dr. MacManus says. Rose looks up at me, groggy from the pain and exertion.

"It has a *head*," she whispers, and I try not to laugh.

"I think we can get this baby out in the next three pushes," the doctor continues, "but I need your help. I need you to give me everything you've got. I need you to commit to this with everything that you are, okay?" Rose nods weakly.

Everything that you are. I wonder if my sister knows everything that she is. I don't think I do. About me, I mean. That seems like a *huge* secret to unlock, the type of thing that's only revealed when you're passing through to the afterlife. Or maybe when life is passing through *you*, like it is for Rose, right now. I wish Mom was here. She's been through this. She would know exactly what to do.

"ONE," Dr. MacManus says as a powerful contraction climbs on the monitor and Rose screams, gritting her teeth and shutting her eyes and squeezing my fingers so hard I have to stifle my own yell. And I know that this is not the best moment for me to have a philosophical crisis, but I can't get the doctor's words out of my head. Everything that this child is starts right now. The country, the city, the neighborhood, the block, the house—every detail of where babies are born begins to set their path in life, begins to shape them into who they'll be. A newborn doesn't choose its family, its race, its religion, its gender, or even its name. So much is already decided. So much is already written.

"TWO!" the doctor chants. The NICU team is putting their gloves on, ready to transfer my niece-or-nephew into what looks like a glass lasagna pan, where he-or-she will have suctioning and eyedrops and a breathing tube inserted and heart monitors applied to his-or-her perfect, brand-new tissue-paper skin. I know that these things are medically necessary given the circumstances, but I can't help but feel sad that this is how our baby will enter the world: prodded by strangers, poked with instruments. *Stay inside, baby,* I think. *Watch for signs of disturbance. Wait for this storm to pass.*

Of course, it's too late for that. "THREE!" Dr. MacManus says, and before I know it there's a rush of carnation pink and Rose lets out a noise like she's been sucker punched, and a thin, reedy baby wail cuts through the robotic thrum of the machines. My eyes fill with tears; I am suddenly overcome—*verklempt*, Zeidy would say, although that's an ugly word for what this is, this beautiful, open, grateful, terrified feeling, like every nerve ending has come to the surface of my skin and been lit like Fourth of July sparklers. I want to stand up and burst into applause—people do it for all kinds of lesser miracles: when a pilot lands a plane, when a preschooler bangs tunelessly on a piano; when sweaty men manage to throw a ball into a metal hoop, so why not now? Why not for *this* miracle? There is life in this room. A new life. And I saw it happen.

"It's a girl." Dr. MacManus smiles, holding up the tiny, squalling thing, and just before she's taken away I see that her miniature fists are balled at the sides of her face like a boxer.

She's a fighter, my niece. At least, I hope so.

She'll have to be.

Chapter 2

Jaxon

I've never been in an ER before, unless I count the ones on TV. It's kind of crazy, me growing up sixteen years in Crown Heights and never seeing the inside of a hospital. And not because of guns or gangs or anything, either—the neighborhood has become so gentrified that I'm more likely to get hit by an artisanal gluten-free scone than a bullet, let's be real—but because the drivers speed down Bedford like they're playing Grand Theft Auto, and the bikers are even worse. People have to jump out of the way if they want to live. There's this one delivery dude from Good Taste Chinese (don't believe the hype; the name's a ploy) who I swear needs to be in one of those countless *Fast & Furious* movies, he's that badass.

But I haven't been run over by the Good Taste driver—not yet, anyway. Tonight I'm strictly on Good Samaritan duty. My best friend, Ryan, almost broke his neck hopping a tree on his skateboard. It was to impress a girl, as most stupid stunts are.

Her name is Polly. She and Ryan and me met in homeroom freshman year, in the H-I-Js (I'm Hunte, he's Hendrick, she's Jadhav). But then Polly—I don't know how to say this without sounding like a perv, but she, um, *grew*. Sophomore year she got curvy and popular and started doing things like joining the step team and chairing dance committees, and we just kind of stopped seeing her. But it was over for me; I was smitten. I mean, a girl who can recite the periodic table of elements in order from memory *and* bhangra dance like her hips are spring-loaded? It's the hot nerd jackpot. I just couldn't manage to talk to her or do anything remotely cool in her presence. It doesn't help that my only real hobby is kickboxing, which I do alone in my basement with a red punching bag and can't show off unless I want to start a fistfight.

Ryan, to his credit, is my boy and has tried to help me get Polly's attention. But he's the kind of guy who has a natural confidence even though he's about the same height as my thirteen-year-old twin sisters. And I just . . . don't. When it comes to girls, I choke. And when it comes to Polly? I completely crash and burn. Like today.

School doesn't start until next week, but today the rising juniors were supposed to go in to get their schedules and new ID photos taken. A lot of kids didn't go because of the hurricane, but my mom's hard line with anything school-related is that unless the building is literally locked or she's in a coma, I'm going (and if the threatened coma ever happened, you can bet my dad would send me anyway). The Asian kids at Brooklyn Tech are under a lot of pressure from their families to do well, and it's taken as a given, like "Oh yeah, Korean parents are *crazy*." Well, West Indian parents don't get

stereotyped as much, but they're just as intense. Maybe back on the
island everyone's dancing to Bobby McFerrin and smoking jays and
getting shells braided into their hair like in some cruise brochure,
but a first-generation kid in the U.S. cannot catch a break. Especially
the oldest and only son. So I took an empty, dripping subway car to
Nevins Street only to find that the photographer had canceled. I was
one of about a hundred students who showed up. Ryan was there,
too—his parents are hippies and probably wouldn't care except he
lives two blocks from school, which takes him thirty seconds on his
skateboard—and lo and behold so was Polly, whose dad drove her
all the way from Jackson Heights. (Mr. Jadhav seems scary like my
mom when it comes to academics, but my grades are even better
than Polly's. I wonder how Indian parents feel about Caribbean boys
asking their daughters out. . . .)

Getting my schedule took about two seconds, and then Ryan
and I went to claim new lockers on the third floor, the junior hallway. I chose 915, the farthest locker on the left in the annex by the
computer lab, since I'm left-handed and I don't need another incident like the time I accidentally gave Jenny Ye a black eye with my
elbow, and Ryan took 913. He was so excited that his skateboard fit
perfectly in his locker that he almost didn't take it home, but then
stupidly I reminded him that we wouldn't be back until Tuesday, so
he stuck it under his arm and we went downstairs, taking the north
staircase to the DeKalb Avenue exit, which is where we ran into
Polly, which is why we stopped, which is how we saw the tree. It's
crazy how one tiny decision can spin out and change the course of
your whole day.

Like right now, instead of setting the table and making sure
that Edna and Ameerah aren't copying off each other's homework

and Tricia's not in some neighbor's yard getting into trouble, and
Joy hasn't gotten into Dad's cutlass collection to play pirates again,
I'm sitting between a biker-looking dude with a bloody bandage
that makes his entire right hand look like a red Q-tip, and a little
boy with neon-green snot crusting his nose so bad that he has to
breathe through his mouth. On second thought, maybe this is an
improvement.

"Okay," yells a flustered-looking doctor with bright blue glasses,
ducking out from under a curtained-off room and checking her clipboard. "Who's here with Tony Hawkins?" I still can't believe Ryan
was stupid enough to give them his fake ID so there'd be no way the
hospital could call his parents. It's a good idea in theory (if you're
into risk-taking, which I'm not), but I know for a fact that Ryan has
never once used that ID successfully, probably because in the photo
he looks like he's ten. Luckily the ER was so crowded when we got
here that the nurses barely glanced at us.

I stand up, not sure what to say. I finally settle on "Uh, me?"
Yeah, I'm about as smooth as chunky peanut butter.

"We relocated your friend's shoulder," the doctor tells me hurriedly after I wade through the crowd, trying not to step on anyone's
open wounds. "Good news is the joint was subluxed, so we were
able to pop it back into place fairly easily. There isn't any cartilage
or nerve damage as far as I can tell, so he won't need surgery." She
leads me over to the curtain and pulls it back to reveal Ryan with
one arm in a sling, texting with his left hand. "What did I say, Evil
Knievel?" she says, sighing. "No cell phones!" Ryan smiles sheepishly and drops it in his lap. "The bad news," the doctor continues,
"is that he cannot use his arm for *at least* seventy-two hours, and then
he needs to see an orthopedist to get a rehabilitation assessment."

She looks at me pointedly. "I'm holding *you* responsible for that, because I don't trust *him* as far as he can jump over a tree stump."

I wait until she leaves and then burst out laughing. "She burned you, man!"

Ryan shrugs. "I could've made it if it wasn't raining."

"Bullshit," I say. "You're lucky it was only this bad. And how are you planning to explain that sling to your parents, *Tony*?"

"Easy," he says with a smile. "I'm staying at your house tonight, which is what I already told them anyway." I feel my jaw tense. I told my parents *I* was staying for dinner at *Ryan's* house. I hate lying to them anyway, and now I'm going to have to do it again, make some excuse as to why we decided to travel two and a half miles through a dangerous hurricane to get home when they think I'm safe and sound in Fort Greene, eating Mrs. Hendrick's quinoa salad and playing video games. The fluorescent lights above Ryan's bed flicker, sending chills down my spine.

"You'll still have the sling on tomorrow," I point out, hoping I can get him to change his mind. But Ryan shakes his head, beaming. He's already got everything figured out, like always.

"I'll ditch the sling, say I fell off my board coming home on Eastern Parkway and felt something pop, and then I'll go to the orthopedist next week per Dr. Ginger's orders." He grins and raises his good hand for a high five, while I fight the powerful urge to slap him in the face.

"Whatever, man," I grumble, turning away. In the next room, I can hear someone getting stitches, making little *ah* sounds every time the needle goes in.

"What, you're mad at me?" Ryan asks incredulously. "This was *your* idea."

"You're kidding, right? I was *joking*, idiot. Why do you take everything literally?" If we were on *Judge Judy* or something, Ryan could probably get me on a technicality. I *did* say, "Why don't you go jump that tree?" but only because he kept egging *me* to do it. In front of Polly. I try to mimic the way my dad stares me down when he's disappointed in me, eyes half-lidded, nostrils flared. It scares me straight each and every time. "Don't you remember me running after you, trying to stop you?" I ask.

Ryan shrugs again. "I thought you were showing off."

"Yeah, running into traffic is my signature move when there's a cute girl nearby," I joke.

"Sorry," he says with a laugh. "I didn't mean to ruin your game."

"No game to ruin, my friend."

"But on the plus side, Mr. Jadhav hates you now, so you've got bad-boy cred."

I have to laugh; this is true. Polly's dad happened to arrive at the curb to pick her up just as Ryan was making his swanlike descent onto the sidewalk, which was convenient as far as rides to the hospital go, but not so convenient in terms of my chances with his daughter. "Do you *know* these boys?" he kept asking Polly angrily on the drive over, as if we were two homeless crackheads she found on the street. I don't think she looked up from her lap the whole time. It was brutal.

"You're right," I say to Ryan. "I should be thanking you." I reach out and bat his stupid cowlick off his forehead, the closest I can bring myself to a show of affection right now. "Now if you'll excuse me, I have to go call my mom and lie for you—*again*. Meet me outside in five minutes."

I push through the curtain, reaching into the pocket of my jeans for my cell, and am almost at the exit when I feel my stomach slosh and realize I haven't eaten anything since breakfast. Out of the corner of my eye I spot a bank of elevators and decide to hop down to the cafeteria for a muffin or something before facing my mother's third degree.

Like I said, it's crazy how one tiny decision can spin out and change everything.

Chapter 3
Devorah

My niece's name is Liya. Liya Sara Kleinman, after our late paternal grandmother and Jacob's late maternal grandmother, because in our tradition it's bad luck to name a baby after anyone living. (It's also bad luck to announce the name of a baby girl before her *simchas bas*, or naming ceremony, but Rose was too excited and out of it to keep the secret from me, and I'm glad.) Liya weighs four pounds, one ounce, and is eighteen inches long, born at 7:19 PM and out of our sight by 7:20, whisked off to the incubator to keep warm and have her breathing monitored for at least a few days, until she gains another pound or so, but otherwise healthy.

"Healthy as a horse!" I report to my mother illicitly from the stairwell, lowering my voice into the receiver of Jacob's cell, trying to imitate her trademark optimism with an idiom I don't really understand.

"No horse in New York City looks healthy," my mother replies wryly, but I can hear the smile in her voice.

I'm afraid that Jacob will react badly to the gender news, but instead he actually *hugs* me and starts jumping up and down. I take him in to see Rose, but it's really awkward since now that Rose is *yoledet*, all physical contact with her husband is forbidden. (Like *niddah*, when a woman has her period, the idea is to keep men from being intimate with a woman when she's "unclean," although when the sages wrote these laws I kind of doubt they took into consideration the decidedly unromantic atmosphere of a shared hospital recovery room, especially with some stranger getting a catheter put in, one curtain down.) So I stand there fidgeting as Jacob beams at Rose and clutches his fists over his chest, and Rose raises a weak hand to her lips.

"I love you," Jacob says, his voice surprisingly deep with emotion.

"Mmmmmm." Rose sighs dreamily. (She needed some stitches, so they gave her painkillers.) Then a lactation consultant shows up to teach Rose how to use a frightening breast pump the size of an air conditioner, and both Jacob and I make ourselves scarce.

An hour later, Rose is asleep, Liya's in the NICU, and Jacob has wandered off, so I'm just loitering in the hallway waiting to be useful again. Adrenaline ricochets through my exhausted shell of a body, and I'm filled with a weird energy that I've never felt before. It feels kind of like the time I ate a pint and a half of ice cream all by myself at Chaya Miller's fourteenth-birthday sleepover and then watched Chaya and her best friends Rachel and Tavi do the "Single Ladies" dance, which they'd downloaded on Rachel's older sister's iPad: My heart was racing and blood was rushing in my ears and tingling in my toes and I felt a little bit sick but mostly exhilarated. I wish I could call Shoshana right now and tell her about Liya, about the miracle I just saw with my own eyes. I wish I could call *anyone*. Almost all my friends have cell phones, but my father jokes that I don't need one because he always knows that I'm right where I should be. "You can have a phone when you start worrying me," he says drily every time I pester him. Even Amos has a refurbished Nokia from like 2003, the kind that you can use only to talk, no Internet. But that's because he never comes home on time, and my parents have to be able to call and yell at him even if he's far away.

I wander through the now-empty Labor and Delivery waiting room and over to the big window that overlooks the parking lot. The sky is dark and thick, and eerily quiet—no sign of the bone-rattling winds that were blowing through when we first arrived. I wonder if we're in the eye of the storm—the evil eye that everyone fears but no one sees. I run my fingers along a strip of duct tape and peer up through the low gray clouds, but there's no moon, not even a hint of one. I listen to the rain drum against the glass, while on TV I hear the news anchors regret to inform me that a young man has been killed by a falling tree in Borough Park.

The rest of the floor may be deserted, but the NICU is buzzing. Through the thick glass of the window made for new parents and gawkers like me, I can literally hear the thrum of electricity. It almost looks like a regular nursery, painted a bright buttercup yellow, with a rocking chair and a few stuffed animals perched on a beanbag, but the rest of the room is filled with giant machines, mostly eight incubators lined up in two neat rows. Dr. MacManus and two of the nurses who were in Rose's room during delivery are going from baby to baby, making notes on a clipboard chart. I crane my neck and try to find Liya, but from where I stand I can see only slivers of skin poking out of diapers and blankets, and I haven't known her long enough to pick her out of a crowd—especially one this tiny.

One of the nurses reaches her hand into an incubator that's glowing blue like the deep-sea life exhibit I saw last year at the Museum of Natural History. The baby inside has a bandage over its eyes; I wonder if it has any idea where it is, or if it thinks it's still safe in the womb. The nurse smiles and begins to massage the baby's tiny foot with her thumb, and I'm so transfixed that I hardly notice the other nurse and doctor push through the door just inches to my left.

"So you think we're definitely going to lose it?" the nurse asks, her voice rising in panic.

"Not necessarily," says the doctor, wiping sweat from under his scrubs cap. "But Lower Manhattan just went dark, and NYU Medical is on its backup generator."

"Oh my God," she whispers, and I turn my face so that they can't see the flush in my cheeks. I've heard plenty of cursing, but no one in my family—*no one*—ever says His name in vain. At school, we're not even allowed to write it out. We have to write *G-d*. (Shoshana says that if she ever becomes a famous Hasidic rapper like Matisyahu, she's going to call herself G Dash.)

"Even in a worst-case scenario, we should be okay," the doctor says. "But until we're in the clear, we have to be prepared. MacManus is done with her deliveries, so she's gonna hang out for a few hours in case we need extra hands."

I let out the breath I didn't even know I was holding. I don't trust many strangers, but I trust our doctor. The thought that she will be with Liya fills me with relief.

"Can I help you?" The doctor has noticed me and sounds . . . not *annoyed* exactly, but tired. He tries to make eye contact as I search for words.

"Oh, no, thanks, I'm just looking." This is the same line I use at the newsstand two blocks from my house, where I sometimes pretend to comparison shop for bottled water while discreetly gazing at the covers of the secular magazines, transfixed by the women with glossy hair and swollen lips and bare shoulders the color of dark honey. But now that the other nurse has gone back inside the NICU, I'm flirting with a violation of *yichud* by standing with a man in an otherwise empty hallway, so I take one last peek at the babies, saying a special prayer for Little Blue, and make a hasty exit.

Rose is asleep when I get back to her room, a bottle of thin yellow milk sitting on a table beside the bed alongside the red enamel mezuzah Jacob brought from home. She seems to be sleeping so deeply that her chest is barely moving, but when I lean in to kiss her forehead I can see her eyes darting back and forth under their lids, the rapid eye movement of deep dream sleep. It would be cruel to wake her, and boring to wait, so I double back through the waiting room to look for Jacob, even checking the hallway by the vending machines and poking around outside the men's room for a few minutes just in case. ("When you don't know what to do, walk fast and look worried," my mother always says, and it's the perfect advice for a hospital.) While I'm loitering by the bathrooms it occurs to me that I haven't peed since Rose and I were doing inventory at the store nine hours ago, so I duck into the empty ladies' room, shut myself in a stall, and savor every vanishing inch of my tights as they peel away from my legs. Even though I don't need to, I roll them all the way to my ankles. Like Dr. MacManus said, the heat makes people do crazy things.

After I reluctantly pull up my stockings and zip up my skirt, I take a good look at myself in the mirror. I'm almost surprised to see the same face I woke up with this morning; with all the rain, sweat, and tears it's been drenched with today, I half expected it to look older and wiser, or at least pale and gaunt from anxiety. But no— there are my cheeks, as round and pink as they were when I was three and my zeidy would pretend to take bites of them during Shabbos dinner. There are my father's thick eyebrows and my mother's (and Rose's) round gray eyes and the dainty nose that Shoshana says she would pay me her allowances for ten years to trade for hers, which is larger and sports a (practically invisible, but she won't listen to me) bump on the bridge. There are my lips, which have been touched only by people in my immediate family and might as well come in a factory-sealed cellophane wrapper. I wet my hands again and clap the cool water on my face, smoothing the rest over my unruly black curls. I may not have grown any cheekbones today, but thanks to the humidity, my hair has at least doubled in size.

I leave the bathroom and find myself facing the elevator bank, so I decide to go down to the cafeteria below the lobby floor and see if Jacob is there. At the very least maybe I can get him to buy me that ginger ale he owes me. Suddenly starving, I step into the brushed-chrome car and reach for the door-close button. As soon as my skin touches it, I swear I feel the lights flicker.

• • •

Labor and Delivery is on the fourth floor, and on the third floor (Neurology), an elderly couple gets on, smiling oddly at me the way people do when they see me, out of the context, in the summertime. Black shoes, opaque black tights, black skirt to mid-calf, white long-sleeved T-shirt with a purple cardigan . . . I wonder, as I often do, what they assume I am. I've gotten Amish (thanks, Anne-Marie!), goth (that one was my favorite), or "in an orchestra?" (from a five-year-old, so I took it as a compliment). On the second floor, Electrophysiology, a young nurse with close-cropped hair and yellow running shoes gets on, wearing a backpack over her pastel blue scrubs.

"My shift just ended, and I'm gonna get myself home before I'm stuck here all night," she says brightly to no one in particular.

Between the second and ground floors, the lights dim again, and the elderly woman gasps and grabs her husband's arm.

"I jinxed us," the nurse says, putting a hand to her temple.

But half a minute later, the doors spring apart on the main floor, and the old couple and nurse rush off. The elevator opens directly out into the ER waiting room, and the wind is whipping against the sliding glass door so forcefully that it's actually banging. I vaguely remember futilely pulling on that same door for Rose when we arrived, not realizing it was automatic, and how heavy it felt—like a slab of granite. For the first time I wonder how I'm possibly going to get home tonight. Both Jacob and I took cabs to the hospital, and who knows if anyone is still willing to take a fare in this weather. At least I know that Isaac and Zeidy are with my younger siblings; that my second oldest brother Niv is with his wife, Rivka, in their apartment on President Street; that Mom and Dad are safe upstate; and that Rose and Liya have doctors watching over them. I'm the only one lost at the moment, and I can't panic yet.

It's not until the elevator doors close again that I realize someone else has boarded. A boy, my age or a little older, who stands with his broad back to me, sinewy muscles spreading his red T-shirt tight across his shoulders, his hands shoved deep into the pockets of his jeans. Skin the shade of the smoky, dark chocolate hidden behind the gold foil of my Hannukah gelt. My pulse quickens. This is *definitely* a violation of *yichud*, although you can't avoid ever being alone in an elevator with a stranger unless you're a total freak, right? *Besides*, I tell myself, *it'll be ten more seconds, at most. What could happen in ten seconds?*

And then the elevator stops.

And the lights go out.

Chapter 4

Jaxon

AUGUST 28, 7:45 PM

At home, our power goes out all the time. We live on the top floor of an old brownstone, which my dad would describe as "quirky" and my mom would deride as "broke-ass." (Our landlady tries to fix everything herself, but she's eighty-two, so mostly she relies on a glue gun and a bottle of Drano.) If we have the TV on and someone plugs in the toaster, a fuse blows. And forget about summer. If we want to run the AC we have to turn off almost all the lights in the house. So I'm used to the dark, but the way the elevator shudders and screeches to a stop is still freaky.

"Aw, shit," I say, and there's a sharp intake of breath behind me. The girl. I forgot about the girl. I only got a glimpse of her when I stepped in, since I was trying to make way for the old couple. But she has long dark hair, I remember, and a pretty face. Which means

I'm probably going to make a fool of myself. My heart thumps so loud in my chest I'm sure she must be able to hear it.

"Sorry," I say with a laugh. "I've just had a long day."

No answer.

It's funny; I forget sometimes how I might look to other people. I could be reading *The Great Gatsby* on the 3 train, or walking down the street listening to a podcast on my phone, or coming out of my orthodontist's office with Invisalign braces feeling like the biggest nerd on the planet, but some people don't notice anything but an almost-six-foot-tall black man. After Trayvon Martin got shot in Florida, Mom wouldn't let me wear a hoodie for six months.

"I'm Jaxon," I say into the darkness, trying to make the most of my warm, deep voice, which makes my sisters laugh when I do impressions of radio deejays. (*"And now, a blast from the past going out to my girl Ameerah, who loves meatballs, Kanye West, and using up all the hot water in the shower, heeeeeere's Sister Sledge, with 'We Are Family'!"*)

But the girl stays silent, and after a minute I start to wonder if she might actually be deaf. "That's Jaxon with an X," I add, just to fill the dead air. "Not, like, the seventh president. Or Michael."

Still nothing. Man, I'm striking out like A-Rod in the 2011 ALDS. But then, finally, a thin, nervous voice says, "Devorah."

"All right, Devorah, I'm going to press the call button," I say. "Hang tight." *Hang tight?* I shake my head at my staggering lack of smoothness. The stakes for my redemption are rising with every stupid word out of my mouth. Now I'm going to have to try to get us out of the elevator MacGyver style to regain any shred of dignity.

I run my fingers over the wall where I know the buttons should be, trying to count floors and guess where the HELP button might fall on the bumpy grid. The worst that can happen is I press the alarm bell, which won't win me any suave points but will still help our case. I tentatively press one button, then the next, and when nothing happens I start punching them harder, hitting everything I can.

"Nothing," I say with a sigh, finally giving up. Devorah doesn't react. In fact, I haven't heard her move *once*, not even just to shift her weight or swallow. I realize she must be scared, or maybe even claustrophobic. I need to make her feel comfortable.

I reach into my back pocket for my phone—even the subways get reception now, and we're barely underground in here—but there are no bars. I hold it up above my head, and its light gives me a few feet of visibility. The elevator is deep, maybe eight feet long to accommodate gurneys, and Devorah is backed into a corner, clutching a rail with each hand. Even though her face is a mask of fear, and despite the low light, I can tell I was wrong. She's not just pretty, she's *beautiful*. I can feel my mouth getting dry. "Is it okay if I, um, move around a little to see if I can get a signal?" I ask.

"Yes," she says, squinting into the light, trying to make me out. "Just . . . I'm over here, so . . ."

"Don't worry," I say. "I won't get too close." I don't know why I feel like such a predator all of a sudden when I'm trying to be the hero.

I inch around the perimeter of the car, keeping the phone up above my head. Who am I even going to call if I get a bar? I can't call 911; we're already at the hospital. And while I do owe my mother a phone call there's no way I'm going to give her the opportunity to chew my ear off, the rhythm of her loud, lightly accented alto voice quickening the more worried and angry she gets, while

I'm trapped five feet from Devorah. Luckily—or unluckily; I guess both—I can't find service.

"Do you think the power's out in the whole building?" she asks tentatively.

"Yeah, probably." I stick my phone back into my pocket, but my eyes have adjusted to the dark now, and I can see Devorah clap a hand over her mouth. "Hey, you okay?" I ask.

She shakes her head no.

"We're gonna be fine," I say. "There's nothing to be scared of in here." I force a smile, my stomach curdling as I realize the thing she could be scared of is *me*.

"It's . . . my niece," she says, slow and high-pitched and kind of halting, like she's trying not to cry. "She came early and she's . . . in the NICU. What if she's . . ."

Relief washes over me, followed by guilt for being glad Devorah's upset about a sick baby and not my company. "No," I say, trying to sound authoritative even though it's just now dawning on me that the other people in the hospital could be in serious trouble. "She's fine. Those babies are the first ones they're going to check on. And they're used to these hurricanes now. They have the backup generators ready to go."

She swallows hard. "Then why is it still dark in here?"

"Because . . . the cafeteria elevator is low priority. They know the worst condition we've got in here is munchies." Fourteen years of big brothering have made me pretty good at making stuff up on my feet. I wish I hadn't said "munchies," though. She's not *eight*.

Devorah nods and slides down to the floor, pulling her knees in close to her chest. And suddenly, there is nothing more important to me than getting this girl back to her niece. I get a rush of dumb machismo.

"You know what?" I say. "I'm gonna get us out of here." As usual, my mouth is a few steps ahead of my brain, but I feel unusually sure of myself, backed up by some Superman-caliber adrenaline. I know I've seen dudes escape from elevators in movies, but I've never exactly taken notes on the process. What I do know is that I have two options: Try to pry apart the doors or bust through the service hatch in the ceiling and climb up the cable. I look down at my beat-up Converse sneakers; I hope they have some tread left.

I think we're between floors, so I'm not going to risk messing with the doors (also, I'm not sure I'm strong enough, and I don't want to look stupid). The hatch, though—I'm pretty positive I could kick that open if I can get in the right position. It can't be heavier than a 150-pound punching bag.

"Is it okay with you if I try something?" I ask, pointing up to the square two feet above us. Devorah looks stricken but nods.

"Be careful," she says as I brace my hands on the railing.

"Relax, I do this all the time," I joke. She doesn't laugh.

I bounce a little bit to get a feel for the strength of the railing and the give of the floor, which moves a little bit under my weight but not enough to do any damage if I can support myself on my arms. I almost can't believe that my basement hobby is going to come in handy. I know my dad wishes I played baseball, or at least something he could come watch me play in the park while eating a hot dog. He's been squirreling away money for years for a college fund, but I know he'd rather I get a scholarship. "Why don't you drop the 'kick' and just do boxing like Muhammad Ali?" he'll comment with a laugh when he sees me padding downstairs in my shin guards. *This is why, Dad*, I think as I launch myself off the floor.

I swing my legs up like I'm doing a handstand on the bar and kick as hard as I can at the ceiling. The muscles in my forearms shake as the soles of my shoes hit the underside of the hatch with a dull, heavy thud. It dents but doesn't open, and the whole car sways.

"Maybe you shouldn't," Devorah says sharply.

"I can do this," I mutter, flexing my hands before trying again. This time I twist while I jump, coming at the hatch from an angle and using the torque of my body to increase the force of my legs against the metal, and even I'm surprised when it clangs open, echoing through the tunnel above and sending soft light streaming in.

"The emergency lights are on in the shaft," I pant. "That's a good sign." I catch my breath and stare up at the steep seven-foot climb. I didn't really think this through. "Hello?!?" I yell, cupping my hands around my lips. "Anybody up there? We're stuck!" I shout two more times before deciding it's a lost cause. On the floor, Devorah is covering her ears.

"Okay," I say. "I'm gonna climb up." Something passes over her face that looks like relief, and a pang of shame blooms in my chest. None of this is impressing her. She'd probably rather be alone in here. I bend my knees and jump up, grabbing the edge of the hatch like a chin-up bar, and hoist myself through.

There are two sets of twin cables attaching the elevator to whatever secures it at the top of the building. In my mind I had seen myself climbing one of the cables like a gym-class rope until I reached the first-floor doors, which I would then pry open with my bare hands, but (A) these cables are no thicker than two inches across, way too skinny to climb; (B) there's a safety ladder bolted into the wall; and (C) even if I *did* climb the ladder, to open the door I'd have to hug the sheer face of the wall, Spider-Man style, which wouldn't give me any room to maneuver. I'd probably fall just reaching for it.

I don't know this girl, Devorah. I don't know her and she's barely said two words, and she seems weird and cold and totally uninterested in me, but for some reason I still have this powerful urge to do it anyway, to step off the ledge and basically sacrifice myself to make her like me. It's *crazy*—especially since we're not exactly in imminent danger. But then I think of my four little sisters, my mom, and my dad, and the shoebox full of bills on the top shelf of my parents' closet that'll pay for my education, something they've worked their whole lives just to give me, and I talk myself down. There's no reason to take such a stupid risk. I saw what happened to Ryan, and he just tried to jump a skateboard over a tree. What would my tombstone say? *Here lies Jaxon Hunte: "A" Student, Hopeless Romantic, Virgin, Dumbass.*

I yell for help again, and when no answer comes I lower myself back into the elevator. "Sorry," I say, wiping my hands on my jeans. "I guess I need a stunt double."

"No," Devorah says, her voice sounding strong and sure for the first time. "That was really brave." She stands up and takes a step toward me, and as the light filters down through the hole above us, like artificial moonlight on a movie set, I can really see her eyes for the first time, big and gray flecked with shimmering hints of sky blue, like someone bottled that moment when Dorothy steps out of her black-and-white farmhouse and into Oz.

That's the moment I know I'm in trouble.

Chapter 5
Devorah

AUGUST 28, 8 PM

The first ten minutes stuck in the elevator are some of the scariest in my life. In fact, they probably would be *the* scariest if I hadn't already been through Rose's water breaking dramatically in the party goods aisle this morning. The first thing that runs through my head when the lights go out is that I'm violating *yichud*, which sends me into a panic. But then I quickly realize how selfish I'm being, thinking about my own perceived virtue when Liya is upstairs, less than an hour old and all alone and stuck in some sort of futuristic chafing dish that's being kept warm only by electricity—electricity that is now gone. For a few minutes I feel afraid I might throw up, or pass out, and so I sit on the floor, trying to pray while this boy—Jaxon, with an X—jumps around like we're in a bouncy castle.

At first I think he's just posturing and showing off, the way boys always do, which makes me irrationally angry, but then he actually *kicks through the ceiling* and tries to climb the cables like a super-hero. And he's trying so hard to put me at ease that I have to admit I'm starting to *kind of* let my guard down.

"You live around here?" he asks. We're sitting on opposite sides of the elevator car now. He's got his legs splayed out in front of him in a big V, and I've got mine shut tight as a steel trap, tucked underneath me, with my hands holding the hem against my knees just in case.

I nod. "Near Eastern Parkway."

"Me, too!" he says. "What block?"

"Um . . ." I know I shouldn't be giving out my address to a stranger, but I don't want to seem like I think he's some kind of criminal. I decide to be vague. "Just off Kingston Avenue," I say.

"What?! Me, too! We're neighbors!" He's visibly excited, like a little kid; it's cute. I don't have the heart to point out that while we might fit the dictionary definition, we are most definitely not neighborly. I'm not allowed to cross Eastern Parkway. The other side—Jaxon's side—is "not our people," according to my father. I give him the benefit of the doubt and believe that what he means is they're not Jewish, not that they're not white.

"Don't leave me hanging," a voice says, and I realize I'm spacing out. Jaxon is holding up his hand, but I'm not sure what he expects me to do in response. I raise my right palm in a little wave, which seems to please him.

A minute goes by, and I examine the beds of my fingernails to avoid making eye contact. Maybe this won't be so hard. Maybe he'll take the hint and we'll just sit here on our opposite sides of the elevator and when I get out no one will be able to blame me, because I've done the best I could.

But you can't control another person, and Jaxon doesn't seem to like the silence. "So, um, what's your niece's name?" he asks.

I amend my rules. As long as I only *answer* questions, I won't be making things worse.

"Her name's Liya," I say, despite a twinge of regret at sharing the name with a stranger when my parents don't even know yet. For some reason I feel compelled to add, "Liya with a Y, not like Jacob's wife in the Bible." A failed, nervous attempt at ice-breaking humor: *definitely* not part of the rules. Jaxon smiles.

"Are you religious?" he asks. It's all I can do to keep from bursting into laughter.

"Um, *yeah*. I mean, yes." My mom always scolds us when we don't use proper words. But she's not here. No one who knows "me" is, which means that I can say anything I want to. I've already started to deviate from the script. This realization fills me simultaneously with excitement and fear.

"Me too, kind of," he says. "Roman Catholic. I mean, that's how I was brought up. But I think I might be . . . what's the word for when you don't really know what you are?"

Tell me about it, I think. "Agnostic?" I say.

"Yes, thank you. That." He smiles, and I can't help but smile back. He's handsome—not in an obvious way; when his face is still, the features look kind of plain and even a little haphazard: eyes a little close together, nose a half inch too wide for the narrowness of his face, bottom lip fuller than the top so that it juts out ever so slightly, like a child's pout. But then, when he breaks into a grin, everything aligns, like a constellation bursting into view through a sky of endless, hazy stars.

"So why are you here?" I ask quickly. (I desperately want to change the subject. I wish I hadn't made that joke about Liya's name. Of all the things we could be talking about, why did I have to bring up religion? Why couldn't I have stuck with something easy like the weather? Especially since we're in the middle of a *category three hurricane*?)

Jaxon laughs. "My idiot friend tried to jump over a tree on his skateboard," he says.

"I heard about that!" I blurt before I can stop myself. Talking to Jaxon feels so natural that I keep forgetting I'm not supposed to be doing it. *Just answer his questions*, I think. *Don't make conversation. Keep it together.*

"Wait, how?" He sits up straight and cocks his head, looking at me for a few seconds longer than feels comfortable. "You don't go to my school, do you? I feel like I'd have noticed—" He pauses and smiles shyly. "I mean, I *know* I would remember you." My cheeks flush, and I'm grateful for the dim lighting.

"The doctor," I say. "The doctor who took care of Rose—my sister—also fixed your friend's shoulder."

"The redhead?" Jaxon relaxes and leans back, drawing one knee up. "Yeah, she was cool."

Conversation dies again, and I let it. *Do not resuscitate!* I think wryly, but that just makes me start to panic about Liya, so I take a few slow, deep breaths. Somewhere above, drifting down the elevator shaft, I can hear faint voices. I idly wonder if they're coming from the main floor or from some other awkward little stage play in one of the other elevators.

"So . . . your whole family must be up there freaking out right now, huh?" Jaxon says. He's not willing to let this go. To let *me* go. And in spite of myself, I'm glad. No matter what it might say about me and my values, I need to talk to someone right now. I need distraction.

"Actually, I'm the only one here," I tell him. "My parents are out of town, and my brothers and sisters are at home with my zei . . . grandfather." For some reason we've always called my grandfather "Zeidy," but no one refers to my grandmother as "Bubbe." She is always "Grandma"—maybe because she converted from being a regular Jew to Chabad when she was eighteen, making her a *ba'al t'shuvah*, or "one who has returned."

"What happened to the baby daddy?" Jaxon asks. "He left?"

"Oh, sorry, no, he's here too." How could I forget about my favorite person, Jacob? "But I had to be with my sister during the birth, because—" And yet again, I've steered the conversation right back where I started it.

I smile tightly and think about how to explain *yoledet* to someone who doesn't know it exists. I've never had a private conversation like this with an outsider. I've never had to explain anything, because in my world everything just *is*. For a second, I consider lying and just pretending I'm someone else. After all, I'll never speak to Jaxon again once the power comes back on. This might as well be a dream. A very lucid and as it turns out very enjoyable dream. But then I decide that this opportunity is too valuable. Where else will I find someone to listen without judgment? This might be the only chance I ever get to be completely honest without worrying about being proper.

"Because," I continue, "according to the laws of our religion,

he's not allowed to see or touch her body for at least two weeks."
Speaking of bodies, I almost feel like I'm having an out-of-body
experience. I can't *believe* I'm talking about this to a *guy*—and not
even a Jewish guy, let alone a fellow Hasid, which would be bad
enough. This is exactly why the laws of *yichud* exist: Plop two teenagers in a confined space, let them get to talking, and sooner or
later the conversation will go to a sinful place, and if they talk the
talk . . . No. I have to shut down that train of thought before my
brain explodes. I am going, my father would say, completely off the
derech. I have to rein myself back in.

"Wow," Jaxon says. "That's intense. What religion *are* you?"

"I'm Hasidic," I say. He looks at me again, his thoughtful brown
eyes taking in my hair, my clothes, everything. I feel the blood rush
to my face.

"Well," he finally says. "That explains the tights." I'm so in
need of tension release that I laugh much longer than I need to.

"Yes. *Yeah*," I say, course-correcting for my newfound freedom
of speech. "I know it's important, but in the summer it totally sucks."

"No disrespect," he says, "but why does anyone care if you have
bare legs? I mean, I get the no-booty-shorts policy, but if you're
wearing a long skirt who cares?"

"It's called *tz'ni'ut*," I explain. "It means modesty. We're not
supposed to attract any attention to ourselves, so we have to keep
covered up. Everything below the elbows and knees, at least. Some
Chabad families are more liberal, but mine is . . ." I search for a kind
word. There's nothing wrong with my family's values. The rules can
feel very strict, but I have always respected them. "*Traditional*," I
finish.

"Chabad?" He looks confused. "I thought you said Hasidic."

"Chabad-Lubavitch is one Hasidic sect," I say. "There are many." And then—because I can't resist—I add, "What, we all look the same to you?"

His eyes widen, and his mouth drops open. "No, no, I—" Then he sees my smile and breaks into a grin, showcasing two deep dimples. "Okay, fine, I deserved that. Now can I ask a few more stupid questions? For educational purposes?"

"Sure," I say, frankly surprised that he's so interested.

"Are you the ones who drive around in that crazy Winnebago with the klezmer music?"

I laugh. "I think you mean the Mitzvah Tank. Those are Lubavitchers, but not me personally."

"Cool. Do you have to wear a wig?"

"No. Only married women cover their hair."

"Do you eat meat?"

"Yes, if it's kosher, but never with dairy."

"So you can't have a cheeseburger?"

"No."

"Not ever?"

"Nope."

"You're telling me you've *never* had a cheeseburger?"

"Never in my life."

"Damn." He sits back, presumably contemplating this hardship. "This is making me hungry now." He shoots me an impish grin. "Maybe I can kick through the floor and make it down to the cafeteria."

"Please don't," I say with a laugh.

"You're not packing any snacks, are you?"

"Unfortunately—" I start to say, and then remember the illicit

M&M's, buried in my pocket, that I forgot to give to Rose. "Wait, I am, actually!" This excites me much more than I know it should. I dig them out and hold them up with a flourish. "They might be soft, though."

"I don't care. Oh my God, I love you," Jaxon says with a sigh, holding out his hands. I toss them across the car and then pretend to fix my skirt so that I have an excuse to duck my head and ride out the blush that I can feel rising in my cheeks. Both of the clauses in that sentence make me extremely uncomfortable, even if the second one does manage to make my stomach flip a little. I know Jaxon wasn't being serious, but no man (outside of immediate family) has ever said those words to me. "Want some?" he asks, his voice garbled a bit by chewing. I look up quickly and shake my head.

"Can't," I say.

"Not even candy?" He seems genuinely sorry for me for a second but then gives me a suspicious look. "Then . . . why did you have them?"

"Inside joke."

"Okaaaaaaay." He smiles as he tosses back another handful. "Shit, these are good. You're not allowed to curse, either, I guess."

"It's . . . frowned upon," I say, fighting a smile. I can't pretend I don't kind of like hearing *him* do it, though.

"My mom frowns on it, too," Jaxon says. "She has this mason jar on the mantel that she makes us throw a quarter into each time we swear. But it backfired, because now we all call quarters 'shits.'" He shrugs. "It's stupid."

"No, it's funny," I say. I've never had a boy try this hard to make me laugh. Most of the boys in my neighborhood just assume I should be impressed with them because they study the *Tanya* and

I can't. Something about Jaxon is so different and so . . . open. So uncondescending. Maybe it's his easy smile or his warm, searching eyes. Maybe it's the way he wears his nerves like a sandwich board, and how vulnerable it makes him seem despite his long, lanky frame that I really shouldn't be noticing as much as I am. *A body is just a body*, I tell myself. But it doesn't stop the strange feeling spreading through my chest and down my legs, like pins and needles from some unseen limb that's waking up for the first time. I want to confide in him, against my better judgment. "Rose and I used to play this game where we'd write down all our mean thoughts and then ball them up and throw them out our bedroom window into the neighbors' yard," I say. I have never mentioned this to anyone, save for Rose. She'd kill me if she knew.

"What?!" Jaxon laughs. "Did they ever find out it was you?"

"They're pretty old, so I don't think they ever gardened," I say. "But if they *did* find them, they were probably confused." I can't imagine the look on Mr. Eliav's face reading the crumpled loose-leaf paper that proclaimed, in big block letters, "TALIA GOLDSTEIN IS A B-WORD AND HER SWEATERS ARE UGLY," or "ZEIDY SMELLS LIKE FARTS!" I stifle a giggle.

"You're close with your siblings?" he asks.

"Sort of," I say. "More with my sisters. My brothers are in school all day."

"You don't go to school?"

"Yeah, but girls get out earlier, to help at home. Boys have to study."

"Huh," he says. "I help at home."

For some reason I immediately picture him in an apron, braiding challah. "You do?" I say with a smile.

"Hell yeah," he says proudly. "I run a mean vacuum. With four little sisters you can't wait too long to clean or you'll be knee-deep in glitter pens and Barbie heads."

"Don't tell me you cook, too," I tease.

"Not really," he says. "But I work part time at Wonder Wings, so I can get you a discount."

I smile as I try to imagine sitting at a table with Jaxon, dipping chicken into blue cheese sauce. A portrait of *treif* if ever there was one.

"How old are your sisters?" I probe. I don't even care, really; I just like hearing him talk.

"Edna and Ameerah, the twins, are fourteen," he says. "Then there's Joy, who's ten, and Tricia, who's eight." It's sweet to think of Jaxon surrounded by a bunch of girls. I bet he's a great big brother.

"I have three sisters," I say. "The littlest one, Miri—Miriam— she's eleven. Hanna's fifteen, and Rose is eighteen."

"Rose is the one with the baby?" he asks, his eyes widening. I nod, and he whistles. "That's young," he marvels.

"Not where I come from," I say.

"My mom was twenty when she had me," he says. Then he looks up at me and grins. "But I was an accident."

I'm blown away by his honesty. Hasidic girls don't have accidents. Or if they do, they're sent away so that no one will ever know.

"I don't know why I just told you that," he says, looking down at his sneakers. "I don't even know you."

"No, I'm glad," I say. "I mean, I'm glad . . . you're here." He looks back up at me, and I look at him, and this silence is much different than the others. It's like the oxygen changes. I think back to what Rose said earlier—*two air masses converging over water*—and wonder if I'm tempting fate.

"So," I finally say, searching for a segue and finding there is none, forcing me back into my census-taker role. "You don't have any brothers?"

"Nah," Jaxon says. "My dad and I are in the minority, but we deal. You?"

"Three," I say.

Jaxon smirks. "Three brothers, three sisters. Your last name isn't Brady, is it?"

"No, it's Blum."

"That was a joke," he deadpans. "You know, *The Brady Bunch*?"

"Am I supposed to?"

"It's a TV show," he says, waving a hand dismissively. "But it's old, like from the fifties or something."

"Oh," I say. "I actually don't watch TV."

Jaxon feigns shock. "By choice?"

I'm not sure how to answer that. It's not allowed in my house, which is my parents' rule, not mine. But I choose not to watch it even when I have the opportunity, like at friends' houses, or in the back of taxicabs, or tonight in the hospital waiting room. Then again, am I choosing not to watch it because I truly don't want to, or because I want to please my parents?

"I was raised to believe that TV distracts us from more important things," I say carefully.

"Isn't that the point?" he asks, laughing.

"I never thought about it that way. Maybe." School and homework, setting the dinner table and helping my mother cook, tutoring

Miri and Hanna, even doing mind-numbing inventory at the store—
in a flash I imagine how light and easy these tasks would feel if I
knew that at the end of them I got a distraction. A distraction like
this.

"No TV, huh?" he says, shaking his head. "No TV, no
McDonald's. No candy. No cursing. No tank tops. What else?"

"You make me sound like an alien," I say, crossing my arms
defiantly. "Aren't there things *you're* not allowed to do?"

"Good point." He thinks for a minute. "I'm not allowed to drive
my dad's truck," he says. "I'm not allowed to make rice, ever since
I accidentally set a dish towel on fire . . ."

I hang my head and bite my lip to contain my smile.

"I'm not allowed to get home after dark," he continues, counting off the rules on his long fingers. "I'm not allowed to illegally
stream HBO on the computer, and I'm not allowed to stay home
from school unless I'm dead . . ."

"Don't joke about that!" I chide, sounding like my mother.

"But I'm serious!" he says. "My parents are crazy. If I don't go
to college, I'm pretty sure they'll disown me."

I feel a flash of jealousy. Jaxon will graduate high school, just
like me, but he'll get to decide where he wants to go and what he
wants to do with his life, while my parents will go to a *shadchan* to
find me a husband, whether I'm ready or not. Forget that my grades
are better than either of my older brothers' ever were. Forget that I
study English and math and science, much more well-rounded than
their almost entirely religious education. It is simply expected that
my education will end when I am married. My father likes to brag
that I will be easy to match into a good family. Some girls, the ones
with plain faces or poor manners or bad reputations, will have to be

paired with husbands outside the community, who don't know about the shame they've brought to their households. But not me. I will be someone's prize. I level my eyes at Jaxon, wondering what he would think of me if he knew. I decide that if he smiles at me right this second, I'll tell him.

It's an easy bet to lose.

"My parents," I say, leaning forward a bit to give my heart more room to bang around wildly in my ribs, "would disown me if they knew we were talking."

He raises his eyebrows. "This right here?" he asks, gesturing back and forth between us. "This is a cheeseburger?"

"I'm not allowed to talk to strangers," I say. "Or to be alone with any man besides my father or brothers."

Jaxon processes this for a minute and then starts nodding slowly. "When I first laid eyes on you, I knew you were a rebel," he says. "I said to myself, I gotta be careful with this girl. She's dangerous. Look at that cardigan! I bet she throws paper onto other people's property, and probably runs around getting stuck in elevators all over Brooklyn just for the rush." He's making fun of me, but this time I don't mind so much. The flirtation in his voice is intoxicating.

"Stop it," I say with a laugh, and then steady my voice. "I'm serious. For me, this *is* dangerous."

"No, I get it," he says, the sly smile disappearing. "I wouldn't want to make you uncomfortable. We can stop talking if you want."

I shrug. I don't want to, but I don't want to *tell* him I don't want to. Then maybe it really will get dangerous.

He holds up a finger in a "give me a minute" gesture and fishes his cell phone out of his pocket. He types something and then slides it across the floor. I pick it up and look at the screen.

Let's not talk, he has written, the words floating inside a bright green bubble. Don't want 2 get u in trouble.

When we first got stuck I balked at having a conversation with Jaxon, but now I feel like I never want to stop. I press the return key and painstakingly form a reply using the finicky touch screen: It's OK. I gather my courage and add, I like talking to you.

He grins when he reads it and points to his chest. "Me, too," he mouths. He types something else and passes the phone back.

Compromise: listen 2 some music w/ me?

I look up at the light filtering down from the darkness above, feeling like G-d is testing me. It's not that I've never heard secular music before—even though I live by Chabad rules, I still live in the world, a world with car radios and custom ringtones and mariachi bands in the subway—although, like television, it's not welcome in my house. But I've already given up so much ground in this little box, stuck in limbo between two floors, what's one more transgression? My English teacher, Mrs. Goldman, has a saying about girls who read or watch or listen to things they aren't supposed to: "*frum* to *frei* in sixty seconds." *Frei* literally means "free," but it's meant like a slur.

I nod at Jaxon, and he pulls a knotted, grimy pair of headphones out of his pocket, making a face as if to apologize for their condition. Then he scoots toward me, and I instinctively freeze. *I have to sit right next to him.* Somehow I had not considered the possibility.

He's respectful and sits a foot away, but as he's handing me my earbud, our fingers brush, and a current shoots through me as though I've stuck my finger in a light socket. The warmth from Jaxon's body radiates across the space between us. He smells like rainwater, heady and sweet. *That's stupid, Devorah*, I think. *It's raining. Everyone probably smells like rain.*

You pick, he types, handing me the phone. Uh-oh. I scroll through the mostly meaningless names, searching for something familiar to grab onto. Finally I spot something: Doesn't Zeidy always say that Grandma Deborah had a soft spot for the Shirelles? I tap the screen, and out of the corner of my eye I can see Jaxon smile to himself, like I've picked something that has a special meaning to him, too. We sit back and listen as the softly metallic clang of a song recorded decades before we were born fills our ears:

> *Tonight you're mine completely*
> *You give your love so sweetly*
> *Tonight the light of love is in your eyes*
> *But will you love me tomorrow?*

One verse in and I'm so scared I'm sure I must be visibly vibrating. It's a beautiful song, but it feels so *intimate*. Worse than talking, almost. I think back to Rose and Jacob's wedding. Even they weren't sitting this close to each other, and they were married. I clasp my hands in my lap, staring at the floor, keeping my head down. No good can come of this. Only—

It *feels* good.

I glance over at Jaxon. He's got his legs pulled up, arms crossed over his knees, with his chin resting on top, his eyes closed, head bobbing with the rhythm of the melody. Maybe it's because he doesn't know I'm looking, but for the first time since I met him he's not awkward at all. And his face isn't plain; how could I have thought that? It's lovely. Beautiful, even. He opens his eyes and looks at me, like he can read my mind. And once again the air stands still.

> *Tonight with words unspoken*
> *You say that I'm the only one*
> *But will my heart be broken*
> *When the night meets the morning sun?*

I don't know what to do. Part of me wants to lean over and kiss him; part of me wants to vault through the hatch and climb until my arms give out. Neither are good options. I am *never*, I decide, even thinking about drinking ginger ale again. It's not worth the ethical or hormonal agony.

But then Jaxon smiles, and my anxiety melts away. In fact, I relax so much that I lean into him more than I mean to, and my hand grazes his thigh. I pull it back like I've been bitten by a snake, accidentally knocking the headphones out of our ears. And almost at the exact same second, the lights come on and the elevator jolts to life.

The only thought I have time to process before the doors clang open is *It's over. It's over before it had a chance to begin.*

Chapter 6

Jaxon

It figures that it takes being trapped in a confined space for me to finally get up the nerve to flirt with a girl, just like it figures that the first time I'm actually *getting* somewhere—sharing headphones and meaningful glances, that's big for me!—the moment is ruined by something out of my control.

I know Devorah didn't mean to touch me. I know we weren't about to make out or anything. I mean, I'm pretty sure just sitting next to me was like second base for her. But I felt something, and I think she did, too. Listening to that song, the one I downloaded during a pathetic, late-night pining session for Polly, after I actually Googled "unrequited love songs"—seriously, I was in pain—I finally realized you can't force moments like that to happen. I've been trying to create chance encounters with Polly for more than a year, doing dumb shit like standing outside her physics class so that I could "pretend" to bump into her, or strategically positioning myself close to her at school dances so that I might be the one she turned to when a slow song started. But just now, with Devorah— that was the opposite of planned. That felt real. And suddenly I'm filled with dread that I'll never feel it again.

The elevator starts moving up, creaking at first but gaining speed, and I know I have only a few seconds. I look at the phone in my lap and sputter, "Can I get your number?"

She shakes her head helplessly. "I don't—"

Of course. She doesn't have a phone, idiot. This girl lives in a bubble, a bubble I'll never be able to get inside.

"Can you remember mine?" I ask as we slow to a stop, springing to our feet, the chaos of the ER already seeping in, voices shouting over one another. Devorah looks so overwhelmed I'm not sure she's even listening, but I start to tell her anyway.

"Jaxon," she says quickly, cutting me off after the area code. "I'm sorry. But I can't. Please, just act like you don't know me." Her eyes are wide with fear.

As the doors open, all I can think to say is "Call me Jax."

There are a few dozen people gathered in front of the elevator bank, way more than I remember being in the emergency room an hour ago, but as soon as they see us, 99 percent of them grumble and disperse, and I realize that they were just waiting to see if their missing friends and loved ones were in here. As the crowd parts, I see Ryan, waving maniacally with his good hand, standing next to a skinny dude with a full beard in a dark suit and hat who looks pissed.

"Jacob!" Devorah cries, rushing out like she's been held hostage or something. "I was going to look for you in the cafeteria and the elevator shut down and—" She glances back nervously at me. "It was *awful*. I was so afraid!" It feels like a punch in the gut. Maybe I did make up all that chemistry I thought I felt. It wouldn't be the first time.

As I jog reluctantly over to Ryan, I hear Devorah ask that Jacob guy if the baby is okay, and he says yes, that she's stable and Rose is in the NICU with her right now, and I steal one last look at those big gorgeous eyes filled with happy tears. That's all I need to start to feel all right again. At least someone gets a happy ending. And hey, better her than me.

"Dude, I am *so* glad to see you," Ryan says, raising his hand for another high five, which I grudgingly accept. "At first I thought maybe you left, but then I thought, 'Nah, Jax would never do that to me,' but then after like an hour when you didn't respond to any of my texts, I started to second-guess myself and thought maybe you *were* mad at me, so I thought I'd call your house to see if you were there—"

"You called my mom?!"

"Yeah, and she's, um . . . not pleased," Ryan mutters.

I look down at my phone, which has finally found a signal and is filling up with increasingly threatening texts.

Ryan just called, says he is at Interfaith in the ER and u have gone missing. Tell me this is a joke.

And:

Bad enough u lied to us, driving in this weather could get
us killed, how irresponsible can u be??

And:

TEXT OR CALL ME RIGHT NOW. I'M NOT PLAYING. >:-(

"Ryan!" I say, low enough so Devorah can't hear me but firm
enough so he knows I'm mad. "I was stuck in an elevator; what was
I supposed to do, climb out?"

"Sorry, man, I didn't know what else to do. And I'm in trouble,
too, because now I have to go home to *my* house."

"Great," I say. "There's a silver lining."

"The good news," he says, not missing a beat, "is that your dad
is picking us up in the truck."

"That is *not* good news." I would rather sleep at the hospital
than have to listen to this story told and retold for the rest of my
life as part of my dad's lecture series, Things I Have Sacrificed for
My Son. I clamp my lips shut in frustration and taste a sweet hint of
chocolate: proof, at least, that I didn't imagine *everything*.

"What was up with that girl, by the way?" Ryan asks as Devorah
and Jacob disappear down the hall. "She looked hot."

"Shut up."

"No, I mean literally *hot*. What is she, an Eskimo?"

"Shut *up*." I'm tired, and I know I'm about to get my ass ver-
bally whupped; would it be so hard for Ryan to let me have a minute
of peace?

Apparently. "During the blackout I tried to talk to this college girl
with an eye patch, but she was pretty heavily medicated," he says.

"That's great, Ryan." I see my dad's red Ford pickup pull up in front of the emergency room doors. He's got the tarps tied down tight, although I'm sure he's moved his gear inside for the night. My father is a contractor/carpenter and professional tinkerer, but most of his income is from house-painting jobs, and there are never fewer than half a dozen paint cans stacked beside the front door, scenting the whole apartment with that tangy titanium dioxide smell.

I lead the way to the exit with my head down. The wind and rain are brutal as we dash the ten feet or so to the curb, shielding our faces from the stinging droplets with our backpacks. Since I'm sure we'll be dropping Ryan off first, I squeeze into the middle seat, panting, and Ryan takes the window, holding his skateboard between his knees. My dad looks down at it like it's a bong.

"I'm sorry," I mutter, but he just stares straight ahead and nods, not like he accepts my apology but more like he knew I wouldn't be able to come up with something better.

"Save your sorry's for your mother," he says, and sighs. "I'm just the chauffeur. And we've got an early day tomorrow."

"We?" I ask, and he fixes me with a warning look.

"Yes, *we*. You're gonna go door-to-door with me offering storm-damage home repairs. And then, you're grounded until school starts next week."

"But Dad," I say, "that's not fair! I didn't do anything—" I'm about to say *wrong*, but I swallow the word before it has a chance to get past my lips. I need to quit lying before I dig myself in deeper.

My father clears his throat. He's a big man with a deep voice, and when he's getting mad you can hear it coming, like a growl emanating from a dark cave. "Whoever told you life was supposed to be fair?" he asks, nostrils flaring. Then he turns the wipers all the way up, shifts the truck into drive, and steps on the clutch, easing away from the curb and into a foot-deep river that's running down onto Atlantic Avenue. A vein bulges in his temple, and I think back to what Mr. Jadhav said to Polly: "Do you *know* these boys?"

Maybe my parents don't know the real me. Hell, I don't know who I want to be half the time. But I do know one thing for sure: I was more myself in that elevator than I think I've ever been anywhere else.

Chapter 7
Devorah

Fridays, in preparation for Shabbos, are normally peaceful days. Businesses close at two or three PM so that commuters can get home well before sundown, and all the shopping and the ironing and the silver-polishing has been done ahead of time, throughout the week, so that Friday afternoons are spent soaking up the smells of homemade matzo ball soup simmering on the stove and sweet yellow-brown challah baking in the oven while neighborhood children play outside on the street before dinner. That's *normally*. Today is anything but normal.

For one thing, there's the aftermath of the storm, which has left the neighborhood looking as if some science fiction creature tramped through, kicking down trees and scattering branches and garbage like confetti across rooftops and power lines. The magnolia tree in our backyard miraculously survived, but the Eliavs' ancient, nearly dead pine did not, falling straight into their glassed-in sunporch and shattering two windows. I slept in Miri and Hanna's room last night (when the Shomrim dropped me off, after Jacob called in a favor, Miri met me at the door in tears and refused to fall asleep until I curled myself around her bird-boned body, singing lullabies and petting her hair), and the crash sent all three of us screaming up into Isaac's room. Then Isaac and I put on rain boots over our pajamas and darted across the front lawn to make sure our elderly neighbors were still alive (yes) and see if they needed help (also yes). So at seven AM, once the skies cleared to a mottled gray-blue, I was in the Eliavs' backyard, ankle-deep in mud and up to my elbows in my mother's gardening gloves, throwing shards of glass into a paper bag. Incidentally I didn't find any of Rose's and my "bad thoughts," even though I poked around for them. Like everything else on the ground, they must have been swept away.

The other abnormal development is that for the first time in my life, I am in charge of Shabbos dinner. Until the storm hit and Rose went into labor, my parents had planned to stay in Monsey for the weekend, and my siblings and I were going to walk to my brother Niv's house on Troy Avenue to eat. But Liya's arrival has changed everything, and now we have to whip up a huge Shabbos dinner out of nowhere, because in addition to being blessed with a new baby, a still-standing home, and all other manner of G-d's good graces, Rose is getting released early from the hospital. I don't know what my parents said or did to Dr. MacManus to get special treatment (I hope the doctor is still alive), but my mother called just half an hour ago and told us to set two extra places—one for Rose and one for my aunt Varda, whom my parents couldn't very well leave behind to fend for herself with one working foot—right before she asked me five hundred questions about every minuscule detail of our prep work. I know she's beside herself that she had to choose between meeting her first grandchild and micromanaging what Hanna and I have taken to calling *the Shabbos dinner to end all Shabbos dinners*. Both activities give her such great pleasure.

So now, just two hours before sundown, I'm frantically shifting pots and casserole dishes around our narrow kitchen, each move of my hands sending some sauce or oil splattering onto the teal-and-white decorative tile that borders my mother's prized double oven, while Hanna sets the table and Miri dusts the baseboards on her hands and knees.

"I cleaned everywhere except places no one can see," Miri reports, sidling up to me like a soldier at attention, clutching a dwindled roll of paper towels in one hand. The knees of her skirt are covered in dust, and her auburn hair hangs limply around her slender, porcelain-doll face.

"Even if someone gets down on all fours and peeks under the rug edges?" I ask, shoving a steaming tray of potato kugel on top of the fridge to make room for challah braiding.

"I think so?" Miri wipes a hand across her cheek, leaving a trail of dirt. It's considered a mitzvah to bathe in honor of Shabbos, but suffice it to say none of us has gotten around to obeying that particular commandment. I can still feel the caked mud on my calves from my morning of manual labor.

"Good girl," I say. "Now go and hide all the wrinkles in the tablecloth with decorative napkins. And find Amos—I need someone to help me braid the challah."

My mother enjoys entertaining and has been known to spend

weeks preparing for celebratory events. It is a fact that at my naming ceremony—seven days after she gave birth to me—she baked and decorated 150 bumblebee-shaped cookies, because "Devorah" means "bee" and also because she is *crazy*. I know that as soon as she walks through the door she's going to redo everything I'm doing, and I can't decide if that will be a great offense or a huge relief. Maybe both.

Miri runs off to cover up Hanna's lackluster ironing skills, and I lean back against the pass-through window, feeling the ache of thirty-six near-sleepless hours deep in my bones. It is the first minute I've had to myself since before the Elevator Incident. And as soon as I let my mind drift from my laundry list of Shabbos chores for even a second, all I can see is his face. *Jaxon*. Even though I've been distracted all day, I can't stop thinking about him. It doesn't help that while the storm cracked to a crescendo overhead last night as I slept in my sister's bed, I even dreamt about him:

I'm walking down the center of the Brooklyn Bridge, in a huge crowd, on a blindingly sunny day. Everyone around me wears dark coats and hats and keeps their heads down to protect their eyes. But I get this strange feeling that someone is looking for me, and so I turn my face up, and there on the top of the first tower is a figure in a red T-shirt, dangling his legs over the side. Jaxon. He reaches a hand down toward me, and then the sun goes black. Everything turns black.

"Did I hear you *challah* for me?" a voice pipes up. Amos is leaning on the doorjamb, and when I look over he shoots me a lopsided grin. Even though he's only about four feet tall and has some telltale signs of puberty, like a smattering of pimples and the three hairs dotting his chin that he calls a "beard," he's the handsomest of my brothers, with clear blue eyes, dark, wavy hair, and a huge, infectious smile.

"Yes," I say with a sigh. "Can you help me roll strands? I'm literally up to my elbows in dough." It's also all over my shirt and somehow in my nose. Amos laughs.

"Sure, but no promises. Mom doesn't let me in the kitchen for a reason." He washes his hands and rolls up his sleeves, and then we divide the thick, pillowy dough into six balls, rolling each between our palms to make foot-long snakes.

"Was it gross?" Amos asks me as he struggles to keep his snake from fraying in two.

"What?" I'm only half listening, my mind running a maddening stopwatch of how long I have before the shower window closes. Heating up liquids on Shabbos is forbidden, which means no hot water once the sun dips below the skyline.

"Rose . . . you know, giving *birth*," Amos says, wrinkling his nose as only a thirteen-year-old boy can when discussing the miracle of life.

"No!" I playfully swat him with a dishrag. (*Yichud* doesn't apply here since Hanna and Miri are in the next room, and the kitchen has no door.) "It was scary sometimes, but not gross." Our snakes completed, I pinch the tops together on a large cutting board and start to braid, drawing the farthest snake on the right over two, under one, and over two, just like my mother taught me when I was three years old.

"What about when the power went out?" he asks. Since he'd be useless at braiding, he's backed away from the counter and is rearranging refrigerator magnets while I work. "That must have been cool." Upstairs, I can hear Isaac shuffling around in the study.

He would never come down before dinner, not even when help is so desperately needed. And it's not for lack of kindness on his part; it's just the way things are: the roles we've learned and come to depend on. Amos is the exception to the rule, too precocious to stay out of other people's business.

"Actually it was stuffy, since the air-conditioning went off, too," I say with a smile. Amos rolls his eyes.

"You know what I mean," he says with a sigh. "Was it like—" He purses his lips and makes a noise like a computer powering down. It's actually pretty accurate.

"Kind of," I say, finishing the braid and tucking the ends of the challah underneath the loaf. I crack an egg against a ceramic bowl from the cabinet over the left-hand sink; everything in our kitchen has a twin to accommodate two sets of dishes, pots, and pans, one for meat and one for dairy.

"What about the guy you were stuck in there with? Was he scary?" Amos says this like it's harmless small talk, but it makes my breath catch in my throat. I freeze with half an eggshell in each hand, one holding the virtuous white, and the other the decadent yolk.

"Wait, how do you—"

"Jacob told me you got stuck in the elevator with a man."

"That's true," I say cautiously, discarding the egg whites into the open garbage can as I simultaneously slip the yolk into the bowl and whisk it with a fork until it looks like custard. I hand Amos the pastry brush and let him paint the challah with the glistening egg, hoping it will distract him. No such luck.

"Jacob said he looked dangerous," Amos says, knitting his eyebrows together in concern.

"What?! No, he—" I struggle to find words that won't

incriminate me. I can't say that Jaxon was nice; how would I know, if I had kept quiet? "It was scary at first, but . . . he was . . . *fine*," I say, shoving the challah into the oven so forcefully the baking sheet clangs against the rack. "He didn't bother me."

Amos shrugs. "I was just *asking*," he says, and bounds out of the kitchen as casually as he arrived. I, on the other hand, am almost trembling with anger and fear. Who else has Jacob told about Jaxon? What else has he said?

"Shabbat Shalom!" my mother trills as she sweeps into the house, cradling a pale, waddling Rose, who looks a bit dazed, her pretty face still puffy from the IV fluids. Jacob and my father—a nursery rhyme duo in the making, one short and scrawny, the other huge and barrel-shaped—trail behind, followed by Aunt Varda, hopping on one leg, and my middle brother, Niv, and his wife, Rivka, who have come bearing trays of roast chicken covered in tinfoil.

We all gather in the entryway and fawn over Rose, asking if we can get her anything. (The one upside to Rose being a *yoledet* is that we're technically allowed to break the Sabbath for her sake. I wonder: If I made myself smell bad enough, maybe she would *ask* me to take a shower?) But my sister demurs politely and settles into the armchair by the front window, holding her belly gently, as if a baby were still inside.

"Can I see a picture?" Miri asks, running and then sliding to a stop on her knees at Rose's feet.

"I . . . I don't have one," Rose says, looking like she might cry.

"*I* do," my mother says, settling her petite, round frame onto the couch next to Aunt Varda. (They wear nearly identical straight, shoulder-length, chestnut-colored wigs, which hide the strawberry-blond curls they were born with, a genetic gift from their mother that no one from my generation has received.) "I took enough for an album." She pulls a slim silver point-and-shoot camera out of her purse and turns it on, peering expectantly at the tiny, glowing screen.

"It's almost sundown, Ayelet," my father warns, but my mother dismisses him with a wave.

"Psssht," she says. "This is my *granddaughter*. Shabbos can wait."

Miri, Hanna, and my brothers crowd around the camera like puppies vying for milk, but I hang back. It's not that I don't want to see Liya again—I'm dying to, I barely caught a glimpse—but I need to keep an eye on Jacob. Specifically, I need to make sure he's not spreading rumors about me to my father. Ever since they walked in the door the two of them have been speaking quietly to each other with squinty, serious expressions. Under the pretense of double-checking the silverware placement, I wander closer to eavesdrop on their conversation.

". . . can't say for sure," Jacob says. "*Something* must have happened." My blood runs cold. Did Jacob somehow find out what happened in the elevator? Could he have heard us through the air shaft? I wouldn't put it past him to press his ear against the doors.

"Well," my father says slowly, "we don't know yet. You shouldn't blame yourself. Or her." *Thank you, Daddy*, I think, regaining my composure. He can be intimidating sometimes, and scary-silent, but my father has always been fair. I have crystal-clear memories of him dividing up the last slice of my eighth birthday cake into seven equal slivers with a protractor so that none of his children would feel favored or denied.

"You're right, I know you're right," Jacob says, nervously

scratching his beard. "I just can't understand. Seven weeks early, after seven months of no complications . . ."

Oh. I nearly crumple with shame as I "count" the last place setting. Of course they're not talking about me; they're talking about Liya's birth. And why shouldn't they? *That's* the huge news today, not my getting stuck in an elevator. What has gotten into me? Why am I obsessing about it? It was nothing.

Except it wasn't.

I ignore my inner voice and take the chicken from Rivka to set on the *blech*, the metal stove covering that keeps food warm once the sun sets and we aren't allowed to use electricity. While I'm in the kitchen, I turn on the faucet in the left-hand sink, cup the cool water in my shaking fingers, and splash my face until my cheeks go numb.

Sundown falls at 7:33 PM, so we're all seated around the big, rectangular dining table that Zeidy's father built back in Ukraine and transported to New York in pieces on a steamship—the same one that brought Zeidy and his eight siblings to the United States—by 7:15. I snuck in a shower just under the wire and have my limp, wet hair tucked behind my ears, dripping onto the back of my shirt. In my house we've always sat men on one side, women on the other, so Jacob, Isaac, Niv, Amos, Zeidy, and my dad sit across from Rose, Hanna, Rivka, me, Aunt Varda, and Miri. My mother takes the head of the table, which evens things out and also makes sense since she has to lead the blessings anyway.

It has already been decided that instead of the usual nine candles, we will light ten tonight, one for the baby in addition to the seven for each of us kids and the two requisite Shabbos candles. My mother lights the first two, then Rose lights two, and then me,

Hanna, and Miri, in age order. Once the tiny wicks are flickering in the otherwise dark house, casting us all in an amber glow, my mother stands and holds her palms out over the candles, drawing her hands in toward her face three times, as if beckoning the light. She covers her eyes and recites the blessing:

"Baruch a-ta A-do-nay Elo-hei-nu me-lech ha-o-lam a-sher ki-dee-sha-nu bi-mitz-vo-tav vi-tzi-va-noo li-had-leek ner shel Sha-bbat ko-desh."

We have to stay silent until my mother removes her hands from her eyes, which we've learned over the years is entirely dependent on her mood. If she's happy, she'll drop them almost immediately, but if she's upset she can hold out for a good two minutes. The idea is that she's using the quiet time to pray, so I guess the more she has to pray about, the longer she takes. Tonight is a two-minute night, and I wait it out trying in vain to pray for Liya instead of thinking about Jaxon.

When I was three I had to have surgery—nothing major, to have my tonsils removed—and as a reward for being brave, my mother took me to see *Annie* on Broadway. This was a big deal; hearing a woman sing in public is usually avoided as part of *tz'ni'ut*, but since Annie was played by a ten-year-old I guess my mom was able to rationalize it. According to her, I was very, very good during the whole show, but I *hated* it whenever Annie left the stage for any reason. "Where's Annie?" I would demand, holding my mother's face in my tiny hand. "Where. Is. Annie???" That's what my brain is doing right now, only with Jaxon. *Where is he? What's he thinking? Does he wonder about me, too?* I stare down at my plate as though the answers will appear, swimming up to the porcelain surface like letters in alphabet soup.

Finally, my mother drops her hands and we all shout, "Shabbat Shalom!" and turn to hug anyone within arm's reach. I leave a wet splotch on Aunt Varda's sweater.

After kiddush, the blessing over the wine, and the ritual hand-washing and the ceremonial breaking of my lopsided challah braid, it's finally time to eat, and my nerves must be burning extra calories, because I'm starving. I demolish three pieces of challah, slurp down a bowl of soup, and eat two servings of potato kugel before most of my family members have even filled their plates.

"Are we being timed?" Niv jokes.

"I like a girl with a healthy appetite," Zeidy says, laughing and refilling his wine. "Go on, *zeeskyte*, *ess*."

"More like *fress*," Isaac chimes in, and my brothers snort. *Fress* means to eat like an animal.

"Enough," my father says, and everyone quiets. There are rules for dinner conversation on Shabbos that include no fighting.

"Devorah," my mother says gently, giving me a pointed look. "Leave some for Rose, please. She needs her strength."

"No, Mama, I can't." Rose grimaces. "I've lost my appetite. I just want to be with her." She looks around the table, her eyes wet. "I'm sorry, this was a mistake."

"There is nothing we can do," Jacob says stoically. "Visiting hours have almost ended. And I don't think it will do you any good to spend the night on a waiting-room chair." He tears off a chunk of challah and hands it to my father, who passes it to Rose. "Please," he continues, making the word sound hard and impatient, the opposite of polite. "Have some bread, at least. You have to eat for your milk to come in."

Rose cringes but takes the food silently and holds it in her lap.

"Good girl," my father says gently. But I wonder if he can see what I see. I wonder if any of them do. Rose might be being "good," but she's not being *Rose*. My sister has always been the quiet one during big family gatherings, but this is different, and scary. It's like she's empty.

I study my mother's face in the flickering candlelight. Her stone-colored eyes are big and bright behind her glasses, her smile easy and genuine as she gazes proudly at my dad and around the table at the big family she'd always wanted after growing up one of only two daughters (I once asked her why Grandma Deborah never had more children, but my mother just bristled and told me it was no one's business but Grandma's and G-d's). Obviously I didn't know my mother before she was married, so I don't know if a switch flipped in her; if a light went out, like it seems Rose's has. She has always been charismatic and commanding and intolerant of what she calls *blote*, which translates roughly from Yiddish as bullshit. But one of the cruelties of teenagehood is that you'll never know what your parents were really like at your age, and they'll never accurately remember—not enough to empathize, anyway . . . maybe just enough for pity.

"Where is the baby sleeping?" Miri pipes up, and we all look to Rose, bracing ourselves for her to lose it completely, but amazingly, she comes to life, laughing as she wipes the tears from the corners of her eyes with her wrist.

"She's in an incubator, *tsigele*," Rose says. The Yiddish word for "baby goat" has been our nickname for Miri since she came home from the hospital colicky and brayed like livestock for six months straight.

"What's that?"

"It's a little bed that keeps her warm and protected until she's big enough to go outside."

Miri smiles and takes a bite of chicken, seeming happy with this answer, and Rose pops the challah into her mouth, reaching for another piece. My mother and father exchange a glance of relief.

"If you ask me," Jacob says—though clearly, no one has—"she could have come home today. She's a good size for a preemie, she's breathing on her own, she's eating . . . Keeping her 'for observation' is just an excuse for them to take more of our money. Why should we trust that doctor? She's not *our* doctor." He doesn't mean Dr. MacManus wasn't Rose's prenatal ob-gyn; I can tell he means that she's not one of us. Not a Chabadnik. Translation: not to be trusted.

Rose's face crumples again, and my mother rushes to comfort her.

"She was very respectful," I say. "Wasn't she, Rose?" Jacob glares at me.

"She was fine," Rose says quietly, dabbing her eyes with a napkin.

"Exactly!" Jacob cries, banging his fist on the table and almost upending Isaac's wine. "*Fine*. We shouldn't pay eight thousand dollars for fine."

"Jacob," my father warns in a deep and weary voice. Money and business are not discussed on Shabbos.

"Rivka's friend just had a baby," Niv says. "She used a midwife from Park Slope. They had a home birth, right in the living room."

On my right, Rivka takes a break from slowly and methodically picking the crispy top bits off her square of kugel and nods politely. She's very nice but doesn't talk much; Niv tends to speak for her, presumably because of her accent—Rivka's family moved to Brooklyn from Ukraine when she was fourteen. Her grandfather is a rabbi there, which impressed my parents when Niv was looking for a bride. But I wonder what Rivka was looking for in a husband. My middle brother is fine as brothers go—a bit bossy and juvenile but not cold like Jacob or oblivious like Isaac—and yet, just like Jacob said, fine isn't enough. Not for the rest of your life, anyway.

I look over at Rose, who is staring into her lap, pale as a ghost, lips cracked and eyes red. I can't believe that this woman is the same brave big sister I looked up to and aspired to become for more than fifteen years, the one whose braces seemed so beautiful and sophisticated to me that I approximated them with strips of tinfoil on my own straight teeth. Maybe it's not fair to blame Jacob entirely; after all, she just pushed a human being out of her body without pain medication. But there's a spark that's gone from Rose—not just gone, but seemingly taken from her against her will. I take a bite of my bread and say a silent vow that I will never let that happen to me.

With Jaxon it wouldn't. The thought takes me by surprise, so much so that I swallow too quickly and nearly choke.

"I told you not to eat so fast," Niv says, and laughs. Jacob just looks annoyed that I've interrupted the conversation.

"Well," my mother says once I catch my breath. "A home birth would be dangerous seven weeks early. Too much risk."

"True," Jacob says. "But for the next one, I would feel much better staying in Crown Heights, with our people to take care of us."

"We'll see," my father says vaguely.

"What we need is more Hasidic doctors," Isaac cracks. Since secular schooling is frowned upon—too much opportunity for insidious outside culture to seep in—there are few doctors, lawyers, and other professionals in our community, or in any of the Hasidic sects.

"What we need is a fence," Niv says, and the boys laugh.

"Maybe all of the goyim could move to Manhattan and let us have Brooklyn," Jacob adds.

"Or we can kick the soccer moms off Staten Island," Isaac says, and laughs.

"You're all being imbeciles," Zeidy grumbles, and I want to give him an air high five like Jaxon taught me. But of course I keep my hands on my knife and fork.

"No one is going anywhere," my mother says loudly, a forced smile stretched wide across her face, the equivalent of a flashing yellow light warning her children to cut it out before she loses patience. "We live where we live."

"And I have an easy way to avoid dealing with outsiders," my father adds. "Ignore them."

"But what if you can't?" Hanna asks, refilling her grape juice. "What if you get *stuck* with one?" I catch my breath. I don't know if this is coincidence or if Jacob has taken it upon himself to tell everyone where I was during the blackout.

My father chuckles, brushing crumbs off his beard with his napkin. His full, wide cheeks are rosy with wine. "How, my dear, would you get yourself stuck with one?" He doesn't know. A good sign.

Hanna casts a sidelong glance my way. "I don't know," she says, picking at her salad. "What if you met in some way through forces outside of your control, almost like it was fate?" Hanna is the hopeless romantic of the family. She's also the most outspoken opponent of our parents' no-TV policy, since it means she can't watch movies to feed her fairy-tale fetish.

"Like if an elevator stopped!" Miri nearly shouts, so excited that she has information to contribute to the grown-up talk. "Like with Devorah in the hospital!"

I glare across the table, first at Jacob and then at Amos, not sure who has betrayed me.

My father turns to me and sets down his fork. "Devorah, enlighten me. What's this about an elevator?" Jacob smirks. He didn't tell my father after all, but he clearly set me up by telling Amos. Okay, fine, I decide; if that's how he wants to play, I'll play. I smile sweetly at him and prepare to unleash my secret weapon, which is that regardless of the spark that was lit in that elevator, I am Devorah "*Frum* from Birth" Blum, and as far as my family knows I am nothing if not a virtuous daddy's girl.

"Tatty," I say calmly, invoking my childhood pet name for him, "after I helped Rose through her delivery and checked on the baby in the NICU, I couldn't find Jacob anywhere, so I decided to look downstairs. While I was on the elevator, the power went out, and I was trapped with a boy my age."

"He was black," Amos pipes up.

"Amos!" I yell.

"Did he try to save you?" Hanna asks breathlessly.

"That doesn't matter," my father says, clearing his throat. "Devorah had no control over her circumstances. What matters is how she behaved, which I know and trust is the right way." I smile at Jacob again, and he rolls his eyes.

"However," my father continues, "the laws of *yichud* exist for a reason, and we should all remember that when circumstances *are* within our control, we are bound to obey them."

"Otherwise you'll end up like Ruchy Silverman," Niv says. Isaac stifles a laugh, and Rivka gasps. My parents seem to freeze in place, and exchange another glance that looks to me to be the opposite of relief.

"Did something happen to Ruchy?" I ask. I'm truly confused, as Ruchy was in the grade above me at school until the middle of last year, when she left suddenly to go on a trip to Israel. She has the shiniest golden hair and a face like a fashion model; Shoshana and I have spent many hours trying to make ourselves feel better by cataloguing her potential flaws.

"Niv," my mother says sharply, "that is not dinner conversation, and certainly not Shabbos conversation."

"I'm sorry," he says. "I take it back."

"Did she get hurt?" I ask. As much as I'm jealous of Ruchy, I would never wish harm on her. Well, nothing worse than acne, anyway.

"She got what she deserved," Jacob mutters, and my father sets down his fork and shoots daggers in his direction.

"No," my father says angrily. "She is fine, and we will discuss it *another time*." The end of the sentence comes out like a growl.

My mother makes a show of changing the subject, and gradually, as my father relaxes, talk turns to the coming school year. But as my family chatters and laughs around me, I retreat into my head, worrying now about *two* people and where they are: Ruchy and Jaxon. Jaxon and Ruchy. Two figures that my memory renders both blurry and larger than life. Two specters I will probably never see again.

Chapter 8

Jaxon

SEPTEMBER 2, 7 AM

I'm already awake when my alarm rings, staring up at the cracks in the ceiling above my bed, which look like two crooked parentheses with nothing in the middle. That's a good analogy for the new school year, too: a big question mark hanging over you that could collapse at any minute. Kidding. Sort of.

I've been grounded since the night of the storm (a Thursday, and today is Tuesday), so I'm actually excited to get up and out, even though my summer-logged brain isn't used to having to function this early. Staying in my room can get claustrophobic, since it's no more than a glorified closet that barely fits a twin bed and a dresser, but that's the price I pay for having my own space, I guess. Edna and Ameerah share a room, Tricia and Joy share, and of course Mom and Dad do, too. I'm the only one with any kind of privacy in this cramped house where we're all practically on top of one another all the time, constantly up in one another's business. It's awesome to hole up in my room when I have my cell and laptop to listen to music and check Facebook and stream movies, but in my family *grounded* means no phone, no computer, no friends, no leaving the building unless it's for work or school, and obviously no basement training sessions. So for the past four days I've been trudging through the last of my summer reading list, *Invisible Man* and *Ethan Frome*. Both are crazy depressing, so I've been taking lots of breaks to read the stash of comics my mom forgot to confiscate from under my mattress.

I'm pretty sure my parents aren't that mad at me anymore. I got a huge lecture about the importance of honesty (and skateboard safety) when I got home on Thursday night, followed by the silent treatment on Friday, but after I did the dishes and two loads of laundry and picked up all the socks (thirteen) and hair elastics (seven) strewn around the living room without being asked, they started to forget to shun me by the weekend. Mom even gave me two extra strips of bacon at breakfast on Sunday, although I was still banned from going with the rest of the family to the West Indian Day parade on Eastern Parkway (which I told myself was just as well since it's flooded with cops, and people get shot or stabbed almost every year). But when they got home, giddy and sunburned, dad slipped me $100 from his shoebox stash to buy some new school clothes. And then yesterday morning mom let me watch NY1 with her, and when I told her (in a fit of shameless ass-kissing) that I wanted to go to journalism school to be like Pat Kiernan, she hugged me and told me I was her favorite son, which is our running joke.

So I'm feeling pretty good walking to school to start my junior

year, even if I am carrying ten pounds of books over my shoulder
and wearing my same old jeans and navy hoodie, the one with the
cuffs all frayed and thumb holes poked through. (My dad may have
given me money, but that doesn't mean I could leave the house to
spend it.) But it's seventy-five and sunny, and I've got a free first
period and Charles Mingus playing on my phone as I walk down
Kingston Avenue, past the neat little brick row houses with red plastic awnings jutting out over front stoops tagged with amateur graffiti, past the nail salons spilling their acetone-laced air-conditioning
out onto the sticky pavement and the liquor stores, all neon signs
and labyrinthian aisles of lotto-ticket-lined bulletproof glass, before
I finally see the broad, leafy lanes of Eastern Parkway, Brooklyn's
own little ghetto Champs-Élysées.

And then I see them.

Black coats, white shirts, black fedoras, and beards on most of
them, just like that mean-looking dude outside the elevator. They're
clustered around a reddish brick building with pointed turrets and
stained-glass windows that looks kind of like a church crossed with
a normal apartment complex. But the really weird thing is that I've
made this walk at least five hundred times, and I've never noticed
them before—not as anything other than scenery, anyway. Just then
a group of girls rounds the corner, in matching black skirts, white
blouses, and cardigans, and out of the corner of my eye I see a lock
of dark, curly hair lifted up by the wind, and suddenly my breath
is gone. I stare for longer than I should, just to make sure it's not
her (of course it isn't, and to add potential injury to insult a burly
middle-aged guy sees me looking and gives me the stink-eye). As
I make a hasty retreat down the steps to the train, Devorah's words
ring in my head—*What, we all look the same to you?*—and I think

about how just a week ago I wouldn't have been able to pick her out of a crowd, and now she's the only thing I'd see in one. Not that I'll ever see her again. I turn my Mingus up, wedge myself into a too-packed 3 train between two Jamaican nurses trading salt-fish recipes, and try to zone out.

When I get to school I take the stairs two at a time to the third floor and step over the other free-period kids, who are sitting cross-legged under their lockers, alternating between screaming greetings at one another and staring into their phones. I don't see anyone I know yet, so I head to my locker, which is just through the doorway that leads to the back stairwell and up to "the cage," a chain-link janitorial supply area by the roof entrance that's supposedly a secret hookup spot. Not that I'd know.

I'm unloading the contents of my messenger bag when Polly passes by about six inches from me, so close I can smell her coconut shampoo. She's got her hair pulled back in a little ponytail with pieces tucked behind each ear, and she's wearing skinny jeans, a tight purple button-down, gray Converse, and thick, black-framed glasses that added up make her look like an impossibly cute hipster librarian. But something about the sight of her doesn't paralyze me for once. And maybe that's why, for the first time in months, she zeros in on me right away.

"Hey," she says, a little hesitantly.

"Hey." I close my locker and try to lean against it casually, which it turns out is impossible if you're actually trying. I give up and shove my hands in my pockets.

"I was actually looking for you," she says. Polly's amber eyes dart nervously behind me, where a couple of goth-looking girls are clustered around their lockers comparing schedules. "I've gotta get to International Relations. But, hey, is Ryan okay? I felt bad not staying, but my dad—"

"Hates us?" I finish.

"No!" Polly smiles apologetically. "He was just in a bad mood."

"Right," I say, raising an eyebrow. I mean it to be flirtatious, but Polly frowns. "I mean, *right*, like of course," I say, clearing my throat.

"Right," she says. It could not get any more awkward.

Or so I thought.

"This freak bothering you, P?" Jason Rivera, the varsity basket-ball shooting guard, who's easily two hundred pounds and built like a tractor trailer, all square shoulders and compact muscle, swoops in and lifts Polly up under one arm like she's a physics textbook (not that J-Riv, which is his ridiculous, derivative nickname, would ever pick up a physics textbook, I'm just saying). Polly squeals delightedly and yells, "Put me *down*, monster! Jaxon and I were just talking."

Jason drops her and looks me up and down, clearly unimpressed.

"Action Jaxon, huh?" he says. No one calls me that. "He don't look so weird to me. Well, except for that pube mustache." My face tingles with shame. I only have to shave like once every three weeks, but if I forget I get some sparse little tufts. I didn't think anything was showing, but Ameerah fogged up the bathroom mirror so much with her long-ass shower this morning, I guess I didn't really get a good look.

"Thanks," I say, attempting to defuse whatever's happening here with self-deprecation. "I'm working on a soul patch, too."

Jason shakes his head, like I'm a lost cause. "Whatever, freak."

"Hey," I say to Polly, who's averting her eyes. "Did I miss a memo or something? Why does he keep calling me a freak?"

"Because," Jason booms, "this is the freak hallway, *freak*." He bangs his giant fist against my locker for emphasis, and a group of seniors passing behind him crack up. I look behind me just in time to see one of the goth girls give him the finger.

"Let's go, P," Jason says, leading Polly away by the arm. She shrugs at me and mouths "*Sorry*."

I'm sorry for you, I want to call after her. *You're better than this*. But the urge to get through my first day without a beat-down is slightly more powerful, so I just watch them go.

I wait around for Ryan, but he's late—really late, since first period is almost over. And I know we have the same schedule on Tuesdays and Thursdays: free first followed by a double AP Bio lab. We also have the same social studies elective: Intro Philosophy on Monday and Wednesday mornings with Mr. Miserandino, whose nickname is "Mr. Misery" because he routinely yells at students and kicks you out of class if you're even a second late. My commute is half an hour door to door, so I'm gonna have to hustle to get here early. I'll probably have to get up at six thirty just to win the race for the first shower. Or nah, I'll just skip the shower those days and spray on some extra Axe. Like my mom says, I have to keep my eyes on the prize, and I'm willing to bet the admissions board at Columbia cares more about grades than a little natural musk.

Finally the bell rings, and Ryan runs through the door so fast he nearly smacks into me. He's still wearing his sling, which he's tagged himself with a Sharpie message that reads, "Keep Calm and Carry My Books."

"There you are!" he pants. "Oh, man, you owe me. I told Miserandino your grandma died yesterday."

"What are you talking about? And that's not cool. Both of my grandmas are still alive, man."

"Philosophy," he says. "The class we just had. Or *I* just had."

I place my hands on his shoulders, making the most of our six-inch height difference. "Ryan," I say. "What are you smoking? We have a free first period Tuesdays."

He swats my hands away, his blue eyes twinkling with some mixture of amusement and schadenfreude. "Jaxon," he says, imitating my condescending tone. "Today's a *Monday* schedule, dude."

"Oh, no." I feel the blood drain from my face. I've accidentally cut my first class of the year. With Mr. Misery, who takes no prisoners. "Oh, *shit*."

"Yup. You so owe me."

"I don't owe you," I say, grabbing my bag. (If today is a Monday schedule, that means I have Spanish in five minutes, which means I need to get halfway around the building.) "I stayed with you in the ER all day Thursday. If anything, *you* owed *me*. And now we're even." I make a break for the stairwell, and Ryan follows. "By the way," I say once we're out of the goth girls' earshot, "did you know our lockers are in the freak hallway?"

"I found out this morning when some chick with a septum barbell tried to scalp me tickets to see a band called Blood Spatter," Ryan says. "I already put in a request with the main office to switch."

"Why didn't you tell me?" I ask.

"I would have, if you would have been *on time*," he says, trying to rub it in some more.

"You could have texted me," I say as we exit the stairwell on the second floor and merge into boisterous teenage traffic. "Or did your phone get dislocated trying to jump the toaster?"

Ryan gets quiet, and I wonder if I've hurt his feelings, but when I turn back to check he smiles at me nervously.

"Look," he says, struggling to keep pace, "I was going to talk about it at lunch, but, um . . . I'm kind of not supposed to hang out with you for a little while."

"What?!" I stop in my tracks, and a tiny freshman plows into me, sending his iPod flying. Ryan retrieves it for the kid and then drags me over to a nearby water fountain.

"I know," he says. "But my parents are pretty pissed about what happened."

"It wasn't my idea," I say, glancing at my phone. I have sixty seconds before I'm late to my second class of the day.

"They kind of think it is," Ryan says, looking at the floor and scratching the back of his neck.

"Why would they think that?"

"Because I kind of . . . told them it was?"

"Ryan!"

"I know, I know," he says, holding up his good hand defensively. "But they were so mad at me for not telling them about it, they were going to take my Xbox 360, so I needed a scapegoat."

The warning bell rings—thirty seconds—and I take my cue. I back away from Ryan and toward the small beige-paneled room where I'll be forced to perform dialogue scenes in which I describe in detail every piece of furniture in my imaginary Mexican hotel room.

"I don't have time for this," I yell. And as I turn my back I wonder if it's remotely possible that this could all be a dream, one of those worst-case-scenario anxiety nightmares in which every-thing that could go wrong, does. I'm an accidental truant and a self-selected freak. My best friend can't talk to me, and my former crush is getting manhandled in front of me by a giant basketball star. I have a patchy mustache and old clothes, and nobody sees past that to the person underneath.

No one but her, anyway. Devorah's different from every girl—hell, every person—I've ever known. She has no game, no agenda. She made me feel like the best version of myself: brave and funny but not trying too hard; romantic but not cheesy. She made me feel like a good man, maybe even good enough to deserve someone as open and guileless and beautiful as her.

But I've got to stop thinking that. I don't know where Devorah is, and I probably never will. Like the saying goes, lightning doesn't tend to strike twice.

Chapter 9
Devorah

People like to say it's a small world. And even if you're talking big picture, that's probably true. But my world sometimes redefines the word "small." Like the fact that my school is four blocks from my house, and my family's store is one block from my school. Which means that on the average day, I travel exclusively within the same quarter-mile radius.

It didn't used to feel so small. I never wanted to venture outside. We're taught early on that strangers can't be trusted and that we are never to speak to anyone who isn't Hasidic (well, except for the boys and men who get to ride around in the Mitzvah mobiles, trying to bring non-Orthodox Jews back into the fold; Chabad is the only Hasidic sect that embraces proselytizing, which in a way is the only reason I exist, since my grandma was allowed to convert). Anyway,

I know it sounds closed-minded, but I never really even wondered about what life was like beyond the borders of my neighborhood. People outside the faith didn't seem real, more like two-dimensional cutouts living in a far-off other world.

Before I met Jaxon, my only connection to life beyond Chabad, ironically, was through the subjects I studied in school. This might sound nerdy, but I really loved learning. I used to pore over my textbooks when I got home, following the words with my pointer finger and stopping whenever I struck something I wanted to commit to memory, like *octopuses have rectangular pupils*, or *every hour the universe expands by a billion miles in all directions*. When my finger hit a sentence that was blacked out by the school censors, it felt like an exciting mystery.

But something about this year feels very different. Suddenly nothing quite fits—and not just my billowy white school blouse, which is straining at the bust for the first time under my thick navy vest. I feel an unrest creeping in, that expanding, unknown universe straining against the confines of my consciousness. And it's paralyzing. This morning I sat through my Hebrew class without raising my hand once, even though as usual I knew all the answers. I forgot to take notes during Halakha because Mrs. Piekarski started talking about the three levels of sin—*pesha*, *avon*, and *chet*—and I got distracted trying to figure out which sin I'm committing by not being able to stop thinking about Jaxon. *Pesha* is purposeful and wicked, deliberately defying G-d, like stealing or killing. *Avon* is uncontrollable lust or emotion against your will or better judgment. And *chet* is unintentional, obviously the best kind. I want it to be *chet*, but I'm pretty sure it's *avon*. It can't be a good sign that I keep thinking about the curve of his lips in profile, or the way his skin felt against my own, like electrified velvet. Incidentally, I don't marvel over the censored pages in my schoolbooks anymore. I *know* what Romeo and Juliet are doing behind those marks. And more than that, I *want* to know.

"Are you okay?" Shoshana asks me when we break for lunch in the courtyard, sitting down at a wooden table and unwrapping our tuna sandwiches. "You seem weird." The sun shines brightly in my eyes, lending Shosh's light brown hair a halo of starbursts.

"What do you mean?" I take a bite of my sandwich but find it hard to chew. My mouth is dry, dehydrated. I probably sweated all my fluids out through stress over the weekend. Mom took us clothes shopping in the city, and every dark-skinned boy I saw made my heart pound. I don't know if I was more scared to find out that it *was* him or that it wasn't.

"Ever since Rose had the baby you haven't been returning my calls," she says, pouting a little. "And you haven't told me anything yet." She lowers her voice and leans in so that the teachers chaperoning lunch won't hear. "*Especially* about the stranger."

"How did you hear about that?" I stage-whisper. But it's not surprising. Gossip travels fast in our community, because the culture is so insular. Everyone wants to know everyone's business. Amos probably told Shosh's brother, Judah, or Hanna told her friend Naomi who lives next door to Shosh's older sister, Aviva. Jacob also sometimes does his Shomrim patrol with Aviva's husband, Michah. The potential paths are endless.

"Come on," Shoshana says with a playful smile. "*You?* Trapped in a confined space with a black man? That's like a joke setup, like 'Two rabbis walk into a bar.'"

"Thanks," I say.

"But seriously," she says. "What did you *do*? Did you freak out?" Shosh has always been easily excitable; the first time I met her, on the street in our neighborhood when we were six, she was literally spinning in circles because she'd eaten too much chocolate babka. I can't help but get worked up by proxy.

"A little," I admit, taking a gulp from my water bottle. "Inside, anyway."

"Did he try to talk to you?"

I nod, ducking my chin to hide the smile that reflexively parts my lips every time I think about our conversation.

"What did he *say*?"

"Not much at first. He told me not to worry. Then he tried to get us out. He actually climbed through a hatch in the ceiling."

"No!" Shosh's eyes have grown perfectly round. She is loving this.

"Mmm hmmm."

"What did you do?"

I look around to make sure that none of the teachers are paying attention, and then I lean forward, my chin nearly trembling from the weight of what I'm about to say. I've been dying for four days to get the guilt off my chest, and if anyone will understand, I know it's Shosh. "I spoke to him," I whisper.

"Shut *up*."

"I know," I say. "But he was being so considerate, and after he kicked open the ceiling just to try to help, I felt bad—or rude—not saying anything."

Shoshana sits back, smiling softly. "I'm impressed," she says. "I never would have pegged you for such a rebel." Of course she's joking, just like Jaxon was when *he* called me a rebel. But still, my face burns with shame.

"It's awful, isn't it?" I ask.

"It's not awful, it's awesome," Shoshana cries, drawing the attention of the nearby tables. I glare at her, and she lowers her voice again. "What did you guys talk about? No, wait, first tell me what he looked like. Spare no details."

"He was . . . normal," I sputter, unprepared for the question.

"Was he handsome?"

"I . . ." *am obsessed with his face, even though I can't remember exactly what it looks like.* "Couldn't really tell. It was dark."

"What about his body?" Shoshana wiggles her eyebrows. Girls in my community tend to respond to the laws of *yichud* in two ways: Some never, ever think about the opposite sex, to keep their minds pure; and some think about them all the time, seeing romance as a forbidden mystery. My best friend is clearly in the second camp.

"Shosh! Stop it," I say, covering my face with my hands.

"Oh, you're no fun, frummie," she says, tearing off the end of her straw wrapper and blowing the paper at me. I raise an eyebrow.

"Hey," I say. "If you must know, my *frum* status has been falling steadily since Thursday."

"Prove it," she challenges, sipping her cranberry juice and feigning disinterest.

"Well, I talked to him," I say. "I listened to music on his phone—"

"What?! Which songs?" Shosh interjects.

"Something old, I don't know it," I say dismissively, rushing to get to the secret I need to spill, that's burning like a wildfire in my chest. "And . . . I keep *thinking* about him, too. About Jaxon. That's his name. His first name, anyway. I don't know his last name."

"Wow, that's manly," she says dreamily. "Like a general or something."

"He spells it with an X," I add, unable to help myself.

"Oooh, edgy!"

"I guess," I say. "He wasn't edgy, though. He seemed pretty nerdy, actually." I smile self-consciously. "In a good way."

"Dev," she says, pushing away her half-eaten sandwich, "this is *literally* the best thing I have heard in months. I'm so glad this happened. Not Rose's baby being born early or any of the dangerous parts, of course, but you getting a crush. On a goy!"

"Shhhhhh!" The girls at other tables don't seem to be listening, but it's a risk to be discussing this out in the open. There's a lot of inner policing at my school, girls turning one another in for bad behavior. Shosh is the only person I trust with this, and I have to be careful, especially since the news is spreading. Not through Jacob, I'm pretty sure—he's too concerned with piety to risk the family's reputation—but through my younger siblings, who don't know any better.

"Oh, what, you don't think half the girls at school don't go home and pine for Ryan Gosling?"

"Who's Ryan Gosling?"

"This is my point," she says excitedly. "You don't watch regular movies. You don't sneak gossip magazines into your room on Shabbos. You don't secretly text boys—you don't even have a cell phone! You don't do *any* of the things most of us do. I love you, Dev, but sometimes I've wondered if you're not some kind of perfect robot. Until now." She grins. "You're officially normal."

I know this is a backhanded compliment, but it fills me with relief. Maybe I've been worrying over nothing. Maybe this really *is* normal.

"I don't know," I say. "It doesn't feel normal to think this much about a boy—*any* boy."

"It definitely is," Shosh says. "It's hormones. Hormones don't care if we're saving ourselves for marriage." I feel my cheeks flush bright red.

"I'm not thinking about him like *that*," I say. Which is true. Even in my fantasies, we just sit and talk some more. Or okay, maybe hold hands. But that's *it*. "I just think about . . . what he's doing. Or if I'll ever run into him again."

"Too bad you don't know his last name or where he lives," Shosh says, laughing.

"Well . . ." I lean in conspiratorially. "He mentioned that he works at some place called Wonder Wings. And I know it's crazy, but I was thinking of going there. One day after school. Just to say hi."

Shoshana's face suddenly changes. Her smile disappears and is replaced by a look of true shock.

"Devorah," she says, dead serious for the first time all day—and maybe ever. "You can't do that."

I'm momentarily speechless. Of course she's right. And I can't believe I even said that out loud. The giggly girl talk gave me a sense of security that I have no business having. Shosh may be my best friend since first grade, but she's still Hasidic. *I'm* still Hasidic. Even if I secretly met with a Chabad boy I could ruin my reputation. And here I am blithely suggesting that I meet Jaxon just blocks from my home, steps from the watchful eyes of my neighbors, my family, the Shomrim. I can't do that. I know this, the way I know my alphabet or my prayers or how to arrange the Shabbos silverware, but it's not until this moment that I actually understand: I can *never* see him again. Not by choice. A lump rises in my throat, and I take a bite of my cold sandwich just to force it back down.

"I mean, think about him, yeah," Shosh says, relaxing a little bit. "Pretend he's your boyfriend in your head if you want. But you know that it can never, *ever* happen in real life. That's not an option."

I know that I should just backtrack and pretend I was joking. But something is overflowing in me now—years of compartmentalization, years of pushing down the questions, years of accepting the pat answer of *Because that's what it says in the Torah* with an obedient nod.

"Why not?" I hear myself say. "What would be so wrong about it?"

"Are you kidding?" Shosh asks, looking at me like I've just started doing cartwheels in the middle of temple. "He's not one of us. He's not even *Jewish*." I press my lips together and try to breathe deeply. *What am I doing?* Just as Jax doesn't understand my world, no one I know will sympathize with this insane crush I'm harboring. I should have known better. "Unless he converted," Shosh continues, "you could never be with him and still live here. And even if he converted, you'd have to be matched . . ." She stares at me like I'm crazy. "You *know* this, Dev. You know the rules backward and forward. And until about five seconds ago, I thought you followed them. All of them."

"I do," I say defensively. "All I'm saying is I *liked* talking to him, and I don't know why it's such a big deal." I emphasize the past-tense verb, feeling a little guilty. It's a lie. Just one more drop in the bucket of sins I seem to be hauling around ever since I stepped off the elevator.

"Well, okay," Shoshana says tentatively. "It's over anyway. Just don't do anything more. If you went away I would die."

I laugh, rolling my eyes. "Where would I go?" I ask.

"Maybe to 'Israel,'" Shosh says, making air quotes. "Like Ruchy."

I perk up. I had been meaning to ask Shoshana about the mystery of what happened to Ruchy Silverman. Getting an answer about her could be the silver lining to what's shaping up to be a totally depressing lunch period.

"You mean she didn't go to Israel?" I ask, trying to sound casual.

Shoshana shakes her head. "She had a boyfriend," she says. "A film student at NYU. Her parents found some texts."

I furrow my brow. That's bad, but not as bad as I thought it would be. Niv made it sound like Ruchy had made some fatal error in judgment. Like she was dead.

"How did she meet him?" I probe. Ruchy may have been beautiful and popular, but she definitely wasn't a "bad girl."

Shoshana smirks. "You know the home for the mentally disabled where she worked after school? The guy had an uncle there. They got to talking, and one thing led to another." She fixes me with an I-told-you-so look.

"But then why is she gone from school? I mean, didn't Mr. and Mrs. Silverman just break them up when they found out?"

Shoshana shakes her head. "It was too late," she whispers.

I frown. "What does that even mean?"

"Devorah, you're so innocent," Shoshana says with a sigh. She glances around nervously and then gestures for me to look under the table, so I "accidentally" drop my napkin. At first I can't make out what she's doing down there, since the sun is reflecting off the mosaic glass set into the stone floor, and my eyes have trouble adjusting. But after a few seconds, I get it, and my breath catches in my throat. Shoshana is drawing an arc between her rib cage and her pelvis. She's telling me that Ruchy got pregnant.

I sit back up and take a deep breath. "Where is she now?" I ask.

"No one knows," Shoshana says gravely. "It's like she doesn't exist."

The conversation with Shosh is still weighing on me after school as I absentmindedly work the register at the store. Since Rose is on indefinite leave from her post as cashier, I get to break up the monotony of my stocking/shelving duties to help out up front when my dad holes himself up in the back office, poring over sales and inventory spreadsheets and making orders. I actually love working the register. Most of our customers have been coming for years, so I can greet them by name and ask after their families, which usually earns me a pat on the hand and a muttered blessing. I love the older ladies especially, because they usually pay cash, and there's nothing better than ringing up purchases the old-fashioned way, hearing the dull chime of the register as it springs open and counting out change. I've never once given incorrect change. My father jokes that he shouldn't even bother balancing the register at the end of the day when I've been working, since it always comes out even, to the penny. That's the thing about math: It's dependable. Math will never give you a blank stare and tell you you're going to end up barefoot and pregnant, some grotesque poster child for the importance of *yichud*.

But maybe I'm being too hard on Shosh. She's just looking

out for me, in her way, which is to overreact. The funny thing is, her tough-love advice has made me think more about Jaxon, not less. I feel more than ever like I need to see him again, just to find out if he deserves to be on this surreal and dangerous pedestal I've placed him on. Was he really that charming? Or interesting? Did it really feel electric when we touched, or were my nerves just jumpy from the day I'd had? Given my mental state that night, I'd worry that I hallucinated Jaxon, except for the fact that Jacob clearly saw him, too.

"Hey, where do the Shana Tova boxes go?" Hanna interrupts my reverie, teetering into view from the greeting card aisle, balancing a dozen gift boxes bedecked with shiny red plastic apples in her trembling arms. Since the high holidays fall in three weeks, we've been spending hours arranging display shelves full of products featuring apples, honey, and the somewhat less appetizing shofar, a ram's horn. (On Rosh Hashanah we eat apples dipped in honey to ensure a sweet year, and my dad blows the shofar to usher in the Ten Days of Repentance, which are as fun as they sound.) We don't normally sell food, but the gift boxes are filled with candy and packets of honey, and occasionally Hanna and I will "spill" one on purpose so that we can hoard and eat its contents. Right now, though, Hanna is threatening to spill them by accident. I rush out from behind the counter and take some of them off her hands.

"Let's put these in the window," I say.

"But we just changed the window for back-to-school!" she groans.

"Right, but now school is back, and it's time for Rosh Hashanah," I say. "Besides, the new year is so much more fun to decorate. It's full of . . . possibility. Think of all the people wishing for something special this year. Like to fall in love." That gets her. Hanna is a sucker for all things romance. As a Hasid, of course, she approaches it from an anthropological distance. She would make an excellent *shadchan*.

"Fine," she says with a sigh, adjusting her grip. "Lead the way."

We spend almost an hour—interrupted only once by Mrs. Gottlieb looking for a disposable waterproof tablecloth—rearranging the crude tableaus that sit behind the streaky windows, underneath the sagging blue-and-white striped awning. Our store isn't fancy, but it has character. A few years ago at a stoop sale Mom picked up some pedestals painted to look like Corinthian columns roped with grapevines, and so now whatever product we're pushing gets special placement. Hanna and I set up three columns side by side, one tall and two short, like an Olympic podium, and have the Shana Tova boxes cascading down them, surrounded by holiday cards splayed out in heart patterns. I think it looks pretty good. And even better, it managed to completely take my mind off what happened at lunch.

I've just resumed my post behind the counter when my father comes out of the office.

"Daddy, we did the windows!" Hanna announces.

"That's great, *shana punim*, I'll look in a minute," he says, frowning down at his watch. "Hanna, listen, I need you to run an errand for me. I forgot to pick up my cholesterol medicine at lunch, the pharmacy closes at five, and I have a call with a manufacturer that I'm already late for. Can you run over and get it?" He peels two twenties out of his wallet and hands them to her. "You can buy yourself something with the change—just no candy, it's almost suppertime."

"Sure, Papa," Hanna says brightly, taking the bills. "Just let me know where to go."

"It's J&R Drugs, on Union and Nostrand," he says. "It's right next to that fast-food restaurant—"

I don't claim to be any sort of mystic, but somehow, I know what my father's going to say before he does. It's like déjà vu. This whole day I've felt sort of fuzzy and out of focus, and now suddenly, everything is lining up, like the mirrors of a kaleidoscope shifting.

"—Wonder Wings," he finishes. And just like that, there it is again, that electric feeling I thought I had made up, crawling across my scalp.

Jaxon works less than half a mile from my family's store. Less than four blocks from my school. Of course I could have discovered this easily if I just snuck onto my father's computer when he was up front helping customers, or stood on a kitchen stool to reach the cabinets above the pantry, where my mother stores the thick yellow phone books that show up on our doorstep once a year, even though we never use them. Those things would have felt wrong. This, though—my father, casually mentioning the piece of information I've been all but obsessing over for the past four days, the only piece of this forbidden puzzle that I'm missing—this feels like a sign. This tells me I *have* to go.

"Daddy?" I say. "It's getting late, and the men will be out in the streets coming home from work . . . let me go with Hanna."

He furrows his thick brow for a minute—it's still bright and sunny outside, after all, and at a big-boned five foot seven, Hanna's bigger than I am, so if anything, she'd be protecting me—but then shrugs.

"Business is slow today," he says. "I'll just put out the bell in case anyone comes in while you're gone."

Hanna is grinning at me, her pale, freckled face slick with sweat. She's excited to have a break and to have the company. She has no idea she's just become my accomplice.

I spend the walk to the pharmacy having two conversations. One is with Hanna, in real life, an inane back-and-forth about some girl in her class who Hanna doesn't like. The other one is more urgent but also much harder to carry on, since it's all in my head: the conversation I'm about to have with Jaxon.

". . . so she told Rachel that Rachel couldn't sit in front of her because she's allergic to her perfume. But then Rachel goes, 'I don't even wear perfume!'"

Hi.

I hope it's not weird that I came by. I was just running an errand with my sister, and I saw the sign.

I have the element of surprise working in my favor. I can plan out what to say, at least at the beginning. After that, who knows.

"—and then she told me that I was too tall to sit in front of her, and finally I just said, 'You know, Haya, if you have so many special needs, maybe you should just sit somewhere else!'"

"Good for you," I say out loud, while in my head I hear Jaxon say:

I've been waiting every day for you to walk through that door and back into my life.

No, that's stupid. There's no way he's going to say that. Maybe just:

It's good to see you.

And then what? I could say . . .

Yeah.

Brilliant. Brilliant, Devorah. Way to think this through.

"—she's just a B-I-T-H-C, if you know what I mean." Hanna is fuming.

"You mean B-I-T-C-H, and don't spell out curse words," I say, distracted by the giant red letters I can already read from a block away. I glance at my reflection in a shop window and realize that I'm still in my school vest, which combined with the long skirt makes me look like some sort of bohemian train conductor. I peel it off and stuff it under one arm. "What? I'm hot," I say when Hanna makes a face.

We push through the doors into the pharmacy—not strictly Chabad but favored by my father for its Orthodox owners and reasonable prices—and are greeted by a cool blast of air-conditioning and the dueling scents of air freshener and cough syrup. It's a mom-and-pop type place, just four modest aisles of ointments and vitamins, nothing like the Duane Reades and Walgreens that look like mini-department stores, lined with refrigerated cases of every conceivable beverage. The pharmacy counter is in the back, and since there's only one employee and it's a few minutes until closing, the line is four people deep. I take a sharp breath—this is my chance. I almost can't believe I'm actually going through with it, but I know that if I don't, I'll always wonder what would have happened, for the rest of my life.

"Hey," I call to Hanna, who's already padding down the center aisle to join the line, "I just saw Shoshana pass by outside. I'm going to talk to her for a sec, okay?"

"Sure," Hanna says gamely, giving a little wave. I feel bad manipulating her natural naïveté, but I don't know what else to do.

I shall be telling this with a sigh, I think, quoting Robert Frost as I will my legs to move me back through the swinging glass door with its loud doorbell chime, out onto the humid street. *Somewhere ages and ages hence: Two roads diverged in a wood, and I, I took the one less traveled by . . .*

I look up at the cheery red Wonder Wings sign and the neon letters in the window that flash OPEN! OPEN! OPEN! again and again in a cascading rainbow of colored lights. I swallow my fear and push through the door.

. . . And that has made all the difference.

For some reason, in my mind I was picturing a vast restaurant full of dark corner tables and balletic busboys, the kind of noisy, crowded place where I could hide in plain sight while I got my bearings. But instead, as soon as I step over the threshold, I'm greeted by a single fluorescent-lit room—maybe fifteen feet by ten at most—with mirrors and bright Caribbean flags lining the walls. There are only four tables, and three are empty; the only patrons are a middle-aged woman and her young son, picking over a plate of bones and celery ribs. A pretty older woman in a bright yellow head wrap and long green beaded earrings stands behind the counter, refilling a dispenser of lemonade. And there is one busboy, but he's tying up a garbage bag with his back to me. His broad, muscular back.

Jaxon.

He spins around, and for a second I'm afraid I've said his name out loud. But he looks completely shocked to see me; he actually freezes with the Hefty bag lifted in midair. I smile awkwardly and raise my hand in a wave, realizing too late that it's completely idiotic to wave at someone who's standing four feet from you. Jaxon blinks quickly a few times, like he's testing his eyes, and then cocks his head and breaks into the slowest and most amazing smile I've ever seen, like a sunrise lighting up his entire face. He straightens up and puts the garbage down.

"Hi," he says.

"Hi," I say.

"Wow. Uh . . . wow," he stammers softly, and I just smile. I can't help it. Already I know that this—whatever this is—was worth it; the feeling I'm having, like every cell in my body is doing a somersault at the same time, is positively euphoric.

"Can I help you?" asks the woman refilling the lemonade.

"Oh, um . . ." I shake my head.

"She's with me," Jaxon says. "I mean, I know her. Sort of."

"All right, then," she says, leaning forward over the counter, voluminous cleavage spilling out of her pink shell top. "You make sure he gets that stanky garbage outside before I faint!"

Jaxon rolls his eyes good-naturedly. "Yes ma'am," he says, and heaves the bag onto his shoulder. "You stay right here," he says as he passes me. "Don't move."

"He's a good one," the woman tells me as the door swings shut behind him. She looks me up and down and then winks. "I always wondered what kind of girl he was hiding away."

"Oh, I'm not—" I ball my vest in my fists and shake my head. "We're not—" The boy eating with his mom—he can't be more than ten or eleven—glances up at me and snickers.

"What is she telling you?" Jaxon says with a laugh, jogging back in from the street. "Don't listen to her. Cora just likes to cause trouble."

"Who, me?" Cora asks with a coy smile. Then she turns back to the lemonade. Jaxon gestures to one of the empty tables.

"Stay awhile," he says.

"I can't," I say. He raises his eyebrows and smiles.

"That's what you said last week, and here you are," he says. "Come on, sit with me for one minute."

I shake my head. "I really can't. My sister is waiting for me next door. I just came to—"

To what? What have I come here to do? My mind is a blank, and my heart is a drum.

"—see you," I finish.

"Okay." He laughs. "Here I am. Looking is free, but a photo's five bucks."

"Stop it. That's not what I meant."

"Then sit," he pleads. "I've been hoping you'd come here, and now you're here, so let's talk, or take a walk, or something."

"It's not that easy," I say, glancing back nervously. Hanna could be coming out of the pharmacy any minute, wondering where I am.

"Fine—can I at least give you my number or my e-mail this time? So you don't have to stalk me?"

I shake my head again, and Jax looks crestfallen. But I suddenly have a better idea. Tomorrow I can make an excuse to run an errand without Hanna. A long errand. Tomorrow I'll have time to think of what I want to say.

"Meet me at the corner of Washington and Montgomery," I say, leaning in and tilting my chin toward his shoulder for privacy, feeling the heat radiate between us like one of the magnetic force fields Shosh and I constructed for our fourth grade science project. "Tomorrow, at five fifteen. We can take a walk then."

He looks confused but intrigued.

"Okay," he says. "What's at the corner of Montgomery and Washington?"

"Just be there," I say. I'm sure Jax is smart enough to figure out the answer to his own question. Washington Avenue is technically where Crown Heights ends; its westernmost border. It's also where the Brooklyn Botanic Garden begins, a sprawling jumble of trees and paths and ponds we can get lost in, and where neither of us will look out of place. And it's the only date spot I can think of outside the neighborhood that'll have me home in time for dinner.

I can feel Cora's eyes on us and fear I've stayed too long already, so I leave Wonder Wings as quickly as I came in. It hurts to turn away from Jax, but this time I know it's not forever. We'll see each other tomorrow. We have a date. A *date*. I have to put a hand over my mouth as I step back down to earth, the warm pavement shimmering in the sun, both to hide myself from anyone who might be passing by and to suppress the nervous scream that threatens to tear from my throat, scattering the pigeons. This is so surreal. But it's happening. And most incredibly of all, I'm *making* it happen.

I don't see Hanna until we're almost nose to nose. She's standing on the sidewalk near the curb with her arms crossed, a white paper bag clutched in her fingers and a devilish grin playing on her lips.

"*That* didn't look like Shoshana," she says.

There's no sense in arguing with her. "It wasn't," I say. "That was—"

"The boy from the elevator," she interrupts, looking both completely shocked and almost uncontrollably excited. "Right?" I nod, and Hanna shakes her head in disbelief.

"Listen, you *can't*—" I start. "*Please* don't tell anyone about this." My mind races to grab on to a reasonable excuse. "I had his keys," I say. "He asked me to hold them while he climbed up the elevator shaft and I put them in my pocket and forgot about them, but then I found them and they had a keychain from this place on them, so when Dad mentioned it before I thought maybe he would be there, and . . ." I trail off, exhausted by my own lie.

"Dev, don't worry," Hanna says, linking her arm through mine as we turn to walk back to the store. "I wouldn't tell anyone anyway." She frowns as we start to walk. "He's cuter than I pictured. It's so sad he's not Jewish. Imagine the story you would be able to tell your grandkids if you guys got married!"

"Hanna, stop it!" I cry, pinching her arm. "I told you, I had his keys, there is nothing like that going on."

"Relax," she says with a sigh. "I'm just saying it would make a good story. I know it's not real. Can you even imagine? What *Dad* would say?" She nearly collapses into giggles, which I guess should make me feel better, but instead I feel impossibly sad and heavy.

I *do* want that fairy-tale ending to my story. But I know that if the boy in my story is Jaxon, I'm never going to get it.

Chapter 10

Jaxon

I hate cleaning the grease trap. It's one of those things that you see people doing on reality shows about the world's nastiest jobs. And at a place like Wonder Wings, which serves french fries, chicken tenders, and battered fish and shrimp along with our signature wings and token salads, there's a lot of fat that gets trapped. They actually have professionals who will clean a grease trap for you, but Cora is cheap, and she knows I know a thing or two about taking stuff apart thanks to my dad, who hasn't had an appliance serviced since 1992 (and even then it was just because he broke his wrist and couldn't replace the dryer belt one-handed).

But today, I am *feeling* the grease trap. In fact, I'm feeling *everything*. I might as well have cartoon birds flying around my head ever since I came home from work last night.

"What happened to you? You fall down?" my mother asked when I helped set the table by spinning in a circle balancing plates in each hand.

"Nope," I said. Then I started whistling.

"Check his irises," Edna—the future doctor—said. "If his brain is hemorrhaging, they'll be different sizes."

"Fayth Griffith's chest must be hemorrhaging then," Ameerah said, and cracked up.

"What in the hell is she talking about?" my dad asked bemusedly from his beat-up La-Z-Boy, where he was nursing a can of beer.

"Boobs, Dad," I called, and my mom whacked me with an oven mitt.

"What is wrong with you?" she asked with a laugh.

"Absolutely nothing, for once," I said, which made her smile turn suspicious.

"Something happened at school," she said. "Didn't it?"

"Nope!" I said again.

"Oooh, was it Polly?" Tricia said, pouring a steaming pot of rice into a serving bowl.

"Polly?" Ameerah laughed. "No chance. Jax can't close that deal."

"I could if I wanted to," I lied—though on the high I was riding, I sort of believed it—"and it's not about her."

"It's a girl, though," Joy said from her prone position on the living room floor, where she was leafing through a textbook. "You can tell by his stupid face."

"It's always stupid, though," Tricia said, kissing my cheek on her way to the table.

"It's just rubbery," Edna said.

"Thank you, *dear sisters*," I said, but all of their chatter just rolled right off. All I could sense was that door swinging open and the burst of warm breeze that licked at the back of my neck and the feeling of stepping off a diving board before I even turned around and saw her standing there, bathed in sunlight. It was perfect. Even though I had been up to my elbows in trash.

"A girl, huh?" my mother said, taking the roast out of the oven. "The last thing you need is a girl to distract you. You're distracted enough."

"What?" I joked.

"Don't be cute," my father called.

"Can't help it," I said, and it was true—I couldn't.

Now, almost twenty-four hours later, I still can't. I'm suffering from what might be the world's greatest mood, even as I scrape big deposits of putrid, gelatinous fat from the sides of the trap into a bucket.

I spent last night (when I was supposed to be doing my philosophy reading) burning a carefully curated mix CD for Devorah. It's called "Elevator Music" (get it?) and has everything from Jay-Z and Childish Gambino to Bright Eyes and Florence + the Machine and, of course, the Shirelles. I tried not to make it too lovey-dovey, but it's kind of hard when every song is, in one way or another, about love: wanting it, getting it, losing it, hating it. And obviously I don't love Devorah. At least not yet.

"Hey, Romeo," Cora says, leaning against the kitchen door. "You almost done? We got orders coming in." Normally I clean the trap around five PM, in between the after-school crowds and the dinner rush, when business is slowest. But today I begged Cora to let me do it early so that I could cut out and meet Devorah. "And please," Cora says, grimacing at my yellow-splattered T-shirt, "tell me you're not wearing that on your date."

"Nope, I brought a change of clothes," I say, scraping the last of the gristle from the trap. "I don't want to smell like wings for this girl, no offense." I glance up at the kitchen wall clock, which is bright orange and shaped like the silhouette of a walking chicken. It's 4:48. I figure it'll take me ten minutes to change my clothes and freshen up in the employee bathroom, and then another ten to walk to the spot where I'm supposed to meet her. I should add on five minutes to pick up some deli flowers, too, the kind that come wrapped up in a big cone of paper that'll drip water on my shoes while I walk. Which means I have exactly two minutes to spare.

"So who exactly is this girl?" Cora asks. I've been working for her for seven months, and since about day two she's been acting like a second mother.

"She's just a girl," I say noncommittally. "I met her around the neighborhood."

Cora nods. "I bet you did," she says. "What happened to Polly?"

I cringe. I can't believe I've spent so much time talking up a crush that never went anywhere. When you let something like that out, it's not yours anymore; people think they know what's going on and that you need their advice. No way I'm making that mistake again. *No one* is going to know what goes on between me and Devorah except for us.

"Polly's just a friend," I say. "I'm over it."

"What about this girl?" Cora asks. "She more than a friend?"

I stand up and wipe my hands off with a dishrag. 4:50. I have to get going. I just shrug and shoot Cora a quick "It's all good" smile.

She takes a deep, slow breath—the kind people take when

they're gearing up to lay the smack down on you. "Do her parents know you're seeing her?"

"I don't know," I say, turning on the hot faucet in the sink and sticking my arms in up to the elbows, scrubbing them with goopy pink liquid soap. "That's her business."

"Uh-huh. Right now it's her business, but once they find out it's gonna be *your* business."

"Maybe they won't find out then." I dry my hands and lean down to grab my bag. I'm going to have to update my route. I should just get out of here before Cora ropes me into a Very Special Episode talk about my love life. There's a Burger King on Bedford Avenue near Montgomery where I can duck in and change.

"How do you plan on that?" Cora asks.

"Well," I joke, slipping on my backpack, hoping she gets the hint, "I'm not exactly invited over for dinner."

Cora sighs heavily. "I know you think it doesn't matter," she says. "And maybe it shouldn't. But you know, Jax, things are complicated. Before you were born, there was—"

"A riot, I know," I groan, cutting her off. I hear enough about it from my parents.

"A race riot's not a small thing," she says, narrowing her eyes. "We may live side by side, but they're not like us. And they *don't* like us. You understand?"

"Yes, ma'am."

"Now one more time like you're not just humoring me."

"*Yes*, I hear you."

"Okay, good."

But I'm not changing my mind, I think as I breeze past Cora and zigzag through the few front tables and hit the door like Superman breaking through brick. I've never felt this way about a girl before, and the only thing that matters—more than color, creed, or keeping kosher—is that she feels it, too. And I'm about to find out. I check my phone: 4:54.

I break into a run.

4:59 and I'm two blocks closer to our meeting place, standing outside a deli trying to decide between two sad floral arrangements that are leaning listlessly against a crate of shriveled oranges, propped up in a janitorial bucket filled with a few inches of water. One has red roses—a clearly superior flower, the international symbol of romance—but they're about half dead already. The other has carnations, which aren't as pretty but look slightly healthier. I've been trying to decide for a few minutes, but I keep getting distracted by the Brooklyn Miracle Temple's cross-shaped sign, which is 3-D and reads JESUS SAVES. *Jesus could have at least saved me some decent flowers*, I think, and then, immediately: *I'm going to hell.* I pick up the roses.

5:01 and I'm almost at the Burger King when my phone rings. It's my mom. I told her I was working late—my second bald-faced lie in less than a week. If I pick up, she might be able to tell I'm not at the restaurant by the street noise. But if I don't pick up, she'll definitely be able to tell I'm not at the restaurant, because she'll call there.

"Hi, Mom!" I say cheerfully, trying not to squeeze the last life out of the flowers as I hold them awkwardly in my armpit. "I just stepped out to grab a . . ." *What don't we sell at Wonder Wings? What would I have to leave to buy?* ". . . a coffee!" Third lie. (And really, fourth lie, since I don't drink coffee, but who's counting?) "What's up?"

"Listen, Jaxon, do you think Cora would let you off a bit early today?"

"Uh . . . I don't know. Probably not." (Fifth lie.) "Why?"

"Your father got a last-minute job out in the Rockaways and forgot to pick up Joy from her track meet. It ended fifteen minutes ago, and I don't want her walking home alone. Can you get her?"

My heart plummets. I feel sick. "There's no one else?" I ask, and I can hear my mother's tongue click against the back of her throat. She was expecting me to drop everything without hesitation. Why would she expect any less? That's what I've always done. "I mean," I hedge, "we're slammed today. Of course I'd *love* to leave early, but I don't know if I can."

"I'd do it, but I'm in Manhattan with the twins getting their teeth cleaned." In the background, I can hear someone—probably Ameerah—singing "Teeth" by Lady Gaga.

My mood has changed so fast I've got emotional whiplash. I know I can't leave my little sister sitting on the curb as the sun goes down, dressed in nothing but a tank top and iridescent shorts. But going to pick up Joy means ditching Devorah. And there's no way I can call or text or e-mail her to let her know what happened. She'll just think I blew her off. And she'll never come looking for me again, I know that much. She'll be gone, this time for good.

"I . . ." I look down at the roses under my arm and at my grease-stained jeans. It's 5:07. I won't even have time to change now.

"Jax," she pleads, "this is my baby girl. She's waiting alone, and I can't reach her. *Please*. Look—put Cora on the phone. She has kids, she'll understand."

I can hear the panic rising in my mom's voice, and I realize I have no choice. It's Devorah—a girl I've met twice—versus my

own sister. It's infatuation versus familial love. It's the audacity of
hope versus the reality of timing. And it *sucks*.

"No, Mom, it's fine," I say with a sigh. "I'll go."

I hang up and think frantically of some way to alert Devorah. I
could run over to our meeting spot and tell her in person, but that's
five long blocks in what's now, cruelly, the wrong direction. And I
would never forgive myself if anything happened to Joy because I
took a hormone-fueled detour. I could send a proxy, find some kid
who'd go tell her for me for $5. But flagging down a strange kid
on the street would look all kinds of wrong, and the people who'd
volunteer—like the homeless guys who loiter around liquor stores,
holding the door in the hopes that someone'll reward them with a
nip of Bacardi—I wouldn't trust around Devorah. If they bothered
to tell her at all.

Write a message on the flowers, I think suddenly. But what are
the chances she'd pass this way—0.01 percent? The girl can't even
eat a Whopper.

Feeling defeated, I leave the roses on a fire hydrant outside
Burger King, figuring at least they'll make someone happy, even if
it's not the right someone. The mix CD, though—I'm keeping that.
And somehow, I swear, I'm going to make sure Devorah gets it.

Chapter 11
Devorah
SEPTEMBER 7, 4 PM

Isaiah 43:18 says, "Forget the former things; do not dwell on the past." And yet here I am, back exactly where I started. As in literally the same gray plastic bucket seat where I waited for news of Liya's birth ten days ago. Only now, the duct tape is gone from the big window, and outside it's gorgeous and sunny, the perfect late summer day. We have school on Sundays, so it's never been a "weekend," but it's hard not to think of it that way sometimes, when everyone else is going to the park, sunning on their stoops, letting their fingers get sticky with ice cream. Or, if you're my family, hanging out at the hospital. Not that I don't want to visit Liya—of course I do—but now this place just makes me depressed. Because I could ride the elevator all day long and there would still be no Jaxon.

On Wednesday I waited for an hour. I stood leaning against the wrought-iron fence that separates Washington Avenue from the squat glass greenhouses of the Brooklyn Botanic Garden. I wore my highest hemline, a skirt that I technically outgrew last year, and a lightweight pink top that I changed into in a Dunkin Donuts bathroom after I left the store, telling my father I had to work on an assignment with Shosh. I plucked my eyebrows in that dingy bathroom mirror, which might as well have been a dented tin can for how little I could see. I put on lip gloss. And then, my stomach performing a series of nauseating flips, I stood there, stock-still, for *an hour* getting catcalls from the beer-bellied, wife-beater-clad men streaming in and out of J & J Food Market ("THE SANDWICH PROFESSIONAL"—a doubtful piece of proud advertising on its awning) across the street. First it was "Waiting for someone, gorgeous? He's a lucky man!" Then it turned into "You can come to my house if he don't show, sweetie. Heh heh heh." Finally, at six o'clock, my humiliation was compounded by their hollow condolences. "He stood you up, princess!" "You're too good for him!" I would have left, hidden in the lobby of the apartment building a block north, or taken refuge in the gardens, but I was convinced that the second I left, he would finally appear, out of breath and grinning, explaining it all away, making nothing else matter.

But apparently, something else mattered more. I've been trying to wrap my brain around it and make it okay, but I can't. He seemed so happy to see me, so eager to meet again. When I left the restaurant I was floating. I could barely sleep that night, planning my outfit, what I would say, what he would say. Debating whether he might try to kiss me, and if I would let him.

I couldn't have made all of that up, could I? Was he just a flirt? Was my crush one-sided? Maybe not having had many crushes (and barely having touched a member of the opposite sex) puts me at a disadvantage when it comes to reading body language, but I thought he really liked me. What could have happened in twenty-four hours to change that?

For the first two days after the failed meeting, I vacillated between sadness and anger, and I'm not sure which felt worse. The intermittent urges to weep in the middle of math were embarrassing, but not as scary as the flashes of shame-laced outrage that made me want to turn my desk upside-down and storm out of class. I couldn't pay attention to anything for more than a few minutes at a time, and I couldn't vent to Shosh because I knew she would be mad at me for going to see him in the first place. At the store, I forgot to restock shelves and priced an entire row of napkins at $199.99 a package. On Thursday I gave Mrs. Goodstein the wrong change, three dollars and ten cents in her favor. She noticed and returned the money right away, but I still knew.

Friday was the first time it occurred to me that something could have happened to him. Like, maybe he got sick or injured, and of course he would have no way of reaching me to let me know. It's so stupid, but on our way home from work for Shabbos, Hanna and I passed a dead bouquet of roses on the sidewalk outside a Burger King, still in their deli wrapper, and I thought for a second that maybe they were from Jaxon, and that he got attacked before he could give them to me. And as unlikely as it was, I became obsessed with the thought of him bloodied and broken, lying in a hospital bed somewhere. I was so upset and out of my head that before my father came home for Shabbos dinner, I snuck into his study on the third floor and opened the web browser on his laptop. (He almost never uses the Internet at home, but he needs it occasionally to place orders and to check the business e-mail, which gets a lot of spam messages from Nigerian diplomats.) I feverishly typed "Jaxon" into the search bar, and then froze. Jaxon what? *Jaxon elevator boy? Jaxon Wonder Wings?* I finally settled on "Jaxon Brooklyn," and ended up watching a video of a fat white baby's first birthday party. Then I realized I didn't know how to erase the search history, so I just shut down the laptop and hid it underneath a sheaf of papers. I hope it's true that G-d protects fools.

"Devorah!" my mother says, pinching my arm.

"Ow, what?" I look up to find her, Hanna, Miri, Amos, Zeidy, and Jacob standing over me. Ugh, *Jacob.* Why can't he be working on Sunday along with all of the other able-bodied men in the family?

"Did you hear me? We can go in and see Rose and the baby now." She tugs me to standing and looks at my face with narrow-eyed intensity, like she's inspecting a melon for bruises. "You haven't been yourself lately. Are you getting sick?"

"No," I say, batting her hand away.

"Well, something's wrong," she murmurs.

"Maybe she's turning into a zombie!" Amos says. "Like on that show!" My mother whips her head around.

"What show are you watching? And where?"

"I saw a poster on the subway," Amos says, holding his hands out and letting his tongue go slack. "Flesh-eating warriors!" Only because he's not using his tongue it sounds like "shlesh eeing awriors!"

"Ew," Miri groans.

"Awesome," Hanna says.

"Let's go," Jacob says impatiently. "Devorah, bring your brain or leave it here, it makes no difference to me."

I look at my mother, expecting her to give him a verbal slap, but instead she just chuckles gamely and takes his arm, and we all file down the hall toward the NICU, where I notice for the first time that the hallways are lined with framed photos of wrinkly, sleeping newborns curled up in watermelons and bean pods, as if they arrived on earth not through the birth canal but rather by special delivery from some idyllic organic grocer.

"Please tell me Rose isn't going to do one of those photo shoots," Hanna whispers, and we snicker.

Just as I'm crafting a retort about how I've always longed to make a nest out of challah, I stop short, the words caught in my throat like a chicken bone. Because that's when I see him, standing at the end of the corridor near the waiting area, where we were just sitting. Jaxon. And he's not bloodied, or broken, or any of the things I feared. Instead, he's smiling at me and raising his hand in a tentative wave.

"Girls!" Jacob says. "Hurry up. These visits are on a schedule."

Jaxon freezes just as I find my legs again. I meet his eyes, but before he has the chance to do anything, I panic. I turn my back. I walk away.

Liya is sleeping in Rose's arms as we circle around them in the NICU, all smelling like the pomegranate hand sanitizer we've just doused ourselves in. I want nothing more than to be present in this moment and to lose myself in the sight of my sister, glowing and grinning and inexplicably already thin again, cuddling her daughter, a blanketed burrito topped with a tuft of downy, margarine-colored hair. But instead I'm focusing all my energy on not letting anyone know I'm completely freaking out.

What is Jaxon doing here? How did he know I would be here? Is it some incredible coincidence, or was he looking for me? And if he's looking for me, is that thrilling or creepy? Did Hanna see him in the hallway? Worse—did Jacob? And what do I do now? I can't let him leave without seeing him . . . but I also can't let anyone else see me see him. For a minute I worry that my racing thoughts will make my head explode. At least I'm already in a hospital.

"She looks like your grandmother," Mom whispers. "Don't you think so, Papa?"

"Well . . . Deborah was a bit taller," Zeidy jokes.

"Can I touch her?" Miri asks shyly.

"Gently," Rose says, and guides my youngest sister's small hand over the baby's head. "She still has soft spots on her skull."

"Cool!" Amos says. It's the first thing about the baby he's seemed impressed by.

"They're called 'fontanelles,'" Jacob explains, bending down to kiss Liya on the head while dutifully avoiding contact with Rose. "Her bones haven't fully fused yet." I stare down mutely at the baby, thinking that maybe *that's* my problem: that I still have soft spots, places where my faith is weak.

"Devorah," my mother says, "you've gone white. Are you sure you aren't getting sick?"

"You should leave if you're sick," Rose says, furrowing her brow and clutching Liya against her chest. "Any germs are dangerous for the baby."

"Another reason why I don't trust hospitals," Jacob mutters.

I shake my head and attempt a smile. "No, no, I'm just hungry, I think. Low blood sugar."

"You ate a whole stack of pancakes before we left the house," Hanna says, and I make a mental note to pinch her later.

"Why don't you go downstairs and get yourself a banana or something?" Mom says, taking out her wallet and pulling out a five-dollar bill. She hands it to me, along with the perfect excuse to roam the halls alone. But just as I close my fingers around it, Jaxon appears in the long rectangular window behind my mother's back. Luckily everyone but me and Rose is facing the opposite direction. His eyes widen as he sees us, and I shake my head quickly.

"You don't want a banana? Fine, get whatever," my mother says as I watch Jaxon retreat behind the heavy white door to the stairwell a few yards away, beckoning me to join him. I glance down at Rose, who is gazing beatifically at Liya, paying zero attention to me. Good. Maybe I can actually pull this off. It's terrifying, though, like the time when I was five and I got stuck in the oak tree outside Aunt Varda's house. Isaac and Niv were supposed to help me down, but they ran off together, and no one inside the house could hear me yelling. I clung to a frail branch ten feet above the ground for what felt like an hour before my father arrived, red-faced and panting from his unexpected sprint, to lift me down. Every second felt like the last second before my inevitable fall.

I slip past my family and out the door, the bill my mother gave me already damp and crumpled in my fist. The closest elevator faces the NICU window at a diagonal angle to the stairwell door. In other words, even if I pretend to wait at the elevator, there's no way to double back without crossing in full view of everyone. But then I realize that I can take the elevator down one floor and enter the stairs *there*, climbing to meet Jaxon. So I push the button and make sure to wave conspicuously as I get on. I see Jacob say something that makes my siblings laugh, and I'm sure it's a joke at my expense. *Someday,* I promise myself as the doors close, *I will tell him exactly what I think of him.*

The third-floor layout is exactly the same as the fourth, so once I get off the elevator I walk the dozen feet or so to the stairs with my heart in my throat. The door is marked with a big red EXIT sign, and as I push down on its wide silver bar with all my weight, a thought drifts through my head like an ominous cloud in an otherwise clear blue sky:

In making this choice, will I ever be able to come back?

Chapter 12

Jaxon

The look on her face, man, when she saw me in the hallway? I almost convinced myself to turn around and go home. I had prepared myself for anger, but I didn't expect her to freeze me out like that. Then again, I guess I took her by surprise. And her folks were with her—plus that dude Jacob who was here the night of the storm. I know they can't know about me, or about us . . . if there is such a thing as us.

The thing that made me stay was actually something my mom said when I got home from picking up Joy (who, by the way, was fine and engrossed in a game on her coach's iPhone when I showed up, greasy and despondent, to rescue her from imagined predators). I was apologizing for taking so long when she interrupted me with a cluck of the tongue and a kiss on the cheek. "I know I can always count on you, Jax," Mom said. "You're reliable, and that's no small thing. You're going to make your wife *very* happy someday." At first I just brushed it off as the kind of affectionate, sort of embarrassing thing a mom says to her kid that's really more of a pat on the back for her. But the more I thought about it, the more I got worked up. I *am* reliable. If I say I'm gonna do something, it's done. If I say I'm gonna be somewhere, I'm there. I don't make empty promises, and I don't start things I don't finish; that's just who I am. It's who I've always been. And I needed Devorah to know that. After a night of tossing and turning and having really obvious stress dreams involving a tidal wave crashing over Eastern Parkway, I decided that if she wanted to write me off I'd let her, but not until she knew why I stood her up, and why that will never happen again.

My first day at the hospital was Thursday. I only work Monday through Wednesday at Wonder Wings, and technically Thursday afternoons are reserved for basketball at Brower Park with Ryan and some guys from the neighborhood, but since Ryan was still avoiding me I felt fine blowing it off. I didn't want to arouse suspicion, so I came in through the ER entrance and hopped right on the elevator without talking to the check-in nurse, acting like I was just coming back from a phone call. My plan was to go up to Labor and Delivery and pretend I was supposed to meet my friend (Devorah) who was visiting her niece in the NICU, to try to get the doctors to tell me when she was actually going to be there. But the nurse I started sweet-talking, a big woman with short, bright yellow hair and an expression my mom would call permanent bitchface, was having none of it.

"So you're not related to the infant in question?"

"Uh . . . no. But—"

"And you don't have your 'friend' Devorah's last name."

"I—"

"*Or* her phone number?"

I tried to change my tack. "Look, we just met," I said, shooting her my best humble nice-guy smile. "Here, actually. We got stuck in an elevator when the power went out. But we made plans to meet today, and I just want to know if she's here."

Big Yellow looked at me without a glint of sympathy in her eyes. "That's cute," she said. "You can tell it to the security guard I'm about to call."

So that went well. I almost didn't come back on Friday, but I couldn't shake the terrible feeling that came from knowing Devorah was out there hating me, or worse, thinking I had just played with her. So even though I had a tutoring job in Park Slope at four thirty, I raced over to Interfaith after my last class. I didn't even have a plan, I was just going to do a quick lap and leave, but as luck would have it the minute I stepped off the elevator (*our* elevator, I couldn't help thinking as I noticed the dent in the ceiling hatch where my Converse All Star had collided with the metal), I ran into the red-haired doctor who fixed Ryan's shoulder. I introduced myself, and she seemed to remember me.

"Your friend, Tony, how's he doing?" she asked.

"Tony?" I frowned, before I remembered Ryan's ridiculous alias. "Oh yeah, he's fine. Still stupid, but fine."

She laughed politely and then looked away, the way you do when you want to end a conversation but not be rude. I knew I had to get down to it.

"I know this is a weird thing to ask," I said, "but I'm looking for a girl I met here last week. You delivered her sister's baby?"

"I deliver a lot of babies," she said with a patient smile.

"This one was early, by like a lot," I said. "And the girl and her sister, they're, um, Hasidic?"

"Oh, sure, of course, I remember them," she said.

"Have they been back here?"

"Well, the child's mother has been here every day," she said hesitantly. "But since you're not a relative I can't let you see her."

"That's okay; it's really the sister I'm looking for," I said. "Do you know if she's coming today?" The doctor smiled again.

"Since it's Friday I'd guess that's unlikely," she said.

"Why does it matter what day it is?"

"Sabbath starts at sundown," she said. "They can't work or drive or turn on lights until nightfall tomorrow."

"Damn," I say, and she laughs, genuinely this time.

"Damn is right," she says. "I couldn't do it." She turns to leave but then pauses, giving me the kind of look you might give a lost puppy on the street. "They might come Sunday," she says. "It's a popular visiting day, especially after their schools let out. Good luck!"

So here I am. Hiding in a stairwell on a Sunday afternoon because I was dumb enough to think she'd come alone, and we'd have one of those slo-mo embraces like you see in movies when one character runs through an airport to stop another character from leaving, and somehow nobody gets Tasered by a rogue TSA agent.

I'm expecting her to come through the door, so when I hear footsteps on the stairs below me I whip out my phone and pretend to be on a call, in case it's a doctor or nurse or someone else who might want to stop and frisk me.

"Grandma's doing all right," I assure the imaginary person on the other end of the phone. And then I see her, looking up at me like I'm crazy from the landing in between floors, those gray eyes big and searching beneath a mass of unruly curls.

"What are you doing here?" she asks flatly, not moving.

"I was . . . looking for you," I say, putting my phone back in my pocket and trying to figure out something new to do with my hands, which suddenly feel like big bricks of cement.

"Then why are you talking about your grandma?"

"That was . . ." I start to explain, and then think better of it. She's already wary of me. "It's nothing," I finish.

"So," she repeats, still not budging from the landing, "you're here looking for me."

I nod.

"How did you know I'd be here?"

"Truthfully?" I ask, just as it occurs to me that the truth makes me sound like a stalker, "I've been here on and off for a few days. Just in case."

"Jaxon," she says with a sigh, exasperated, but her face visibly softens and she takes a step forward, her hands leaving the railing. "Why didn't you just come meet me on Wednesday if you wanted to see me?"

"My sister needed to get picked up," I say, so relieved to have a chance to plead my case that the words tumble out too quickly, too inarticulately. "It got sprung on me. And I couldn't tell you, so I needed to see you so I could tell you that I'm sorry. And that I want to see you. Again. I mean, this doesn't really count."

"Why not?" Her hands are on her hips, but she's almost smiling now; I can see it in her eyes.

"Because . . . we don't have any privacy," I say, "and your

family's waiting outside the door. *And* I'm not wearing my special outfit." She smiles and starts to climb the stairs. Progress.

"What special outfit?" She raises an eyebrow.

I grin. "You'll see it when we have our date. That's incentive." She takes another step.

"You want to go on a date?"

"Absolutely," I say, walking to the top of the stairs with my palms out. "Please give me another shot."

She breaks eye contact. "Jax, I like you, but—"

"Uh-uh, no buts," I interrupt. "You like me. I'm gonna hold you to that, it's on the record now." She bites her lip to stifle a smile, which is exactly what I need to give me the balls to keep going. I take a deep breath, feeling the words swell again and knowing I'm powerless to stop them. "And I like *you*. More than like you, actually. And I hear it when you tell me this can't happen, but I still can't let it go. And even if I could . . ." I shrug helplessly. "I don't want to."

She looks at me like I'm crazy again and shakes her head. "You don't even know me."

"I know I've never felt this way about anybody," I say, grabbing the railing, gathering my courage. "And I know I don't care if you're different from me. I mean, aren't we past that? The Civil Rights Act and shit?"

"I wish it was that simple," Devorah says, climbing one step and whispering now, like she's afraid someone's listening in. We're only a few feet apart, and I can see her free hand trembling by her side. "But it's not. I'm not allowed to date *anyone*."

"Why not?" I say, knowing the answer. I just want her to say it out loud, so she can hear it.

"Because," she says, getting flustered, her cheeks flushing

crimson, almost the color of the roses I bought for her, and just as beautiful. "It's the way I was brought up. It's a sin. I have to wait."

"For what?"

She narrows her eyes, aware that I'm baiting her. "For *marriage*."

"You know it's 2014, right?" I joke, and she shoots daggers at me from underneath those thick eyelashes. She's getting mad now, but I don't care. The air between us is electric, and I know she feels it, too.

"Look," she says. "I know you don't understand. And sometimes I'm not sure I understand, either, but . . . it's just the way it is."

"So you're telling me you don't feel anything?" I ask, taking a step down. I half expect her to bolt, but she doesn't budge. Instead she lets out a slow, shaky breath.

"I didn't say that," she says. My heart beats wildly in my chest.

"What about Wednesday?" I say, taking another step. We're face-to-face now, or would be, if we weren't on a flight of stairs. As it is, her face is about in line with my ribs. "What if I had made it? What would have happened?"

"I don't know," she says softly. I'm towering over her, maybe scaring her. Without thinking, I jump down and around so that I'm two steps below *her*. She turns and smiles. Our faces are perfectly aligned.

"Was that a *date*?" I press, grinning. She averts her eyes and says nothing. "Oh," I say, "so you were just waiting there to tell me you can't see me, right?"

"No."

"Then what?"

She laughs nervously. "I said I don't know, why do you care?"

"Why do I care?" I ask softly, rhetorically, knowing I care way too much already not to freak her out. "Because I can't stop thinking about you," I say. "And maybe you're right and I don't know you that well, but . . . just tell me you don't like me that way, and I'll leave. I swear, I'll never bother you again."

We stare at each other silently for what feels like forever, our breathing falling into sync, out, then back in again, like overlapping waves as I watch her eyes flash gray, then blue, then gold, like some hypnotic kaleidoscope. I'm so dumbstruck by Devorah that it takes me almost a minute to realize what this silence means. I asked her a question, and she's answering. Or not answering. Which is an answer in itself.

"So I'm not crazy?" I murmur. She shakes her head. And it's too much. I can't help myself. I lean in, and I kiss her.

I've kissed two girls in my life before this moment—two and a half if you count Hallie Fuller's ear in fifth grade, when she turned her head at the last minute. Both were nice but awkward, a jumble of tentative false starts and unruly tongues and accidental teeth. Don't get me wrong, I thought I saw fireworks. But it turns out they were just some dollar-store Roman candles. With Devorah, it's fireworks. It's the Fourth of July over the Hudson. Everything clicks instantly, and there are no false starts, no wrong angles. Just me tumbling head-first into her soft mouth and sweet, hot breath, which catches in her throat as I press my lips to hers. I'm afraid to touch her with my hands, not sure how far is too far, but then she raises hers and cups my face, her index fingers tracing my jaw. I don't know who pulls back first, but I know the kiss ends too soon. Suddenly we're staring into each other's eyes again, and this time I *do* see fear, even though her fingers are still on my neck, digging in like her life depends on it.

I want to tell her it's okay, that we'll figure it out, and that I'm scared, too. I want to confess that I'm falling in love with her. Hell, most of all I just want to kiss her again. But I can't do any of that, because someone starts to bang on the door to the stairwell. Devorah drops her hands like I'm on fire.

"Go," she whispers.

"Not without knowing when I'm going to see you again," I say. The knocking gets faster.

"*Devorah?*" a male voice calls from outside. Her eyes widen with terror.

"I'll find you; please, Jax, just *go*," she begs.

That's all I need to hear. I run down the stairs all the way to the lobby, where I throw open the heavy ER door like it's made of tissue paper. I've never felt adrenaline like this before, never felt the air fill my lungs so sweetly or the sun bathe my skin so gloriously. I run all the way home, half a mile, my feet barely touching the pavement, my heartbeat flooding my ears again and again like a bass line that sings, *Devorah, Devorah, Devorah.*

Chapter 13
Devorah

"Devorah?" Jacob calls again. "Are you in there?"

I'm pretty sure he'll hear me if I move, but I can't stand still. I feel like I'm on the Cyclone at Coney Island, back before it reopened, when it was so jerky and screechy you had to hold on for dear life or you thought you *really* might fly out.

That kiss. I can't believe it just happened. My lips are still tingling—is that normal? And there's a weird, fluttery feeling in my chest, which gets worse (or better, I should say, since it feels like floating) when I think about how I could feel his breath on my neck. As I walk on rubbery legs to the fourth-floor landing, it occurs to me that maybe I'm not on the roller coaster after all; maybe I've already fallen off. Maybe I'm suspended in the popcorn-scented air over the boardwalk, about to come crashing back to earth.

"Hi," I say as calmly as possible as I step back out into the hallway outside the NICU, coming face-to-face with a frustrated-looking Jacob. It's all I can do to keep from trembling uncontrollably; I'm *sure* he can tell. My face must be bright red, my pupils dilated, lips swollen from the shock of being used for the first time for what it seems like they were designed to do; after all, why eat or speak or whistle when you could do *that*? I put my hand up to my face as if I'm scratching an itch, covering my mouth, which feels like it might as well be a three-story neon sign flashing the news of my sin across Times Square.

"What were you doing in there?" Jacob demands. "I came out to look for you and heard voices."

"I . . ." For a second my mind draws a blank, but then a lie comes into focus; I'm getting very good at coming up with them now. "I was afraid to take the elevator," I mumble. "And there were some orderlies talking on the landing downstairs." I hope I'm reading my lines right and sounding casual. I feel like my own understudy. *Tonight*, I think maniacally, *the part of Normal Devorah will be played by Off the Derech Devorah.*

"Hmmm." He squints at me for a second like he's trying to see through me, but then seems to let it go. "Well, the others are already waiting down the hall. You missed your chance to hold the baby."

"I'm sorry," I say. Usually when I apologize to Jacob I'm secretly calling him names in my head, but this time I'm sincere. There's so much that I want to escape, but being part of my niece's life isn't part of it. I'm ashamed that my selfishness has caused me to miss a moment I'll never get back—even if it also created a moment I'll never forget.

As I walk back to the waiting area, following a good ten feet behind Jacob, I realize for the first time that what I'm doing with Jaxon can't be undone. If I keep seeing him, I'll have to keep lying, or worse, reveal to my parents that I've ruined everything they've hoped for me. Devorah, the *frum* princess, who would make any *shadchan*'s job easy—gone. Devorah, the doting daughter, eager to please and quick to obey—gone. I will just become another cautionary tale whispered to teenagers around the Shabbos table: *You heard what happened to Devorah Blum. Don't end up like her. She kissed a black boy, and then—*

"There she is!" my mother says, standing up as I round the corner.

"You missed it," Miri squeals. "The baby burped and threw up all over Rose!"

"It was sick," Hanna says, just as Amos says, "It was great!"

"What did you eat?" Mom asks, studying my face. "You look better."

"Oh, um . . . an apple," I mumble, not realizing the parallel before it's too late. *Like Eve, and look how well that turned out.*

"There's a blush in your cheek," Zeidy says, reaching forward to poke me in the arm. "You look just like your grandmother when we would go dancing."

"She climbed the stairs," Jacob says dismissively.

"*Why?*" Amos asks. "Just because you didn't want to get stuck on the elevator with a—"

"Amos," my mother warns, and I take the opportunity to change the subject.

"I'm so sorry," I say to Rose, who is cradling Miri, stroking her hair as gently as if she were Liya. "I wanted to see her. My stomach"—(*my heart*)—"had bad timing." She smiles serenely.

"It's okay," she says. "You were the very first person she met; I don't think she'll forget you. And besides, the doctors say she can come home next week!"

"As soon as she gets to five pounds, one ounce," my mother says, clapping her hands.

"Which is only three ounces away!" Rose beams.

The tears come unexpectedly, as if they've been spring-loaded, waiting for this bit of good news to bring relief to what's come to feel like a permanent ache deep in my bones.

"*Zeeskyte*," Zeidy laughs, "what's wrong? This is a cause for celebration."

"Hormones," my mother whispers, as if I'm not right there.

"It's not *hormones*," I say, sniffing, wiping my eyes with my shirtsleeve. "I'm just *happy*."

"We can all see that," Jacob says quietly, almost to himself, and as the rest of my family moves in to embrace me, all I can do is look over their shoulders at him, a dark shadow puppet in his black suit against the bland beige hospital walls, and wonder if I was wrong. Maybe he can see through my lies after all.

It's two AM, and I can't sleep. I used to have bouts of insomnia in middle school, but that was when Rose still shared my room. In the clutches of that acute but somehow unidentifiable anxiety, as I would listen to the faint thrum of night traffic drifting in from Eastern Parkway through the cracks in the windows, the sight of her chest rising and falling beneath the blankets just a few feet away never failed to calm me. But now I'm on my own. And I know exactly what's making me so anxious.

The rational part of my brain keeps telling me what Shoshana told me over lunch last week: I do not have a choice. This is not one of those Choose Your Own Adventure books I used to leaf through in the library on rainy weekend afternoons; there is only one path to take, and that is to forget about Jaxon and get back to the only life that I know, which has been plotted out for me long before I was even born. In this life, I will go back to school and to work at the store, make good grades and braid challah every Friday, celebrate the high holidays and usher in a new year with apples and honey, a new year that will see me turn seventeen and enter my senior year of high school. Before I know it I'll graduate and it will be two Junes from now, and as the streets fill with the sounds of children playing on the hot cement my parents will meet with a matchmaker and will pick a boy to become my husband. And then I'll be married and will choose a wig—long and sleek and black like Rose's—and move into an apartment that's probably less than five blocks from where I'm lying right now, stock-still, with my covers up to my neck and my eyes wide open with worry. I try to imagine what it will feel like to share my bed with a strange man. Will I be able to choose when I want to touch him, or will I be at the mercy of his urges? Will I like the way he smells? Will his smile light up his face like a slow sunrise, or will he be like Jacob, gruff and moody? In the life I have set out for me, my husband seems like the only unknown variable.

And then there is the irrational part of my brain, the part that tells me to go find Jaxon and lie with my head in his lap in the park, listening to his jokes and watching his eyes flash with warmth and laughing until I can't breathe. This story is much more unfinished; in fact, I have no idea where it will lead. I know only that in this alternate reality, I will have Jaxon. He is the only thing I know for sure. The only nonvariable.

I told him I would find him, and I desperately want to make good on that promise. But all my life I've been told that there is nothing for me outside the Chabad community, no opportunity for any happiness in the greater world. I only wish I knew if this were true.

And then it hits me, as I stare up at my ceiling: One floor above me, there is a way to find out.

I leave my slippers on and the hall lights off, creeping like a burglar up to my father's study, taking care to skip the creaky step at the top of the stairs. As usual, my parents' bedroom door is shut tight, which means I'll have at least a second of warning if one of them gets up to use the bathroom—long enough, at least, to shut the laptop.

As I pry it open with delicate fingers, a chime rings out, causing my heart to lurch. I spring to my feet in case I need to abandon my mission, but after a few seconds with no discernible movement from the next room, I gingerly sit back down and squint into the bright blue screen littered with tiny icons. Once again, I open the web browser and type a name into the search bar. But this time I enter a full name: Ruchy Silverman.

The very first link that pops up is a Facebook profile. I know about Facebook, mostly thanks to the fact that when I was in ninth grade, my school made us all sign a form pledging not to use it, and anyone who got caught with a profile got fined $100. I don't know if Ruchy had a profile back then, but apparently she doesn't care now. And why should she? I click on the bright blue text and hold my breath.

Instantly, a photo appears of Ruchy, as beautiful as ever, with a cute, layered short haircut, grinning and holding a chubby infant in

her arms. Underneath the photo there are boxes that read "About,"
"Photos," and "More." I start with "About," hoping, I guess, that
there will be some biography or something that will tell me everything I want to know about her life now. But instead, it just says
that she lives in New York, New York, and is in a relationship with
someone named Matteo Barone.

I click on "Photos" next, hunching forward guiltily as I scroll
through an album of Ruchy's life. They don't seem to be in chrono-
logical order, because the first batch are from the past few years.
In these she is posing arm in arm with friends, all of whom wear
the telltale crew necks and wrist-length sleeves of Hasidim (even
though, with her glowing skin and Barbie-doll hair, Ruchy looks
like her head was pasted on the photos from a swimsuit catalog).
But then there seems to be a jump. Suddenly Ruchy is embracing
a tall, olive-skinned man with a shaved head and stubble across his
chin. Here they are on a beach, her with a big straw hat and a toothy
smile; him with a sunburn and a cigarette hanging from his lips.
Here they are kissing in close-up, out of focus. Here they are at a
dinner table, him with his arms around her waist, cupping her belly.
There are a series of pregnant shots that Ruchy must have taken by
setting up an automatic timer on her camera, showing her standing
sideways with a window and a radiator in the background, her outfit
changing in each shot as her middle grows rounder and rounder.
And then, she is in a hospital bed, swollen and sweaty, holding a tiny
pink burrito-baby that looks just like Liya. There are a lot of shots of
the newborn—"Sal," according to her captions—lying limply in a
bassinet. And then I come across the most shocking picture, one that
nearly makes me gasp out loud.

It's Ruchy, her baby, her boyfriend . . . and her parents. Mr. and

Mrs. Silverman, who still live on Carroll Street in a big maroon brownstone with Ruchy's younger brothers, who still go to temple, who still come by the store from time to time to buy paper plates in bulk. From the way people whispered about her, I just assumed that Ruchy was excommunicated from her family. But here are her beaming parents, holding their grandson with tears in their eyes and embracing the man who led her astray. I shut the browser window and push myself back from the desk, not knowing what to think.

Ruchy doesn't look ruined at all. Certainly being an unwed teenage mom must be an incredible hardship not without its low moments, but the thing that strikes me the most about her photos is that she doesn't look like she's suffering, at least not on any grand scale. Instead, she looks joyful and grateful. At peace. It's hard to reconcile what I'm seeing with what I have been taught to believe. There is supposedly no happiness to be had, no chance to succeed outside our small and insular world, and yet here is a glimpse through the looking glass that tells me different. My own slideshow starts playing in my mind: Me in a cap and gown, not from high school but from college. Maybe even nursing school, so that I could become a nurse-midwife, so that I can take care of scared Hasidic women like my sister and Ruchy. Then, me and Jaxon, holding hands in public, posing with my family. Jaxon at Shabbos dinner, lighting a candle. Our sisters playing together. Could my parents ever accept a different path for me?

Almost without thinking, my fingers drift back to the keyboard. If I can find Ruchy so easily on this Facebook site, then maybe . . . maybe . . .

Holding my breath, I type "Jaxon" into the search bar and hit enter. A sea of faces appears on the screen, but none are his. I scroll through four pages and am about to give up and tiptoe back down-stairs when I see a search toolbox at the top of the screen, with the word "Location." I type in "Brooklyn, New York." And then, from the thousands of Jaxons, there are only thirteen. And number seven is mine. Jaxon Hunte. Student at Brooklyn Technical High School. Busboy at Wonder Wings. Elevator hero. First kiss.

Do you know Jaxon? his page prompts me. *Send him a message.*

I grin stupidly into the darkness as I click on his photo, feeling relief wash over me. I promised him I would find him. And now I have.

Chapter 14

Jaxon

When Devorah said she'd find me, I thought that meant she'd come to Wonder Wings again. I even packed a special bag when I got home from the hospital, with a nice change of clothes and extra deodorant and the mix CD and one of my mom's off-season tablecloths I figured could double as a picnic blanket if we had time to go somewhere (no actual picnic, though; other than water I'm still not sure what the girl can eat).

But then my phone pings at 3:12 AM on Sunday night, with an e-mail telling me I have a Facebook message from someone named Pandora Bloom. I almost sleepily delete it, thinking it's spam, since I don't recognize the name and the picture is blank, just one of those generic silhouettes with a big question mark where the face should go. But then I have a nanosecond of pause, because if—hypothetically *if*—someone had to create an alias to protect her identity and *if* that person also happens to be the most wonderful kind of nerd alive, then *maybe* she would name herself after the first human woman in Greek mythology, who was too curious not to open her infamous box.

And I'm right. She wrote, and I quote (yeah, I'm a poet and I just don't know it):

Jaxon,

I told you I would find you, didn't I? Sorry I'm not using my real name, but I have to be careful. Also I might not be able to check the computer very often, so it might be better for you not to write back.

Meet me at the Kingston Avenue subway station tomorrow (today, that is—it's late; I can't sleep) at 3. I don't have to work, and we can take the train into the city. You'll see me on the platform, but don't talk to me or act like you know me. I'll let you know when it's safe.

Devorah

I have work at three, but I don't have to think about what to do; it's no contest. First thing in the morning I text Cora and tell her I'm sick with stomach flu, which no one ever challenges because of the puke factor. Then I tell my mom that I have a tutoring job and that Cora let me swap my schedule. I know I'm taking a slight risk going back to the Kingston Avenue stop after school, but I figure I'm probably safe. In a city like New York, with eight million people streaming all across it each day, the chances of running into someone you actually know at any given moment are pretty slim.

So my Monday already feels charmed, but it gets even better when Ryan comes up to me at my locker before first period and apologizes for being such a dick for the past few days. He says that his parents know the skateboarding accident isn't my fault and that I can come hang after school whenever. I have to tell him an abridged version of my week since we have only a few minutes before class, but we make plans to meet up later. The rest of school is a blur; my feet barely touch the ground. I pray that some subconscious part of my brain is still working to keep me from academic ruin, and I hope it shows up for my calculus quiz on Friday, because God knows I can't remember a damn thing except for three o'clock, Kingston Avenue. (That's almost like a math problem, right? If a Manhattan-bound 3 train leaves Kingston Avenue at three PM, going sixty miles per hour, carrying both Jaxon and Devorah, what time will it be when they get to Times Square, which is eight miles and seventeen subway stops away? Extra credit for calculating how many feet from Devorah Jaxon must stand at all times to keep his heart rate under 160 beats per minute.)

She's already there when I get to the platform at 2:58. Dressed in a white button-down and a navy skirt to just below her knees, with the ever-present tights and flat black shoes, her hair a waterfall of ringlets. She's staring out into the tracks with her hands clasped in front of her, holding an unmarked paper shopping bag, but she smiles as soon as my feet hit the bottom step and reaches a hand up to tuck a lock of hair behind her ear—her way of waving.

The station is full of kids letting off steam after school, punching

one another and laughing like hyenas and every so often some girl
shrieking at the top of her lungs like she's getting stabbed. I notice
one or two Hasidic men standing reading their Hebrew newspapers,
but there aren't too many. Usually they commute the other way, so
there are always a ton on my ride to school. Now whenever I see one
I wonder if he knows Devorah. Maybe that's racist, though, to think
they all know one another.

The train lurches into the station, and it's medium-full; no empty
seats but no armpit-to-armpit sardine can, either. I follow Devorah's
lead, so when she stands by the pole in the middle of the car, I lean
on one of the doors down at the end, keeping her in my line of
sight but trying not to look too much. We meet eyes once, as the
train leaves Grand Army Plaza, and both duck our heads, folding our
smiles into our chests.

At Hoyt Street two seats open up, right across from each other,
and as Devorah makes a move to sit down in one of them, I break
protocol and all but dive for the other. "Relax, son, there's no cash
prize," grumbles an elderly man a few seats down, and Devorah
shakes her head gently, biting her lip to keep from laughing. So to
get her back, for the next five stops I play a game with her. The way
the game works is, I stare at her until she feels me looking. Then, as
soon as she looks at me, I look away. It's driving her crazy, I can tell.

In lower Manhattan the train fills up so that people are standing
between us, and at Fulton I give my seat to a pregnant lady (at least,
I hope she's pregnant; my mom taught me to just get up, never ask)
and maneuver so that I'm standing in front of the sleeping Asian
man sitting next to Devorah. She keeps her eyes down until the train
pulls into Forty-second Street, and then she coughs, primly but pur-
posefully, into her palms. That must be my signal. I follow her out

onto the packed platform, and as we walk up the stairs, I reach my right hand up to squeeze her left, just for a second. "Wait" is all she says, not even turning around. This time, I'm the one going crazy.

(So back to that math problem. There are two answers, depending on how you look at it. From a mathematical perspective, it takes us forty-five minutes from the time we step onto the train at 3:02 to when we emerge into the throngs of sunburned tourists at 3:47. But in reality, time almost ceases to exist. You hear things like "time stood still," and it sounds impossibly corny, but that's what it feels like. So. We could have been on that train for thirty seconds or thirty days, I have no idea.)

"Hi," she finally says when we reach the street, squinting like moles into the bright afternoon sun.

"Hi," I say. "So what now?"

"I don't know," she says, laughing. "I just thought this would be a good place to get lost."

"It's a good place to get run over," I say, pulling her out of the way of a bike messenger trying to circumvent a stopped tour bus by riding up on the sidewalk. "But you know, to be honest I was hoping for somewhere we could be alone."

"What's more alone than standing in the white-noise center of the free world?" she asks, gesturing to the mob streaming around us.

"See, now you're just showing off." I grab her hand, but this time I don't let go. She stiffens for a second. "Can I hold your hand?" I ask, to make sure, and the Beatles' famous refrain rings in my tingling ears.

She nods. "I have only two requests. One is that you please not kiss me again." That knocks the wind right out of my sails, but she must notice my face fall because she quickly adds, "Not because I didn't like it but because I *did*, and I don't want it to get in the way of us being able to talk."

"Okay," I say, relieved but also reluctantly mentally deleting the steamy makeout session I've been hoping for. "What's the second one?"

She smiles self-consciously and holds out the shopping bag. "That you help me change my shoes." I peer inside and see a pair of bright red Converse pull-on low-tops.

"These are sweet!" I say, holding out the sneakers one by one as she stands beside me under the flashing Quiksilver marquee, grabbing my shoulder for balance. She slips off her flats and steps gingerly into the Converse, doing a little twirl.

"I've always wanted them," she says excitedly. "Shosh—my friend Shoshana—has a pair in black, but her parents are a lot more laid back than mine. And she's only allowed to wear them on weekends."

"She sounds wild," I crack, and Devorah punches me lightly on the arm.

"You have to remember, Jax, this is a big deal for me," she says, suddenly shy again. "I'm risking everything coming here. My parents think I'm visiting Rose at the hospital, since we were"—she blushes, stumbling over her words—"since I didn't get a chance to visit yesterday."

"Rose is covering for you?" I can barely hide my excitement, even though I know she's trying to be serious. If her sister is cool with us, then there must be a chance her parents might come around. But Devorah looks stricken.

"*No*," she says, like I've just suggested we go streaking down Broadway. "She has no idea. I'm just praying she doesn't talk to my mom before I get home." She looks down at her sneakers, shifting from foot to foot, as if she's still testing whether they truly fit.

"Hey, don't worry," I say, trying to stop her confidence from nose-diving. "Let's forget about everybody else and take these fancy new kicks for a spin."

"I'm not like you, Jax," Devorah says, still not meeting my eyes. "It's not that easy."

"You're not like anyone," I reply, and she finally looks up at me and it's all I can do not to break my promise and kiss her right then and there. Devorah smiles nervously and takes a tentative step toward Broadway.

"Okay, fine, I'll let you help me break them in," she says, holding out her hand. I take it.

"You know," I say as we snake our way through the hordes of tourists and day workers and comedy club–voucher hawkers clogging up the crosswalk, "this is what it could be like for us anyplace else."

"What?" Devorah asks distractedly, gazing up at the bright theater marquees.

"We'd just disappear," I say. "No one would look twice."

"That's a nice thought." She smiles dreamily.

"It's true."

Devorah doesn't respond, and I realize we've wandered our way to the foot of the red steps that stretch out over the TKTS booth. She looks up at them longingly.

"Go on," I say.

"No." She laughs. "It's okay."

"C'mon, the girl in the red shoes climbing the red steps at the center of the free world? It was meant to be."

She shakes her head, suddenly looking uncomfortable again. I wonder if it will always be like this, a mini roller coaster from happiness to terror every ten seconds. "I don't want anyone to see me," she whispers. I look around, but there's not a black fedora to be found for a block in any direction.

"No one's looking," I assure her.

"You don't know that."

"Why did you pick Times Square then? If it makes you so worried?"

Devorah looks up at me, frowning apologetically. "I don't know. I guess I thought it would feel safe, but it doesn't. It just feels claustrophobic."

"Then let's get out of here."

"Really?"

"Yeah. Let me take you someplace where I guarantee you no one will be looking at us."

"How can you be sure?"

"Because," I say as the idea takes shape in my head, "it's a place nobody goes."

As we scamper back down into the subway, a gust of ninety-degree air blowing our shirts back against our skin like shrink-wrap, I say a silent prayer that I'm not lying.

We get off the 7 train at Vernon Boulevard–Jackson Avenue in Long Island City, which is luckily just as desolate and industrial as I remember from when I used to come here to tutor Vinnie Chan, who lived with his family in one of two luxury high-rise apartment buildings facing Midtown across the water.

"Where are we?" Devorah asks in a tone that manages to be somehow both impressed and underwhelmed.

"Queens!" I announce proudly. "The ass end of it, anyway."

"It's perfect," she says. "Where should we go?"

"Let's just walk." I hold out my hand. "See where the wind takes us." She looks at me funny for a second but then breaks into a grin.

"Remind me to tell you a story later," she says.

Fiftieth Avenue is the bleakest, blandest, most unromantic street I've ever been on, so when it veers off onto an overpass after a few blocks I steer us left, onto the Pulaski Bridge. Speaking of unromantic, we're not exactly talking Brooklyn Bridge here; the Pulaski's just a highway on stilts. But still, there's sort of a view of the city, once you look past the E-ZPass toll lanes on the way into the Queens-Midtown Tunnel. And it's got red trim, which is in keeping with the color of the day.

"So did I get you in trouble?" I ask Devorah as we start off on the footbridge, which sandwiches us in between two gray lanes of traffic and a six-foot chain-link fence. "At the hospital?"

"No," she says. "But it was close. I had to lie." She takes a deep breath of the exhaust-tinged air. "I hate lying."

"Me, too," I say softly. "It's awful. But the alternative is not seeing you, and that's worse."

She smiles. "You always say the right thing."

I make a face. "Are you kidding? I never say the right thing. I'm always putting my foot in my mouth."

"I don't see that," she says, frowning.

"Well, maybe you're not listening."

"Or maybe you aren't talking to the right people."

There's that urge to kiss her again. I have to bite my tongue to keep from trying.

"So what if we stop lying?" I blurt out. "Just be together and make people deal with it?"

She smiles. "That would be nice."

"Let's do it, then."

"Go ahead," she says, a little sarcastically. "Your parents probably wouldn't care."

"Yes, they would!" I try to imagine bringing Devorah home: My mother's strained smile, the eyes she and my dad would make back and forth at each other. Mom serving meat loaf and au gratin potatoes, the awkward exchange when Devorah politely declines ("Just scrape the cheese off" . . . "Jaxon, why didn't you tell me she was lactose intolerant?" . . . "Separate dishes? You mean like a dessert plate?"). Dad's paint-stained coveralls, his thick-soled bare feet propped up on the coffee table. "They wouldn't know what to do with you," I say with a sigh. Which is depressingly true.

Devorah grimaces. "My parents would probably call the police. Or the Shomrim."

"The Shom-what?"

"Shomrim," she repeats. "Like Hasidic police. Only they don't have guns."

"Phew," I joke, "'cause I'd be a moving target."

Now *that* is definitely the wrong thing to say. Her face goes blank, and her smile disappears. She looks out at the skyscrapers, shimmering in the distance like stalagmites against the watercolor-pink sky.

"I don't know why it has to be like that," she says softly.

"It's bad blood," I say. "*Old* bad blood."

Her jaw tenses; she's mad, too. "But whatever happened . . . doesn't have anything to *do* with us."

"I know," I say, hearing my dad's angry voice in my head: *Whoever told you life was supposed to be fair?*

"We should just be able to be with whoever we want." She kicks a bottle cap on the walkway that ricochets off the railing and onto the asphalt.

We stop and face the skyline, weaving our fingers into the rusty chain link fence. Conversation stalls, and when I looked over at Devorah her face is still dark and tense.

"So tell me that story," I say, trying once again to lighten the mood.

"Oh, it's nothing." She shrugs, but she smiles a little, sun breaking through her cloudy eyes. "There's just a story my mother likes to tell about my grandmother being lifted up by the wind on the beach. You made me think of it when you said we'd go where the wind took us. But I don't even know how much of it really happened. My mother tends to exaggerate."

"It makes you happy, though, I can tell."

Her smile spreads, and her eyes drift up again toward the sky. "Yeah, it does. It just—I like the image of it. Of her flying. Sometimes I wish she was still alive so I could ask her."

"If it's true?"

"No, how it felt," Devorah murmurs. "To be so free."

I squeeze her hand. "Don't you feel that now?"

"A little," she says. "But not enough. We're not far enough."

"How far would we have to be?"

She closes her eyes. "Far enough so no one could find us." I start to lean in, but then her eyes flutter open and she takes a step back.

"Sorry," I say sheepishly.

She smiles and playfully pushes me away. "You know, I never broke a single rule in my life before I met you."

"Me neither," I say. Mostly the truth.

"So does that make us bad influences on each other?"

"No." I grab onto the fence with one hand and swing my free arm like Gene Kelly in *Singin' in the Rain*. "This feeling can't be bad. It's like no other feeling I've ever had. It does—"

I'm trying to be poetic, but suddenly Devorah lets out a guffaw and points up at a green traffic sign above our heads, hanging from the red-painted metal archway that marks the Pulaski's end in Greenpoint. WELCOME TO BROOKLYN! the sign reads, the big white letters flashing in the last of the day's sunlight. LIKE NO OTHER PLACE IN THE WORLD!

"Great—I'm trying to pour my heart out, and instead I'm quoting the New York City Department of Transportation," I say with a sigh.

"No." She laughs, putting her arms around my neck. "It was beautiful. And I'm sorry I interrupted you. Please finish what you were saying."

"I was just gonna say that it *does* feel like flying. To me at least."

Devorah stands on tiptoe and gives me a soft, sweet kiss.

"Let's run away," she whispers, and this time I close *my* eyes, letting Brooklyn fade to black, imagining nothing but white sand and blue-green ocean stretching out in front of us, on and on, sprinting toward an endless horizon.

• • •

When we leave each other at the G train in the ass end of Queens, we make plans to meet the next afternoon at the same time and place. But Tuesday morning I get another of Pandora's Facebook messages, and this time it makes my heart skip a beat for the wrong reason.

Dear Jax,

Good news: You were right, I didn't get caught in my lie. Maybe the shoes are magic? Maybe you are? Bad news: Business is picking up and Rose is still at the hospital every day and I don't think I can get out of working tomorrow without arousing suspicion. But I thought of a way we can still "meet": If you happen to be standing outside of Wonder Wings at 4:30 and I happen to pass by then we could see each other at least. I hope?

I won't be wearing my magic shoes but hopefully you'll recognize me. I'm your bad influence. :)

Devorah

This sucks on a number of epic levels, but mostly because I have a whole trip planned this time, much better than hoofing it over a seventh-rate bridge in the relative middle of nowhere: I was going to take her up to the planetarium at the Museum of Natural History, where we could have sat together in the anonymous dark and let the universe swallow us. I had it all planned out so we could get home by six, too, since when I came in at 6:31 on Monday, my mother raised her eyebrow (only one—she's skilled like that) and said she thought my tutoring sessions were only supposed to be an hour, and I had to invent some serious subway trouble that not only accounted for my lateness but also for the fact that I didn't call to *say* I was running late.

But all that has to be scrapped, so instead I go to work like normal, and since I'm "recovering" from a "stomach bug," Cora makes me wear one of those face masks doctors wear when they're dealing with pandemic diseases, and all the kitchen guys laugh at me and call me "J1N1," like the code for swine flu. And the only thing that keeps me going is knowing I'll see Devorah at four thirty and that I can *finally* give her the CD—which I have so far ironically been too excited to remember to bring with me, and which is as close to a love letter as I can come up with on short notice.

At 4:15 I can tell we're about to get swamped, since about ten middle-school kids start gathering on the sidewalk out front, all pooling their dollars, counting and recounting, trying to figure out if they can afford the daily special: five pounds of wings for $29.99. So I tell Cora I need some air, which she gladly gives me just so I won't pretend-puke on any of the customers. I grab a Coke from the bodega next door and walk around the block a few times with the dinky dollar-store jewel case getting sweaty in my hand until I spot Devorah walking down Union Street. I intercept her at the corner and hold out my gift.

"I made something for you," I say, but instead of the flirty smile I was expecting, she looks horrified.

"It's not safe to talk here," she whispers, darting around me. "I just wanted to see your face."

I jog after her. "Do you want to go somewhere?"

She shakes her head and pretends to study a sign in the bodega window advertising a sale on condensed milk. "No, I just—I'm sorry, Jax, I thought we could just *see* each other. As in look, not talk."

"Yes, you did write that," I say with what I hope is an irresistibly charming grin. "I just didn't know you were being literal."

Devorah glances around nervously and gestures for me to keep walking. We fall into awkward step, keeping a few feet between us. She still hasn't acknowledged the CD.

"So how are you?" I ask, settling for small talk—whatever will get me more time with her.

"Fine." It's like talking to a ventriloquist; I can barely see her lips move.

"Do you miss me?" I'm sort of joking, but not really. I just need something to get me through until we can see each other again, for real. But she just nods once, and then looks away like she doesn't know me.

"Okaaaaaay," I say with a sigh, giving in. "I get it. But will you at least tell me when I can see you again? As in spend time with you, not just gaze at your face from a predetermined distance?"

"Yes."

"When?"

"Soon. Please stop walking next to me."

"At least take the CD." I press it into her hands, and she stops in her tracks, looking at me helplessly; a deer in headlights.

"Where would I say I got it?" She crosses her arms, rejecting the gift, and I tuck the case back into my pocket, trying not to let her see how much it stings. Devorah lowers her voice to a whisper, her eyes softening. "Of course I want it," she says. "And of *course* I miss you, but if we're keeping things a secret then we can't leave any kind of trail." She touches my arm, but before I can so much as blink, she's gone. And I'm left to serve five pounds of wings to ten loud preteens who find my face mask hilarious, to say the least.

If Monday was a 10, Tuesday rates a 1. Maybe. Maybe less.

On Wednesday I'm listening to my own perfect mix CD and refreshing my Facebook page every thirty seconds, but there's still no new message. And I don't know what to do. I am officially in full-on Devorah withdrawal.

"Dude," Ryan says from his bed, where he's paging through a comic while I monopolize his MacBook Air, "I thought you said things were going *great*." (I called in sick again today; I just couldn't go through the motions of work with this pit in my stomach.)

"They were. They *are*," I say. "I'm just waiting to hear from her."

"Quit giving her all the power, man."

"What's that supposed to mean?"

Ryan just makes the sound of a whip cracking and laughs, and I give him the finger.

"I'm serious, though," he says. "If there's one thing my parents learned from their couples therapy it's that communication is key to any relationship. And it sounds like your communication with Devorah is, to borrow from the Yiddish, *fercockt*."

I'm about to shoot something back about how what's really *fercockt* is that his parents talk to him about their marriage counseling, but then I realize that Ryan actually has a point. It's *not* fair that I never get to decide when we see each other, or when or where. It's *not* fair for her to expect me to act like I don't know her if we pass on the street. If we're actually together—and I think we are—then we need to spend time together and figure out what we're going to do and how this is going to work. We need another day like Monday, on the bridge. Hell, we need a whole month of days like that. I know I could convince her of this if I could only *find* her and talk to her.

"How do you find someone who doesn't want to be found?" I groan.

"She didn't give you her number?" Ryan asks absentmindedly.

"She doesn't have her own phone."

"That's messed up."

"Ryan," I say, turning away from the computer for the first time since we got to his room, "she's Hasidic. It's against her religion to use electronics."

"Nope, you're thinking of Amish people," Ryan says, not looking up from his vintage copy of *Amazing Spider-Man*. "Jews can use electricity. Take it from a member of the tribe."

"You're a *quarter* Jewish," I say.

"Which is a quarter more than you."

"Fine—so tell me, Rabbi Hendrick, what am I supposed to do, call her house and ask her dad if I can talk to her?"

"Why not?" he says. "Just say your name is Shlomo or something."

"I don't know why I'm even talking about this with you," I say, and sigh. "I should know better."

"Hey," Ryan says, putting down the comic. "I care a lot about this."

"Shut up."

"I *do*. I want you to get your woman, Jax. You deserve it."

"Thanks." I drop my head down on Ryan's graffiti-covered desk and bang it lightly three times. "It's just making me so crazy that I can't get in touch with her! She can send me messages, but I'm not supposed to e-mail her back. She knows where I work, but I don't have any way of finding her apart from this fake Facebook page she set up and doesn't even check."

"Wait," Ryan says, jumping off the bed and elbowing me away from the laptop. "I might be able to get the IP address she sent the messages from."

"Since when can you do that?"

"Since I didn't have shit to do all summer but try to hack into Lindsay Lohan's Twitter account." He brings up Devorah's latest message, opens a command window, and starts typing letters that make no sense to me. "See?" he says proudly after a few minutes. I stare at the chain of meaningless numbers.

"That's . . . not an address."

"Give me a second; now I have to trace it," he says, rolling his eyes, and opens a new browser window. After a few clicks he points to the screen with a smug smile. "Aaron Blum, 482 Crown Street, you're welcome."

I know he's expecting to be thanked, so I clap him on the back and smile, but inside I'm more terrified than anything else. Now I have to follow through. I can't just sit licking my wounds and listening to moody emo songs. I have to go stand outside her window declaring my love like some ghetto Shakespeare character and hope no one calls the cops, or the Sham-Wows or whatever that Hasidic mafia is called.

"Maybe I should write her a letter first," I hedge, but Ryan shakes his head firmly.

"We're going," he says. "I'm not letting you back out."

I know he's right. It's a dangerous and possibly stupid plan, but it feels like all I have left. If I see Hasids on my side of Eastern Parkway, in Times Square, and even on Jones Beach in the summertime, then it's got to be at least sort of normal for non-Jews to wander over to their side occasionally, right? Ryan and I could pass for rubes who just made a wrong turn—couldn't we?

I compulsively refresh my Facebook page one more time and feel the pang of rejection and longing bloom fresh in my chest when my inbox comes up empty. I don't want to disrespect Devorah by showing up at her house unannounced, but she's making it impossible for us to be together. We have to get face-to-face time. And if she's not willing to make that happen, then I will.

Chapter 15
Devorah
SEPTEMBER 11, 5:15 PM

"Ahhhh! Ahhhh! Ahhhh! Ahhhhhh! *Ahhhhhhgggggghhhh!*"

I look down at the miniature, contorted face of my scream-ing niece, which is turning a deep magenta pink, at least ten shades darker than the pale blush cashmere blanket she's wrapped in, the one made from the possibly cursed yarn that her mother believes may have caused her premature birth. Every ten seconds the poor thing chokes on her own tears, gags, and then immediately resets, as if programmed on an endless loop of ear-splitting sounds, like a car alarm.

"Shhhh, bunny, shhhhh," I purr, poking the soft nipple of a pac-ifier between her angry gums, but Liya's tiny body only stiffens in protest, her cries getting louder and more guttural. I am not the one she wants, clearly. The one she wants (Rose) is out having her *mikveh*, the ritual purification bath that will end her sentence as a *yoledet*. (Another sign—as if I needed one—that boys are the chosen ones: after having a girl, a mother has to wait fourteen days to be "pure," but after a boy it's only seven. So unfair.)

Up to the moment she was left alone with me, Liya alternated between two states: sleeping or blinking disinterestedly, her eyes impassive and unfocused. All afternoon, ever since she arrived home bundled in her cream-colored car seat on Jacob's arm, we siblings have taken turns holding her, studying her face for signs that she has acknowledged and anointed us as the favorite aunt or uncle. My parents came home briefly but then had to return to the store, where Rosh Hashanah business is clearing out shelves now on a daily basis. Hanna went back to the store, too, and while I was awarded the privilege of babysitting, Miri, Amos, and Zeidy wouldn't give me a moment's peace . . . until, that is, the baby started to cry. Now they've all disappeared, the kids to the street and Zeidy to his bedroom, leaving me to sing loud, off-key nursery rhymes alone, roaming the parlor floor and bouncing like my life depended on it.

"Would you like the swing?" I ask Liya, placing her gingerly in the podlike contraption that vibrates and sways at the touch of a button, which Jacob set up between the couches in the living room (they're staying with us for a week, until the nursery is assembled in their apartment, so I get to see Jacob first thing every morning—lucky me).

But no. She would not like the swing.

"Do you need to burp?" I pick her up and lay her over my shoulder like Rose showed me, her body like a wriggling sack of sugar, her soft, sweet-smelling head nestled into my neck. I pat her back once, twice, then three times without so much as the slightest variation in the volume and spacing of her wails; but then, on the fourth pat, she heaves, and I feel warm liquid spill down my back. The good news is that this development shocks her enough to give my ringing ears five seconds of rest before the crying starts back up again. The bad news is that there's vomit in my hair.

I wipe Liya's face and set her down in her bassinet while I wring out my curls in the sink (I choose the dairy sink, which seems if not very palatable then at least technically correct), letting the running water drown out her screams. Then I take a deep breath and use the hall phone to call Shoshana.

"Is that the baby?!" she cries when her mother puts her on the line. Then: "She sounds upset."

"Yes, either she's hungry or tired or she hates me," I say with a sigh. "Maybe all three. Want to come over?"

"I'm supposed to set the table."

"That takes five minutes," I plead. "I'm literally covered in throw-up, and I can't make Liya stop crying. Please, Shosh? I need you!"

"Isn't your zeidy around somewhere? Newborn babies love old men," Shoshana says, audibly examining her nails. "Maybe it's because they look so much alike."

"Thanks anyway," I say miserably, and hang up. I know I should feel grateful that Rose and Jacob trusted me with their tiny preemie, but it's hard when my once-colorful sister is a barely ambulatory zombie and her formerly tolerably if obnoxiously arrogant husband is suddenly acting like some villain of Victorian literature, appearing around corners in dark robes, drumming his bony fingers like he's plotting to destroy me.

Once she has my attention again, Liya cries with renewed

energy, her little pink fists clenched in despair. I pick her up and kiss her tear-streaked face, knowing that there is only one person I could call who would be here in a heartbeat to help me with whatever I needed. And I don't even know his number.

I feel awful about the last time I saw Jaxon, when he tried to give me the CD outside the restaurant. I could tell he was hurt that I didn't want him to talk to me out in the open. And after what we shared on Monday I can't blame him; it's hard to go back to pretending to be strangers after having such an amazing afternoon. I can't stop thinking about it, either—I play it over and over in my head instead of sleeping—and of course I want to see him every day. But he still doesn't seem to understand what's at stake for me. If even one person from the neighborhood sees us talking, my life as I know it will be over, and there'll be no chance for us to sneak out ever again. I even hid the red Converse at the back of Isaac's closet after he left for yeshiva on Tuesday so that just in case they were found they couldn't be traced to me.

But I know I'm being the worst kind of hypocrite. I told Jaxon we can't leave any trail, and yet I'm the one who made a Facebook page for the express purpose of the forbidden act of writing to him, a page I had to link to my father's business e-mail account so that I could activate it and prove I wasn't a robot. I deleted the "Welcome to Facebook!" e-mails that popped up right away, but it was the middle of the night and I was desperate and sloppy, so now I have to sneak up to the study three or four times a day just to refresh the inbox and cover my tracks if necessary. I should just delete the account, but then I would have no way of contacting him, and closing that window would mean resigning myself to—

"*Ahhhhhhgggggghhhhhhhhhh!*" Liya screams, interrupting

my train of thought to conveniently remind me exactly what I have to look forward to if I cut off contact with Jax. Not immediately, of course, but two years down the line, this could be *my* baby that I don't know how to take care of, and I would be just as alone, only in a different and unfamiliar house—an apartment, probably, cramped and dark—decorated with useless, expensive wedding gifts, like the handcrafted hourglass someone gave Rose and Jacob.

But maybe not. That photo of Ruchy and her family at the hospital swims up through my consciousness. Ruchy, who made the dangerous choice. Ruchy, who seems not to have gotten what she "deserved," according to Jacob, but what she wanted for herself. What she consciously *chose.* Not that I would ever let myself get pregnant, not even with Jaxon's baby. But maybe we could re-create the rest of that photo. Maybe . . . maybe . . .

I bounce Liya faster, whisper-singing the lullaby my grandmother taught my mother when she had her first child: *"How the winds are laughing, they laugh with all their might . . . laugh and laugh the whole day through, and half the summer's night."*

When Jaxon and I kissed on that bridge I felt like the world was limitless, spinning out to infinity in all directions, making anything seem possible. Now three days later I feel like the world could fit inside that ugly MoMA hourglass that Rose keeps on her bedside table, and I'm drowning in the sands.

My nerves are so shot from Liya's incessant strangled cries that I'm actually relieved when Jacob lets himself in at five thirty. It's early for him to be getting home—normally he studies until just before dinner—but I don't question it, especially not when he takes the baby from my anxious embrace and holds her close, bouncing and humming for all of sixty seconds before she quiets and falls gratefully asleep in his arms (but not before sending one last defiant fart in my direction). I've never seen Jacob successfully comfort another human being before. Maybe fatherhood is changing him. One can always hope.

"Thank you," I whisper, moving toward the stairs to take a much-needed shower.

"Devorah, wait," he says, in a voice that makes me freeze in fear. Jacob never talks to me when there isn't someone else nearby to ensure that *yichud* isn't being violated. I turn to see Jacob lay Liya down in the swing.

"Should I get Zeidy or Amos?" I ask innocently.

"Frankly," he says, giving me a hard stare, "I don't think you'd want them to hear what I have to say."

My blood runs cold. "Okay," I say evenly, staying where I am, clutching the banister so hard the white bones of my knuckles press up against the skin. "What is it?"

"I know." Jacob sits on the couch, folding his hands in his lap and giving me a look that defies me to ask him what he means.

"You know what?" I have no choice but to play along.

"I know you've been seeing that boy," he says. "I saw you with him."

"You couldn't have," I say with a laugh. "Your eyes must be playing tricks on you. It might be time for some new glasses."

"Don't," he says sharply, standing up and taking a step toward me. "I was on my way to the store on Tuesday to talk to your father when I saw you leave at a few minutes past four. I also saw you look around to make sure no one was following you. So—"

"You followed me," I finish hollowly. My chest is starting to feel tight.

"Smart girl," Jacob says. "Yes, I followed you down Union Street and saw you meet him at the corner of Nostrand. I saw you lean in to him."

I want to protest and to make up another lie, but my brain feels stunned and sluggish. All I can do is shake my head slowly.

"You saw him in the hospital last weekend, didn't you?" Jacob continues quietly. "I knew it was fishy that you took the stairs. And I'm sure I heard you talking to someone."

"No," I say, but my weak voice gives away the lie.

"You left your family, your sick premature niece, to run around with a *schwarze,*" Jacob whispers, the words tinged with hateful venom. Suddenly I feel like I can't breathe.

"Do you have any idea what this means?" Jacob asks. "Not just for you but for all of us? The shame we would all suffer if this got out? What it could cost the business? Your father's standing in the community?"

"Please, Jacob, I've done *nothing*," I say with what I hope is believable conviction. "All I did was talk to him."

"Good," he says. "I hope for your sake that's true. Because if you're lying, you do realize that no self-respecting Chabadnik is going to want you for a wife, not even with that pretty face. They'll have to find someone out of state for you, someone with a limp or a lazy eye or some other defect lowly enough to qualify him for damaged goods."

Jacob wipes his hands on his trousers like he's just touched something slimy and gives me another of his penetrating stares. *I know.* The words are still echoing in my head. How could I have ever thought I could get away with this? How could I have been so careless and stupid? If I had only waited to meet Jaxon somewhere it would be safe, instead of risking everything in broad daylight . . . and for what? For a selfish glimpse of the boy I'm falling for so hard just the sight of him makes me light-headed?

"I hope it goes without saying that you are never to see him again," Jacob says, a self-satisfied smile playing on his lips. He is relishing this moment, I can tell. "Unless of course you'd like me to share what I know with your father."

He walks off into the kitchen, and I finally let my hand slip from the banister, where it falls, shaking, at my side. Now that Jacob knows my secret, I have no options left. I know what I have to do, and it breaks my heart. Tears spill down my cheeks as I climb the stairs two at a time up to the study, where I erase every trace of our correspondence, wiping the computer's memory clean and wishing that someone could do the same to my heart.

Chapter 16

Jaxon

Standing on the north side of Eastern Parkway looking across the seven lanes of traffic bisected by two broad, paved walkways dotted with benches and lined with elm trees still in their leafy summer prime, it's a little hard to feel the sense of foreboding I know I should be feeling.

It's not like I haven't crossed the parkway before—hell, Wonder Wings is on the other side, so I'm over there three times a week at least—but there's a difference between just crossing over and really going in. If I had to sit down and map out territory, us versus them, I'd say that between Eastern Parkway to the north and Empire Boulevard to the south, between Nostrand to the west and Utica to the east, that's the Hasidic Crown Heights. And then everything west of Nostrand and north of Eastern Parkway is black Crown

Heights. Or *was* black Crown Heights. The hipster contingent has taken over a lot of the commercial streets, and now you can't go two blocks without running into some up-its-own-ass artisanal shop with a name that's just two random nouns thrown together with an ampersand. Satchel & Dove. Twig & Petal. Those are the places where you find out there's such a thing as boutique tarragon mayonnaise and that a baby onesie can legitimately cost sixty dollars.

But even though strangers of different backgrounds and skinnier jeans have seeped into our neighborhood, we still don't cross Eastern. Mom always told us the Hasidics liked to be left alone; that was all she would say. And it seemed true. I remember seeing families on the subway, clustered together, all in dark colors and long hems like they'd stepped out of some old painting, or in the Botanic Garden, little boys with yarmulkes running around crazy like any other kids, but if they got too close to us, their mothers would swoop in, ushering them away with whispers in another language. But then sometimes we would see the Mitzvah Tank, that big beige Winnebago driving around with boys and men jumping out to ask people if they were Jewish, and ask our parents how that figured into the whole being-left-alone thing.

"They want other people to join them, but only if you convert to their religion," Mom would explain.

"Why don't they ever ask us?" Ameerah asked once, and my father just said, "We're the wrong color." That was the end of that discussion.

"Jax!" Ryan calls, hopping out of the subway station brandishing his skateboard and a giant Nalgene bottle. I hope it wasn't a mistake to bring him, but if I've learned one thing from the movies it's that you don't go into uncharted territory without backup. In fact, it's usually the wingman who ends up getting killed in some over-the-top gory way, like getting impaled on a fence post. I decide not to share this nugget of trivia with Ryan.

"Hey, man," I greet him. "I thought we decided no skateboard. In the interest of stealth."

"Yeah, I know," he says. "But then I thought, what if we need to make a quick getaway?"

"'We'?" I ask as we cross the first lane of traffic. "Is that thing a two-seater?"

"Good point. Well, I can go get help, at least."

"That's comforting, Ry."

Yesterday we Googled the area around Devorah's house and found a bakery on the corner that we can use as our cover. We're going to browse, pretending we're looking for a cake for my sister's birthday. After that, we'll walk past her house a few times and check it out, and if it feels safe, Ryan will ring the doorbell and create a distraction so I can run around the back and try to find Devorah's window. I even brought some pebbles from Tricia's mini Japanese rock garden so I can do some old-school romantic gesturing. But I hope I won't have to use them. I'm hoping she'll answer the door.

As we're waiting at the light to cross the center section of through traffic, two Hasidic men stop next to us. They're a little older, both with mustaches, short beards, and glasses. I stick my hands in my pockets and try to look casual, just as Ryan sticks his water bottle in my face and yells, "Hydrate!"

Yup, this was definitely a bad idea.

Two blocks past Eastern Parkway, anyone else who looks even remotely like us has disappeared, and Ryan and I are officially lost in Chabadland. Suddenly all the names on the Kingston Avenue store awnings are Jewish: Weinstein's Hardware, Kesser Cleaners, Mermelstein Caterers. The dudes from the crosswalk are a few feet ahead of us now and keep looking back as if they're surprised that we're still behind them. In fact, everybody we pass seems to let their eyes linger on us for a beat too long. And it's not just in my head; Ryan notices, too.

"Maybe we should have worn darker clothes," he says under his breath. And it's probably true that Ryan's neon green T-shirt decorated with cartoon panda bears doing tai chi isn't helping our cause. But we would have looked even stupider trying to blend in, like two high school exchange students auditioning for a production of *Fiddler on the Roof.*

"How does it feel to be a minority?" I ask him as we pass a big store called Judaica World.

"Fine," he says—the only answer that a privileged white kid can give to that question without getting a beat-down.

I keep my chin tucked in, eyes on the ground, the same stance I have when I pass by the guys from my neighborhood who laugh and call me Urkel because I wear a big backpack and don't hang out on the street all night smoking Kool XLs—and by the way, we need a new black nerd archetype; also, when are these wannabe gangstas watching reruns of *Family Matters*? But here, on the other side of Eastern, no one says a word to us. There are no jeers, no jokes, no names called out. Just eerie, observational silence, punctuated by the occasional scrape of Ryan's skateboard dragging on the pavement as he loses his grip.

"Should I be on the lookout for anyone?" he whispers as we wait at the light at Carroll Street.

"The only one besides Devorah who knows what I look like is her brother-in-law," I say, keeping my voice low.

"What does he look like?"

"Oh, you know, black hat, black suit, beard, glasses, look of distrust," I say. "Knock yourself out."

He laughs, but what Ryan doesn't know is that I'm secretly terrified. Like, run-screaming-in-the-other-direction terrified. Stalking a girl's house is messed up to begin with, but stalking a girl's house when her family is historically programmed to hate you must be some kind of sick suicide mission. It's my only hope of seeing Devorah again, since she seems to have cut off all communication with me (and it can't be because she doesn't feel something, too; I *know* she does), but it's seeming riskier by the second. What am I going to say to her if I see her? And if she wasn't willing to talk to me on the street outside a fast-food restaurant with no one around, do I honestly think she's going to have a heart-to-heart with me outside her home, with her parents right inside? These questions all make perfect sense to my brain, but that's not the part that's in control now, driving me to keep putting one foot in front of the other, each step taking me farther and farther down the rabbit hole. I miss her so much that it's starting to physically hurt. My heart's got the reins now, and all it wants to do, apparently, is find Devorah and spill its entire contents at her feet. Failing that, I have a plan B ready in my backpack, but I don't even know if it's going to work. There might not be enough wind.

As we approach Crown Street, I slow down. Devorah could literally appear any second, and I know I need to be ready, although the only thing I'm really ready for, thanks to the crazy adrenaline pumping through my system, is to use the bathroom. I practice what

I've decided should be my opening line: *I'm sorry, but I love you.* I could even cut out the first three words if I have to.

"There!" Ryan cries, and I nearly have a heart attack before I realize he's just pointing out the bakery. I'm way too jumpy; I've never felt this raw before, like my nerves were hanging off the outside of my body. I know love is supposed to make you vulnerable, but how anyone can actually live like this long-term is beyond me.

We get coffees from the rheumy-eyed old man behind the counter but then are ushered out the door before we can even carry out our cake-hunt cover story, because it's almost five o'clock, and he has to lock up before sundown. I could kick myself for planning this stakeout for a Friday. Of all the days to show up unannounced at Devorah's door. And if I can't talk to her today she's off the grid (even more than usual) for the next twenty-four hours. Awesome.

"I guess we'll just have to loiter here like normal riffraff," Ryan says as we stand pointlessly in the still-strong late afternoon sunshine.

"Well, we can't wait until it gets dark," I say. "We have to get home for dinner."

"We could go in there," Ryan says, pointing his Styrofoam cup in the direction of a little store across the street that has its door propped open." I glance at the awning and wish I had some kind of J.R.R. Tolkien invisibility cloak.

"*Blum* Quality Goods," I whisper. "As in *Aaron* Blum. That's her family's store, man."

"You don't know that," he says.

"Well, I'm not going to risk it," I shoot back.

Just then, a redheaded girl appears in the doorway with a broom. She looks up and immediately catches my eye, cocking her head and frowning like she recognizes me. And in the half a second that our eyes lock, I vaguely remember seeing her at the hospital on Sunday, laughing with Devorah in the hallway.

"Shit," I say, spinning around. "Don't look, don't look."

"Was that her?" Ryan asks.

"No, but I think it's one of her sisters. We have to get out of here. Abort mission." I start walking down Crown in the opposite direction, at a fast clip, and Ryan jogs to keep up with me.

"Jax," he pants, "we came all this way. We've at least got to walk by her house."

"I don't know," I say, tossing my coffee into a trash can on the curb. "I'm not feeling very lucky today."

"Well, I know you, and I know you'll torment yourself if we don't at least look," he says. It doesn't happen often, but occasionally Ryan can actually say something insightful.

"All right," I agree. "But just a walk-by." I stop and put a hand on his shoulder, looking him dead in the eye and breaking into a smile. "And if things get dicey," I say, "*I'm* taking the skateboard."

We make a big loop around the block before we venture closer to Devorah's house. 482 Crown Street is a three-story redbrick building with a turreted roof and a sloping stone stoop lined with curving hedges. It's not that much different from my house, actually, except that instead of being flush up against the neighboring houses it has narrow strips of balding grass on each side leading around to a backyard. The street is quiet and empty, which makes it that much weirder for me and Ryan to be there. Still, my heart feels like a balloon in my chest. Just knowing I'm close to where she is gives me some kind of contact high.

"What do you want to do?" Ryan asks, taking a slug from his water bottle. Both of us are damp with sweat, and Ryan's freckled nose is starting to glow as red as Rudolph's.

I guess, best-case fantasy scenario, I had hoped that Devorah would be outside, alone, communing with the neighborhood birds or something, like Cinderella, giving me easy access. But no one's outside, and I can't even see anything through the dark front-window drapes. I know I have no shot at getting time to talk to her, but I don't want to leave, either, not when I'm this close. My feet feel glued to the pavement.

"Should I ring the doorbell?" he asks.

"Nah, man, what would you say?"

"Uh . . . 'Do you have a minute for Greenpeace?'"

I can't help but laugh. With his Toms shoes and Nalgene bottle, Ryan definitely looks the part. "That's okay," I say.

"Well, should we leave the thing you brought?" he asks. I start studying the nearby trees and fences to scout the right spot, and just then the redheaded girl from the store rounds the corner about two hundred feet from where we're standing, followed by a big older man with linebacker shoulders spreading his jacket out so it flaps behind him like a cape.

"Hide," I croak, and duck down behind the black Ford SUV that is thankfully parked right in front of us. I think I saw them before they saw us, but I hold my breath anyway, shooting daggers at Ryan's stupid skateboard, which even though he's crouched down almost to curb level is sticking out ever so slightly beyond the car's rear bumper. I hear their footsteps getting louder and then the scuff of shoes climbing concrete stairs, the jingle of keys.

"What are you looking at, Hanna?" the man's deep voice asks, and I freeze even more than I'm already frozen. If they've seen us, I decide, I have two choices: Ask to see Devorah or run as fast as I can. It's one of those man-or-mouse moments, and I don't know which I am . . . although the fact that I'm currently cowering behind a parked car certainly points in one direction.

"Nothing, Daddy, just open the door," an annoyed teenager's voice replies. I allow myself to take a breath, letting it out slowly and shakily as I hear the door open, and then close. I can see Ryan start to open his mouth, so I clamp a hand over it and shake my head fiercely. I count out twenty seconds as slowly as my racing pulse will let me, and then, pointing at Ryan to stay where he is, I rise a few inches, peering through the Ford's tinted windows just in time to see the door fly open and the redhead—Hanna—step back out.

"I dropped my notebook!" she calls through the door before shutting it behind her. I duck back down and roll my eyes at Ryan. As soon as she's back inside, we have to get the hell out of here. I listen for her footsteps, but instead of getting softer as she goes back down the street they get louder and louder until—

"Hi," she says, poking her head around the hood of the car and staring down at us quizzically. I can see Devorah a little bit in Hanna's face: in the eyes, around the chin, and in the way she's kind of smirking at me right now.

"Hey," Ryan says with a wave. I start to stand up—no point in hiding now—but Hanna holds a hand out to stop me and whips her head around to look at the house. After a second, she looks back down at me.

"You're the boy from the elevator, right?" she whispers. I nod, and she smiles. "Does Devorah know you're here? Is she meeting you?" The fact that Devorah told her sister about me is as good a sign as I've gotten all week. I have to fight the urge to leap up and hug this girl.

"No," I say as low as I can. "She doesn't know I'm here. But we've met. I mean, since the elevator."

"I knew it!" Hanna says, looking pleased with herself for a second before she glances back nervously at the house. "No one can know you're here. Even staying on the street is pretty risky. But if you can get around to the backyard, I'll make sure Devorah sees you. Her window is on the second floor."

"Is the backyard really safe?" I ask. "You guys don't have, like, a pair of Dobermans back there?"

"No," she says, laughing. "And my mom hasn't cleared the weeds in about three years, so no one will be back there, I promise. There's an old playhouse near the fence that you can hide behind, but everyone is getting ready for Shabbos so I don't think anyone's going to be looking as long as you don't make noise."

"Thank you," I say gratefully. She shrugs self-consciously and then runs back across the street, where I hear the door open and shut with a thud.

"You're *in*, man!" Ryan whispers, punching my shoulder.

"Don't congratulate me yet," I say.

We make plans to meet back in front of the bakery, and Ryan jogs off, leaving me to decide how best to get across the street and into the Blums' backyard without looking like a shady intruder. Which I am, I guess. Something my mom likes to say when she's up on her equal-opportunity soapbox floats through my head: *People have enough reasons not to like you just based on how you look; don't give them any more based on how you act.* Creeping around a lily-white neighborhood with a big backpack and climbing into people's yards is probably exactly what she's talking about, but Hanna is giving me a shot that I can't turn down. I have to see Devorah. It's like breathing at this point, or eating. It feels like I need her to live.

There's still no sign of anyone outside on the street—I must have lucked out and arrived just late enough so that everyone is already home from work—so I figure my best bet is to simply make a dash for it, around the car, across the street, through the thin passageway between Devorah's house and her neighbors', and into the yard. I'm about to spring into action when my phone vibrates in my pocket. It's a text from my mom:

Where are u? Never can find u these days. Need milk. XO Mom

As I'm reading that one, trying to ignore the guilt it stirs up, a text from Ryan appears on the screen:

Dude you described just came out of store. Be careful.

Jacob's on his way. There's no time to wait now. Still clutching my phone, I jump up and sprint as fast as I can across the street and into the alley between the houses, where I have to turn sideways to fit through. I shuffle along, wincing at every twig that crunches under my sneakers, until the red brick spills out into an overgrown square of grass littered with rusted toys and shaded by a big magnolia tree. The entrance to the backyard from the house seems to be a basement door that's padlocked from the outside, so at least I know there'll be no element of surprise. I see the playhouse Hanna described, which is bowed and rotted through in some places, but it gives some cover so I crouch behind it and stare up at the three windows on the second floor. I don't know which one she'll appear at, but I want to be ready when she does. I realize too late that I probably should have spent my energy making a sign, instead of dreaming up the metaphorical statement I've got in my backpack, tied to a very risky gift. But it's too late now.

I see movement in the center window and duck my head. There's the sound of the storm window being shoved open, and then Devorah's voice drifts down through the warm evening air: "I can't believe you're hot, Hanna, it's *freezing* in here!" I smile to myself and silently thank my girl Hanna for being so sly. Devorah definitely doesn't know I'm here. But now it's up to me to make my presence known.

I stand up and hear her gasp before I've even had time to lift my eyes up to her face. She's framed perfectly in the window, her arms above her head pushing the storm window up, her face a pale circle glowing in the center of a dark square. Her eyes widen, and her mouth drops open.

"No, it's nothing, I just saw a squirrel and it scared me," she says, turning back into the room for a moment. "Go downstairs, I'll just be a second."

She looks back down at me, and I open my mouth to say what I came to say, but she raises a finger to her lips and shakes her head urgently. So I do the only thing I can, the only thing I feel, which is to raise one hand to my heart like I'm about to say the Pledge of Allegiance, only not to any flag but to Devorah. And I just stare up at her and think, *I love you I love you I love you.*

The light is getting hazy, that soft orangey glow that will soon give way to purple dusk, but it's bright enough still that I can see her features perfectly as they crumple, her chin quivering, her eyes folding into little winks. I was a little afraid she'd be angry that I showed up at her house, but I never thought she'd cry. I start to feel awful, until she breaks into the most heartbreaking smile, laughing and crying at the same time, and puts her hand up to her chest, too, so that we're just standing staring at each other, knowing we're both thinking the same thing.

I don't know how much time passes—probably only seconds, though it feels like hours—but somebody must be calling her down to dinner, because she turns again and yells, "I'm coming!" and then looks back at me again, wiping her tears away. She holds up a hand, and then she disappears from the window. Is she asking me to wait?

I crouch back down and tuck my chin, pressing my forehead against the warm, spongy wood of the playhouse. Hanna was right: It seems like no one has spent time back here in decades. The sun's almost down, but in the light streaming in through the half-sunken roof I can see toy cars and plastic dolls buried in the weeds, crusted over with rust and dirt. It's a sad tableau, but it's also the perfect place to hide the cell phone.

It's one of those old-school Nokias that no one uses anymore; I got it from the T-Mobile store near work for $19.99 plus $20 to buy us three hundred minutes' worth of phone calls, which, based on the amount of time Devorah has free to talk, I figure should last us about eight years. I set everything up last night and already committed the number to memory, although of course it's in my phone under both "D" and "Pandora," just in case one of them accidentally gets erased. In Devorah's new phone, I've programmed my number in under "J." That seems like the safest choice in the hypothetical, worst-case scenario event that one of her parents or someone else finds it before she does. Oh, and I've set my outgoing voice mail to the default female robot voice that just says my number, not my name. Covering all my bases. The ringtone, though, that's pure Jax; I couldn't help myself. I know it's risky not to just leave it on silent, but she can always turn the volume off. I just need her to know that I put thought into every detail. I'll give you one guess what the song is. When I call, I want it to sound like what falling in love feels like.

After a few minutes, when Devorah still hasn't resurfaced, I decide to get to work, putting plan B into fast and decisive action. (*Action Jaxon—maybe J-Riv was on to something after all.*) I unzip my bag as quietly as possible and pull out the string, which is already tied on one end to the Nokia. That should be enough to anchor it to the ground, but just in case I loop the string around a nail on the back of the playhouse, too, letting the phone drop into the yellow grass inside. As for the other end, I had hoped to let it loose—which would probably be more romantic—but the breeze isn't strong enough, and besides, then it might fall, forgotten, into the weeds after I've left. And if she doesn't see it, she won't find the phone. Or get the sappy metaphor. Because it's more than a decoy hiding the real present; the next time Devorah looks out her bedroom window, I want her to know that it's a message from me, to let her know that I love her, and that I won't stop until she feels that freedom that she's always dreamed of. Until she feels like she's flying.

Chapter 17
Devorah

"*Baruch a-ta A-do-nay Elo-hei-nu me-lech ha-o-lam a-sher ki-dee-sha-nu bi-mitz-vo-tav vi-tzi-va-noo li-had-leek ner shel Sha-bbat ko-desh.*"

My mother's sweet alto rings out over our Shabbos table, and I know I'm supposed to be praying and giving thanks and channeling joy and positivity. After all, Liya is finally home, blissfully unconscious in a sling on Rose's chest. The storm has passed, the neighborhood is clean again (and so is Rose, having emerged from her ritual bath just as the baby started sleeping for five-hour stretches at night, which has helped her to dezombify somewhat). We're all healthy, and Rosh Hashanah, the new year and first of the High Holy Days, is practically around the corner. But all I can think as I light my Shabbos candle is: *Shit. Shit. Shit shit shit shit shit SHIT.* I would owe Jaxon's mother two dollars for cursing that much. And all because her son is stupid and romantic enough to show up unannounced *in my backyard.*

My inner monologue goes something like this:

I mean, what is he THINKING?

(He loves me.)

Someone could see him! Everyone *could see him.*

(I might love him, too.)

Not that any of that will matter once he gets caught.

(This is the bravest thing he could do.)

This is the most selfish thing he could do.

(Hanna knows now. At least she can help, and that's a relief.)

Jacob knows now, and if he catches Jaxon here, we're dead. Maybe literally.

(How can I sneak off to see him again?)

How can I get rid of him without arousing suspicion?

(When he raised his hand to his heart, I cried.)

Every time anyone turns toward the window, I feel like puking.

(He loves me.)

I hate him!

(I love him.)

SHIT.

I manage to make it through the kiddush and the washing of the hands without anyone noticing my silent panic attack. But after the HaMotzi blessing, as we're passing around the challah, I shove the basket to my right without paying attention and accidentally drop it right into Rivka's lap. My brothers snicker.

"Keep your eyes open, please," my mother says with a laugh. And I know she's just joking about my butterfingers, but she's right on a deeper level, too.

"Maybe she's got something on her mind," Jacob says, taking a sip of his wine.

"More like nothing in my stomach," I shoot back. Our eyes meet, and I try not to think about Jaxon. At this point, I half believe Jacob could read my mind if he tried.

"Well, there's no shortage of food," my father says, passing me a platter of brisket swimming in gravy. He smiles at Mom, laying his big, chubby catcher's-mitt hand on her shoulder. "You've outdone yourself yet again."

Mom beams, her face as bright as the flames licking up at the ceiling from the tapered white candles between us. "Well, I'll never forget the very first thing your mother said to me during our *bashow*," she says with a laugh. (A *bashow* is the first meeting of a newly matched couple, usually with the groom and his parents visiting the potential bride in her family's home.) She sets her features into an accusatory scowl and shakes her finger, impersonating my late Bubbe Sara. *"Can you cook?"*

My father chuckles and shrugs. "What can I say—she was looking out for me!"

Hanna leans forward in her chair. "What did *you* think about Mama the first time you saw her?" My father rolls his eyes good-naturedly. This is not the first time Hanna has asked this particular question. In fact, it may be the seventeenth.

"I thought she was very nice," he says carefully.

"That's it?" Hanna asks, unimpressed.

"What more do you want?" Isaac asks, spearing a potato with

his fork. He's one to talk, the eldest son who's already seen his younger brother and sister both married off and who has already had not one but two failed attempts at *shidduchim* because he didn't like the girls the *shadchan* picked. I start to open my mouth to say as much when I think better of it. I don't know if Jaxon is still waiting for me, and I need to make sure he's not doing anything crazy—or crazier than what he's already done. If I can eat quickly and get to my room without anyone suspecting anything, I can check to make sure he's well-hidden, and then write out a sign on a piece of paper, something to hold up in the window to tell Jax where to hide until I can sneak away later, when everyone leaves for *tish*.

"Hanna wants love at first sight," Niv says, laughing derisively. "Fairy-tale stuff."

"That is why," my father says, clearing his throat and reaching for the water pitcher, "you should not be reading fairy tales."

"I don't read them," Miri says proudly.

"Neither do I," Hanna cries. "I just thought when you met your soul mate you'd come up with something better than 'very nice.'" She kicks me under the table—now that Aunt Varda's back in Monsey, Hanna has resumed her usual seat—and I grit my teeth. Hanna might be more of a liability than a confidante.

"Ahh, I see," my father says, drumming his fingers together in front of his wiry black beard. "Well, that's because we don't know our *bashert* by sight. Only Hashem knows."

"And He brings you together through the *shadchan*," my mother adds.

Or He cuts out power to your elevator, I think. Across the table, Jacob is staring off disinterestedly while chewing, his eyes drifting up toward the window behind me. I have to get his attention so that he doesn't accidentally spot Jaxon, but it feels like poking a sleeping dragon.

"What was your first meeting with Rose like?" I ask, smiling what I hope looks like a real smile. He looks at me quizzically and then dabs at his mouth with his napkin.

"It was very . . . traditional," he says, drawing out the last word for my benefit.

"Bo-ring," Amos mutters under his breath.

"Weren't you there?" Rose asks, furrowing her brow, and I shake my head.

"I was in the house when the Kleinmans came over, but I wasn't in the room." This is not exactly a lie; I was crouched at the top of the stairs, trying hard to eavesdrop but failing miserably. I turn back to Jacob and force myself to grin again, ever the obsequious sister-in-law. "Rose was giddy afterward," I tell him.

"That's silly," he snaps, throwing down his napkin. "It's not just unrealistic to fall in love before marriage, it's destructive to our faith. Because to have romantic thoughts about someone before being joined before G-d constitutes a sin, and a union based on sin is by definition unholy." It sounds like he's yelling at Rose, but I know that Jacob is talking very specifically—and very threateningly—to me.

"All right, all right," Zeidy says with an annoyed wave, trying to reroute the dinner conversation, but Jacob is just warming up. His thin lips are wet with spit as he leans in to deliver his sermon.

"In Chayei Sarah, what does it say about Isaac?" he asks pedantically, tapping his finger on the table like a frustrated grade-school teacher. "*He married Rebecca, she became his wife, and he loved her.* Not he loved her and she became his wife, but she became his wife and *then* he loved her. Love takes a long time—years, even."

"Excuse me," Rose whispers, as she pushes her chair away from the table and walks into the kitchen, cradling the still-sleeping Liya.

"Thank you, Jacob," my mother says loudly. Her tone is polite, but her eyes are flashing. "I'm sure Devorah only meant that Rose was excited to be matched with such a fine young man. As we all were."

"Okay," he says, sighing, clearly upset at being cut off mid-rant. "But it's important for the children to understand these things. Love is not romantic. Love is *earned,* through virtue."

"Well said," my father booms. "Now, would someone please pass me the peas?"

Silverware starts clinking, and Niv and Isaac start debating what kind of car Niv and Rivka should buy when the lease on their Corolla runs out, and just as I'm letting out a shaky breath into my untouched brisket, thinking that the worst is over, Rose lets out a gasp right behind me. And I don't even have to turn around to know that she's standing directly in the center of the big, five-foot window that looks from the dining room out into the yard, directly in line with the little abandoned playhouse that, when last I checked, my six-foot-tall secret boyfriend was using for camouflage.

"What's wrong?" my mother asks, leaping up. "Is it the baby?"

"No," Rose says. "But there's something outside."

I push back my chair like the house is on fire, but Amos is smaller and faster and is already at the front door before I can even stand up.

"Amos, wait, let me go first!" I cry, nearly barreling into Zeidy as I struggle to get out from behind the dining table. I push through the heavy front door and race down the steps after my brother, knowing full well that it actually makes me look *more* suspicious to spring into action like this, when the "something" my sister saw could be a psychopath holding a chainsaw, for all my family thinks I know. But the force that drives me out into the moonlit knee-high grass isn't rational; it's animal. Jaxon could still be out there, and I have to protect him. I cannot let Amos get to him first. Ignoring the cramps in my calves and the bile climbing my throat, I sprint through the narrow passage between the Eliavs' house and ours, scraping my elbow on the rough stucco siding. "*Amos!*" I yell again.

"Cool!" I hear my little brother pant. That slows my heart somewhat; despite his affinity for zombie movie posters, I doubt Amos's first reaction to finding a stranger hiding in the bushes would be that it was *cool*.

Sure enough, when I reach the backyard, I can see immediately that Jax is gone. But he's left something for me: a kite, candy-apple red with a long string that twists down through the branches of the magnolia tree. It's beautiful—or would be, if I were the only one who could see it. I look back over my shoulder and see Jacob, peering through the glass alongside my parents and brothers. Without thinking, Jaxon has raised a red flag in front of a bull.

"It's a kite!" Amos yells to Hanna, who is rounding the corner with Miri on her heels. He gazes up at the fluttering streamers. "Where'd it come from?"

"It must have gotten blown over from someone else's yard," I say quickly.

"But there's no wind," Miri points out.

"Maybe it's a *present*," Hanna says.

"From who?" Amos asks, leaping for the string.

Shut up, I scream at Hanna through telepathy.

"Devorah," she calls, ignoring my glare, "why don't you check and see if there's a *note*?"

I freeze. Would Jaxon have been bold enough to leave an actual love letter? That doesn't seem like his style—more likely, the kite *is* the love letter, a way to say it without saying it, risky but at the same time completely hidden in plain sight. Still, I'd be stupid not to check. If there is anything more damning, I have to see it before anyone else does.

"Stop it, Amos, you'll break it," I say, darting over to where my brother is fruitlessly tugging on a length of string snagged around a knot in the dusky brown trunk. I stand on tiptoe and run my fingers under the string slowly, feeling in the dark for a hidden scrap of paper but finding only scratchy branches. Behind me, I hear some- one rapping their knuckles on the glass, but I don't turn around. I'm almost to the kite. Just a few more inches . . .

"Can I be the first to try it?" Miri asks.

"I saw it first!" Amos cries.

"*Rose* saw it first," Hanna scoffs. My fingers close around the diamond of nylon, and I pull back, dislodging the kite from the tree and nearly falling on my butt in the process. Amos grabs for it, but I elbow him away, turning it over in my hands, my eyes frantically searching the fabric for handwriting. I'm both incredibly relieved and unexpectedly disappointed to find none.

The window groans open, and my father's voice fills the still night air. "Leave it alone!" he yells. "We're in the middle of dinner. Come back inside right now."

"Sorry, Tatty," I call, mentally preparing how I'll talk my way out of this. Blowing in from someone else's yard isn't that far-fetched, is it? And even if it is, there's no way to trace it to me. Not unless Jacob speaks up. And he couldn't, not without proof. He's too careful and calculating for that.

"Amos, let it *go*," Miri says. While the three of us girls are obediently walking back toward the front of the house, smoothing out our skirts, Amos has picked up the kite where I dropped it and is yanking at it, getting snapped back again and again like a dog leashed to a post.

"It's still stuck," Amos says petulantly.

"*Leave it*," my father commands from the window.

"But there's something at the end!" Amos cries.

Hanna and I exchange a panicked look, and she doubles back, crouching to fit her head and shoulders through the door of the play-house. A second later, the kite springs free, and Amos happily loops the string around his arm, running back toward the house, where I'm sure he will ferret it away among his toys and claim ownership. But I guess I have to let him.

"It was just a rock," Hanna yells up at our audience in the window, running to join me by the basement door. But as we file along the dark brick side of the building, bathed in shadow, she taps my shoulder and opens her hand to reveal a small silver cell phone. She raises a hand to her lips, slips it into her sleeve, and hurries ahead.

I couldn't say what the rest of dinner was like, because I was too busy spiraling into a panic attack, convinced that at any moment the phone hidden in my sister's blouse would go off like some sort of explosive. That, combined with Jacob's third degree, was nearly enough to stop my heart completely.

"Maybe it was for you, Devorah," he kept suggesting, repeating it a couple of times throughout the meal until I finally had to dignify it with a response.

"That's impossible," I said coldly. "I've never flown a kite."

"Some things you can't explain," my mother said, sighing, with a shrug. By the time dessert was finished, everyone seemed to have forgotten about it. Except, of course, for me.

Now I'm in my room, in pajamas, under the covers, with the sheet rolled up tight under my neck, the way I used to insist my mother tuck me in when I was young because I believed that bogey-men couldn't get me as long as I was hidden. The phone is under my pillow, a hard little knot under the back of my skull. I know it's just a dinky piece of plastic, but it feels much more thrilling, and dangerous.

I wish I could talk to Rose or my mother about what's going on. Growing up, I was taught that it was a blessing not to have to worry about dating and romantic love. I felt grateful to be able to focus on my studies, and to give all my love to my family, thanking G-d that He in all His infinite wisdom took away the choices that kept so many other women across the world preoccupied and dis-tracted from the divine: how to dress to attract a man, how to keep his interest, how to make him commit. I always assumed, just like Jacob said, that I wouldn't experience love or romance until I was introduced to my husband, and this gave me a great sense of peace. I truly believed that freedom of choice was a burden, and that girls who wasted their thoughts on dating were pathetic.

But the deeper I get into whatever this is with Jaxon, the more I question all of that. I can still understand why Hasidic kids are never taught about love, or sex—according to the Torah, those things just aren't allowed to happen—but we're human beings with human hearts; surely *someone* must have realized that it wouldn't always be possible to control romantic love. Or maybe Jacob's right and there is something really wrong with me to even be having thoughts like these. Maybe my entire *frum* self-image has been a lie, and I've actually always been *frei* without even knowing it. Either way, having no one to turn to for advice is terrifying.

Ever since our heart-to-heart on the night Liya was born, Rose has closed up again, a wifely watercolor of her former self. And my mom—well, I'm not sure how she would react. I know she wouldn't approve, but she might listen, at least. After all, she knows better than anyone what it's like to have an "other" in her life. Her own mother came late to the faith, a blonde, blue-eyed *ba'al t'shuvah*, and had to be accepted by a family who didn't fully trust her at first. Or so I assume; Mom and Zeidy never talk about Grandma that way. I once heard Rabbi Perl, from our shul, say that it's a serious offense to remind a repentant sinner of his or her "evil deeds," and I guess the "evil" of not being observant until she was eighteen years old extends to her family, too. It's just not spoken about. All my mom has ever said on the subject is "What's past is past."

I roll onto my side, keeping the covers pulled tight around my shoulders. I often wish Grandma Deborah were still here, but never more than I do right now. She could tell me exactly what she went through. She could tell me what it was like on the other side. She could tell me if it was worth it.

All of a sudden, the phone buzzes alive under my pillowcase, sending vibrations through my jaw and into my teeth as a little chime rings out like a doorbell. I sit up straight and clamp my hands over my pillow, trying to smother technology into submission. Since it's after sundown, I'm not supposed to use any electricity, and even though the phone isn't plugged in (I'll have to remember to poke around in the grass tomorrow for a charger), it definitely 100 percent counts.

Turn off the phone and call him tomorrow night, my somewhat still-intact conscience echoes. *It can wait.*

But can it? If I don't respond to Jax tonight, will he come back tomorrow with an even bigger, bolder declaration of his feelings for me? I can't risk that, even if it means breaking Shabbos rules.

And it's just a drop in the bucket now, isn't it? (My conscience is starting to get bitchy.)

I cautiously slide the phone out from its hiding place and kick off my covers, lowering myself down to the carpet on the side of my bed farthest from the door. It figures that I have to make myself vulnerable to my imagined bogeyman if I want to communicate with Jaxon. No risk, no reward. I hold my breath and look down at the screen.

Did u find it?

I squint through the darkness and struggle to type a reply. I've used a cell phone before, but I'm not adept at texting, and I keep forgetting that I have to hit keys multiple times to find the right letter. After a few minutes of gibberish attempts, I manage to put together a semicoherent, vaguely punctuated thought:

Yes but amos almost found it first. could have been bad,
You are crazy!!

Less than ten seconds go by, and the chime rings again, amplified now that there's no pillow to muffle the sound, and thanks to Shabbos all the appliances in the house are silent.

Crazy about u :)

How do I turn off sound? I type frantically, panic tamping down the bloom of euphoria.

Another chime. SHIT. I grab the pillow from the bed and stuff it into my lap, perking my ears up and listening for motion outside my room. After a minute or so, when it feels safe again, I look at the screen.

Should b a volume button on the left side

I find it and click it down to the lowest setting. It's not muted, but it's quieter. It's something.

Thanks for the kite, I type. Now stay away from my house :)

Sorry, he replies immediately. Won't need to again now that we can talk.

I smile giddily into the faint green glow, but I know I need to wrap it up. Can't talk now, I write. Shabbos. No phones :(Text tomorrow after sundown?

Wait, he shoots back. And he means it. I sit still with the bed frame poking into my spine for what feels like ages before the phone buzzes again in my fist.

Can u get away tmrw? Jaxon has written. And then: I can take you on special shabbos date, no electricity.

I drop the phone into my lap and lean back, letting my head fall against the mattress with a satisfying *thunk*. Poor Jax. He doesn't realize that even if we spent the whole day praying in a pitch-black synagogue together, we would still be desecrating Shabbos just by virtue of the fact that we're together. Of course, the bitter irony is that Saturday is by *far* the easiest day of the week for me to sneak out for a real date with him; the men are at shul, and the women are resting and relaxing, visiting friends . . . not really doing much or going anywhere more than a few blocks from home, since driving a car is forbidden. I could say I was hanging out with Shosh or anyone else from school. And almost everyone takes a long nap after the midday Shabbos meal. No one would be looking for me or expecting me to show up anyplace before dinner, and the chances of running into anyone from my family would be virtually nonexistent.

The cell buzzes against my inner thigh, and I blush even though I know no one else—not even Jax—knows about this accidental thrill. I bite my lip, feeling guilty, yes, but also magnificently unbidden. I've lived my whole life according to a strict set of rules, yet here I am breaking one after another. And lo and behold, the sky is not falling; no one is coming to drag me away to some sinners' prison, even after I've had kisses that turned my entire body into a wildfire. I sit up straight, feeling a little woozy.

Pls say yes, the screen pleads.

Yes, I type, before I can talk myself out of it. I know I've crossed a line, for better or worse, that there's no turning back from. And despite the pull of my conscience, I'm not all that sorry. Because following rules never felt this intoxicating.

$\mathscr{C}$hapter 18

Jaxon

SEPTEMBER 13, 10:30 AM

$\mathbf{S}$ o thanks to Wikipedia I'm basically a Shabbat Jedi now. And thank God for the Internet, because when I told Devorah last night I would take her on a Shabbat (or "Shabbos," but that's the Yiddish, so as a "goy" I think I should stick with the normal spelling) date, I had no idea how crazy the rules were. There are *thirty-nine* major no-gos, and while some of them, like slaughtering or plowing (get your mind out of the gutter, they're talking soil), seem easily avoidable, others (like, um, "carrying") are trickier. *I* don't have to abide by the rules of Shabbat, but she does, and planning a date that is both awesomely romantic *and* doesn't require Devorah to carry anything, take any form of public transportation, or use any kind of electricity is a little more challenging than I was anticipating. I had wanted to pick her up on my bike and take her someplace special, but the message boards I found are pretty divided when it comes to whether bike riding violates the "no plowing" rule, since theoretically you could turn over dirt if you rode through a patch of grass.

I'm probably getting a little carried away (I might have even stayed up until three AM planning), but I need this to be perfect. The last time Devorah and I were alone together was five days ago, and with everything we have to deal with, it could be another whole week before we get our next chance. Each of our dates has to be like a dozen normal dates, to tide us over during the fast. I don't know how much longer I can stand it.

Luckily I'm off the hook in terms of coming up with an alibi for today. After a week or so of post-storm cooling, summer is back with a vengeance, and it's supposed to hit ninety-five this afternoon, so Mom took the girls out to Rockaway Beach on the A train. I was invited, but I said I had too much homework, which is never an excuse she'll argue with. And Dad still has repair work from the hurricane keeping him busy; he'll be fixing a broken skylight on a Park Slope townhouse all day.

I know I'm gonna be dripping with sweat by the time I get to our rendezvous point, but I still take an extra-long shower, double up on deodorant, and run my electric shaver over my chin and upper lip. I'm on my way out the door, grabbing my Mets cap and some five-dollar wraparound shades for stealth purposes, when I hear the unmistakable weary stomp of my dad's size-eleven Timberland work boots in the stairwell.

"Hey, J," he says as I open the door, awkwardly cradling my backpack full of damning, unexplainable items. He frowns, confused. "I thought you were studying today."

"Yeah, I am . . . I just thought I'd go to the library for a while. Fewer distractions." I swing my bag onto one shoulder and give my dad my best *what can you do?* smirk.

"Oh, sure," he says, patting my back as he steps past me into the cool AC. "Good idea." He bends down and shuffles through a pile of tools stacked haphazardly on the entryway table we use for mail, finally pocketing a paint-encrusted slide rule. Then he walks to the kitchen, and I hear the hiss of tap water. When he comes back his face is dripping wet, but he's smiling. "Hey, want a ride?" he asks. "It's hot as Hades out there."

"Thanks," I hedge, "but I don't want you to go out of the way."

"It's on my way," he says, wiping droplets from his neck with a yellowed handkerchief. "I gotta drive down Prospect Park West anyhow."

It's not on *my* way, though. And I'm meeting Devorah in half an hour, so I can't afford to lose the time.

"Nah," I say, trying to sound disappointed. "I shouldn't. I have a Spanish lesson on mp3 that I was gonna listen to on my walk. Kill two birds, or whatever."

He laughs, revealing a mile-wide row of big white teeth and red gums. "Man, I wish I had your discipline," he says. "Probably would have got me farther than this." He gestures down to his dirty T-shirt and cargo pants, a tool belt slung low on his hips. "You know, your grandmama used to say to me, 'Goats don't make sheep.' Meaning children always turn out like their parents. But not you, Jax." His dark eyes turn serious, his smile a little sad now. "You're so much better than I could ever be."

"Dad—" I protest. I'm half embarrassed by the earnest compliment, half horribly guilty that it's based on a lie. The only thing worse than betraying trusting parents is having them reward you for it.

"Don't be modest," he says. "I'm proud of you, and you should be proud of yourself." He claps me on the back with another laugh. "Now get on," he calls, as I start out the door. "Go hit those books." I take the stairs two at a time and break into a run on the street, even though the thick, hot air makes me feel like I'm moving through stew. I just want to get around the corner before my father comes back out to his truck. I can't look him in the face again, or else I might not be able to go through with it.

By the time I get to Wonder Wings, my T-shirt is damp to the touch and stuck to my skin in places, but being the detail-oriented guy I am, I packed a fresh one in my bag. Now I just need to get inside without drawing attention to myself. Cora doesn't open until noon on weekends, since even in the most desperate circumstances our hot wings don't qualify as brunch, but she'll be rolling up around eleven thirty, which means I have only twenty minutes or so to get in and out, provided Devorah shows up on time. I try to look confident and nonchalant as I pull my key ring out of my pocket and open the padlock at the bottom of the grate that pulls down over the storefront like big steel window blinds at night. I squat down and pull up on the grate to get it off the ground, and then transfer the weight from my biceps to my shoulders as I push it up, Superman style, above my head. I leave it at about six feet since I'm just going to drag it back down in a few minutes, and then let myself in through the glass front door, leaving the sign turned to CLOSED.

The bathroom is around back next to the kitchen, invisible from the street, so I don't bother to close the door as I peel off my shirt and set my backpack down on the sink. I sift through all the clothes in my bag until I find my red T-shirt, the same one I was wearing when I first met Devorah in the elevator. I hold it up for a sniff test and catch a glimpse of myself in the mirror, my bare chest glistening with sweat under the fluorescent lights. What would she think if she saw me like this? I think about seeing Devorah naked way more than I probably should, maybe because she's always so covered up. And it's not even the dirty parts, either, although those cross my mind more than she would like to know. But I also want to see those jet-black curls cascading over bare shoulders, the small of her back, her knees, her ankles. I wonder idly if she ever fantasizes about me that way, and my face starts to get hot in a way that has nothing to do with the weather.

"Oh!"

I hear her voice before I see her in the mirror, standing frozen in front of the grease trap, taking in the sight of me with a mix of shock and amusement. I snap out of my daze and pull the shirt over my head as quickly as possible.

"Hey," I say, trying to regroup, my tongue suddenly feeling heavy, as useless as a mop in my mouth. "I was, um . . ." Devorah blushes and breaks eye contact, examining a poster one of the line cooks has taped up to his work station, which shows a busty model eating a chicken wing in a . . . suggestive fashion. I clear my throat. "You're early."

"Only by about sixty seconds."

"Well." I sigh, launching into a nervous comedy act, "Still, I'm sorry you had to see that. My striptease usually has better choreography."

"No need to apologize," she says. We stare awkwardly at each other for a minute. I'd wanted to hug and kiss her as soon as I saw her, but now that she's just seen my nipples, that seems way too forward.

"I need to tell you something," Devorah finally blurts out. "Jacob knows."

"Oh no." I sit down on the closed toilet lid, my heart in my stomach. "I'm so sorry. I should have known leaving the kite was way too obvious."

"No, not because of that," she says quickly. "He saw us, last week. On this block. He followed me."

"What? That's crazy!"

"I know," she says. "He thinks he's some kind of one-man morality police force."

"What's he gonna do?" My eyes drift up to the kitchen wall clock. It's 11:21; we have to get moving.

Devorah shrugs, but her eyes are full of fear. "He says he won't do anything, as long as I stop seeing you."

"So I guess you've made up your mind." I know it's serious, but I can't help but smile. Knowing Devorah risked getting in major trouble to come meet me solidifies what I've been hoping the past two weeks: that she's falling in love with me, too. Why else would she put everything on the line like this?

"It's not that simple," she says. "But I can't let him control me. I'm not going to give him that power."

I stand up and make a move to hug her, but she holds out a hand like a stop sign. "We can't," she says with a nervous smile. "Shabbos rules, remember?"

"Damn," I whisper, and she laughs.

"Speaking of which, where are we going?" She's warming up

now that she's gotten the Jacob business off her chest, and bounces excitedly from foot to foot.

"Not far," I say. "But just to be safe"—I hold out my backpack—"I brought you a change of clothes."

"What do you mean?" she asks, her eyes sparkling with curiosity.

"I figured you might feel more comfortable undercover," I say. "Especially now that I know you're being tailed." As soon as Edna and Ameerah left this morning, I raided their closet, taking all the hoodies, long dresses, and hats I could find.

Devorah starts to rifle through the backpack. "Don't worry," she says. "There's no way Jacob followed me today. He's at shul until at least noon. Plus, I had Hanna walk me over." She holds up a floor-length teal cotton dress and a yellow-and-white striped sweatshirt with the word PINK scrawled across the back. "You're a genius." She grins.

"I try," I say. "The only downside is, you're gonna be sweltering." She laughs gamely. "What else is new?"

"Do I look okay?" she whispers, keeping her back to the street as I lock the grate back up a few minutes later. Cora will be showing up any second; we're cutting it dangerously close.

I look my date up and down: The breezy summer dress reaches almost to the sidewalk, barely showing the soles of her black leather shoes. She's got the hoodie zipped up tight, with the hood on and her hair tucked in. A pair of Ameerah's enormous, bug-eyed black sunglasses covers about two-thirds of her face.

You look like the Unabomber went shopping at Victoria's Secret, I want to say. But I know that will make her feel even more nervous than she already is, so instead I say, "You look beautiful." Which is also true.

I take her hand, and she reflexively stiffens, but I lean in and whisper, "The more natural you act, the less people will look." I drape an arm around her shoulder and pull my Mets cap down so it's shielding my eyes. "Just trust me. Talk normally; stay close to me. Pretend you don't even see anyone else." I look around; the restaurant's corner doesn't usually get a big Hasidic crowd since it's on the Caribbean fringe, but until we get across Eastern Parkway, I won't be able to relax, either.

"Just think," I say under my breath, trying to distract her as we rush across the street to make the light, "someday soon we can go wherever we want without worrying about who sees us."

"Promise?" she whispers.

"Promise." I hope I'm telling the truth.

It's hot and relatively early for a weekend, so there aren't too many people milling around as we start down Nostrand, trying to adopt the unhurried, in-sync steps of a normal young couple in love. A couple of old dudes sitting in plastic lawn chairs outside of a pizza place look at us a little funny, but it's probably because my costume-design efforts have turned Devorah from a pretty, unflashy Orthodox girl into what probably looks to a lot of people like a bougie, over-the-top Sikh.

"Want to know something funny?" she asks, loosening up as we near the big Dunkin Donuts near the intersection at Eastern Parkway. "I've never worn sunglasses before."

"What?!"

She shrugs helplessly. "We just don't wear them. I only see them at Purim."

"That's like Hasidic Halloween, right?" I ask.

"Sort of," she says, laughing. "There are masquerade parties, but it has nothing to do with ghosts or pumpkins. It's about a woman named Esther who saved the Jews."

"So what do you go as? Let me guess: a Ghostbuster!"

Devorah looks at me blankly. Oh, right. The great pop culture divide.

"I usually go as Esther," she says with a self-conscious smile.

"What does she look like?"

"Well, she's a queen. So my mom sewed me a dress out of red velvet and gold brocade. But other than that I just look like me."

Devorah stops at the corner and looks over at the flashing red hand at the other end of the crosswalk, totally unaware that she's just summed up exactly what it is that makes me love her so much. Right now she's dressed ridiculously, but that's my doing; if left to her own devices, Devorah would never be anybody but herself. It would never even occur to her. Other people put on disguises every single day—brand-name clothes to make them seem cooler than they are, makeup to cover up their flaws, personas carefully cultivated to make them more popular—but Devorah never does. She is always, almost helplessly, genuine. And that is endearing as hell.

The light changes, and we start to walk across the street, when I hear a sharp male voice call out after us.

"Hey! You two! Hey, stop!"

It feels like every muscle in my body clenches at once. Devorah grabs my elbow and digs her nails in.

"What do we do?" she whispers. The crosswalk light is already starting to flash, counting down from 25. *24, 23, 22* . . . We could run. I think we can make it if we run. But—

20, 19 . . .

—there's no point in running blindly. If it's Jacob, fine. But if it's Devorah's father, or the police—

17, 16 . . .

—not that we've broken any laws, unless letting myself into Wonder Wings counts . . . the Korean man who runs the deli next door has always seemed suspicious of me, I bet he called it in—

"*Jax,*" Devorah whispers, more urgently this time.

"*HEY!*" the voice calls out again.

13, 12 . . .

I turn around.

"Oh, good," says a middle-aged man in flip-flops and a wife-beater. "I thought you couldn't hear me." He holds out my wrap-around sunglasses, which I had stuck in the outside pocket of my backpack when we left the store. "You dropped these." Devorah lets go of my arm with an audible sigh of relief.

"Thanks, man," I say.

9, 8, 7 . . .

"Run," I tell Devorah.

We make it. Just barely, but we make it. And ten slightly less dramatic minutes later, we're standing in front of our destination: my perfect, secret Shabbat date spot.

"What is this?" she asks, pulling off the hood and sunglasses and peering up at the crumbling brick facade.

"Welcome," I say, with a stupid little bow, "to *my* house."

The basement of our building is only partially finished, which is a nice way of saying butt-ugly. There's a cement slab for a floor, cinder-block walls, exposed beams on the ceiling, and one entire corner is taken up by a huge gas boiler, which looks kind of like a super-sized file cabinet with pipes sticking out all over. The rest of the basement is lined with boxes and furniture the tenants aren't using, and of course I have my little training corner, which has always seemed action-movie badass but feels sort of embarrassing now that Devorah's seeing it, the duct-taped vinyl bag standing proud on my mom's old yoga mat. At least the candlelight helps make it look classier.

Under the guise of kickboxing practice, I came down this morning and pimped out the space a little bit. First, I cleared the center of the room and laid out a blanket. I stole some throw pillows off the couch, too, plus a few big Yankee Candle jars left over from Christmas and a folding breakfast tray. Then I went out and got some kosher snacks (again, thank you, Internet): pretzels, grapes, almonds, and—you learn something new every day—Twizzlers. It looked a little bit too much like a make-out den, though, especially with nothing but candles, so I brought down an old game of checkers to up the wholesome quotient.

We stand on the bottom step, and I watch her eyes as she takes it all in: the puffy rolls of insulation leaning against the wall, the bin of half-clothed, lazy-eyed baby dolls in the dim light, the musty smell barely hidden by the unseasonal synthetic scent of fresh-baked gingerbread.

"It's perfect," Devorah says, throwing her arms around my neck.

"Hey, hey—I thought you said we couldn't do that," I say, leaning in for a kiss. It's downright sexy in here, and the checkers aren't doing much to kill the vibe.

"You're right; we shouldn't." She hops down the last step to the floor and kicks off her shoes. Gathering her long dress in one hand, she climbs gingerly between the candles and settles onto the blanket cross-legged. "Come sit," she says. "Let's talk."

"Well, to be fair, though," I say, playing devil's advocate, "we're already breaking *yichud*, so we're batting oh for one."

She claps her hands together and laughs, throwing her head back. "Jaxon!" she cries. "You're speaking Yiddish!"

"I try," I say with a grin as I slide onto the blanket across from her.

"So, first of all, Shabbat Shalom," she says, waving her hands around her face. She looks at me expectantly. "Now you say it."

"Oh, um, Shabbat Shalom."

She grins. I've never seen her this happy, and it's contagious.

"Now we do the kiddush," she says. "Do you have anything to drink?" I slap my palm to my forehead, and she laughs. "It's okay; grapes are almost the same as grape juice, right?" Devorah picks two grapes off the bunch and tosses one to me. Then she says a long string of Hebrew words, and at the end we raise our grapes in a symbolic "cheers" motion and pop them into our mouths. She shows me how to mime washing my hands in preparation for the challah— which will be played this afternoon by its understudy, strawberry Twizzlers—and then blesses the neon red candy with her eyes reverently closed.

"You're good at that," I tell her once we've eaten our snack-food feast.

"I should be," she says, lying back on a pillow contentedly, her ringlets spread out like satin ribbons. "I've sat through at least two Shabbat meals a week for my entire life, which means I've heard it . . ." Devorah whispers to herself as she does math in her head. "One thousand, six hundred, and sixty-four times."

"Wow," I say. "I don't think I've done anything that many times."

"Well, my life is all about routine," she says, and sighs. "There's nothing new—*ever*." She props herself up on her elbows and smiles. "Except you, obviously."

"Does that get boring?" I ask. "Having so many rules?"

"Not for most people," she says with a frown. "Everyone around me seems to thrive off of it. That's why I feel so trapped sometimes. There's literally no one who understands what it feels like to want anything else. I feel like a total—"

"*Freak*," we say simultaneously.

"Jinx," I say with a laugh.

"You, too?"

"It's not the first label I'd choose for myself," I say. "But it's what I get called."

"Who would *say* that?" she asks in sincere disbelief.

"Just this caveman on the basketball team who thinks he's the love child of Kobe Bryant and Kanye West." Devorah looks even more confused by this biologically unlikely analogy. "He's just a bully," I explain. "And it doesn't help that I accidentally picked a locker in a place that people at school call the freak hallway."

Devorah gasps. "That's so mean!"

"I know."

"Why do they call it that?"

"Maybe because it's full of kids who . . . do things differently. Dress funny, or whatever. Girls with shaved heads, boys who wear makeup, that kind of thing."

Devorah sits back up and hugs her knees. Orange dots—reflections of the candle flames—dance in her pupils. "What do you do that's so different?" she asks.

"Nothing," I say. "I mean, I don't run with the popular cliques, but I'm not on the lowest rung of the social totem pole, either. I guess I just don't fit in anywhere."

"That's not how I see you at all," she says, her chin jutting out defensively, as if in disbelief that anyone could ever not think I'm awesome. I picture her, all five feet and change, marching up to J-Riv and his crew like David confronting Goliath.

And that's why you're wonderful, I think.

"Thanks," I say instead. "But I can't help but feel aimless. I feel like I'm just reaching for . . . *nothing* right now. I don't know what I want to do. My only real life goal so far is to go to college, and that's only because I don't have a choice." As soon as the words are out, I want to shove them back in, rewind like one of the scratchy VHS tapes my mom still hoards under the TV. I know Devorah would probably do anything to have my kind of problem. She's trapped by too few choices, while I feel trapped by too many. It's too bad we can't share some choices and even it out.

But instead of looking angry, Devorah just smiles. "You don't know what you want to be when you grow up?" she asks, teasing a little. "Maybe a Ghostbuster?"

"Ha ha, very funny." I toss a grape at her. "But no, of course I don't know what I want to be yet. Why, do you?"

Devorah rests her chin on her crossed arms. "I didn't even consider it until recently," she says. "But if I got to pick, I think I would go to nursing school and become a midwife. Deliver babies."

I raise my eyebrows. "Why?"

"Seeing my niece get born was a turning point for me," Devorah says, her eyes lighting up so bright that for a second I could swear someone flipped on the naked bulb dangling over our heads. "It happened the same night I met you," she continues, smiling into her knees. "That night changed everything. In the span of an hour my whole world cracked open, and I saw *life*. Literally, I saw life being born, and then I met you, and I saw a life that was so different from the one I'd been living. I saw a future that could be so different. And that's what I want to do. I want to bring more life into the world, you know? I want to be there when other people experience that moment."

I am in love with you. The words are on the tip of my tongue, and the only thing I can do to beat them back is kiss her, so I do. I crawl over on my knees and take her face in my hands and I kiss her, long and gentle, wanting her so bad it almost scares me. When I finally pull back, she smirks at me and runs her fingers through my hair.

"I didn't know you felt so strongly about childbirth," she says.

I roll my eyes and kiss her forehead, settling back against the pillow with her head nestled in the crook of my arm. "I don't," I say. "But what you said, how *you* feel about it, is amazing. I don't feel that way about anything."

"Nothing?" She turns on her side and rests her hand on my chest. I could get used to this. I never thought I'd pray to be stuck in my elderly landlady's mildewy basement for all eternity, but here I am.

"I don't know," I murmur. "I mean . . . I like music, but I don't know if I want to be a producer. I like kickboxing, but I don't want to train rich white ladies at a gym." Devorah laughs, and I get bolder.

"I love being with you," I say slowly, "but that's not a career . . . unless you need a houseboy when you're a big famous midwife."

"You can be my househusband," she says. "You can stay home and raise the kids."

After that, we're both silent for a long time. It's crazy scary to think that far into the future (although maybe it doesn't feel that far for her, if her friends are all getting married at eighteen), but it's also unspeakably exciting to imagine that something like that could be in the cards for us someday. I want to say exactly the right thing, to reassure her without overwhelming her, but I'm too afraid of saying the wrong thing. Finally, after five or ten minutes have gone by with nothing but the clank of the boiler and the faint strains of a TV upstairs, I find the ability to form words again.

"Can I ask you something?" I say.

Devorah nods into my neck.

"Hypothetically, can we really do this?" I ask. "Can we choose each other?"

"I don't know," she says softly. "I didn't think so at first. But then . . ."

"What?"

Devorah sits up and turns to look at me. "There's this girl I went to school with, Ruchy," she says. "She disappeared from the neighborhood abruptly, and I hadn't seen her in a long time. And then last week, I found out that she left."

"What do you mean, left?"

"I mean she left the community," Devorah says with a far-off look in her eyes. "She moved in with her boyfriend. She just . . . left."

"That's allowed?" Now I sit up, too.

"No!" Devorah's small hands ball reflexively into fists, but then she relaxes. "Or at least, I never thought it was. I grew up being taught that the world outside was immoral." She casts her eyes down. "Honestly, I didn't know better. I looked down on it, on all of you."

"So do we," I say guiltily. "About you."

"It's convenient, at least," she says, sighing. "Mutually exclusive."

I tuck a curl behind her ear, letting my fingers trail down her cheek. "But it doesn't have to be," I say. "Your friend Ruchy—she broke through, right? That means we can, too."

Devorah smiles, but her eyes are sad. "Maybe," she says. "But it's easier for you. You can pass back and forth. I'm afraid that if I leave, I won't ever be welcome home again. And I don't hate it, you know?" Her chin trembles as tears fill her rain-cloud eyes. "My family is everything to me, and there's so much I love . . . I want to be able to have both. You *and* them."

"Listen," I say. "No matter what, you've got me, okay? You'll always have me."

Devorah stares at me for a long minute, the light flickering across her face, almost like we're back in the elevator. Except this time, no one's waiting outside for us. And this time, we can't control ourselves anymore.

I'm not sure who moves first, but within seconds we're all over each other, Devorah's hot tears staining my cheeks as I pull her against me and taste her lips, breathe her oxygen. She grabs the back of my neck, and my hand leaves her waist, operating as a free agent from my lust-paralyzed brain, tugging at the zipper of her hoodie, reaching in, cupping her breast. She moans, and I gently ease her back onto the blanket. The tension that's built up in me over these weeks of waiting is overpowering. I feel like I'm going to explode.

But then Devorah turns her face away, puts a hand against my chest, and pushes. It's the universal sign for *stop*, so I roll off, panting. "I'm sorry," I say.

"No," she says, her face plump and flushed, her eyes wild and dazed. "You didn't do anything I didn't want. We just . . . can't."

"I know," I gasp, trying to turn off the electric current buzzing through every inch of my body.

We lie there for a few minutes listening to each other breathe, until her hand migrates over to mine, and we just hold on, splayed out on the basement floor like stargazers.

"I should probably go," she whispers.

"When can I see you again?" I ask.

"I don't know. But soon. I can't stand this." She gets up and finds my backpack, pulling out her clothes. "Could you . . ." she says awkwardly, and I turn over and I close my eyes as she stands in the corner to change.

"This is just how it's gonna be, huh?" I mumble into the blanket. "Underground meetings, sneaking around, no time to do anything but talk about how we can't do anything?"

"For now," she says. "We just have to wait until Jacob stops hovering. And he will. He has a new baby, and his rabbinical studies. I'm actually amazed he has so much time to stalk me as it is." It's a joke, but I can't laugh. I'm suddenly in a kind of terrible mood, all my endorphins dive-bombing, reality seeping back in. As long as we stay in Brooklyn, we'll always be hiding. The only way to get the time we need to give our relationship a running start is to get away somewhere. And not permanently or anything—I know we can't go the white-picket-fence route at sixteen without so much as GEDs—but just for a few days. Even just for one night.

"Hey," I say, a spark of hope igniting in my chest. "Are you allowed to have sleepovers?"

Devorah laughs. "With you? Doubtful."

"No, with other girls. You know, popcorn, pillow fights, frozen bras."

"You've never actually been to a sleepover, have you?"

"Just answer the question," I say, laughing.

"Sure," she says. "Sometimes."

"Could you have one next weekend?"

"Why?" She pauses. "You can look now." I pop up onto my knees to find her sitting on the bottom step, buttoning up her cardigan.

"Ryan's parents have a house out in the Hamptons," I say, the idea taking shape as I talk. "They only use it in the summer; by now it's empty most of the time. I could get the keys—"

"Jax—" she says, but I won't let her finish.

"Just think," I say hurriedly. "We could go up on a Saturday, come back Sunday, have a whole twenty-four hours to ourselves. Take walks in public, go out to dinner, lie on the beach. Go to sleep together, wake up next to each other . . ."

"There's a pretty loaded time lapse buried in there," Devorah says, blushing.

"That's not what I meant," I sputter. "I won't try anything, I swear. All I want is time with you."

Devorah nestles her chin into her palm and looks at me for a long minute. "We'd have to be back early on Sunday, since I have school," she says.

"Is that a yes?" I can barely contain my glee.

"It's an 'I'll think about it,'" she says.

I take her up to the street and say goodbye, but it's not bitter-sweet this time. I know I can reach her whenever I want. I know she's just as crazy about me as I am about her. And most importantly, I know that if I can just get Devorah away from all of this for a weekend, we can figure it out, find a way to make it work, for real. Not just as some secret star-crossed fling, but forever. Out in the open. The way it should be.

Chapter 19

Devorah

This morning I stayed in the shower much longer than is probably considered polite in a ten-and-a-half-person household. But I just couldn't tear myself away from the warm rivulets of water coursing down my back. It felt too good. I could chalk it up to it being my first post-Shabbos shower, but it's only been a day since my last one. And it's not just the shower. *Everything* has felt too good for the past eighteen hours. Eating. Walking. Running my fingertips along the wood banister as I head downstairs for breakfast. And I think I know why. It's because I know for sure now: I've met my *bashert*.

I know my father says that only G-d can know when two souls are meant to be together, but my feelings for Jaxon have developed into something so deep and profound that I don't know what else it could be but fate. And it's made me question the future my parents expect for me even more. How can anyone commit themselves to a life with a person they don't already feel this way about? How can you blindly trust that love will follow marriage? How can you put so much of your happiness into the hands of a stranger who doesn't even need to take a class or earn a certificate to become a match-maker claiming to do the work of G-d? These questions don't seem irrational or disgraceful to me, and I can't believe that no one else is asking them.

But I try not to get too bogged down in crises of faith on this sunny Sunday morning. Breakfast has morphed into a casual affair ever since Liya moved in, and the circle of my siblings on the liv-ing room rug, surrounding the baby, who's working on her "tummy time," is too warm and inviting to resist. Plus, thinking about Jaxon and our date puts me instantly back in a good mood. I pour myself some cold cereal and sit down next to my mother, who is tickling Liya's feet and singing.

"You know," she says to Rose, "you can just move in here. I won't mind a bit."

"We'll only be four blocks away, Mama," Rose says, stirring her cup of odd-smelling fennel and anise tea, meant to help with milk production. (If the wet spots on her blouse are any indication, it's working.)

"The nursery is almost ready," Jacob calls from the dining table, where he is reading the paper with my father—and also, apparently, eavesdropping. "We'll be out by Tuesday."

My mother makes a pouty face, but this piece of information just buoys me even higher. Of course I'll miss having Rose and the baby here all the time, but it will be worth it if it means I have to endure Jacob's miserable, accusatory glances only two or three times a week from now on.

Liya burps loudly as if to punctuate this announcement of good fortune, and we all laugh. But then, once it's quiet again, another sound rings out, farther away and decidedly less funny.

It's my cell phone. And it's *ringing*.

My mother has a cell phone. So do my father, and Rose, and Jacob, and Amos. It's not an all that out-of-the-ordinary thing. Or it wouldn't be, except that my phone is playing "our" song. The one we listened to in the elevator. It's playing music—*secular* music, sung by a woman, which is the worst kind!—and it's playing it *loudly*. So much for the volume controls. I can't believe I didn't just turn it off after Jax and I were done texting last night. After we were so careful all afternoon, one tiny oversight is about to bring every-thing crashing down.

"What *is* that?" my father asks, furrowing his brow and looking up at the ceiling. Hanna looks at me with wide, dramatic eyes, and I see Jacob look over at her, and then at me. I wish she would stop being so obvious about everything.

"Sounds like the radio," Miri says.

"Probably outside," Hanna jumps in. "A car with the windows down."

"No," Jacob says, standing up and looking right at me. "It's definitely coming from inside the house."

As the tension mounts in the living room, the Shirelles blithely continue their distant, moody crooning.

"No!" I spring to my feet, milk sloshing out of my bowl onto the carpet. "It's—" My mind races to come up with some excuse, but I can't think straight with everyone staring at me. "I'll go see what it is," I sputter, and run up the stairs two at a time.

The phone has stopped ringing by the time I get to my room, but I slam the door behind me and pick it up off the floor next to my bed. With shaking hands, I struggle to turn it off and then, in a blind panic, stuff it into the band of my tights, far enough down my thigh so that it doesn't make a bulge under my skirt. So much for a lifeline. (But at least for once, I'm grateful to be wearing stockings.) I stand helplessly, trying to concoct a reasonable explanation, when the door swings open and in walks Jacob, followed by my mother, looking smug and flustered, respectively.

"Hand it over," Jacob says, holding out his hand, the thin, bony fingers flexing in anticipation.

My only choice is to play dumb. "Hand what over?"

"Jacob seems to think you have a cell phone," my mom says, in a tone that lets me know she's not willing to believe it until she sees it with her own eyes.

"What? No!" I feel the chunk of warm plastic inch down toward my knee.

"There's no use lying, Devorah, we all heard it," Jacob says testily.

"I couldn't find anything," I say, my eyes flashing with real anger. "Go ahead and look around if you'd like." I may be guilty of keeping secrets from my family, but I don't deserve to be treated like a criminal.

Jacob pushes past me and strips my bed, shaking the pillow out of its case, lifting the mattress to examine the wooden slats underneath.

"I just cleaned," my mother says sharply. "You'll be making that bed when you're done." She crosses her arms and sighs.

"It's in here somewhere, I know it," Jacob mutters, moving to my dresser. He opens my top drawer and starts rifling through my underwear.

"Jacob!" my mother shouts, horrified. "Stop it right now!"

Jacob calmly closes the drawer and looks at us defiantly. "Ayelet," he says, "she's pulling the wool over your eyes." I can tell he wants to say more, but I also know that Jacob is too concerned with his place in my father's estimation to reveal what he knows without any supporting evidence. He wipes his hands on his trousers and stalks out of the room.

"Mama," I say, not sure how to undo this damage. "I—" But she doesn't let me finish.

"Please," she says, holding up her hands. "I don't know what you've done to set Jacob off, but make it right before dinnertime. I've had my fill of drama for the morning." She turns to leave but then pauses in the doorway, looking around my room as if seeing it for the first time.

"Devorah," she says slowly, "if you were hiding something, you would tell me, wouldn't you?" I nod mutely.

As soon as she's gone, tears (of shame? relief?) flood my eyes, and I shut the door softly, leaning against it just in case anyone tries to ambush me again. I take my phone out of its hiding place and press the power button.

Can u get away & talk? About to spend whole day @ library with the sisters . . . missing u :)

A knock on the door behind me gives me my second near–heart attack of the morning.

"Don't worry, it's only me," Hanna whispers from the hallway. "But we have to leave for school. So, whatever you're doing . . . you should probably finish up."

I shut off the phone again and wipe my eyes. I know Jax was trying to help, but now I feel like I have a grenade that could explode at any second. I have to get it back to him, and I have to do it without getting caught, expelled from school, or disowned by my family.

You know, just your normal weekend plans.

The Brooklyn Public Library looks like some grand Egyptian temple rising up out of the intersection of Flatbush Avenue and Eastern Parkway. I could stare at it for hours, studying the brilliant gold figurines inscribed on its massive front columns, but seeing as I'm limited to my thirty-five-minute lunch period (ten minutes of which I've already squandered taking a car service to get here), I don't have time on my side. In fact, right now it doesn't feel like I have much of anything, or anyone, on my side. Except, of course, for Jax. Knowing I'm standing within yards of him instantly calms my nerves, although my bones still ache under the weight of the message I know I have to deliver.

Since it's a gorgeous weekend day for the secular masses, I counted on the library being empty, but instead it's teeming with people—kids in grass-stained shorts slapping their way across the marble floors in candy-colored Crocs; skinny-jeaned hipster twenty-somethings clutching sweaty cups of iced coffee; elderly ladies in modest church wear tottering on pastel high heels. I scan the crowds for Jaxon, but it's impossible to know where to start looking. The only clue I have is that he's here with his sisters, so I head left into the children's section, dodging unsteady toddlers and moms pushing strollers the size of tractors.

I walk along the rows of stacks feeling my heart beat wildly in my chest. Any second could bring us face-to-face, in full view of his unsuspecting family, and the buildup is almost unbearable. Is this how Jaxon felt crouched in my backyard? This hunger tinged with terror? I slip between two rows of chapter books to catch my breath. On one side the books have slid over into a haphazard avalanche, opening up a crooked window in the middle of the shelf that looks out onto the bright children's play space in the center of the room. And that's when I see him.

He's sitting in a child-sized chair next to a big, low wooden table, his lanky frame folded awkwardly, adorably into the tiny piece of furniture. Next to him, a coltish young girl in braids and a floral sundress—that must be Tricia, the eight-year-old—sits with rapt attention as Jax reads to her from *The Princess Bride*, his hands waving animatedly, making her giggle. Two taller preteen girls—these must be the twins—sidle up wearing matching cutoff shorts, each holding an armful of paperbacks.

"Can't you read it yourself?" I hear one of them ask Tricia, and the little girl shoots back a saucy look.

"I like the way he does the voices," she says, and my heart melts a little.

"All right, Trish, we're almost done with this chapter anyway. Let's check it out and finish at home," Jax says, easing out of the chair. I know I have to get to him soon, before they leave. And as I'm agonizing over how to make him see me without drawing the attention of his sisters, it suddenly occurs to me that they don't know who I am, and they certainly don't know what I look like. So with a deep breath, I simply step out of my hiding place and into sight.

Jax looks up, and I let our eyes meet for a fraction of a second, just long enough for the air to stop between us, sending that invisible electric current I'm almost used to now—almost. I turn as a familiar tingle travels down my spine, and pretend to leaf through a dog-eared copy of something called *Twilight*.

"I forgot," Jax says loudly. "I have to find a book for school up in the history section. Can you guys hang here for a few minutes?"

"Whatever," one of the twins replies in a bored tone, and then I feel him brush by me. I count out ten long seconds before I follow him, out into the din of the cavernous lobby, up a creaky escalator, and into a long room lined with rows and rows of towering book-cases, each identified by a series of letters and decimals. There are a few people in between Jax and me, and so I'm not quite sure which row he's ducked into until I feel his hand close around my upper arm and pull me in to the historical biographies, letters G through I.

"What are you doing here?" His warm, deep voice is hushed and excited, his broad shoulders filling the aisle, blocking out the light like some kind of human eclipse. Without even thinking, I stand up on tiptoe and press my lips against his. Someone passing by us snickers, and I pull back abruptly. I can't let myself get swept up. I have to remember the reason I came here.

"Jax—" I start, but he interrupts me.

"Don't you have school?" he asks, his arms still wrapped around my waist.

"*Yes*," I say, signaling for him to let go. "But I had to see you."

"I haven't stopped thinking about you."

"That's what I need to tell you—" I say.

"That you're obsessed with me?" Jax winks, and I laugh in spite of myself.

"*No*. About the phone." I press it into his hand. "You have to take it back. Jacob knows." Just saying his name makes me cringe and look behind me, half expecting to see him standing there in his dark suit, his forehead dotted with sweat, his eyes narrowed, his lips twisted in a self-satisfied smirk.

"Shit," Jax says, his smile fading rapidly. "Did he find it?"

"No," I say. "But it went off this morning, and everybody heard it, and I know he knows I have it—and I think my parents are starting to suspect, too."

"Shit," he murmurs again. He slips the phone into his back pocket with a crestfallen look.

"It's just getting too risky," I say. "He's getting too close, and I'm afraid that he's really going to go digging now for something he can use to catch us."

"Like what?" Jax's face is tense, his normally warm eyes dark with worry.

"He's seen you," I say, fear flooding my chest. "He knows what you look like, and I'm pretty sure he knows where you work."

"Don't worry about me," Jax says firmly. "I can handle that guy."

"But I can't not worry!" I say, my voice rising in panic. "There's too much at stake. That's why . . ." I swallow, hard. "I think we should take some time. Apart." I've been rehearsing saying it for hours, but it doesn't hurt any less this time.

"No," he says, looking crushed. My heart breaks into a million tiny shards.

"Just for a few weeks," I say. "Until it's safe again."

Jax frowns. "It's never been safe. It's never going to be safe, Devorah. Not if we stay here, anyway." I know he's right. There aren't enough stacks in this library to hide us for another hour, let alone forever.

"I just . . . I'm getting really scared," I sputter, and he pulls me in close.

"I love you," he whispers into the top of my head. "Do you know that?"

I nod, holding my breath, feeling his pulse race under the smooth skin of his neck.

"What about you?" he asks, tipping my face up to his. "Do you . . ."

"Yes," I whisper, trying to quell the fireworks display that has suddenly been set off in my stomach. "I love you, too."

He laughs with relief and lifts me up, twirling me in a tight circle to avoid bashing me into the stacks. "Good," he says as he sets me down. "Good. And then, no."

"No what?"

"No to taking some time," he says. "We *do* need time, Devorah, but not apart. We need time together, away from all this."

"What do you mean?"

"That weekend trip we talked about? Let's do it now," he says. "Tonight." I study his face for signs that he's kidding, but if he is, he's playing it really straight.

"Jax, no," I whisper, hoping that his sisters have kept their word to stay downstairs. "We can't."

"Yes, we can!" he says. "Like you said, that day on the bridge. Let's run away."

"That was a daydream, not a suggestion."

"It doesn't have to be." He frowns. "You said it yourself, they're gonna find out anyway. At least this way we're in control."

"I can't," I say. "It's one thing to go behind my parents' back, but it's another thing to disappear completely."

"We're not talking *forever*," he says. "One night, maybe two. And by the time we come back, everyone will have had a chance to recover from the initial shock."

One or two days won't be enough, I think. I try to picture my parents' reaction to this kind of betrayal, but apart from the time Amos accidentally threw a dart into Hanna's shin, I've never seen them really lose it. And this would be so much worse. But I also know Jax is right: Everything is coming to a head, and I'm kidding myself if I think Jacob is just going to forget about it. Somehow, he's going to find a way to catch us, and soon. Unless we stop seeing each other completely. Which, at this point, would be a fate worse than anything my parents could come up with.

"Okay," I say. "But I need a little time."

"Tomorrow?" he asks, a smile peeking out from between his lips. "After school?"

I nod, scarcely able to believe this is actually happening. "How will we—"

"Train," he says. "I already checked online; there's a five fifty-one and a seven thirty-one every day out of Penn."

"Seven thirty," I say quickly, thinking on my feet. "It will be easier if we wait until after dark."

"I'll book the tickets," Jax says, and I nod again, trying to picture myself somewhere far away from Brooklyn, away from the noise and the smells and the heat. Away from everyone who knows me and everyone trying to drag me down. Someplace where I can hear the ocean. Someplace where I can feel the wind.

"What about school?" I ask. School is the farthest thing from my mind right now, but I can't afford to get expelled if I want to hold on to any hope of going to college someday.

"Like I said," Jax continues, "it's only a day or two. We can make up the time." He smiles hopefully. "So are you with me?"

"Yes," I hear myself say.

"Okay, all right," he says, looking just as shocked as I am. "You go home and pack. I'll get the tickets. Where should we meet?"

My mind is racing. I can pack tonight, smooth things over with my parents. Then tomorrow, I can leave a letter; that's probably the best plan. I'll leave a letter for my family explaining everything, and once I'm back we can all sit down and discuss it like adults.

"There's a bus stop on Kingston and Montgomery," I say.

"Great." Jaxon squeezes my hands. "I'll pick you up in a car."

"After sundown," I say.

"At six forty-five," he says.

"Six forty-five," I repeat in a daze.

"Promise you won't change your mind on me," he says, and laughs, and I shake my head, thinking, *I have just changed everything.* The books packed in all around us are full of stories of people who made decisions that changed history. Of course, not all of them ended well. But luckily I don't have time to dwell on that. I have to go home and get ready to say goodbye to life as I know it.

Chapter 20

Jaxon

September 15, 10 AM

I didn't sleep last night. Not a single second. I was too wound up. I couldn't believe it was actually going to happen, and I kept having to reread the e-mail confirmation from Long Island Rail Road: two round-trip, off-peak tickets, Penn Station to Westhampton. For twenty-one hours and thirty-one minutes, it will be just the two of us.

I feel a lot of guilt, though, about not telling my parents, which is why I showered and dressed at 5 AM and made a preemptive secret apology breakfast: scrambled eggs and Vienna sausages—Mom's favorite, the one she always asks for on Mother's Day—and Dad's preferred brand of toaster waffles. The eggs came out a little weird and brown, but no one seemed to care; I think they were all just in shock that I'd cooked.

"What's this about?" Mom asked, giving me a sleepy kiss.

"Nothing, I was just up early," I said, digging in the fridge for the creamer.

"Got a test today?" Edna asked, plucking a sausage from the pan with her fingers.

"Something like that."

"Well, whatever it is, keep doing it," my father said with a laugh, helping himself to a plate. "I could get used to this."

I slapped on a smile and tried not to think about what the scene in that kitchen would be like twenty-four hours later.

Sometimes when I'm nervous I'll ask the universe for little random signs that everything's going to work out. Like, if the subway comes right as I get to the platform, that's a sign; or if I hit shuffle on my iPod and the first song that comes up is one I really love, like "So What" by Miles Davis or some pre-Kardashian Kanye. Today, not only was the subway pulling in right when I got there, but the doors stopped smack in front of me *and* there was a seat. And then the first song on shuffle was "Love Train" by the O'Jays, which normally I'm embarrassed to even have (I copied all my mom's old CDs onto my hard drive the summer I turned twelve, which I blame for my predilection for all things old-school) but which is just about the most perfect sign you can get if you're about to hop a flight to follow your heart.

And then I got to school—early, since I have Mr. Misery first thing this morning, good times—and took the back entrance up to the freak hallway and was about to open my locker when my eyes fell on the little number plate up at the top: 915. My locker number. Today's date. Now, if that isn't some kind of big-ass neon sign from the universe, then I don't know what is.

"Hey, man." Ryan appears in the hallway door, looking a little cagey. I know he's freaked out to be giving me the keys to his parents' vacation house without their permission. He already made me swear up and down not to order anything on cable or turn on the lights at night.

"Hey!" I say, opening my locker and taking off my hoodie. "All good?"

"Sort of," he says. "There's only one problem."

"What?"

"On your date with Devorah this weekend, did you guys go anywhere, like, public?"

I feel the color drain from my face. "Why?" I ask.

"Because there's a rumor going around school that you have a Hasidic girlfriend," he says, "and I thought you said you were being careful." Ryan stares me down while I, speechless for once in my life, just lean my head against the cool metal door of my locker and close my eyes. *Shit*.

"Dude," Ryan says, "what, were you guys on the JumboTron at Yankee Stadium?"

"No, I'm not *stupid*! On Saturday we were in my basement—where I seriously doubt we had company—and yesterday we met up for like five minutes in the library." I lower my voice. "Who knows?"

Ryan sighs. "Well, I don't know the extent of it, but I heard about it from Megan Miranda, so it's gotta be pretty bad," he says. I cringe. Megan Miranda is a step-team girl, one of Polly's popular friends.

"I guess it's good I'm getting out of here," I say.

"Ha ha," Ryan deadpans. "Listen, if anyone finds out where you went, I swear I'll say you stole these." He rummages in his pocket for the keys and holds them at hip level, concealed, like some kind of drug deal. "Now come on," he says. "We have to get to Intro Philosophy like *now*."

"I need a minute," I say.

"Well, I'm going," he says. "If you're late, don't say I didn't warn you." Ryan leaves me with an awkward pat on the shoulder, and after he's gone I lean against my locker and mentally retrace my steps this weekend, trying to figure out who could have seen us and when. It must have happened at the library; since I wasn't expecting her, I wasn't being careful. Then again, it won't matter soon enough. By this time tomorrow, the cat will be out of the bag.

I slip my backpack on one shoulder and venture out into the mostly empty hallway, ducking my head and steeling myself for those whispers of recognition that tend to follow gossip subjects around school like a falling stack of dominoes. But no one seems to notice me at all—until what looks like the entire basketball team, plus Megan, Polly, and a senior girl named Candee Cuisimano (who looks exactly how it sounds like she should) round the corner.

"Action Jaxon!" J-Riv says it like he's the announcer at a game show, drawing out the vowels. "I underestimated you, son." He holds his hand up for a high five, but I know he's just patronizing me so I keep my arms at my sides.

"What'd he do?" one of his thick-necked friends, whose name I think is Jordan, asks.

"You ain't heard?" J-Riv crows, busting out in a girlish cackle that's mostly for his cronies. "I saw Romeo here macking on some ultra-Orthodox girl in the library. This boy's got jungle fever!"

"Not exactly," I say, crossing my arms. "A black person can't have jungle fever, because Jews don't live in the jungle. Jungle fever is when a white person falls for an African, and it's racist as hell."

"Oh," J-Riv says, not seeming to absorb the dig at his complete ignorance. "Well, you got dreidel fever then!" His basketball friends crack up—everyone but Polly, who looks like she'd like to sink into the floor.

I know I should brush it off and go to class. I know this. But exhaustion, adrenaline, and shame are mixing a powerful Molotov cocktail in my blood, and as I look at this big, bland bully, whose lips are pulled back in a sneer at my expense—lips that have proba- bly been all over Polly, in some horrible movie-of-the-week, under- the-bleachers cliché, I realize I've currently got nothing to lose.

"You don't know anything," I practically yell, my voice echo- ing through the hallway, stunning J-Riv and his friends into silence. "You think you know me because you *think* you saw me for a split second on your way to the I Can Read shelf in the kids' section? You think you know *her*? Man, shut up. If you don't have better things to do than talk about my girlfriend, then your life must be pretty lame."

J-Riv's face clouds over. "Guess I hit a nerve," he says, talking even louder as some sort of show of confidence. "I'd have some pent-up anger, too, if my girl had to wait for marriage."

I run at him, hearing the guys snicker and the girls shriek. I wish I could say I execute some perfect roundhouse kick to the temple, or pummel him with an uppercut-cross combo, but all of my training flies out the window and I just collide with him like I'm trying to break down a door. Luckily, (A) Jordan and some other guy catch me by the arms before I can land a real punch, and (B) J-Riv has too much weight on me for me to be able to knock him down. I say "luckily" because only as my forearms are connecting with his chest does it occur to me that getting expelled from school for assault could permanently derail my plans with Devorah.

Apparently J-Riv is having similar thoughts about his basketball career, because he just shakes his head menacingly and spits, "This isn't over, *freak*," before shoving me aside and stalking off with his friends. Polly and Megan hold a brief powwow in the corner near the water fountain before Megan hurries down the hallway after them, and I just lean against the wall between two classrooms and rub my hands on my face, taking stock of the streak of luck that has decidedly left the building. Somehow, between 8:10 and 8:15 AM, I have become the laughingstock of Brooklyn Tech and the mouthy archnemesis of someone who could probably bench-press three of me. Plus, I'm officially late to Mr. Miserandino's first-period torture chamber for the second time, which according to his five-page "conduct memo" will cost me a full letter grade for the semester. Not, I realize, that it matters much anymore. When we get back from our trip, by the time my parents are done with me, I'll probably be begging for a tongue-lashing from Mr. Misery. *Begging.*

"Are you okay?" Polly asks, appearing next to me, wearing pigtails and a look of concern.

"I don't know," I say with a sigh.

"You need to talk?" she asks.

"Not to you." Behind her black frame glasses, her big brown eyes crinkle with hurt. "I mean, not right now."

"I'm still your friend, Jax," she says.

"Yeah, well, it hasn't felt that way for a while, and I'm having a bad morning, so now's probably not the best time to do this."

"Do what?"

I ball up my fists and press them against my thighs. "Why are you with that asshole?" I groan. "Come on. You're better than that."

She takes a step back and looks at me quizzically. "I'm not 'with' Jason. We're just friends."

"Okay, then why are you *friends* with that asshole?"

Polly laughs. "He's not so bad one-on-one. But you're right. He can be a jerk. I can't defend what I just saw."

I rub my eyes again and try to pull myself together. Since I've blown off first period anyway and staying on school grounds will only invite more opportunities for me to get my ass kicked, I figure my best bet is to cut the rest of my classes and just go home. I still need to pack and go beg for my paycheck from Cora so that I have enough cash to take Devorah out to a nice dinner. That's the part I'm most dreading, since I called in "sick" to work all last week and have been half-assing it since then. But what's that saying, all's fair in love and . . .

"You seem distracted," Polly says, putting a hand on my arm and smiling awkwardly. "I should let you go." Just a few weeks ago this whole interaction would have had me doing cartwheels, but now it takes all the energy I have just to nod disinterestedly. Polly starts walking down the hall but stops and turns back after ten feet or so.

"Hey, Jax," she says, "she's a lucky girl."

I nod silently again, but as soon as she turns away again I look up at the ceiling and give the universe my best *are you kidding me* eyes. I asked for a sign, not a goddamn labyrinth.

• • •

I decide not to go home right away. Instead, I walk through Fort Greene Park, past babies lurching around after pint-sized soccer balls, watching the sun glint off the clock face of the Williamsburg Savings Bank in the distance. It's only nine, but I know Cora's probably already unlocking the metal grate that keeps Wonder Wings safe from robberies at night (but not from graffiti—there are a couple of tags bleeding across the front in big balloon letters), so I walk up DeKalb, hang a right on Washington, and take it all the way through Prospect Heights, past DIY churches, Caribbean bakeries, and barbershops, all still blinking awake in the stark morning light, until it opens up into Eastern Parkway across from the leaping fountains of the Brooklyn Museum. My calves are starting to cramp—I've walked two miles already, and Converse isn't exactly the industry leader in arch support—but instead of slowing down I break into a run once I hit Union, flying through intersections with my backpack barely hanging on, my headphones streaming out of my pocket. If I can get my heart pumping fast enough, maybe I can get back that feeling from yesterday in the library and this morning when I woke up, that dizzy conviction that anything is possible.

I'm panting by the time I roll up to Wonder Wings, where Cora is sitting at the corner table, drinking her café con leche from the Dominican place up the block.

"Why aren't you in school?" she asks by way of a greeting. This does not bode well.

"Oh, um, I'm still not feeling great," I say, wiping my forehead with the back of my hand.

"Get your butt home, then, I don't want your germs," she says with a semiannoyed smile. "I can call Jamal to cover for you again."

Jamal is Cora's fourteen-year-old son. I feel bad for the kid, doing my thankless job for free.

"Actually I needed to ask you a favor, too."

"Oh?" She puts down her coffee and looks at me with a mixture of concern and suspicion.

"Yeah . . ." Deep breath. "I was hoping I could get an advance on next week's paycheck." Cora purses her lips. "I hate to ask you," I say quickly, and I avert my eyes, hoping I don't look as guilty as I feel.

"Are you in trouble?" she asks.

"Nah," I say, forcing a laugh. "I just . . . gotta make ends meet, you know?"

"I do know," she says carefully. "But you're still a minor, Jaxon. So it seems to me the people who have to make ends meet are your parents, not you." She frowns and places her hands together under her chin, like she's praying. "Besides," she says, "you've been all over the place for the past week. And frankly I don't want to reward that kind of behavior with trust. It would set a bad precedent."

"I know, but it's just this one time," I plead. "I've never asked before, and I swear I'll never ask again."

"What is it for?" she asks. I wrack my brain to come up with some plausible excuse, something that my parents wouldn't be responsible for paying for. I could say I was being bullied (which isn't totally untrue), but then knowing Cora she would step in and call the school, start a big campaign. I'm getting flustered when all of a sudden she sighs and says, "It's the girl, isn't it?"

I stare at the floor.

"I thought so," she says softly. Then, wordlessly, she takes her purse off the table and opens her wallet, slipping out two twenties.

"It's not much," she says, holding the money out to me, "but this should get you through a cheap date. Let's call it a personal loan and not a paycheck advance, okay?" I step forward to take the money, and she pulls it back with a wry smile. "And if you tell *any* of the kitchen guys, you're scrubbing toilets for a month."

"Wow, thank you," I say, folding the bills over in my hands. My luck seems to be turning around, just in time.

Chapter 21
Devorah

SEPTEMBER 15, 6:35 PM

How do you write a letter that will break your family's heart? Maybe there's no good way to do it.

I've been sitting on my bed trying to write one for the past half hour, after suffering through a last supper that no one else knew was happening. I'd wanted it to be perfect, one last memory of togetherness before I confessed my sins, but instead my parents were late coming home from the store and we had to fend for ourselves, ordering in kosher pizza (which arrived with half the cheese pooled on one side and the other half a stretch of sad, bald dough), and Miri and Amos fought the whole time while Liya screamed in my lap and Rose cried quietly into a dish towel, not to mention that the tomato sauce gave Zeidy acid reflux, which we all thought was a heart attack for about three minutes. At least Jacob was on Shomrim patrol tonight, so he couldn't be there—the sole bright spot of an otherwise disastrous meal.

I'm still wearing my school uniform, the clothes I'll be wearing on the train, which I plan to take off as soon as we get to the beach. The first thing I'm going to do is put on a bathing suit (Jax said he'd borrow one from his sisters) and dip my toes in the ocean; I don't care if it's dark and the water's freezing cold. In my overnight bag I have my toothbrush, face wash, hair elastics, a nightgown, a few pairs of underpants, the red Converse, and the first edition of *Little Women* that my mom gave me for Hannukah when I was thirteen. I stashed everything down behind the washing machine in the basement early this morning. I took the padlock off, too, so all I have to do to leave the house is get down the stairs from the kitchen without anyone seeing. And everyone has already retreated to their bedrooms, except for Rose, who's rocking Liya to sleep in the living room. And she's so tired, she should be easy to slip by.

You don't have to do this, I think as I stare at the blank notebook paper in my hand. *He loves you, and he'll forgive you*. Downstairs, as if feeling my pain, Liya lets out a primal wail. I glance at my bedside clock. Only ten minutes left.

I abandon the letter for the moment and walk out into the hall in stocking feet, where I can hear Hanna and Miri talking in their shared room. I want to go in and say good night to them, but I'm afraid I'll cry or act funny, and then Hanna will figure it out and try to stop me, and I can't risk that, not when I'm so close I can almost taste the salt in the air. So instead I climb the stairs to the third floor, where my parents are huddled shoulder to shoulder in the cramped study, going over receipts. As usual, my mother is talking out loud to herself, while my father remains so stoic he could pass for a statue.

I've gotten used to skipping the creaky top step during my late-night Facebook binges, but tonight I put all my weight on it, and my mother turns around with a tired smile.

"Hi, *mamaleh*," she says. "We're a little bit busy right now. Can it wait?"

No! I want to scream. But instead I say, "I just wanted to say good night."

"Did you finish your homework?" she asks.

"Not yet," I say. "I'm working on it in my room."

"Good girl," she says, adjusting her glasses and peering down at her calculator.

"Well, good night, then," I squeak, trying not to let the lump in my throat give me away.

"Good night, love," she says.

I realize that this isn't the last time I'll ever see my parents or anything, but I don't know for sure that it's not the last time they'll truly love me. So I can't help myself. I rush in and wrap them both in a tight hug, breathing in his stale cigarette smoke, her fading jasmine perfume.

"Please, Devorah, we're trying to work," my father says, patting my cheek without turning from his desk. "We'll see you in the morning."

I nod silently as the tears start to come, and run back downstairs before they have a chance to notice. Back in my room I grab my pen and paper and without even thinking, scribble out a farewell:

*Dear Mama, Tatty, Zeidy, Rose, Hanna, Isaac, Niv, Miri,
and Amos (& Liya & Rivka & all the extended family)—*

First of all, I love you all so much. Please know that.
I've gone away, just overnight. There are a lot of things
I've been questioning lately and I need to find the answers
for myself, outside of the community. I know this comes as
a shock and that you might be worried, sad, or angry that
I've left without permission, and without telling you first.
But I promise that I'm safe and that I'll be back tomorrow
night and will explain everything then. Again, I love you!
Please forgive me.

Devorah

And then it's time. I leave the note folded on my pillow and slip down the stairs with my shoes in my hand, my toes sinking into the thick living room carpet, to find Rose and Liya both finally sleeping, their faces flushed but peaceful in the glow of a Tiffany table lamp inset with red and purple dragonflies. I kiss them each softly and turn out the light. No one is there to watch me as I make my exit. And since I'm abandoning everything I love, I figure I might as well abandon something I hate, too. I peel off my tights and toss them in the kitchen garbage. And then I'm gone.

When I reach the bus stop, which is just a chipped plastic bench bolted into the concrete without any sort of cover, the street is all but deserted. The sun has just set, and Kingston Avenue is a long strip of indigo punctuated by streetlamps reflecting off dark storefronts. There's a van idling on the corner, with a sleeping man in the driver's seat, but that can't be Jax's car. I check and recheck the cars parked for fifty feet in either direction, but they're all empty.

A shiver runs through me; gooseflesh breaks out on my legs. What if he's not coming? What if he had second thoughts, too, but unlike me actually listened?

An older man and woman pass by, pushing a stroller with a sleeping toddler slumped inside. They look so familiar that I instinctively turn to hide my face, just in case they recognize me. I can't place them, though—are they friends of my parents? Do they go to our shul? It's only when the baby stirs and the woman whispers, "*Gay shlafen*, Sal," that I realize it's the Silvermans. Ruchy's parents—with her *son*. I watch as they turn the corner, and Ruchy's father puts his arm around his wife. They look happier than my parents have looked in a long time, even with their "ruined" family, their errant daughter, and their illegitimate grandchild. I close my eyes and smile, thanking G-d for sending them across my path tonight. Seeing the Silvermans is exactly what I needed to give me hope that everything might work out for us. Not a fairy-tale ending, maybe, but not a cautionary tale, either. Just a regular tale of two young people in love.

I open my eyes again to see headlights round the corner on Montgomery; seconds later, a black Town Car pulls up to the curb. The door opens with a mechanical yawn, and Jaxon leans out, the sight of him filling me with a warm calm, like the pins and needles you get after coming in from the bitter cold without gloves.

"Your chariot, my lady," he says with a big grin, and I climb in next to him on the ripped leather seats patched with duct tape, pulling the door shut behind me.

"You're here," I say, my eyes filling with tears of relief.

"Of course I'm here." He takes my face in his hands. "I wouldn't miss this for the world."

"Me either," I say, leaning into a kiss that erases every doubt from every bone in my body.

"Penn Station or Grand Central?" the driver asks from the front seat. Jaxon reluctantly breaks off and leans forward to answer, when suddenly I feel a rush of cool air. My first thought is that I must be extra sensitive without my tights. My second thought, more of an observation, really, like I'm watching this happen from a seat in an audience ("Where's Annie, Mama? Where's *Annie*??"), is that the door behind me is opening, which is odd since I'm sure I closed it.

And then I'm being pulled out of the car by my collar as Jaxon winces into the beam of a flashlight.

My feet scrape against the sidewalk as I'm pulled to standing, shocked and gasping for air. I'm staring into another flashlight now, held by the driver of the van I'd seen across the street—the man who was sleeping, or pretending to be. But it's not just him. There are at least five men surrounding the car, all in matching black coats emblazoned with the insignia of the Shomrim.

"Hello, Devorah," I hear Jacob purr into my ear. "And just where do you think you're going?"

Chapter 22

Jaxon

he first thing I think is: *We're getting carjacked*. East Flatbush is only a couple of blocks south, and it's a hell of a lot sketchier than Crown Heights. I see Devorah get yanked out by the neck, and my heart stops, because whatever a hopped-up carjacker would want with her is something I'd rather die than think about. But then once my eyes adjust to the flashlight I can tell the guy pointing it at me is wearing a yarmulke. So the second thing I think is: *They caught us*. And it's actually a relief, because at least now I know they won't hurt her.

I feel the door behind me open, and two hands grab the back of my T-shirt, ripping it as they pull me out. My left leg catches on the door, and whoever's holding me loses his grip for a second so that

I come down hard on the asphalt onto my right shoulder. A searing pain shoots through my arm, and then I'm getting dragged again, forced upright with my hands behind my back, bound by the wrists by the same asshole who dropped me. I make a mental note to punch him with my left arm as soon as I can turn around.

There's a screech of tires as the Town Car peels off, running the red light—not that anyone's around to care, but then I remember that my duffel is in the trunk with my clothes *and* the keys to Ryan's parents' house inside, and I instinctively yell and jerk toward it, trying to run. A burly guy with thick eyebrows and a mole on his cheek shoves his flashlight inches from my face.

"Shut up," he barks.

I can make out at least three guys, not counting Moley or my own personal assailant, who smells like he works at a restaurant, eau de grill smoke and grease. They're all wearing matching black windbreakers, all with thick brown beards, none particularly jacked or anything—one guy even looks like he might be in his fifties. The only one I recognize is Jacob, who's holding Devorah by pinning her upper arms at her sides. She looks terrified, and I feel hot anger flood my chest.

"We don't want any trouble," Jacob says. "We'll let you go if you just get out of here and go back where you came from."

"I come from Brooklyn," I say, feeling my nostrils flare. "And get that thing out of my face," I shout at Moley. He looks to Jacob, who nods, and I see stars as the flashlight shuts off abruptly. I can make out shuffling around, and when my vision adjusts I see that Jacob has handed Devorah off to Moley and stepped down from the curb. He's standing a foot from me now, with his arms crossed and a scowl on his pinched little face.

"If you're from around here, then you should know that this girl is not the girl for you," he says, gesturing over at Devorah.

"Leave us *alone*, Jacob!" she cries. In the apartment above the bakery, a woman opens the window and peers out. In my peripheral vision, I can see passersby crossing the street to avoid walking close to us.

"How is this any of your business?" I ask, returning my attention to Jacob. But he ignores us both.

"There must be plenty of girls in your neighborhood," he says, looking me up and down. "Girls more . . . like you."

"What's *that* supposed to mean?" I ask.

"You know what it means," the guy behind me whispers, and I have to use every ounce of restraint not to whip my head back and break his nose.

"Listen, man," I say to Jacob, trying to keep my cool. "I can appreciate your concern, but this is between me and Devorah. And I think she wants to go with me."

"I don't think so," he says.

"Let us go, Jacob!" Devorah cries. "This is none of your business!" She tries unsuccessfully to wriggle free from Moley's grasp.

"Could you have Cindy Crawford over there let go of her, please?" I snap. Moley looks confused. He clearly does not get the reference.

Jacob frowns and shakes his head. "I'm not about to return my sister-in-law to her kidnapper," he says.

"Whoa, whoa, whoa. I didn't *kidnap* her." I jerk my arms, trying to knock the guy holding me off balance, but he doesn't budge.

"So you didn't coerce her into an idling car against her will?"

"No." He's playing with me now, and I don't like it.

"Jacob, *stop*," Devorah says angrily.

"That's what I saw," the older dude says. "In fact, you pulled her into that car."

"*Screaming*," Jacob adds.

"Fuck you," I shout. "This is not a kidnapping, man. We're *together*. She's my *girlfriend*."

"Really?" Jacob smiles and bites his lip, scratching his chin. "That's surprising to me."

"Why's that?"

"Because you're a piece of trash," he growls, getting up in my face. "And I don't want you coming within ten miles of my family."

I notice that my wrists have more wiggle room; my captor must be getting bored and losing focus. If I just wait one more minute . . .

"Too bad that's not up to you," I say. "Too bad you're not a real policeman, and just some pathetic little neighborhood-watch Napoleon."

"Oh, I'll say whatever I want to the police," he says. "After all, it's your word against ours."

"No, Jacob," Devorah says, loudly but calmly, holding her head up, the stoplight casting her face into neon red relief. "It's your word against mine. And I'll tell them *exactly* what happened."

"Shut up," Jacob barks. "You lost the right to speak the minute you opened your legs."

The guy holding me laughs, and I take the opportunity to deliver a swift kick to his shin with my right heel. He groans and lets go of my wrists, and without even looking I shoot my left elbow back into his chest.

"Don't talk to her like that," I say to Jacob, stepping forward and massaging my wounded shoulder. "We can do this two ways. One, we walk away and no one gets hurt. Two—"

"Jaxon, behind you!" Devorah shrieks, and I don't even have time to turn before I feel a blunt object come down hard between my shoulder blades, sending fresh spasms of pain through my back and driving me forward onto my hands and knees. *Do these guys have billy clubs?* I wonder as I blink at the shimmering asphalt, but when Jacob shouts, "Turn them off!" I remember: Oh, right. Flashlights. And then someone steps on my back, and my chin hits the pavement with a dull crack that shudders through my skull.

My senses are dulled by the pain and Devorah's screams, but I know I get pulled to standing again and put in another armlock, one I'm now too disoriented to escape. Moley and a tall guy with glasses, who must be the dick who pulled me out of the car, take turns punching me: in the jaw, on the side of the head, in the stomach, the chest. These guys aren't fighters, so it could be worse, but I can't defend myself except to turn my head, so instead of a broken nose I get a busted lip. I close my eyes as the coppery blood coats my tongue.

"What's going on down there?" a woman's voice calls out, high-pitched and anxious. The punches stop abruptly, and I crack an eye open to see the lady from the window upstairs, leaning out with a scarf covering her head.

"Call 911!" I yell, just as Jacob shouts, "Shomrim! We've got it under control."

"Mmmmmmpppph!" screams Devorah, whose mouth is being covered by one of Moley's wide hands.

Along the streets, more windows squeak open as other people

stick their heads out to rubberneck, murmuring to one another in hushed, morbidly excited tones. Jacob frowns and shakes his head discreetly at the rest of the group.

"Don't hit him again, not while they're watching," he whispers.

"*Fuck* you, man," I gasp, and then I use all the strength I have left to jerk and flail, ignoring the throbbing in my arms and back, until I pull loose from the amateur lock.

I shove past Jacob, and I must look scary now—blood dripping from my mouth, shirt ripped, eyes red as an angry bull's—because Moley drops his hands from Devorah before I even touch him.

"Come on," I say, holding out my good hand. She just stares at me, her eyes frozen wide with fear.

"Get the cuffs!" Jacob yells.

"Come *on*," I say again, grabbing at her arm, but Devorah doesn't move.

"Run," she says in a hoarse whisper.

"Not without you." I hear a car door slam, then the jangle of metal on metal. I feel like I have the right—no, the *responsibility*—to not remain silent right now, but Devorah doesn't seem to agree.

"Jax, *run!*" she screams, her voice cracking from the effort, her abruptly unfrozen face contorting into a red mask of pain.

And so, reluctantly at first, I do. I run. Then adrenaline kicks in, drowning out the pain, and I'm sprinting down the sidewalk as fast as my shaking legs will carry me, tripping and tumbling onto the pavement a few times but barely even feeling the scrapes. I run until my lungs burn and bile rises in my throat, until Kingston Avenue spits me out into the broad, leafy, familiar embrace of Eastern Parkway lit up by a thin sliver of yellow moon, and then I run across seven lanes of traffic against the light until I reach the other side, where I collapse against a scaffolding pole and dry heave onto the sidewalk. I keep waiting for my breathing to get easier, but I'm dizzy and gasping for air. The stars seem to spin overhead, vertigo turning the world on its side.

Am I dying? The thought floats through my brain right before I throw up, but as I crumple to the pavement I realize that I don't care what the answer is. She's gone, maybe forever.

I might as well be dead.

Chapter 23

Devorah

SEPTEMBER 15, 8:15 PM

The last time I was in my living room (only an hour and a half ago, my rational brain reminds me, but somehow it feels like days) it was the picture of peace, nothing moving in the gentle dark except Rose's chest rising and falling beneath the sleeping baby curled on top of her.

Now, it's a war room.

All the lights are on, and I'm sitting in the chair by the dragonfly lamp, flanked by Jacob, who doesn't seem to trust me to move more than six inches on my own. His hand, the nail beds grimy with dirt (*but not blood, oh no—he was just the sadistic director, standing by and watching as they beat him*), rests on the chair arm to my left, his body conveniently blocking my path to both the front door and the stairway. Across from me, my father sits in his now-rumpled work clothes, his wide feet stuffed into beige slippers, taking up the whole couch as if his body has expanded with rage, like steam collecting under the lid of a boiling pot. In the kitchen, my mother is making coffee for Rabbi Perl, who like his name is almost perfectly round and translucent, the veins purple and blue under his elderly skin. After some impassioned debate that I was not a part of—but which involved many furious glances and gesticulations in my direction— my father called him at his home and got him out of bed to come and bear witness to my shame. Some others didn't have to be called; over the shuffling in the kitchen I can hear subtle squeaks in the planks of the floor above that tell me Miri, Hanna, and Amos are listening from the landing, their faces pressed up against the smooth wooden rails.

"All right," the rabbi says as he enters, his trembling hands clutching a ceramic mug emblazoned with the joke slogan I ❤ TANYA—the sacred Chabad text, not a woman. "Tell me what's been going on." Out of the corner of my eye I can see Jacob shifting from foot to foot. He must be beside himself that it's not his place to speak first and that he, like everyone, must look to my father out of respect. Everyone, that is, but me. I can't bring myself to meet his eyes.

"Our daughter," my father says slowly, his voice thick with anger and fatigue, "has been seeing a boy."

"What is the nature of the relationship?" the rabbi asks, lowering himself onto the love seat to my right. He's not asking me. My opinion on the subject is not expected or required. For the first time in the presence of a religious elder, I feel no subservience, only a stab of defiant anger.

"I only learned of it tonight," my father says, "But as I understand from my son-in-law, they have been secretly dating for some weeks, and she was planning on leaving on a trip with him this evening."

"All without our knowledge," my mother adds, choking back tears. Her hands fly to her face as she sinks into the couch beside my father, who bristles at the sound of her sobs. Jacob leans across to pass her a handkerchief.

"I assumed," the rabbi says kindly. He turns to Jacob. "Tell me what happened tonight."

"I was out on Shomrim patrol," Jacob says soberly, "when I saw Devorah standing alone in front of Eliyahu's Bakery. This was after sundown, so naturally I was concerned. A black car pulled up, and I watched her get inside. That's when I decided to intervene, and I found her with the boy in question. In quite a compromising position." Clearly he has been rehearsing his lines. I almost want to clap.

"I understand there was a struggle," the rabbi says.

"Yes, unfortunately the boy lashed out at us violently, and we were forced to restrain him." In a flash I see Jaxon down on the ground, a black boot driving into his back.

"That's not true!" I cry. "The Shomrim hurt him first. They dragged us out of the car."

"*Quiet*," my father says threateningly.

"They punched him!" I say, hearing my voice rise hysterically but unable to control it. "He did nothing to them, and they beat him with his hands held behind his back!"

"That's not true," Jacob says. "But I'm sure it's difficult for Devorah to tell truth from lies at this point." He turns to my parents. "I told you she had a cell phone, didn't I? *Now* do you believe me?" Then he smiles ever so slightly, relishing the moment, and I lose what little restraint I've been clinging to since I was brought home and forced into this chair, just one more in a series of waiting rooms I get to live in while other people dictate the terms of my freedom.

"You're a monster," I shout. "And you're a liar, too!" I turn to face my parents, who look at me like I'm a frightening trespasser they've never seen before. "He knew about Jaxon from the beginning," I say. "He saw us together. He threatened me and told me he would tell you if I didn't stop seeing him."

"Devorah, STOP!" my father yells, a cannonball boom that reverberates through the house. He collects himself and then fixes me with a steely stare. "What has happened to you?" he asks. "You are not the daughter I raised."

"I found the letter," my mother jumps in. "The idea that you would leave without talking to us first, that you would go to such lengths to hide, even when I gave you a chance to tell me—" She starts to tear up again. "I just don't understand how you could disrespect us like this."

"I'm so sorry," I blurt, so upset and anxious that I trip over my own words. "I never meant to—I don't want to hurt anyone. You have to believe me, Mama, I didn't want *any* of this to happen. It just—" I feel hot tears cascade down my cheeks. "I'm still your daughter," I plead. "I just didn't know what to do."

"You could have done anything but this," my father mutters, raising a napkin to mop his brow.

Rabbi Perl holds up his hands. "Let's all try to calm down," he says. "Devorah, I'd like to hear from you now." His eyes are wet and cloudy, the lids above them papery-thin. "Is it true that you were planning on leaving the city tonight with this young man?"

I wipe at my eyes with the back of my hand. "Yes, but—"

He waves my explanation away. "Where were you planning on going?"

"It doesn't matter now," I mumble.

"Devorah!" my father barks. "Show some respect and answer the rabbi's question."

"Just Long Island," I say reluctantly, as if it's no big deal, and my mother shakes her head, looking like she's sitting shiva after a death. Rabbi Perl nods encouragingly. It almost feels reassuring, but then I remember that it's just his job to be a mediator. He *wants* me to trust him.

"Why Long Island?" he asks.

"There was a house," I say. "His friend had a house we were going to stay in. Just for the night." It all feels so far away now, a fading photograph in a family album that will never exist.

The rabbi coughs. "I'm going to ask you a very personal question now, one that may make you uncomfortable," he says. "But it's crucial that you answer honestly. Was your relationship with the boy . . . physical?"

Humiliation burns in my gut as I think of the moist warmth of Jaxon's lips, and those moments in the basement when his hips pressed against mine as we lay tangled on the floor. I shake my head.

"Your legs are bare," Jacob says disgustedly, and I glare up at him.

"I did nothing," I say to the rabbi, hoping that he can't see the lie pulsing in my lips. "I admit to breaking *tz'ni'ut*, but nothing . . . happened." I can't believe I'm alluding to sex in front of my parents and the rabbi who has known me since I was a toddler. I wonder if it's possible to literally die of shame.

"So it wasn't of a sexual nature," he prods.

"No," I whisper into my lap.

"There's some good news," the rabbi says, turning back to my parents, who remain rigid and silent.

"Why should we believe you?" Jacob interjects. "If you had gotten away with what you pulled tonight, you would have ruined the lives of everyone in this family. And for what? Some teenage fling?"

"You don't know anything," I snap.

"Enlighten me, then." Jacob chuckles. "Because frankly I can't imagine what you or anyone would see in him. He looks like every other thug on that side of Eastern Parkway."

"Jacob, *enough*," my father says.

"With respect, Dad, if it wasn't for me Devorah would be on a train right now," Jacob says petulantly.

"And I appreciate your help," my father replies. "But what's done is done, and now it is up to her mother and me, and Rabbi Perl, to decide how to proceed."

"What about me?" I ask. "Does anyone care what I want?"

"I think you've made that very clear," my mother says sharply. "And you're going to get it." She leans forward. "You want to act grown up and live alone with a man? Fine. I'll call the *shadchan* tomorrow morning."

"No," I say, horrified. "I don't want *any* man. I want Jaxon."

"You are a child," my father says with a sigh. "You don't know what you want."

"But I love him!" I cry. My mother shuts her eyes as if trying to block me out. Rabbi Perl looks startled and sets down his coffee cup on the side table.

"Devorah," my father says stonily, "you may go to your room. This conversation no longer concerns you."

Chapter 24

Jaxon

Despite puking up what feels like all my internal organs, it turns out I'm not dead, so I sit on a bench on Eastern Parkway for a while like a zombie, just watching the headlights whiz past. At home I have this writing book from my English comp class last year, and I remember one phrase jumping out at me when I first read it, something about how writing a story is like driving at night down a dark road: You can see only as far as your headlights, but you can make the whole trip that way. Well, I feel like Jacob and his buddies bashed in my headlights tonight, and now I'm lost. I have no idea which way to go.

That's not some heartsick attempt at poetry, by the way; I'm being literal. Do I head north, back to my house, where I'll have to spin a crazy lie for my parents about why I'm bruised and bloody and also not, in fact, sleeping over at Ryan's house? (They said no to my cover-story request initially, but then I invented a college application workshop at 7 AM, arguing that being right around the corner from school would guarantee I wouldn't miss a single second.) Do I go south, back to Devorah's house, and risk trying to get her back from the Shomrim? Or do I hail a cab to Penn Station and catch that train, use my savings to stay in some cheap motel for a night or two until I figure out how to proceed? I give the third option serious thought for about ten seconds, until I realize I've got no phone and nothing but a ripped T-shirt and bloodstained jeans for my wardrobe. Yeah, I'm sure hotels all over the Hamptons are going to welcome me with open arms.

I have no idea how much time has passed, but my shoulder is throbbing and I'm starting to get chills, so finally I force myself to stand and walk slowly back home. It would be suicide to go back for Devorah tonight. I'd probably get arrested, or worse. But I know where she is. And the only chance I have to be with her now is to get some rest and go back tomorrow, in bright daylight, when Jacob and the Shomrim can't pull any of that Rodney King shit. Provided, of course, that my parents don't kill me first.

I open the front door of our building as quickly as possible with my gimpy arm and slip into the front hall, where I can hear our elderly Puerto Rican landlady and her live-in Jamaican nurse watching some *telenovela* at a ridiculous volume. As the soap opera organ music swells, I check out my battle scars in the hall mirror, which is arranged over a small wooden console table displaying a gold cross in the center of a doily. I need to know how bad I look so that I know how much to brace myself for seeing my mom.

It's pretty bad. There's a cut across my left temple, crossing the eyebrow, which looks a little bit like grape jelly oozing out of pumpernickel bread. My lower lip is caked with dried blood, there's a scrape across my chin, and my right shoulder is visibly swollen and covered in dirt-smeared scratches. But the worst part is just how hollowed out I look, as if I've lost ten pounds since this morning.

I climb the stairs, shuffling through various stories that could conceivably explain my current state—a mugging, maybe, or a skateboard accident—but I'm too spent and depressed to even care anymore about what anyone thinks. I just want to stand under a hot shower and then face-plant in my bed, waking up tomorrow to realize this was all a bad dream.

I hear excited cries as I turn my key in the lock, and sure enough, as soon as I step inside, my sisters are upon me. It's the best reception I could have hoped for, although the fact that they were waiting for me gives me a sick feeling in my stomach. Somehow, my parents must already know.

"It's Jaxon!" Tricia squeals. "Mama, it's Jax!" Then she sees my face, and her eyes widen.

"You're bleeding," Joy gasps, touching my jaw. I wince, and then try to smile.

I look past their disheveled heads to my mother, who's standing in the living room in her nightgown with her curlers in, clutching her phone and taking me in with some combination of weary relief and frightening indignation.

"You're alive," she says, letting out a heavy sigh. "Thank God."

"What *happened* to you?" Edna asks. "You get jumped?"

"Was it those guys from across the street?" Ameerah demands. The twins each take an elbow and help me to the couch, where

Tricia bursts into tears and throws her arms around my neck while Joy brings me some water.

"Mama called Ryan's house when she couldn't reach your cell," she says, almost hyperventilating. "We thought something happened! Daddy went looking for you!" I picture my dad's face on Saturday when he told me how proud he was, and cringe when I think about him now, hunched over the wheel of his pickup, sick with worry, wondering what could have happened to his upstanding, responsible son.

"Shut up, nobody thought that," Ameerah says, rolling her eyes.

"Yes you did," Joy cries. "*You* were the one who said if Jax didn't come home you were going to die."

"Awww," I say, kissing Tricia's forehead. "Y'all know I would never abandon you."

"You *scared* us," Edna says angrily. "Where *were* you?"

"Girls!" my mother interrupts, laying a hand on my knee. "Your brother is home now, and I know you have a lot of questions, but it's time for you all to get to bed. You can pester him in the morning, but right now *I* need to have a talk with him."

"Uh-oh," Joy whispers in my ear. "Next time we see you, you're gonna look worse!"

I hug Tricia again, gently detaching her skinny limbs from my torso, and watch as my sisters shuffle off toward their bedrooms, stopping every few feet to glance back, hoping, I guess, that my mother will start to lay into me while they still have a decent view.

But my mother isn't one to waste words or cater to an audience. She stays where she is, looking me over for a long minute before she speaks.

"I wanted to call the police," she finally says, her voice shaking with what I realize now is not anger but another emotion. She's fighting tears. "You're lucky your father held me back."

"Mom," I start, improvising sloppily, "I was on my way to Ryan's, and—"

"Don't lie," she says softly. "You don't think I know you weren't staying at Ryan's? His mother told me he and his father were out at a Yankees game."

"I can explain—" I say, but she holds up her hand.

"I called *hospitals*," she says angrily. "I called Cora at home. I even called that family of the boy you tutor, just in case you were there."

"You called the Schwartzes?"

"I didn't know their first name, so I called every Schwartz in Park Slope," she says. "They were number twenty-nine."

"Mama, you didn't have to—"

"Of *course* I had to," she shouts, balling her fists and shaking them in front of her chest. "You're my *son*." This burst of passionate anger seems to surprise even her, and she takes a deep breath before resuming her more stoic stance.

"I'm sorry," I say softly. I mean it.

"Someone hit you," she says. Her tone is matter-of-fact, but her eyes crinkle in pain.

"Yeah, well, you should see the other guy. He doesn't have a scratch."

"Get in the bathroom," she says. "I'm going to call your father, and then I'm going to clean you up."

I sit in my boxers on the edge of the claw-foot porcelain tub as my mother lays out supplies from the medicine cabinet: Band-Aids, hydrogen peroxide, cotton swabs, Q-Tips, nail scissors, tweezers, and a jar of Vaseline. She's the office manager for a podiatrist in downtown Brooklyn, but for all her competence in makeshift first aid, you'd think she was an EMT.

"Your shoulder looks bad," she says, wiping it gently with a damp washcloth. "What happened?"

"I fell on it."

"From where? Onto what?" My mother isn't the type to just flat-out interrogate; she'll nudge away gradually, collecting small details until she solves the puzzle.

"From the backseat of a car," I say.

"Whose car?"

"A car service." I look up at her, wincing as she applies peroxide to the scrapes. "You want to know the make and model?"

She gives me a look that tells me she's not softened enough for jokes yet and opens the medicine cabinet again, rooting through old razors and Tylenol bottles before locating a tube of ointment that she squeezes out onto her palm and applies to my shoulder in light strokes. "This'll help with bruising," she says. "Based on your level of pain and mobility I'm guessing you tore your rotator cuff. About half the time it can heal on its own."

"And the other half?"

"We'll wait and see how you feel tomorrow." She turns her attention to my eyebrow, dabbing at the wound with a cotton ball. "You know when I called Cora looking for you, she told me you haven't shown up for work for the past week. Asked me how you were feeling." She raises an eyebrow. "That wouldn't have anything to do with *this*"—she gestures to my face—"now, would it?"

"You could say they're related," I say, gritting my teeth as she rubs Vaseline on the torn skin with her index finger.

"She also told me you came by the store to borrow money from her today, at nine in the morning," my mother says, replacing the cap with a purposeful smack. I hang my head. "So you're cutting school now?"

"Just today," I admit with a sigh.

"Just today?" she asks skeptically, tipping my chin up with two fingers so she can get at the cuts around my jawline. "What were you planning on doing tomorrow morning, during your 'college application seminar'?"

I hang my head, too exhausted to come up with another excuse and too guilty to want to. Mom exhales heavily through her nose, her nostrils flaring in momentary anger, but doesn't say anything for a minute. Instead she finishes with my chin and cleans the blood off my lip. Then she sits on the closed toilet seat and rests her elbows in her lap.

"Jaxon," she says, "I don't know what's going on right now, but I can tell you what I do know. You are my son, and I love you. You're a good boy on his way to becoming a good man. You deserve everything you can get in this life."

"Stop it," I say. I try to play it off like she's embarrassing me, but really it's that I'm afraid I might start crying if she keeps it up.

"It's *true*," she says. "And don't let anyone tell you different. Why do you think your father and I push so hard? Because we know you can do anything. You can *have* anything. You're a straight-A student with amazing talents, and you are going to have your pick of college scholarships. And I'm not about to watch you throw that away getting caught up in some"—she throws her hands up help-lessly—"some gang, or whoever did this."

I shake my head. "It's not a gang, Mom."

"Oh Lord," she says, clasping her hands in front of her face. "Please tell me it's not drugs."

"It's not drugs."

"Then what?" she cries, looking helpless for the first time all night. "Why else would you skip school, and come home looking like you got into a bar fight? Who would do this to you?"

I look down at my bare feet on the tiled floor. I'm sitting here nearly naked in front of my mother, and I can either tell her the truth or feed her a line. It's now or never.

"I met a girl," I say with a sigh. She sits up straight, looking relieved but confused.

"I don't understand," she says.

"Her family doesn't like me."

"What's wrong with them? Are *they* in a gang?"

"No. But they're what you could call an exclusive group."

My mother frowns. "So . . . this girl's family beat you up?"

"Sort of indirectly, yeah. It's a long story, Mom."

My mother nods slowly, leaning forward, and when she speaks the frost is gone from her tongue. "I guess you must really like this girl, huh?"

I nod. The less specific I am, the better—at least until Devorah and I can figure out where to go from here.

"She go to your school?"

"No," I say. "She lives . . . across town."

"How did you meet her?"

"We got stuck in an elevator the night of the hurricane. At the hospital."

Mom cracks a smile. "That's very romantic," she says. "But if being with this girl has you coming home looking like raw rump roast, I have to tell you I don't think she's worth it."

I shake my head vehemently. "She is."

My mother falls uncharacteristically quiet for a minute, and then looks me in the eyes with a pained expression. "I know what young love feels like, Jax. I know it feels like you'll never have it again, and that this is your only shot at happiness, but trust me when I tell you that it can be fleeting. So before you see her again or put yourself in any danger, you'd better ask yourself if you really like this girl as much as you think you do."

I don't have to think. "I *love* her, Mom," I say softly.

She studies my face with a sad smile. "Love is a strong word."

"I know," I say. "I wouldn't say it if I didn't mean it."

"I believe that's true," she says, sighing. "And I meant what I said earlier, too. I think you deserve everything you want out of life. *Including* who you love."

"So you don't think it's crazy?" I ask.

"What love isn't crazy?" she says. "When your father and I met, I was seventeen and he was the twenty-five-year-old painting my house. I thought my dad was going to murder him!" She straightens up, her eyes flashing. "Don't get me wrong, if you see the men who did this to you again, you call 911 on their asses, you hear me? All I'm saying is, don't you let anyone else tell you who you can or cannot love. That's between you and her. Her family's got no business messing with that, no more business than I do. My mother used to say that no one knows what's going on in a stew but the pot and the spoon." She stands up and rests her hand on my head, running her fingers along my hairline. "You know, you're still my favorite son," she whispers, leaning down to kiss my forehead. "Even if you *are* grounded for the next six months."

I stay sitting on the lip of the tub as my mom brushes her teeth, thinking about how everyone should be lucky enough to feel this unconditionally loved. Devorah's family might not be able to love her that way, but I will. I can show her. And maybe, just maybe, that's all we'll need.

Chapter 25
Devorah

I sit up in bed gasping for breath. I was having that dream again, the one on the Brooklyn Bridge. Same as last time, I was walking down the center path under the big arches, but instead of blue skies above me there were swirling, soot-colored clouds that dipped lower with every step I took, and all of the black-coated Chabad men were standing with their backs to me, looking out at the water. Again I looked for Jaxon on the top of the first tower, but this time he wasn't there. The clouds started to envelop me like a thick fog, and suddenly I got a terrible feeling that something had happened to him, and so I ran into the crowd, pushing aside the stoic onlookers, until I could lean over the railing and look down at the river. And sure enough, there he was, treading water, his red shirt clinging to his dusky skin, his arms reaching up for me, his eyes wide with fear.

And then Rose appeared beside me and laid a cold, bloodless hand on my back, whispering in my ear, "Now it's your turn, Devorah. *Jump.*" That's when I woke up.

"Devorah," Rose says, in real life this time, backing away from my bedside looking alarmed. "It's okay. Relax. I just said you need to jump in the shower now if you want to take one before we leave." She's already dressed in a crisp navy shift, a white cardigan, and black boots, her synthetic hair gleaming over her narrow shoulders. Did I sleep in? Was I supposed to be someplace? Pale sunlight is filtering through the ivy-covered window and onto my bedspread, and I have to wrack my brain for a minute to remember what day it is. But then I feel the stiff collar of my school shirt rubbing against the back of my neck, the one I was too exhausted to take off as I lay across my bed after the confrontation with my parents and Rabbi Perl, burying my face in the pillow and praying for sleep. Suddenly I feel an emotional hangover settle in, sending pulses of grim pain through my temples.

"Where are we going?" I ask groggily. It's Tuesday, a school day. Could I still be dreaming? Did my brain just replace the nightmare with something really mundane to calm me down?

"Oh, to Monsey," Rose says breezily as she opens my drawers and begins pulling out tops, skirts, and balled-up tights. "To see Aunt Varda."

I swing my legs over the side of the still-made bed and smooth my wrinkled skirt over my knees, pinching the flesh just to make sure I'm awake. "Since when were we going to Monsey in the middle of the week?" I ask, and Rose frowns into the mirror before spinning around with a sympathetic smile.

"Since last night," she says. "After all the drama. Mom and Dad thought it would be good for you to get away today, for everyone to cool off. And besides, Varda hasn't met the baby."

"Is Jacob going?"

"No," Rose says quickly, looking away and busying herself with continuing to pack my things. "Now come on, either take a shower or get dressed. We have to be downstairs in fifteen minutes."

I reach to my waist to roll down my stockings, but then I remember I'm not wearing any, and the shame of last night's interrogation rekindles its embers in my stomach. I wonder what Rose knows, how much her husband has told her, and what she must think of me despite her outwardly sunny disposition. Hopefully we'll have a chance to talk on the way to Monsey, I think as I slip past my sister and into the bathroom. I'm desperate to be cleansed, even if it's just on the surface.

When I get downstairs, dressed in the outfit Rose left on my bed for me—a fancier-than-usual silk blouse, a black skirt and jacket, and, of course, thick, opaque tights that stick to my damp legs in spots—I find my mother scuttling Hanna, Miri, and Amos out the door for school. The three of them pause in the doorway to stare at me, and Hanna raises her hand in a meek wave.

"See you guys tonight," I say, trying to sound normal. But I know they heard everything. When I get back later I'll have to find a way to explain it to them from my perspective and make sure they aren't scared.

Miri turns her face up to my mother and frowns. "But I thought you said—"

"Time to go!" my mother cries nervously, cutting her off and ushering them outside, shutting the door behind her with a bang.

"Bye," I mutter after them. During my shower I steeled myself for another confrontation, but I never thought my own mother would just ignore me. I look to my father, who's sitting at the table next to Zeidy, eating oatmeal and sipping from a big mug of coffee as he reads the Yiddish paper. Neither of them look up, and Shoshana's whispers about Ruchy Silverman ring in my head: *"It's like she doesn't exist."*

Rose lifts Liya from her swing and kisses her nose. "Go ahead and eat something, Dev," she says. "The van's outside."

"The store van?" I ask, confused. "Why aren't we taking the Camry?" Rose and my father make eye contact, and some unspoken message passes between them.

"Because . . . Mom needs it," Rose says. "For errands."

"Who's driving us?" I ask, and another silent communiqué shoots over my head.

"Dad," Rose says, as if this should be obvious.

"Dad," I repeat incredulously. Our father tolerates our aunt, but the idea that he would volunteer to spend the day with her—her *plus* a colicky baby and his disgraced daughter—without my mother to serve as a buffer is unlikely. "Don't you have to work?" I ask him. Rosh Hashanah is only a week away, and the high holidays always coincide with my father putting in twelve- or fourteen-hour days at the store.

"I didn't realize you were my employer, Devorah," he says gruffly, still not looking at me. Zeidy pushes back from the table abruptly and shuffles into his room, which used to be a screened-in back porch until my grandma passed and he moved in, along with his arthritic joints that can't climb stairs.

"What's wrong with Zeidy?" I ask. "Does his chest still hurt?"

"In a manner of speaking," my father says. "He's very upset by what you did."

It feels like an open-hand slap, intended to leave a mark. I can understand my parents and Jacob wanting to punish me, but my sweet, doting zeidy? The one who always winks at me and tells me I'm his *zeeskyte*, his sweetheart, the spitting image of my grandmother? I swallow the tears climbing my throat and turn to Rose. "I'm ready," I say. "I don't need to eat."

My father gets up and pulls on his blazer, and Rose puts a pink knit cap on Liya's head, inciting a bout of screaming. I'm stroking the baby's cheek as I walk out the front door, which is why I don't immediately see Jacob, or my mother, waiting on the other side of the threshold. But then Jacob's thin fingers close over one arm and my father grabs the other, and suddenly I'm being all but carried down the front steps toward an idling van, driven by a man who is instantly, chillingly familiar as he turns to look at me. It's Jacob's Shomrim friend, Moshe, the one with the mole. The one who beat up Jaxon.

"No!" I cry out, but it's useless now; it's obvious I'm going into the van whether I like it or not.

"It's all right, Devorah," my mother calls after me. "This is for the best, you'll see." I crane my neck to look back at Rose, whose chin is trembling as she joins her daughter in tears.

"Where am I going?" I shriek. "Don't send me with him! I hate him!"

"You're making a scene," Jacob says quietly. "Do us a favor and leave the family one shred of dignity, will you?"

"Daddy, *please*," I beg, but he still won't meet my eyes, even while he lifts me into the van, buckling me in as Jacob holds me down.

"You'll be fine," he says curtly. "We'll see you next week." And then he slams the door.

Panic blinds me as I lurch for the door lock, forgetting that I'm strapped in. I fumble with the seat belt, but my fingers feel thick and clumsy. I try to breathe in, but it feels like someone is sitting on my chest, and I gasp for air like I'm choking.

"Relax," Moshe says from the front seat. "You're only making it worse."

There's no room for worse, I want to tell him. *This is the bottom.* But I can't waste what little breath I have. He shifts the van into drive and is pulling away from the curb when I hear muffled shouts from outside and then someone banging on the window.

"Open the door! Open this door!" Rose is yelling. "I'm coming with her!" Through the tinted window I can see her struggling with the door handle, jerking it up and down so hard it sounds like it might break off.

Moshe steps hard on the brakes, and Jacob runs up to the front window on the passenger side, yelling, "Don't stop, just drive! I'll handle her."

"Don't you dare let him leave without me!" Rose screams—the first time since her labor that I've seen her exhibit any force of will. She shoves a manicured finger into Jacob's chest. "If you don't get out of my way, I'll make you regret it for the rest of your natural life." If I wasn't having a panic attack, I would laugh; even in her wilder years, Rose has never been this aggressive. It's like watching Gandhi upend a dinner table.

"Fine," Jacob says, stalking away from the car and back toward the house. "Do what you want. Abandon your child."

"It's three hours round trip," Rose shouts back over her shoulder as Moshe unlocks the door and she swings it open. "I think she'll live. There's a bottle in the fridge; you just have to warm it on the stove in a pot of water."

"Rose," my mother calls from the stoop, "Devorah is fine. Rabbi Perolman will take excellent care of her, and—"

"She's not fine, she's scared!" Rose cries. "She's my sister, and she's scared out of her mind. I don't blame her, either, the way you've been treating her. Devorah stayed with me during the scariest experience of my life, and I owe it to her to do the same." She pulls the door shut, panting, her normally wan cheeks glowing a radiant pink. "Okay," she says to Moshe, "*now* you can drive."

"Thank you," I whisper, my breathing starting to return to normal.

"Anytime," Rose says as we pull out into the street, leaving Jacob to express his helpless, angry pantomime to my stupefied parents. Now both of their eldest daughters have gone off the *derech* in less than twenty-four hours.

"So where are we really going?" I ask as the van rumbles down Crown Street.

"To Monsey," she says. "That wasn't a lie. There's a Chabad house there for teens who need"—she looks down at her lap—"guidance."

"So I'm going to Hasidic rehab," I say.

"Something like that."

"For how long?"

"I don't know. Dad made the arrangements. But it sounds like you'll be back by Rosh Hashanah."

"Shanah Tovah," I say sarcastically, and Rose gives me an odd stare.

We pick up speed as we get out of Crown Heights, barreling into the staccato traffic of Atlantic Avenue that swarms around the big brown beehive of the Barclays Center and then races down toward the waterfront. When we turn onto the access road for the Brooklyn Bridge, Rose takes my hand and squeezes it gently.

"I'd like to apologize for Jacob," she says.

I lean my forehead against the glass and close my eyes, shrugging her off. "Too late," I grumble.

"I know he can be difficult," she says—the understatement of the year—"but believe it or not he's just trying to do what he thinks is right. What he *believes*."

I look at my sister in horror. "You're defending him?"

"Of course I'm defending him," Rose says quietly. "I'm his wife."

"You're my *sister*," I say.

"That's different," she says.

"Right, because why side with your own flesh and blood who you've known for sixteen years when you could side with a stranger you met last year."

"He's not a stranger, Devorah," she says with a frown. "He's my *husband*."

"But he was a stranger. Before you met him. Before you married him." I can't help myself. "Before you changed."

"What?"

"You're a totally different person around him," I say angrily.

"You used to speak up for yourself. Now he just pushes you around. You're like a zombie."

Rose blinks back tears. "You have no idea what I've been through this year," she says. "Being pregnant and caring for a newborn is incredibly draining. Plus that week in the NICU was the worst week of my life. I've been sleep-deprived and depressed . . . No one tells you how hard it is." She wipes her eyes with the back of her hand, and I feel terrible. It occurs to me that I haven't asked Rose how she's been doing, not once, since I met Jaxon.

"I'm so sorry," I say.

"And Jacob's *not* a bully," she continues. "Not to me anyway. He can be argumentative, but he has a soft side, too. You've seen him with Liya."

"Whatever," I say with a sigh. "You wouldn't defend him so much if you saw what they did to Jaxon's face." I wish there was some partition I could close to keep from seeing the silhouette of Moshe's wiry muttonchops. Every time I look at him I feel sick to my stomach.

"Maybe I wouldn't," Rose concedes. "And I can't speak for all of the Shomrim. But at his core, Jacob is a good man. He's just trying to help."

I bite my tongue and stare out at the Brooklyn skyline across the East River as we fly up the FDR Drive. I can never tell my sister that I think she married the wrong person, no matter how much I want to. "Okay," I say, unconvinced.

"You know, I remember when you used to get horrified when I read teen magazines and talked about boys," Rose says, folding her hands in her lap and twirling the wedding band on her left ring

finger around and around. "If you want to talk about people changing, the Devorah *I* used to know would never approve of what's
going on with Jaxon."

"Yeah," I say. "I know."

"So what changed?"

"The only thing that changed," I say slowly, "is that I met him.
And if circumstances had been different and I had never met him,
then we probably wouldn't be here. But it was like I had been looking down at the ground my whole life, and he was the first person to
point my chin up to the sky."

Rose looks at me with pity. "I'm sure he's a very nice person,"
she says. "But the novelty will wear off."

"He's not a *novelty*," I snap, sorry that I even tried to explain.
If Rose is too blind to see the truth of her own marriage, there's no
way she could ever understand the beauty of what I have with Jax.

"Dev, he's not even Jewish," Rose says gently. "You had to have
known from the start that it was never going to work out."

"But that's what made it possible," I say. "If he had been Hasidic
he never would have spoken to me, and I never would have had the
opportunity to talk to someone so different."

"Different is overrated," Rose says, sounding exactly like our
mother.

"Really?" I ask. "You've never, *ever* even thought about anyone
outside?"

"Not in that way, no."

"And if you could choose from all the men in the world you
would still pick Jacob as your husband?"

"Yes."

"Okay," I say, sitting back, giving up. "Then I'm glad you're happy."

We sit in silence for a moment as we pass through the thick block of tollbooths that lead out onto the George Washington Bridge into New Jersey.

"Why aren't you happy?" Rose asks quietly.

"I've been trying to figure that out," I say.

"You have so much to look forward to in life, Devorah," she says, leaning back in her seat and lolling her head toward mine. "You're beautiful, smart, and kind." She pauses, and cocks an eyebrow. "*Most* of the time, anyway. Everyone adores you, and you make good grades on top of it. I don't know why you think you have no options."

"Because I don't want to be a housewife," I say.

"Then work," she suggests. "You could get a job any number of places."

"Sure, as a cashier. Not exactly my dream."

"Well, you can help run your husband's business, then," she says brightly. "Look at Mama. The store would collapse without her."

"She doesn't like it, though."

"How do you know? You can learn to like things; it's not always right away."

I think of my childhood distrust of the pale blobs of gefilte fish my mother would cook in a huge cast-iron pot for our Passover seders, and how now the cold, boiled white fish and matzo meal tastes like love incarnate. How high and scary the temple ceilings always seemed, until I noticed the stained-glass treasures hidden between the beams. The first time I saw Jaxon and how I hardly noticed he was even there.

"I guess I believe in the trust-your-gut method," I say. "Like how you knew Liya was going to be a girl."

Rose smiles faintly. "I know it sounds silly, but even with all of the exhaustion and hormonal changes, being a mother is the best job I can think of having," she says. "Ever since Liya was born I feel spiritually fulfilled in this way that's hard to describe. Like, I'm raising a person. I'm teaching someone how to be a decent human being. That's my job."

"Pretty impressive," I say, without a trace of sarcasm.

"It'll surprise you, Dev. You don't think you're ready, but then it happens, and you are."

I shake my head. "I know I'm not ready. Not now and not anytime soon."

"Well," she says, "maybe you'll change your mind."

"Maybe I won't."

Rose laughs and makes a motion like she wants to throttle me. "Since when do you question *everything*?" she groans.

I've been asking myself the same thing countless times over the past few weeks. What really caused this avalanche of an identity crisis? Was it as simple as meeting Jaxon in the elevator? Or has it been more insidious, something that took seed years ago and was just waiting for the right time to bloom?

"I don't know," I say as I gaze out at the lush, late-summer trees whizzing past us on the Palisades Parkway. I can only hope that wherever I'm headed, I'll have time to figure it out.

Chapter 26

Jaxon

"Up and at 'em, Cassius Clay," my mother yells through the door, rapping on it with her knuckles. My eyes flutter open and I try to sit up, but my body screams in protest. My shoulder is stiff and throbbing, my legs seize when I try to move them, and my back feels like I slept on a bed made out of broken bowling balls. Last night filters down through my consciousness in flashes, pieces of a dream I can't quite make sense of. My synapses have been firing for all of ten seconds and already I'm a physical and emotional wreck; I can't *believe* my mom expects me to go to school today.

"I feel like crap," I moan from my bed.

"That's what happens when you try to live out *West Side Story* east of Flatbush," mom quips. "Be downstairs in fifteen minutes, or you'll be late for your first class." A second later, my preset iPod alarm goes off, ironically set to play yet another Shirelles classic that fits in perfectly with today's theme.

"Mama said there'll be days like this, there'll be days like this, Mama said . . ."

I drag myself out of bed and hobble to the bathroom, where my mother has left a bottle of ibuprofen and the tub of Vaseline on the lip of the sink along with a note that reads, "Apply on all cuts, DO NOT skimp!!" I manage to turn on the shower water with my left hand. It's too hot, but I'm too sore to bend and adjust the cold-water knob once I'm in there, so instead I just grit my teeth and let the scalding water knead my muscles to ropy shreds, which hurts, but in a good way. I know the Marines have that hard-core mantra "Pain is weakness leaving the body," and it's never felt more true than right now. As the boiling water beats down on my back and the gathering steam heals my aching lungs, I start to feel stronger, braver, and clearer in purpose. I have to find Devorah and make sure she's okay. And this time, I'm not going to try to smuggle her out under cover of darkness. I'm not going to hide behind sunglasses and a hat or stand under her window tying kites to trees to make visual metaphors that only she will understand. Nope, this time I'm going to stand up like a man and tell her I don't care who knows I love her and that she shouldn't care, either. We don't have to hop a train to some upscale beach enclave to be free; freedom is a state of mind. (I read that last quote in my Intro Philosophy textbook, but I still think it applies.)

When I get downstairs after painstakingly pulling on some jeans and a striped polo shirt, my mother is waiting for me.

"Dad took the girls to school," she says, setting out a plate of eggs that I immediately wolf down standing up, both because I'm in a hurry and because it hurts to sit down. "And I am personally escorting your butt to the subway this morning to make sure you get on it."

I roll my eyes. "I'm going to school, Mom. You can relax."

"Actually I can't," she says. "Not until you prove to me that I can trust you again." She checks her watch and motions at me to speed up my chewing. "Also, every single day that you don't have work—the work at which I will be checking in to make sure you show up," she continues, "I expect you home at four PM on the nose, okay? And please believe that if you're even ten seconds late I *will* be alerting the authorities."

"Yes ma'am," I say, taking a swig of orange juice and mentally calculating the fastest route to Devorah's house from school. My last class gets out at 2:15, which should leave me just enough time to duck over there and see what's going on before I'm due at Wonder Wings. Unless something happens, I'll make it to work on time. And if something happens, well . . . I'll burn that bridge when I come to it.

My mother wasn't kidding; she literally walked me all the way to the Kingston Avenue subway station, escorted me down the stairs, and waited on the platform with me until the train came. Normally she takes the C to work, but since she had already gone so far out of her way she got on the 3 with me and took it two stops to Franklin to switch to the 5. The train car was sardine-packed as usual when it arrived, and I nearly died when she elbowed her way in and cut a swath through the rush hour crowds with her purse, yelling, "My son is injured, give him room!" I kept my eyes down, but I noticed a lot of Chabad men file on after us. I hope Mom didn't give them the stink-eye.

I relax a little once she's off the train, and lean back against the door with my heavy backpack wedged between my feet. I should probably be doing the homework I've completely ignored since last Friday, but it's next to impossible to get my mind turned to school. I promised my parents I'd bring my physical body into the building, but that's about all I can guarantee, seeing as how that body is currently the flesh-and-bone equivalent of a pile of junkyard scraps. And seeing as how I have no idea what's going on in any of my classes, I'll just have to sit in the back today and count on my battle scars to get me a pass from being called on. So I close my eyes and focus on the one thing I've managed to study lately: her face, thick eyebrows setting off those striking eyes and dark lashes, freckle-spattered nose sliding seamlessly into those wide, creamy cheeks that look like cherry syrup poured over shaved ice when she blushes. Rosebud lips parted in a nerdy, adorably crooked smile. Wild, dark curls that smell like lavender honey.

But as the train hurtles through the darkness between Eastern Parkway and Grand Army Plaza, I all of a sudden get this prickly feeling like I'm being watched.

I open my eyes just enough so that I can see the grimy subway floor (but so my lids still look closed to other people) and try to pick up where the stalker vibe is coming from. After a few seconds I'm pretty sure it's across the car to the right; in my peripheral vision I can see there's a guy sitting by the door who's holding a newspaper but not turning any pages. I know I'm probably being paranoid, and it's some old dude who just fell asleep sitting up, but after yesterday I don't feel that safe in a sea of black fedoras, even if we're on a commuter train in broad daylight.

I open my eyes and lift my head in one swift motion, and sure enough, there is someone staring at me from across the car. His face is partially hidden by the paper he's strategically raised for cover, but I don't need to see his nose and mouth to recognize those dark, calculating eyes.

It's Jacob.

The instant he sees me see him, he looks down, but for a split second his shoulders jerk in surprise, and I know I've got the upper hand now. He's by himself, without his wannabe cop sidekicks to protect him. And I'm not about to start a brawl or anything, but I'll be damned if I let that scrawny little narc off the train without telling me what he did with Devorah.

I lift my bag from the ground, trying to keep my facial muscles calm and steady even though deadlifting twenty-five pounds feels like being stretched on a medieval rack. I sling it over my left shoulder and then, turning the stare-down tables on him, start to snake my way through the car to where Jacob sits.

He folds his paper primly and stands up, even though we're still in between stops so standing just makes everybody squish against one another even more and get annoyed because he's blocking a perfectly good empty seat. Without looking back at me, Jacob starts to push his way toward the far end of the car, causing people to suck their teeth and mutter expletives in his wake. I, on the other hand, break out my best dimples and say, "Excuse me, so sorry," as I nudge past the familiar early bird crowd of nurses, students, and Wall Streeters. Everyone winces when they see my face and lets me pass without comment. At least I've got pity on my side.

The train pulls into Grand Army Plaza, and a huge herd of Park Slope/Prospect Heights yuppies gets on board. I can still see Jacob's hat bobbing slowly through the straphangers about fifteen feet away, but I'll never get to him in a straight chase. So I make a split-second

decision and squeeze out the middle doors, hit the platform running, and throw myself back in the doors at the end of the car just as
they're straining to shut against the crush of bodies. My legs kill me,
but it's worth it, because now I'm almost close enough to touch him.

"Hey," I say, loud enough for him to hear me but hopefully not
loud enough to command the attention of the entire train. "I just
need to know she's okay." But Jacob just launches himself through
a trio of nerdy Asian kids and slides open the exit between the cars,
his black coat disappearing as the train rounds a corner and the silver door slams shut. At the next stop I hop cars again, but he's gone,
swallowed by the sea of sleepy travelers streaming in from Atlantic
Avenue who force me back against the doors again, trapping me
inside.

The school day passes by like I'm watching it in fast motion.
Everyone, even people I don't know, stops me to ask how I'm doing,
and somehow I manage to convince the entire student body that I
got jumped by a gang in Prospect Park (thanks for the inspiration,
Mom!). Ryan loses his mind when I show up in our AP bio lab; he
thought I was in the Hamptons. But then he acts really sympathetic
about my shoulder, and I decide I'm not going to tell him I lost
the keys to his parents' place until I've healed more fully. I make a
mental note to call the car service company when I get home, and
see if our lead-footed driver still has my duffel.

Polly finds us during lunch in Fort Greene Park and plays nurse,
bringing me some Ayurvedic ointment for my face. It's weird how
now that I don't obsess about her anymore she's suddenly interested
in hanging out with me again, but I'm trying not to read too much
into it. She tells me that J-Riv is spreading a rumor that *he's* the one

who jumped me, and we crack ourselves up planning a police report to call his bluff.

As the end of the day closes in, I think about asking Ryan to come back to Chabadland with me, but (A) I'm pretty sure he'd balk, and (B) just in case I actually get the chance to talk to Devorah I don't want to do it in front of a wingman. Plus, after Jacob ran away from me this morning I'm actually feeling pretty badass. When I find myself alone in the third-floor boys' bathroom between fifth and sixth periods, I even do a little Travis Bickle routine in the mirror. "How you like me now?" I whisper at my reflection, jutting out my gnarled chin. "I thought so."

I leave my books at school, emptying my backpack into my locker before my last period, which is my weight-lifting gym elective, so I get an easy excuse note from the nurse and am breathing in the fresh air on DeKalb at 2:05, ahead of schedule. I won't be able to do homework without the books, but the heavy bag would weigh me down, and now more than ever I have a need for speed.

Kingston Avenue is much more crowded than it was last Friday just before sundown, and in the bright glare of punishing three o'clock light I can see every Hasid as they react to me in their own personal way. Most flat-out ignore me, but some peer after me like I'm an animal on exhibit at the Museum of Natural History. (*Please don't feed the black boy*, I think, punch-drunk from exhaustion.) A minority change course to avoid me, but from what I understand they've always been taught that strangers are bad news, so I try not to take it personally. The way I look right now I'd probably avoid me, too.

As I approach the intersection of Kingston and Crown, I feel a little hesitation creep in through the bravado that I've been wearing like a Halloween costume since this morning—*What if I can't find her? What if she freaks when she sees me? What if she told her parents some cover story I know nothing about and am about to ruin? Why didn't I just go home and write her a letter like a normal person, with my e-mail address and phone number, and let her reach out in her own time? Why am I acting like some action movie star and trying to be a hero when I'm so obviously not that guy?*—but I try to shake it off. If I give up now, I might never see her again. And I'm willing to risk one last humiliation, or even another beat-down, to keep that from happening.

I take a deep breath as I reach her house and climb the nine steps to the front door, which is inset into a little brick entryway that thankfully hides me from passersby. Alongside the mahogany door is a little gold rectangle engraved with Hebrew letters and a Star of David, set at an angle like an askew photograph; underneath it is a buzzer. I've been coaching myself up to this moment since I got off the train, and just like I planned, I reach out and press down on it before I can convince myself not to.

I shift my weight and listen for movement in the house, but apart from cars on Kingston and the far-off ambient noise of some construction crew drilling into the sidewalk, I can't hear any. It's only two thirty, so it's conceivable that no one could be home yet, but didn't Devorah say she had a grandfather living with her? Where would he have to go on a Tuesday afternoon? I ring the buzzer again, then a third time, and loiter for five minutes before I give up and turn back to the street. I know I could wait here, catch them coming home, but then I'm trespassing, setting myself up in case they panic and call the real cops. I wish there was a way I could confront them in public, someplace I'm legally allowed to be. And then I remember the store.

The door of Blum's Quality Goods is propped open when I reach the corner, letting the perfect seventy-two-degree air drift in off the street into the neat, narrow aisles piled with boxes of note cards and plates wrapped in cellophane. There's a standing fan oscillating lazily inside, ruffling the tattered trim of the fading striped awning, and as I step across the threshold a digital doorbell rings out. So much for stealth.

"One second!" a familiar female voice calls, and my heart leaps into my throat. There's no one at the register, the store is empty, and by some stroke of amazing luck, Devorah is right here. I can't help myself; I drop my bag in the doorway and run down the closest aisle, back toward the voice, and come face-to-face with a startled-looking Hanna. She's bent over a box of blue streamers, her red hair falling in a limp curtain over one shoulder, and gasps when she sees me.

"Hi, sorry," I say, trying to collect myself, the disappointment like a knife in the ribs. "Where's— I'm looking for Devorah."

"You have to get out of here," she whispers. "My parents are in the office." She nods her head toward a door about ten feet from where we're standing. I stand my ground.

"Not without Devorah," I say.

"She's not here!" Hanna whispers, and then raises her voice. "Hi, Mrs. Yenkin," she says loudly, looking panicked. "How can I help you today?"

"Then where is she?" I press, leaning on a nearby shelf for balance, knocking a bag of multicolored dreidels onto the gray carpet. Heavy footsteps shuffle around behind the closed door.

"Hide behind that stack of boxes and I'll tell you," Hanna says. "If they see you, you'll never get the chance—" Then the handle turns, and I drop to my knees, the four-foot shelf becoming my makeshift hiding place. Anyone who walks in off the street will see me. So will anyone who walks more than five steps out of the back room. I hold my breath.

"I thought I heard someone come in," a male voice says. No footsteps; he's still in the doorway. A good sign.

"Oh, um, Mrs. Yenkin came in, but she forgot her purse," Hanna says, her voice high and nervous. "She's coming back."

"What did I tell you about regular customers?" Devorah's dad sighs. "You can always offer a one-time credit. We reward loyalty with trust. It makes them feel good and want to give us their business."

"Oh, right," Hanna says. "Sorry."

"Did you finish shelving those streamers?" a female voice calls.

"Almost done," Hanna says cheerfully.

"Put some up in the windows, too, like you did last year. Those were nice."

"Devorah always does the windows," Hanna says, and there's an awkward silence.

"All right," her father says finally. "We're just finishing some personal business, and then we'll be out. Make sure to break down the shipping boxes." The door hinges squeal, and I'm about to unpause my aching lungs when it stops abruptly. "Whose bag is that?" he asks slowly. I freeze. My army-green backpack is still slumped at the base of the fan by the entrance.

"Oh, someone must have left that," Hanna stammers. "I'll just stick it behind the counter." The hinges squeal again, and then the door bangs shut. Hanna crouches down, visibly shaking. "You have to leave now," she whispers. *"Please."*

"As soon as you tell me where she is."

"She's in Monsey," Hanna says. "That's upstate."

"What's she doing there?"

"*Go*," she pleads.

"*Where* in Monsey?"

"Some rehab place," she says quickly. "It has an acronym, CRT or something like that, I don't know. I only overheard."

The digital chime rings out, and Hanna shoots to her feet as a young woman in a long skirt enters with a toddler on her hip and another, barely much older, at her feet. Both boys have mini yarmulkes pinned in their hair. The woman stops abruptly when she sees me, and grabs her walking child's hand.

"I'll be with you in just a minute," Hanna chirps, but the woman shakes her head and turns around, triggering the doorbell yet again as she makes a hasty exit.

"Hanna!" her father cries angrily through the door. "Could you hold *one* customer in the building, please?" I hear him get up from a chair, and know I've worn out my nonexistent welcome. My hamstrings snap painfully into action as I spring to my feet and make a dash for the door, grabbing my bag on the way.

"Thanks," I pant over my shoulder as I leap past the strip on the carpeted floor that would announce my presence and seal my fate. I'm already on the sidewalk by the time Devorah's parents make their way out of the office, but as I break into a run I could swear I hear Hanna call out after me, her voice wafting through the still afternoon air like a trade wind, steering me on my way: *Good luck.*

Chapter 27
Devorah

The Chabad Residential Treatment Center of Monsey (CRTCM for short, which really rolls off the tongue) is a ranch-style complex inset from the main road by about half a mile by way of a twisting gravel driveway and nestled almost invisibly inside a small clearing in a forest of trees. A series of low wood cabins are connected by quaint stone paths trimmed with round hedges, and there's even a little square in the center with benches where you can read or gaze out at the birds. Ironically, it actually looks exactly like the type of secular college campus I've fantasized about attending.

Rose stayed with me through the intake process, which consisted of me filling out a series of highly personal and frankly presumptuous forms (sample question: *What made you decide to abandon your faith?*) and being shown to my room, an airy ten-foot cube with high, beamed ceilings, a big bed with a firm mattress and a down comforter, and a broad desk stocked with blank journals and felt-tip pens. I have my own bathroom—a luxury I've never experienced—but only because my bedroom door is locked from the outside. Normally, Chana the bubbly residential advisor told me, I would have a housemate in the adjoining room, but September is a sleepy month for CRTCM, as most families use the Jewish new year as an excuse to finally take action. "But we celebrate Rosh Hashanah," she assured me. "We have a special service and every-thing. We get a ton of families from town who don't even have rela-tives here come up just to hear Rabbi Perolman sound the shofar." Rabbi Perolman is the CRTCM's founder and head counselor, and I have my first meeting with him in ten minutes.

I am not allowed to leave my room—or go anywhere—without a chaperone, and so I'm waiting for Chana to return and take me over to the rabbi's offices, which she says patients call "P-House." This is supposed to make me feel like I'm in on some familial joke, I'm sure, but despite the cozy surroundings I can't forget why I'm here: to get fixed, reprimanded, and realigned. To forget who I want to be and remember who I'm supposed to be. To that end, there is a stack of books on my bedside table that includes *The Blessings of Jewish Marriage* and *Finding Hope and Joy: Timeless Wisdom from a Hasidic Master*. I crack open the latter to find cheerful snippets of advice like "Never despair!" and "Get into the habit of dancing."

I toss the book onto the nubby maroon area rug in the center of my room and walk to the window, which looks out on a path leading into the trees, where Chana has informed me there is a brook, and a few meters beyond that, a high chain-link fence to prevent anyone from getting any ideas (she didn't actually say the last part, but I could tell that's what she meant). I watch the trees sway gently in the mid-afternoon breeze and feel a sense of calm wash over me. If I'm going to be trapped anyway, it might as well be someplace beautiful, far away from my family and the mess I left behind.

I'm expecting an old, creaky, rheumy-eyed rabbi like the ones I'm used to at home, so when a slight, energetic man with a toothy grin, wireless glasses, and all his natural hair greets Chana and me at the door of "P-House," I'm momentarily taken aback.

"You must be Devorah," he says, smiling warmly. "I'm Rabbi Perolman, but you can call me Perry."

"Your name is Perry Perolman?" I ask incredulously, not sure whether to be more shocked at the prospect of calling a holy man by his first name or at the injustice clearly committed by his parents.

"No," he says with a laugh, gesturing for me to come in. "It's just a nickname. If it feels more comfortable for you, call me Rabbi."

The rabbi's office has the same exposed-beam ceilings as my room, but it's about twice as big, with a picture window that looks out on the square at the center of the grounds. It's lived-in and quirky, with overstuffed couches, a low coffee table littered with markers and construction paper, and big, colorful paintings of smiley-faced flowers lining the walls. "My daughter did those," he says proudly. "I think they're very joyful, don't you?

"Please excuse the mess," he adds, gesturing to the table as he guides me to the couch facing the window. (The door to the office is, as usual, left wide open, and Chana busies herself at a desk outside; even rabbis aren't exempt from the laws of *yichud*.) "In the mornings I often do outpatient counseling with children, and drawing helps them to relax." All I can do is nod. Rabbi Perolman is unlike any rabbi I've ever seen. In fact, he strikes me as more of a touchy-feely art teacher than a religious scholar. I must be making a face, because he stops and asks, "Is something wrong?"

"No," I say, mortified that I'm starting off on the wrong foot by being disrespectful. "I've just . . . never met a rabbi like you before."

"I'll take that as a compliment," he says. He sits on the couch across from me and places his hands on his knees. "So, I'd like to start by listening to you, Devorah. Tell me why you're here."

Why I'm here. As if there's a simple answer to that downright existential question. "You don't know already?" I ask, and he smiles patiently.

"I know the basic circumstances, yes. But I want to hear it in your words."

"Oh." I stare at my hands, interlacing my fingers. Where do I begin? I'm here because the night of the hurricane, my parents were just three miles from here, sitting around my aunt Varda's kitchen table having instant coffee instead of sitting in the waiting room of Interfaith Medical Center. I'm here because I got thirsty, and the stairs seemed like too much work. I'm here because I let myself talk to a stranger, whose kind eyes managed to light a flame in a heart I had always just assumed was fireproof. I'm here because once I questioned why I wasn't allowed to be with Jaxon, I started to question everything. But maybe I should start with something more concrete. "I tried to run away," I say finally. "With a boy."

"What made you want to do that?" the rabbi asks, his voice devoid of judgment.

"I knew my parents would never approve, and he had a place at the beach where we could go." As I say the words out loud, they sound increasingly ridiculous.

"You're shaking your head right now, Devorah. Why is that?"

"I don't know."

"You don't?" He leans forward and smiles encouragingly. In spite of myself, I'm kind of starting to like him.

"Well . . . I guess I just realize it wouldn't have worked."

"What aspect?"

"Using a night away as some sort of statement to let our families know we were in love," I say. "As if the act of rebellion itself would somehow make them understand." I should have just talked to my parents, I chide myself. Maybe if I had been honest with them, and not let things get so out of hand, I wouldn't be here.

"You're right; that does sound far-fetched," the rabbi says, and chuckles. "So why did you agree to go?"

"I didn't want to stop seeing him."

"Why is that?"

"Because . . ." I can feel my face getting red. "I . . . love him."

Rabbi Perolman sits back against his couch and takes a deep breath. "Did your parents ever discuss love with you, Devorah? Do you know the definition?"

I frown and try not to look as offended as I am. No, I was never taught the *definition* of love—Hasidic kids are told only that one day they'll be married, and even that subject isn't dwelled upon until the mid-teens—but I know what love *feels* like. "It's when you have . . . a strong affection for someone," I mumble.

"I see," the rabbi says. "Then what makes your love for Jaxon different than your love for, let's say, your sister Rose?"

"Well, because . . . I'm not attracted to my sister." I close my eyes, both out of shame and so that I don't give in to the strong temptation to roll them at the rabbi. He's starting to treat me like a small child, and it's making me squirm.

"So affection plus attraction equals love, in your estimation," he says.

"Yes," I say hesitantly, wondering if he's trying to trap me.

"What about lust, then?" the rabbi asks, not meeting my eyes. "What makes lust different?"

"It's not lust," I say quickly.

"Okay, but how do you know?"

"Because," I sputter, "I just know. Because I was attracted to his soul more than his body."

Rabbi Perolman cocks his head. "Really? You look unsure."

"I'm not!" I shout, and then lower my voice. "I'm sorry," I say. "I'm just upset."

The rabbi waves away my apology and sits silently for a moment. "You grew up in a Chabad household, so I know you understand the rules and have lived by them your whole life," he finally says. "I'm not here to lecture you about something you already know. But having met you only a few minutes ago, I can already sense that you're uneasy with your situation."

"Of course I am," I say with a sigh. "I was brought here against my will."

"Fair enough," he says with a faint smile. "But I'm talking about your relationship with the boy—"

"Jaxon," I say. I can't stand to hear one more person refer to him as *the boy*.

"Okay, with *Jaxon*," the rabbi continues. "I can tell you're struggling with your feelings for him. Can you tell me about that struggle?"

"I just . . ." I look out the picture window at the cobblestone paths, each winding its own way through the grass but all leading to the same central square. "When I'm with him I feel so happy— so much *love*"—(take that, *Perry*)—"but the knowledge that being with him hurts my family takes it away a little. And I don't want to hurt anyone. I don't want to hurt Jaxon *or* my family. I want to love them *both*."

"I can see that," the rabbi says. "There are many beautiful things about love, but love takes deep commitment and often sacrifice. It's not easy." I feel tears spring to my eyes, and I blink them away. "I'm sure you've noticed that your parents don't always have an easy relationship," he says. "Neither do your sisters and brothers who are married. And that's because marriage is hard work.

"I like to tell people to think of a marriage like a new job," Rabbi Perolman continues, perching on the edge of his seat and beginning to talk with his hands. "And it's a job we have zero experience for, from a practical standpoint, because we've never been on a date. Our ancestors were betrothed from birth, and dating was simply never something we did historically, right? So we're coming into marriage knowing that we've got to learn the ropes on the job." He pauses and smiles. "And our co-worker knows nothing about the job, either. So you can imagine the bumpy road ahead."

I nod, but he's starting to lose me. Why is he talking so much about marriage? Does he think I was going to run off and marry Jaxon? The whole point was to avoid getting forced into marriage before I was ready.

"The reason we don't date before marriage in our faith is that any type of relationship between a man and a woman—or a girl and a boy—brings up a lot of confusing feelings in both the body and the mind, and even the soul, as you mentioned. And it's only through the lens of a sanctified marriage that we gain the perspective to understand and process those feelings. To use the job metaphor again, dating before marriage would be like trying to get a job as a *sofer* without knowing Hebrew."

"Of course I know I wasn't supposed to date him," I say softly. "That's why I didn't tell anyone."

"And I believe it's why you didn't follow through with running away with him," the rabbi says, smiling. (Does he know I fully intended to make the trip, and that I simply never got the *chance* to follow through? Or did my parents do a little lying of their own when they admitted me?) "You have strong values, Devorah, and you simply could not reject them to live in sin." I dig my nails into the soft brushed cotton of the couch cushion. Suddenly I really don't like where this conversation is going.

"I *do* have strong values," I say. "But can't I have values, and faith, and also question the fact that I'm supposed to marry someone I don't even choose for myself?"

"Yes, you can," he says. "In fact, you'll be happy to learn that what you're expressing is a common concern, especially for women. You wouldn't believe how many girls just like you I've counseled who feel scared that they don't have more control over what's arguably the most important decision of their lives." He casually picks up a notebook and a pen from the coffee table and scribbles something down. "Tell me," he says, "is that your fear?"

I shake my head and stand up. I can't play this game with him, not after the morning (or the week, or the month) I've had. "I

appreciate your help, Rabbi," I say, "I really do. But I don't feel like
having a therapy session right now. Maybe if I have a day or two to
rest—"

"This isn't therapy, Devorah," the rabbi says, his smile replaced
by a look of grim concern. "And this session is not optional. I can't
confidently recommend a union unless both parties complete at least
two hours of premarital counseling."

"I—I don't understand," I stammer, my unease growing by the
second.

"Your parents met with a *shadchan* this morning," Rabbi
Perolman says. "And they've already found a match. Your family is
meeting him tomorrow, and assuming all goes well, he'll be coming
this weekend to visit you."

My legs buckle under me, and I sit down again. My whole body
feels numb.

"Congratulations, Devorah," the rabbi says, his grin returning.
"You're a very lucky girl."

Chapter 28

Jaxon

Fun fact: Here is what you need to buy a gun in Brooklyn (I'm not talking about a New York State licensed firearm, mind you; I'm talking about an unregistered, probably-stolen-and-used-for-a-crime-that-will-one-day-get-traced-back-to-your-stupid-ass street gun): $100 cash or a very large bag of weed. At least, that's what I gather from the *Law & Order: SVU* reruns I sometimes watch with the twins. Yet *here* is what you need to rent a car: a valid driver's license proving that you are over age twenty-five AND a major credit card in your name. With actual credit on it. For the record, a debit card with access to funds in the amount of $107 does not qualify as a major credit card. And a learner's permit issued in May of this year does not qualify as a driver's license. So here I am on the bus to Monsey, yet again a lone black man in a sea of Jews.

I had to campaign hard to get permission to go, but I decided that after the heart-to-heart I had with Mom after the fight, I couldn't just run off again with no warning and risk losing the little trust my parents had left in me. So we had another talk (in which I selectively omitted the fact that I had just willfully defied her and gone to the other side of Eastern Parkway to visit Hanna), and my mom begrudgingly agreed that if I hit the books hard and got back on track at school, I could go to Monsey for a few hours over the weekend to visit—with a chaperone. Initially, I balked at this deal—four days without Devorah seemed like forever, and having one of my parents with me when we got reunited would totally screw up my game. But Mom told it to me straight:

"You're not old enough to understand women yet," she said, chuckling to herself. "Trust me that the girl needs a few days to clear her head and figure out where she stands with you. If you go running up there like a lovesick bat out of hell, preening and crying and begging, it is going to freak. Her. *Out*. If you give her some space, she'll be much more receptive. And besides, from where I'm standing, you're out of options, unless you want to disobey me and get shipped off to military school."

So I listened. I brought my books back home on Wednesday and caught up on my homework, which was actually a welcome distraction from missing Devorah, although every few hours I'd get overcome and have to stop what I was doing to write out a page or two of angsty sonnets just to get it out of my system. On Thursday I went to Mr. Misery's office hours and asked him for the opportunity to boost my grade, and to my surprise he agreed to give me an extra-credit assignment, a paper on—wait for it—the philosophical treatment of love. It must be true that God protects fools, because amazingly I didn't miss or fail any tests in the few days that I completely checked out. So by Friday, I was back on my way to a B average, with plenty of time to get it back up over the rest of the semester. Which was good, because by the end of the week I was also a complete mess.

My heart physically hurt from not seeing her. I got in the habit of sitting on a bench on Eastern Parkway for fifteen minutes every day after I climbed out of the subway from school, just watching the other side, looking for Hanna, Jacob, hell, even Moley, *anyone* who might be able to tell me where she was and how she was doing. I spent $25.88 of my cash reserves on another dinky prepaid bodega cell phone just so I could spend my nights cold-calling every business in Monsey with "rehab" or "center" in the name. Most of them told me flat out that they had no one by the name of Devorah Blum, but the receptionist at this one place called the Chabad Residential Treatment Center paused and then said, "We don't share information about patients with anyone whose phone number isn't listed on the intake form," and I knew, right then, that I'd found her. The only hurdle left was to convince my parents I didn't need a chaperone. And while I didn't completely win that battle, we reached what I hope is a compromise I won't regret.

"Shark gummy?" Ryan asks from the bus seat next to mine, holding out a brightly colored bag of candy. We're stuck in traffic on the Palisades Parkway, inside a huge cabin that smells like gasoline and stale pretzels, and I'm tapping my foot against the floor so nervously that the man in front of me, a short guy with curly blond sidelocks, has turned around twice to glare.

"Still not hungry," I say impatiently. Ryan has consumed a truly disgusting smorgasbord of neon-colored snacks since we left the bus stop in front of the main library at Forty-second Street and Fifth Avenue—the one upside being that when his mouth is full, he can't talk as much.

"Swhashu gundo wenseah?" he slurs through a mouthful of gummies.

"What's that, Chewbacca?"

"Sorry," he says, swallowing. "I said, so what are you going to do when you see her?"

"I don't know," I answer with a sigh. "I think I just need to see her to know what I need to do. Like a catch-22."

"You gonna break her out?" Ryan asks, smiling. "I just need to know the legal ramifications of this trip, for me."

"If she'll come with me, *willingly*," I say, "yes, I'd like to take her home." He must be able to see my *Officer and a Gentleman*–style fantasy sequence in which I carry Devorah out of the compound while everyone around us slow-claps, because Ryan snorts and rolls his eyes, popping another shark into his mouth. "What?" I ask defensively. "I think my folks would like her. And the couch folds out."

"Jax," Ryan says, "that's crazy. You know that's crazy, right? You can't keep her at your house. That's a really good way to get your parents arrested for kidnapping." He's right, of course. I drop my head and close my eyes, trying to drown out the noise of the crying baby a few seats back so that I can think, calculate a plan.

"Whatever; I'll figure something out," I say. "They can't stop her from seeing me forever."

"Actually, they can," Ryan says. "That's kind of what they're doing right now, if you haven't noticed."

I squeeze my eyes shut tighter, seeing red-black blossoms bloom under the lids. "We'll find a way," I mutter.

"If you say so."

"Why are you grilling me, man?" I ask, starting to get annoyed. The bus lurches forward but then stops abruptly.

"Because . . . I don't want you to get hurt," Ryan says. "I just want you to think this through."

"It feels like all I've been doing for the past three weeks is thinking," I grumble.

"Yeah, but where has it gotten you? I mean, other than this lovely urinal on wheels?"

I don't answer. Maybe he's right. Maybe everything I've tried *has* failed. But I can't accept that the answer is just to stop trying. Not when being without her makes me feel this miserable. Not when I know I've met my soul mate.

"I just want you to think about why you picked a girl who's so ungettable," Ryan says gently. "Like maybe it's the chase that's keeping you going, and not her."

"That's bullshit," I snap, drawing another disapproving glare from Goldilocks in front of me. "And I didn't *pick* her, I *found* her. We found each other. Plus, what do you know about love? Your longest relationship was two days." I know I'm being mean now, but the closer we get to Monsey, the more nervous I feel.

"Okay," Ryan says, backing down and returning to his candy. "I just feel like it's my duty as your wingman to make sure you know what you're doing."

I sit back and chew on my lower lip, jiggling my leg and trying to calm the cold panic spreading through my chest. If I knew what

I was doing, I wouldn't be making a Hail Mary pass like this. If I knew what I was doing, Devorah would be sitting next to me, not Ryan. I feel the contents of my stomach climb up my throat and realize there's a very real possibility I might puke for the second time in a week.

But right then, just as I'm contemplating climbing over Ryan and sprinting down the length of the bus to reach the probably vile closet at the back to empty my breakfast into a trapdoor toilet, traffic starts to move, clearing instantly and miraculously, like Moses parting the Red Sea.

I know I haven't been great at reading the universe's signs in the past week, but I have to hope that I've got this one right. Because every second is hurtling me closer to what feels like my destiny. And there's no turning back now.

Chapter 29
Devorah
SEPTEMBER 21, 2 PM

"Are you ready to meet your in-laws?" Rabbi Perolman smiles excitedly at me from his cross-legged perch beneath an absurdly picturesque willow tree. We're in a public park in Monsey, as it was decided by my parents that a rehab center was an unorthodox—no pun intended—site for a first date, regardless of how many times I remind them that it's also going to be a *last* date. It's been five days now since I left Brooklyn; five days that have been, surprisingly, more relaxing than they've been harrowing. But as comfortable as I now am with my new surroundings, and as much as I've grown fond of the rabbi—who, while didactic, has also proven himself to be charming and considerate in our twice-daily sessions—I haven't changed my mind about the prospect of my own imminent marriage.

"I think you know the answer to that," I say, crossing my arms over my chest and squinting into the bright afternoon sun. My parents are on their way up from the city, too, and will be waiting when I get back to CRTCM to try to talk me into signing my life away on a *ketubah*.

"Well, keep an open mind," the rabbi says. "All anyone's asking you to do is meet them."

This is a lie. As good as they sound, most of the emphatic platitudes that pour forth from Rabbi Perolman's mouth are misleading. His big thing, that he repeats over and over, is that I should feel "in control of choosing my destiny." But what he really wants me to do—what they *all* want me to do; the rabbi, his staff, my parents, Rose—is "choose" to recommit myself to a *frum* life and agree to marry David, an eighteen-year-old from New Square, eleven miles northeast of Monsey. Apparently David's father, Mendel, served time in state prison for money laundering when David was a boy, and this black mark on the family's permanent record has made David difficult for the *shadchan* to match. But David himself, everyone assures me, is perfect. "It's a blessing," my mother informed me by phone when I was finally allowed to call home Wednesday night, with Chana over my shoulder listening to every word. "You should be on your knees thanking Hashem for such a good match. Some other girls who have never stepped an inch out of line don't get this lucky!"

Right, that's another thing I'm supposed to feel, according to everyone else: *lucky*. So incredibly lucky. Lucky that Jacob caught me with Jax before I did any real damage to the family name. Lucky that my parents love me enough to send me to CRTCM so that I can be set back on the right path. Lucky that an eligible Chabad boy has been found who will take me—me, the defiled daughter, who once held such promise. Lucky that I get a second chance for the life I didn't want the first time.

But even with everything that's happened, I'm still me, the girl who aims to please, who loves to be liked by authority figures, who would sooner leap out the window than flip on a light switch on the Sabbath (let's just not talk about cell phones). And so, except for a bout of crying and shaking after I first learned about my match with David, I've been tolerating the circus around me, trying to be respectful and abide by the rules of the community here. And some aspects have actually been welcome and healing. Back home, even though Shabbos meals are fun, the Sabbath itself has become a boring day of homework and cold lunch bookended by two interminable temple services. At CRTCM, Sabbath is a quiet day of reflection. Instead of sitting through a traditional service, I took a walk around the property with the rabbi, who reminded me that the Sabbath is supposed to represent a single day of perfectness in an otherwise broken world. Similarly, he said, the human soul is fragmented and splintered, which causes internal strife on all days except the Sabbath, when the fragments gather together within the body in peace.

I spent the rest of Saturday afternoon praying quietly in my room, begging for help to find that peace. I certainly feel the splinters the rabbi spoke about—my devotion to my family versus my magnetic attraction to Jaxon; my lust for freedom and new experiences versus my need for safety and stability—but bringing them all into harmony seems impossible. Rabbi Perolman is right: I have to take control and make a choice. But there is no choice that will bring all of my fragmented soul together. No matter what I decide beneath the flimsy shelter of the willow's branches, part of me will be forever lost.

Mr. Kaplan is tall and rail-thin, with large, angular features, hollow cheeks, and a beard that makes him look like an Abraham Lincoln impersonator as he stalks stiffly across the lawn from the parking lot. Mrs. Kaplan is his visual opposite: barely five feet and as round as a snowman, with bright eyes, a shoulder-length feathered wig, and an infectious laugh. David, their son and my *shidduch* match, is tall like his father, but still apple-cheeked, with a graceful gait and the dancing blue eyes of his mother. He smiles sheepishly as he sits down between his parents on one side of a sun-dappled picnic table. Rabbi Perolman and I sit on the other side, grinning and fidgeting, respectively.

"We've heard such good things about you, Devorah," Mrs. Kaplan says. During the matchmaking process, the parents of the girl and boy are expected to call around the community asking all sorts of personal questions. I'm assuming at this point the Kaplans know that, in addition to my penchant for kissing strange boys in the stacks of the library reference section and planning ill-advised elopements to affluent beach communities, I'm allergic to cashews, can't snap my fingers, and wear a size seven shoe. I nod politely as they ogle me, glad I took the time to shower this morning and pin my hair back at the temples. In spite of my resolve to sabotage this meeting, old habits die hard, and I first want to make a good impression.

"So what do you want to know?" Rabbi Perolman prods. "Hobbies? Values? Grades? Shabbos linens?" The Kaplans chuckle good-naturedly; it's a cliché that parents ask what color and style of tablecloth the girl's family sets out for Shabbos dinner, as a means of detecting social class.

"No," Mr. Kaplan says, smiling at his wife. "We'll leave the questions to David."

David smiles nervously as I study his face and try to imagine seeing it every day. It's an odd feeling, like trying on a dress with the understanding that once you buy it, you can never take it off.

"Go ahead," Mrs. Kaplan prompts, physically nudging her son.

"Uh, how are you doing today?" David asks shyly.

"To be honest, I've been better," I say. The rabbi shoots me a look of warning, but to my pleasant surprise, David immediately laughs.

"I appreciate that," he says. "Me, too. I've felt sick all day from nerves."

"You were nervous to meet me?" I ask.

"Of course," he says. "The *shadchan* said you were at the top of everyone's list, and that you were very beautiful and intelligent. Which obviously are true."

Did she also tell you I'm on final sale? I think, but I force the sass back down and thank him for the compliment.

"So, Devorah, what are you looking for in a husband?" Mrs. Kaplan interjects eagerly.

"Mom," David says with a laugh, "that's kind of abrupt." He has a sweet smile, one that transforms his features from plain but pleasant to almost handsome. *Shit*, I think, channeling Jaxon. I wasn't expecting him to be cute.

"This is how these things work," Mr. Kaplan says, and his wife nods enthusiastically.

"It's like a job interview," she explains. "You just have to ask as many questions as you need to before you know." She pauses and looks back and forth between us conspiratorially. "Unless you two *already* know. It's love at first sight, isn't it?"

"Mother," David groans, and I bite my lip to keep from smiling. I'm starting to feel sorry for him.

"It's okay," I say, turning to Mr. Kaplan. "I'll answer. I'm looking for someone who is . . ." *not looking for a wife.* But of course I can't say that. I have to find a way to be honest without being rude. "Someone who's *patient*," I begin. "Someone who is warm and kind and tolerant." I'm picturing Jax's grin now; I can't help it.

"Very good, Devorah," the rabbi cuts me off, as if sensing that at any moment I might say what I'm really feeling and ruin everything. "And now, David, what are you looking for in a wife?"

David takes a deep breath and adjusts the collar of his white dress shirt. He's sitting in direct sunlight, and sweat is beading around his nose. "I, um . . ." He smiles helplessly at me. "This feels so formal and weird, doesn't it?"

"It does," I say, almost laughing from relief. I had been fearing Jacob Part II, someone who would be immediately dismissive and domineering, treating me like property at an auction house. But David seems nice and decent, someone I might really like under different circumstances—an instinct that is instantly proven right when he looks at the rabbi and asks, tentatively, "Would it be possible for us to have some time one-on-one first?"

"Yes, yes," Rabbi Perolman says, springing to his feet and gesturing to a dirt path that snakes alongside the picnic area and over to a small stone gazebo with a sagging green roof overlooking a shallow pond, its perimeter thick with trees. "You can go take a walk if you like, and whenever you're ready we'll resume the questions."

The Kaplans look momentarily disappointed, but then the rabbi asks them about a recent trip to Montreal and they light up, even brandishing a small digital camera.

"He'll regret that," David says, leading the way along the path.

"Thank you," I say as soon as we're out of earshot. "That was getting painful."

David sticks his hands in the pockets of his black trousers. "I saw an opportunity for freedom, and I took it," he says simply. Birdcalls shoot back and forth over our heads in the trees above, and I take a breath as I prepare to rip off the Band-Aid.

"I should tell you up front, I don't want to get married," I say, staring at the ground where patches of light, filtered through the leaves, dance at my feet. "My parents are trying to keep me from seeing another boy."

"I know," David says after an uncomfortable pause. "About the other boy, anyway. I mean, you're here, after all."

"So are you just here as a favor to your parents?" I ask.

"A little. But I was genuinely curious about you. All of those things I said the *shadchan* said are still true."

We arrive at the gazebo and lean on the railing facing the pond. I gaze out at the still green water, which reflects the wispy cirrus clouds above. "Am I your first match?"

He nods. "My birthday was two weeks ago, so I just turned eighteen. That's when they flip over the hourglass, I guess."

"So you still have a year of school left, then?"

"Yup." He shakes his head self-consciously, course-correcting. "I mean, *yes*."

"And then what?" I ask. "Yeshiva?"

"No," David says. "I have a job. My dad works at B&H, and

I've been working part time on the sales floor." B&H Photo Video is a huge, Hasidic-owned electronics emporium in Manhattan that has a Monsey outpost. "Next summer I'll go full time," he says.

"That sounds . . ." I search for the right adjective. "Fun?"

"It's a living," he says with a sigh, sounding exactly like my father.

"That's exactly how I feel about getting married," I say. "It's just the way things are supposed to be. Not good, not terrible, just *meh*."

"It doesn't sound that bad to me," David says. "But if it makes you feel better, I don't feel ready, either. Although I would never tell that to my family."

I furrow my brow. "Then why are you here?"

"Because it's important to them," he says, shrugging. "And because I'm eighteen, and it might take me a while to find a match, with my father's conviction."

"That's why the whole system of *shidduchim* seems antiquated to me," I say. "Why should it matter what your father did, if a girl likes you?"

"I'm hoping it won't," he says, laughing. "Does it matter to you?"

"No!" I cry. "Of course not. But then, I'm not a prize myself."

David looks at me. "I wouldn't say that. You're spirited and direct, and obviously very smart. Maybe we shouldn't dismiss this match out of hand."

"That's kind of you," I say carefully, not wanting to lead him on or insult him. "But . . . I think we want different things. You want a wife. Even if you're not quite ready for one, you're of age and you're a good catch and you have a good job lined up. You want what your parents have. Right?"

"I guess so. They have a happy marriage, a nice house. But isn't that what everyone wants?"

"Not me," I whisper, clutching the wooden railing of the gazebo.

"Don't you want a family?" he asks.

"I do," I say. "I want to get married someday and have children, but—my sister just had a baby. She's eighteen, like you. And seeing her go through that, I realized it's just not . . . *all* I want. I want to be more than that."

"More than what?" David asks, and I realize I must be testing his patience. I should just thank him for coming and leave now, spare us both the tedium of continuing this pointless display. I decide that there's no point in being polite anymore, no matter how nice he is.

"More than a mother," I say. "Frankly, thinking about being home with five kids just makes me want to run screaming into the nearest body of water." I gesture to the pond and rest my head on my arms, hunching down on my haunches in a very unladylike way. I half expect him to turn and walk off in anger, but instead David just smiles.

"It's a good thing my mother can't hear you," he says, looking back toward the picnic table. Mrs. Kaplan, who has been watching our every move as Mr. Kaplan and the rabbi talk, waves when she sees us looking. "What you just said would have killed her."

"I'm sorry," I say, straightening up. "I'm wasting all of your time."

"Not necessarily," he says. "I'm interested to know why you feel the way you do. I've never met any Chabad girl who's against *shidduchim*."

"I guess I just think people should choose their lives for themselves," I say.

"We *do* choose," David argues.

"You choose, maybe," I say pointedly. "Girls don't have that freedom."

"That's life," he says, sighing.

"It doesn't bother you at all?" I ask, taking a step back.

"Not much, no."

"I can't stand it," I say.

David clears his throat; I can tell he's looking for an out. "Well, not everyone believes in the importance of tradition," he mutters.

"But I do," I say, suddenly defensive. Until I met Jax, I had never been happier than when I was sitting around a table with my family, all of us joined not just by blood but by something so much deeper and more meaningful—by faith. Having grown up surrounded by people just like me, who know exactly where I come from—down to the village my great-great-grandfather was born in—is a blessing and a comfort, and I wouldn't trade my childhood for anything.

"Then what?" David asks.

"It's . . . the limitations," I say. "What binds us together may be beautiful, but I just can't accept that my happiness is against Hashem's wishes. I can't let tradition dictate my place in the world."

"You don't think wives have places of honor?" he asks, and I give him a dubious look. "I'm being serious," he continues. "A woman is the foundation of a household. Without her it all falls apart."

"I know," I say slowly. "It's just that the foundation of a house by definition is in the basement."

David falls silent for a minute.

"It's a shame you devalue yourself, Devorah," he says finally. "You really are quite pretty. You'd make any man very happy."

"Thanks," I say curtly. I never wanted to marry him, but it still disappoints me that I was so wrong about David. He's no better than Jacob after all. "What will you tell your parents?" I ask.

"I'll tell them exactly what you said," he replies, grimacing. "That should be enough."

"I'm sorry," I say again, even though I'm not sure I am.

"I'm sorry, too," David says. "I don't know what you want from your future, but I hope you find your way back to the fold."

What I want from my future. It's a question I've been skirting since I arrived in Monsey. Ironically, having nothing but time to think has made me adept at avoiding thoughts that threaten to upset the tranquil numbness that has enveloped me like a fog for the past five days. I know I have to decide what I want, to make sense of the war being waged in my heart, but I don't owe these strangers any answers. And I don't have to face the future today.

Except, apparently, I do. Because when I turn to leave, Jaxon is standing in the doorway of the gazebo, staring at us with naked, furious hurt in his eyes.

"Oh my God," I whisper. And in that terrifying instant, I know what I have to do.

Chapter 30

Jaxon

SEPTEMBER 21, 2:30 PM

"What are you doing here?" she gasps, looking horrified.

"Is this him?" the Adrien Brody–looking dude asks.

Blood pulses noisily through my ears. I don't know what I was expecting to find in Monsey. But it wasn't this.

"Yeah, this is him," I say, clenching my jaw. "Who are you?"

He doesn't get a chance to answer. Behind me, a woman shrieks, and I look back to see two men get up from a picnic table and start walking quickly toward us across the grass.

"Please step away!" the shorter, younger one calls out. "This is a private meeting." He's trying to sound authoritative, but even from this distance I can see the fear in his eyes. I'm still an other here; Monsey is just the suburban version of Crown Heights.

"Listen, man," I yell, holding my hands up. "I'm not touching anybody. I just need to talk to Devorah."

"That's not possible!" he says sharply, stopping short about ten feet from me. "She's in the middle of a treatment program, and only approved visitors have access to her during this time."

"Who, like him?" I nod at Adrien Brody as he speed-walks past me to join the taller guy and the lady who screamed on the other side of the gazebo.

"That's none of your concern," the short man says, and motions to Devorah like he's calling a dog. "Come on, let's go. We can continue back at the center."

"I think we'll just go home, Rabbi," the tall man says gruffly, putting an arm around his frightened wife. "We've seen enough."

"You don't have to go with him," I say. Devorah rubs her eyes, and then looks back and forth between me and the rabbi, her lips parted in an expression of soundless anguish.

"Your parents signed you into my personal care," the rabbi says, his eyes hardening behind his dainty glasses. "If you go with him right now you might as well have gone to Long Island last week; it's the same impulse to run away instead of facing your problems."

"What are you, her shrink?" I ask, and he glares at me.

"I'm her premarital counselor," he says. The words hit me like a sucker punch.

"What the hell is he talking about?" I yell.

"David, let's go," the woman says.

"Who's David?" I ask.

"Someone who dodged a bullet," Adrien Brody mutters.

"Jax—" Ryan pants, finally catching up to me. When I spotted

Devorah in the park, I opened the door of the cab without even tell-ing the driver to stop first. "Hey, man," he says, taking in the cast of characters with his trademark nonchalance. "Things look like they're getting a little heated. Let's go walk it off, okay?"

"I'm not going anywhere without her," I say.

"You are not going *anywhere* with him," the rabbi instructs Devorah.

"Stop it!" Devorah cries suddenly, so loud I'm pretty sure it causes ripples on the surface of the nearby pond. "I'm sick of every-one telling me what to do, so just STOP!" She holds her hands over her face for a few seconds, and when she lowers them, her expres-sion is strangely calm. She turns to me, her irises two gathering storms of mottled gray. "I need to talk to Jaxon," she says. "*Alone*. I'm sorry if that's against the rules, Rabbi, but it's nonnegotiable. And if you want to leave me here instead of waiting, that's okay; I can get back on my own." The rabbi scowls, and Devorah turns to the couple and their son behind me. "David, Mr. and Mrs. Kaplan, I'm sorry for what I put you through today," she says evenly. "But I didn't want this, and it's not personal. I hope you can understand." Finally, she turns back to me and says the words I've been waiting to hear for almost a week:

"Let's go."

She takes off running through the tall grass near the edge of the pond, not even looking back, expecting me to follow her. There are woods about a hundred yards off, but there's no path leading into them, just unruly green brush spilling out through the tree trunks like Easter grass. Devorah doesn't hesitate, though, tramping in like she owns the place. As she leaps over a fallen branch, her tights get ripped from the left knee down to the ankle, but she doesn't seem to notice.

My legs are getting scratched to shit (note to self: cargo shorts not ideal for rural rescue mission), and I can barely keep up with her, so I'm relieved when she finally stops and spins around, breathing heavily, her cheeks feverish from the exertion. She looks around, a little spooked, as if she was dropped here blindfolded and has no idea where she is, and without even thinking I reach forward and pull her into my chest. There's resistance in her limbs, which wrap around me coiled tight like they're tethered by rubber bands to some unseen place, but then she relaxes and rests against me, long enough to let our breath start to sync up.

"I looked all over for you," I blurt out, cupping her face in my palms. "I'm so sorry I left you after they—"

"No," she says firmly, "I wanted you to go. If you had stayed, God only knows what they would have done." She reaches up and gently touches the cut above my eye, which has scabbed over but still looks pretty bad. "Does it hurt?"

"Nah," I say. "Not anymore." I lean in to kiss her, but she pulls away. It seems like she's always pulling away. I'm starting to get tired of it.

"Jax," Devorah says in a tone that tells me I'm not going to like what I'm about to hear, "you can't keep showing up like this."

"I had to see you," I say, smiling apologetically. "I needed to know you were okay."

"Thank you." She takes a deep breath. "I'm not really okay yet, but I think I'm getting there."

"They're trying to marry you off," I whisper in disbelief. "That's what this whole road trip was all about."

Devorah nods. "I didn't know," she says. "If that makes it better."

"Man, they must really hate me." I can't understand the logic otherwise. Dating at sixteen is morally wrong, but marriage at sixteen is A-OK, as long as the guy's a Jew? How can they not see how messed up that is?

But Devorah shakes her head. "They're not hateful. They're just scared."

"Of me?" I ask. She pauses, her hands fluttering to her left calf; she's noticed the rip and scratches the bare skin.

"More like what you represent," she says wryly. "My escape."

I grin and scoop her up again. "Well, they're going to have to get used to it, 'cause I'm not going anywhere." I kiss her smooth alabaster forehead, and she buries her face in my T-shirt. "It's gonna be okay," I whisper into her curls.

"Jax," she says, sighing, into my chest—that tone again—"I've been here for five days, and I've had nothing but time to think. I've had so much time to think that I've outlined every possible scenario for us over and over again in my head." She pulls back and looks up at me, knitting her brows together, her eyes glistening, reflecting pools. "And not a single one has a happy ending."

"You want a happy ending?" I ask. "You and me together. Bam. There's your happy ending."

She laughs. "It's not that easy, and you know it."

"You can't have thought of *everything*," I say. "What if we just tell your folks we're not hiding anymore? Make them deal with it?" She shakes her head.

"They won't accept it, Jax. They can't—it's against everything they believe."

"Fine, so I won't be welcome at your house. So what? You can still come to mine! My sisters are crazy, but they'll love you. And my parents already know."

"Wow." She smiles wistfully. "They sound incredibly understanding. But I did think about that, and I know it wouldn't feel right to disrespect my parents' wishes while I'm still living in their house."

"You can move in," I say desperately, grabbing her hands. "Live with us. Live with *me*." I can see Devorah shutting down, her eyes hardening, her jaw tense. I know she's already resigning herself to the idea that there's no hope, and it's my job to convince her otherwise, to prop that window open before it slams shut forever.

She runs her fingers over mine, smiling like you would at a kid who just suggested that the 3 train stops on Mars. "But where would I go to school?" she asks.

"My school." I try to picture her leaning against my locker, laughing at my jokes, taking my arm as we walk to class. I know it could work. It would be hard, but it could work.

"So we'd live together," she says slowly. "We'd go to the same school, we'd have no privacy or any time to ourselves . . . it would be like we're *married*."

"Is that so bad?"

"Jax," she groans, dropping my hands and balling hers into fists. "Why won't anyone listen to me? I'm not ready to be married at sixteen. Not to you, or anyone."

I drop it; I have to—I'm losing her. "Okay, then, we could just see each other on neutral ground," I say, trying to stay positive. "Meet at the subway every day, take trips into the city. Just like we were."

"You mean sneaking around behind our parents' backs," she says, frowning.

"It's not sneaking," I protest. "Like I said, mine already know about you. In fact, they know I'm here right now."

"Then you're lucky," she says sharply. "But I come from a very different kind of family."

"I'm sick of that excuse!" I say, my voice rising. "You keep defending them like they have no choice. They could let us be together if they wanted to." I reach for her again, but she bats me away.

"No they couldn't!" she yells. "You'll never understand. You and me is just *wrong* to them."

"Sounds like it's wrong to you, too." I feel a lump in my throat. I can tell she's already decided that we're not worth fighting for. And there's no hatch for me to kick in and save the day this time. I could throw myself against it until I'm bloody and bruised and never make a dent. "You're breaking up with me," I say, and the nauseous feeling from the bus returns.

Devorah gets quiet. "I wish it could be different," she says, choking back tears. "You have no idea how much I wish we were older, or that we came from the same side . . ."

I swallow hard. "I still think we can make it," I say. "If we give up, they win."

"Jax," she says, her voice cracking. "Meeting you has changed my whole world around, and I feel like I owe the rest of my life, whatever it ends up being, to you." She shakes her head softly. "But the timing is cruel, and I don't see a way past it."

"There's got to be." We're standing a few feet apart now, our arms tight against our bodies like strangers in a crowded subway car.

"The only one I can think of is to wait until we're eighteen," she says. "But who knows where we'll be by then. I can't ask you to wait that long."

"Yes you can," I say. "I'll wait forever." I'm not exaggerating.

She smiles. "That wouldn't be fair to all the other girls," she says.

"There's no other girl," I say.

"But there will be," she says. "And there should be."

I ignore her. "What if I convert?" I ask.

She laughs, wiping the tears from her cheeks. "No TV, no music, no jeans, no cheeseburgers?" she asks. "That's not who you are, Jax."

"But it's who *you* are."

"Exactly," she says. "That's the problem: who we are." She starts to laugh again, harder this time, until it turns into gasping sobs.

"So I've got it," I say, my voice trembling, my chest feeling suddenly weak and empty, like the weight of everything I've been carrying around inside for the past few weeks has collapsed on top of me, pinning my body to the ground. "So if I weren't me and if you weren't you . . ." I trail off, feeling the tears start to win the standoff with my Adam's apple.

Devorah looks at me with a radiant smile, fresh tears spilling down her cheeks. "Then we could be so happy," she whispers, and runs into my arms.

We stand together for a few minutes, holding on for dear life, before I reluctantly take a step back. I let my fingers trail from her face down her arms to the tips of her fingers, drawing a map with my senses, knowing it's probably the last time I'll touch her.

"When do you go home?" I ask.

"I don't know. Next week, I think. It's Rosh Hashanah on Wednesday."

"Happy new year," I say, and she smiles.

"Thanks."

I know I have to be the one to leave, that she'll wait until I'm ready. But I can't force my feet to move. And then I remember that I have one thing left to do before I go.

"Oh, hey," I say, reaching into my back pocket, "I've been meaning to give you this." I hand her the CD I've been carrying around for weeks and watch as she turns it over in her hands.

"I'm never going to be allowed to listen to this," she says after a minute. "You should keep it."

"No, I want you to have it," I say. "It's valuable." It cost about a dollar to make, total, but that's not what I mean. On the bus to Monsey, on the back of the liner, I wrote out all my contact information. I don't know if part of me knew this was going to happen or what, but I just felt this intense need to know that she can reach me if she ever needs to. And not just because I'm clinging to the hope that she'll change her mind—although there is that, I can't deny it—but because it gives me peace to know that if she ever gets in trouble again, or needs a place to go, she can find me, wherever I am. I guess it's my way of kicking in the escape hatch and letting her know there's light out there if it ever gets too dark for her to see.

"Okay," she says, closing her fingers around the scratched plastic case.

"Take care," I say hoarsely. Anything but goodbye.

"You, too," she says.

I turn and start to walk away, my heart breaking into a million tiny pieces that fall silently to the ground, mixing in with the twigs and rocks under my feet. I'm almost at the tree line when I spin around to take in the sight of her, a small but stark figure against the thick trees, her hair a defiant halo of corkscrews shooting off in all directions.

"Hey," I call out, unable to help myself. "I love you."

Devorah smiles. "I know," she says.

When I get back to the gazebo, Ryan is waiting for me, sitting on the steps with his shoes off and his Ray-Bans on, staring into his phone. In the parking lot, the rabbi is leaning against the side of a minivan with his eyes closed, as if he's praying, maybe, or just taking a breather in the warm afternoon sun.

"What happened?" Ryan asks. But I can tell he already knows.

"It's over," I say.

"Dude, I'm sorry." He gets up and puts an arm around my shoulders.

"I tried," I say.

"I know you did," he says. "You tried your ass off."

"That's poetic, Ry," I say with a laugh, grateful for the levity. I give him an affectionate pat as we start to slowly make our way back to the road that will lead us home.

Chapter 31
Devorah

September 21, 4 pm

On my first day at Monsey, I thought the bright flower paint-ings hanging on Rabbi Perolman's office walls were simple and childish, no more than geometric blobs floating on thin, anemic stems. But as I stare at them now, I see chaos teeming below the surface, a mess of haphazard brushstrokes, shapes reaching in vain for one another across vast rivers of blank nothingness. Then again, maybe I'm just trying to distract myself from the fact that I'm in the middle of being mercilessly prosecuted for ruining my own life.

My parents, who arrived from Brooklyn just as the rabbi and I were returning from our disastrous outing in the park, are serving as both judge and jury on this case. Rabbi Perolman is their lawyer, and I am the fool representing myself.

"I was perfectly polite," I say, defending my behavior with the

Kaplans, which my parents seem to think they know an awful lot about considering they weren't even there. "But how could you honestly expect me to be enthusiastic about something I never wanted?"

"You have no idea what you've just squandered," my mother says. "David was the best you will ever do. Believe me, I've already been through *shidduchim* with Rose—and two disasters with Isaac—and I know what's out there. And now, after what happened today, who's going to even want to meet you, knowing some crazed lunatic might show up at any moment?"

"I already told you," I say as calmly as I can manage, "I ended it with Jaxon. I thought you'd be happy." It still breaks my heart a little to say it out loud, that it's over. That I sent away that wonderful boy who wanted so desperately to prove to me how things could be different. Who wanted to marry me, someday.

"We are a long way from happy," my father says, his voice deep and threatening like far-off thunder.

"Devorah," Rabbi Perolman jumps in, "ending your relationship with Jaxon was a crucial step, and I think everyone feels positively about it." *Not everyone*, I think. I feel a twinge of longing but try to push him out of my brain, at least for now. Jax paved the way for all of this, and even if we can't be together I'm not going to let everything we went through be in vain. I have to make them understand. "But the concern now," the rabbi says, "is that you get reinvested in the Hasidic faith rather than distancing yourself even more. If I'm hearing right, your parents are fearful—and so am I, frankly—that if you continue to criticize and reject the Hasidic lifestyle, you'll lose opportunities that you'll later regret."

"I understand that you don't want to be married right now," my mother says. "But trust me, Devorah, within a few years you will change your mind. And if you burn all your bridges, you'll end up alone."

"Childless," my father adds, which causes my mother to recite a prayer under her breath.

"But I see it in reverse," I say. "*I* fear that if I continue on the path that's been set for me, I'll look back later with resentment."

"Who will you resent?" the rabbi asks, adjusting his glasses.

"My husband, my children, my parents . . . *you*," I say. "It's not that I reject our entire culture. I just want to see what else is out there. I just want to feel more free."

"Free will is an illusion," my father barks. "There is no freedom in deciding what kind of skirt to wear or who you would prefer to marry. The only real freedom comes from living your life according to Hashem's will."

I look down at my lap. There's no way I'm getting into a theological argument with my father. He'll never understand what I'm feeling. "By that definition I'll still never be free," I mumble.

"Devorah, you've said a few times in our sessions over the past week that you desire freedom," the rabbi says. "And I'm interested to know what that means to you. Can you tell me what you associate with a feeling of freedom? It seems as if you have something specific in mind."

"Well," I say, glancing over at my parents, "actually, it's from a family story my mom used to tell me." My mother's face pales as I recount my favorite legend; she must be mortified that she unwittingly planted the seeds for my rebellion.

"Hmmmm," the rabbi murmurs as I finish, massaging his beard. "You see, to me that seems to indicate the presence of Hashem, not free will. Your grandmother was moved by a force of nature, not by her own desires."

"Ayelet, are you okay?" my father interrupts. My mother's eyes have filled with tears. She nods, but I can tell that she is definitely not okay. When she's in a room, Zeidy likes to say, she uses up all the oxygen. My mother is many things, but a pale, shivering mute she is not. I don't know what I've said to upset her so much, but I wish I could unsay it.

"Could you give me a minute alone with my daughter?" she asks the rabbi softly.

"I'll get us some coffee," he says as he rises and heads for the door. My father joins him, and soon my mother and I are alone in the bright, homey office, staring at each other from opposite couches. As the middle child of seven, it's possible I haven't been alone in a room with my mother in years, and I've forgotten how much I crave her undivided attention. All I want to do is leap across the coffee table and bury my face in her sweet-smelling scarf, have her hush me and sing to me, telling me it's all going to be all right in the end.

"I'm sorry, Mama," I say.

"*Sha shtil*," she says tearfully. "I'm the one who owes you an apology. I shouldn't have told you that story."

"Why not? I love it."

My mother gazes out the picture window at the empty courtyard. "I was making a fairy tale out of something that wasn't," she says. "Maybe I was editing history a bit to deal with my own feelings."

"What do you mean?"

"Devorah," she says, "the night your grandmother was out on the beach in the storm, it wasn't because she was feeling happy and free. It was because she felt trapped. She was out by herself late at night because she was trying to run away."

The words sink in like footsteps in wet sand, the way I always imagined her running, picking up speed before her unexpected lift-off. "But . . . they had just gotten married," I say. "Weren't they on their honeymoon?"

"You couldn't call it that, really," my mother says. "They didn't even have much of a wedding. It was very rushed."

"Why?" I can't believe I've never heard this before. Or—yes I can. There are many things good Hasidic girls just don't discuss.

"Because once they were discovered," my mother says, bristling, "there was a lot of pressure on my mother to convert."

"What do you mean, 'discovered'?" I ask.

"She was a secretary at the office where he worked," my mother says. "His first job. They were both seventeen." Her cheeks flush pink with embarrassment, and I realize that what my mother is trying to tell me is that Grandma and Zeidy had an affair before marriage.

"Did she even *want* to marry him?" I ask.

"I doubt it," my mother says. "They were never what you would call happy. Or at least, she wasn't." My grandmother died two months before I was born, so I have no firsthand memories of her and Zeidy together. I only know that in family photos, they wear glossy, faded smiles. And that Zeidy still talks about her all the time, calling her "my *motek*." My sweetness.

"How did *you* know?" I ask breathlessly.

"She used to sit in the armchair in the living room at night when we were getting ready for bed, drinking beer," my mother says. "In the morning, Varda and I would find the cans lined up by the fire-place. Once I remember counting nine of them."

"Did Zeidy know?"

"He tried not to see it, I think," my mother says. "Almost every-one tried not to. But I couldn't ignore it. She was my mother, and I felt her sadness like it was my own." She looks at me for a long moment, her eyelids crinkling with concern. "I hope you don't feel that way," she says.

I shake my head. Before the night of the Shomrim incident, in fact, I can barely remember a time when I saw my mother truly unhappy. She seems to love the life she leads, which may be why I feel so guilty for not wanting to emulate her path. After all, how can something that brings my mother—and my idolized big sister—such joy and fulfillment feel to me like such a desolate prison? Doesn't one of us have to be wrong?

My mother must be thinking the same thing, because she gets up and moves to my couch, putting a cool hand on my cheek. "I have no idea what it's like to feel so trapped," she says. "But I know how much it hurt my mother, and I don't *ever* want that for you."

"I wish I didn't feel this way," I say.

"I know, sweetheart," she says, pulling me into a tight hug. "But you do, and we have to deal with it." She holds me out at arm's length and studies my face. "What would make you happy?" she asks.

I take a deep breath and prepare, for the first time in a long time, to tell her the absolute truth.

"What do you mean, college?" my father asks. He's been invited back in at my request, after my mother briefed him on the finer points of our heart-to-heart. But unlike my mother, my father doesn't feel a deep-seated emotional compulsion to see my forbidden dreams come true.

"Not yeshiva," I say, gathering my courage. "A regular four-year college."

"A secular college?" he asks with a derisive laugh. "No. Absolutely not."

"Aaron," my mother says patiently. She's taken on the role of the rabbi since Rabbi Perolman got called away to counsel another patient, which is fine by me. "She's just asking to look, and only at local schools. We're not committing to anything."

Like the rabbi telling me I "just" had to meet the Kaplans, I decide to allow my parents to believe that they will have a choice when it comes to my higher education. "I want to start looking now," I say, "And when I apply next fall I'll pay for all the applications."

"What if you get in?" he asks, raising an eyebrow.

"Then I'll go."

"Feh, why not just move out now?" His tone is still angry, but his eyes have gone slack and sad.

"Because I'm still sixteen," I say. "I can't make it on my own yet, and I don't want to. I miss my family, and I just want to go home and sleep in my own bed."

"She's promised to abide by our rules in the house," my mother adds.

"She'd better," my father mutters.

"But I have some rules, too," I say. My father's eyes widen at my chutzpah. "First, you can't meet with a *shadchan* about me behind my back or involve Jacob in any discussions about my life. I tried to run once, and I swear I'll leave if you ever pull anything like that again.

"Two, I want a cell phone with my own number. One that you know about, no secrets. You'll get the bill each month, so you'll be able to keep tabs on who I call, and that way I can have more free time out of the house without you having to worry."

"More free time?" my father asks.

"Yes, that's number three," I say. "I want a later curfew."

"Naturally," he says, smiling a little bit despite his furrowed brows.

"So what do you think?" I ask hopefully.

"I think you're making a mistake," he says, frowning. "I had hoped for a different life for you, and I pray you'll come to your senses before it's too late."

I clutch the couch cushions underneath my skirt, holding my breath, waiting for the three-letter conjunction that will tip the scales in my favor.

"But," he says with a sigh, "I suppose I would rather have my daughter under my roof than out on the street. If I had to *choose*."

"Is that a yes?" I ask.

It is. Twenty minutes later my father is shaking the rabbi's hand as he signs a release form at the CRTCM front desk, and twenty-five minutes later we are turning left onto NY 59 E on our way back home, where I will step back over the threshold of my same-old house into what I hope with every fiber of my being is a brand-new life.

Chapter 32

Jaxon

It's Monday morning in the freak hallway, and even though I don't feel back to normal, not by a long shot, I've got to fake it for now—at least until after first period, when I've made it through Mr. Misery's first philosophy test, the one I forgot I had until I got home last night. Ryan has taken pity on me (he says it's because he knows I need the grade, but I suspect it also has something to do with the epic dumping I sustained about seventeen hours ago) and is quizzing me as I forlornly eat a banana while slumped against my locker. To paraphrase Descartes, I mope, therefore I am.

"Okay," Ryan says, reading from the practice questions that end the chapters of our philosophy textbook, holding it open so that creepy-eyed marble bust of Aristotle is staring me down from the cover. "'Which of the following is not considered an aspect of the soul by Plato? (A) The appetitive part, (B) The spirited part, (C) The emotive part, (D) The rational part.'"

"Uh . . ." I stare up at the ceiling. Those all sound like valid soul parts to me.

"You know this," Ryan says. "Here's a hint: You use this aspect all the time."

"Wait, I thought the answer was *not* an aspect."

"Well, right," Ryan says. "According to Plato. But you still do it."

"D, the rational part?" I say hopefully, and Ryan snorts.

"If that was true, we wouldn't have spent two-thirds of our Sunday on a bus just to get yelled at by a rabbi."

"Point taken. C, emotive."

"Correct!" Ryan cries triumphantly, but I don't feel like celebrating. I can accept that it's over between me and Devorah—hell, she didn't give me a choice—but it hurts whenever I think about it, like breathing with a cracked rib.

"Ask me another," I say.

"'Why do we make mistakes, according to *Meditations on First Philosophy*?'" Ryan reads. "'(A)'—"

"Seriously?" I interrupt.

"What?" Ryan looks confused.

"The question is seriously 'Why do we make mistakes?'" He nods. "Oh," I say guiltily. "Sorry, I thought you were screwing with me."

"I wouldn't do that," Ryan says. "And for the record, I don't think you made a mistake. You went for it, man, balls to the wall. And I respect that."

"Thanks," I say, laughing. My mom said the same thing last night—not in so many words, and definitely not saying "balls," but the sentiment was still there. She told me that when it comes to telling people how you feel, you'll only truly regret *not* saying anything, and that the temporary humiliation that comes with rejection can't compare to the agony of wondering what could have been if you only spoke up when you had the chance. And when I think about it that way, I do start to feel better.

"Do you still want the question?" Ryan asks.

"Nah," I say, tossing my banana peel into the garbage can at the end of the hall—a three-point shot. "I know why we make mistakes. Because we have to realize that we're imperfect, right?" This was written somewhere in my notes, but I don't have to read them over again to know it's true. I'm far from perfect, and I've even done some things in the past week that start to cross the line from harmlessly imperfect to actually pretty douchey—like bailing on Cora with no explanation—but it's not too late to undo some of the damage, clean out that grease trap, and start fresh before I gunk it up again. I'll go over to Wonder Wings after school and give her back her forty dollars, plus interest. And then I'll take out the garbage.

"I think we're good to go," Ryan says. "We should go now to get seats early."

"We have fifteen minutes!" I protest.

"Yeah, but there's some kind of electromagnetic force that keeps you from getting there on time," he says, hoisting his bag onto his shoulder. "So we need a buffer." And as if on cue, Polly appears in the doorway, her sneakers squeaking against the brown-and-black-checkered linoleum floor. She smiles at us benevolently, like some visiting dignitary from the land of the popular.

"Hey, guys," she says. "Where you headed?"

"We've got a test," I say.

"And unfortunately no time," Ryan adds.

"Oh, okay." She kind of lingers in the doorway as we slide past her into the rush hour hallway traffic. "I'll walk with you, then!" She jogs to catch up and squeezes in on my right side. Ryan shoots me a look. "How are you feeling?" Polly asks. I'm about to give her the honest answer—my good old emotive aspect kicking into gear—but then I realize she's talking about my more visible injuries.

"Better," I say. "My shoulder is still sore, but it's going away on its own. Must not have been too bad."

"Sometimes things feel worse than they are at first," she says warmly, and I smile down at the top of her head, her thick black ponytail swinging with every step as she struggles to keep up. I hope she's right about that.

"Where's your posse?" Ryan asks as we hit the stairwell up to the fourth floor, swimming against the current of freshmen on their way to the science labs.

"I don't have a posse anymore," Polly says self-consciously. "I quit step."

"Sorry," I say.

"Don't be sorry. I'm glad."

"But wasn't that, like, your dream?" Ryan asks.

"*No*," she says, laughing. "I have bigger dreams than that. And the people were kind of . . . not awesome."

"That's one way of putting it," I say under my breath as we reach the landing. Ryan and I start down the hallway toward our classroom when Polly stops short by the water fountain.

"Hey, guys, give me one second," she says, shifting nervously against a flier advertising the Model UN's "Around the World" luncheon. "I just want to say that I'm really sorry I ditched you guys last year. It wasn't cool, and I've been feeling horrible about it." She smiles apologetically and adjusts her glasses. "I think I just wanted to feel accepted so badly that I kind of ignored the warning signs that it wasn't right for me, you know?"

"Yeah," I say, smiling despite the ache in my chest. "I think I do."

"So . . . maybe we can hang out again on the regular?" she asks hopefully. "Like we used to?"

"Playing it close to the vest, Jadhav," I say, raising my hand for a high five. "Why don't you just admit that you love us?" Ryan cracks up, but Polly just blushes and taps my palm gingerly.

"You got me," she says, not looking up.

The test goes okay. No bells and whistles like you see on TV when someone's the thousandth customer at the Food Emporium, but okay. I'm pretty sure I pulled at least a B–, which should be enough to keep my average from plummeting before I have a chance to get my head back in the game.

I'm on my way to Spanish when Mr. Zenarian, the guidance counselor who heads up the tutoring program at Brooklyn Tech, pops his head out of his office. "Hey, Jax!" he calls. His receding brown hair is streaked with gray, and his gray button-down is streaked with brown coffee stains; a perfect inverse. I grin and jog over.

"Hey, Mr. Z!"

"You've been a hard man to track down," he says. "I've been looking for you since last week."

"Yeah," I say, shoving my hands in my pockets. "I've been a little distracted lately."

"Listen, do you have a minute?" he asks. "I have a proposal for you."

I make a face. "Sorry, I can't—I've got class," I say. "How's tomorrow morning?"

"Might be too late," he says, frowning. I look down the hall to the door of my Spanish class, where Señor Diaz is already doing his *bienvenido*. "Okay, here's the thing," Mr. Zenarian continues. "There's this citywide Big Brothers mentoring program that the borough president is starting up."

"Marty Markowitz?" I grin, remembering our laughter on the bridge.

"Right, right," Mr. Z says, getting distracted. "Anyway, I've been asked to nominate a student for the program, and I think you'd be perfect."

"Why me?"

"You're great with your tutoring kids," he says. "I get glowing reports from parents. You have a natural charisma, you're motivated, you're top of your class. I don't know, I just thought it was a no-brainer. You're a natural-born social worker."

"Right," I hear myself saying. And he *is* right. I've never thought about it that way, but the one thing I know I want to spend the rest of my life doing is helping people find their way in life, whether it's my sisters, my tutees, or other people I love who shall go unnamed.

"Anyway, the deadline for applications is Friday," Mr. Z is saying. "And I'm happy to work with you on it if it's something you think you might want to do."

"I don't know," I hedge. "I've got a lot of work to catch up on."

"Well, just think about it," he says, stepping back into his office. "I think it could be great for you. And those kids."

"Okay," I say. "All right. I will." And it occurs to me, as I break into a sprint down the hall to get to class before *la puerta* closes, that maybe, just maybe, I'm not lying. I mean, who knows, right? I could do it. I could find the time.

Crazier things have happened.

Chapter 33

Devorah

September 22 (One Year Later), 3:15 pm

It's funny; once you open your eyes to certain things you start to see them everywhere. For instance, right now, the man walking in front of me on Nostrand Avenue is wearing a black jacket and black pants—the standard-issue Chabadnik uniform—but beneath his coat I can see the hem of an untucked shirt in a bright pattern peeking out, and a cord snakes its way from his pocket up to a set of large white headphones covering his ears. At least once a day now I spot the markings of a Hasidic rebel. And I guess I should know. I'm one of them now.

Okay, fine—it's not like I've joined a band and shaved my head. That will never be me. But since I got back from Monsey last year I've adjusted to living a bit on the fringe, still a part of my community but able to observe it from the outside, too, like a curious Alice crawling through the looking glass. It hasn't been a smooth transition—it took a while to get used to the whispers at school, the sudden silent treatment from teachers who had loved me before, and the disapproving stares from people on the street when I passed by in my bright red sneakers, the picture of modesty from neckline to ankle walking in shoes that were clearly meant for less sacred ground. But knowing that my time here is limited—if I can get financial aid, I'll be living in a college dorm come September!—has taken so much pressure off, and I've been surprised to find that I can actually appreciate the blessings in my life even more now. Like my noisy, meddling, tolerant, wonderful family. Or my incredibly forgiving best friend, who now prides herself as the *frum* voice of reason to my *frei* adventurer.

"I'll keep that in mind," I say, laughing.

Although they resisted at first, telling me I would feel differently by the time I started my senior year, my parents have ultimately made good on their promise to support my decision to leave for college—to a point, anyway. I think my dad still hopes I'll change my mind, but even he's become invested in my research lately and is pushing hard for the Stern College for Women, the female campus of Yeshiva University on Lexington Avenue, within spitting distance of the Adereth El synagogue. I'm going to look at it, along with Brooklyn College, Baruch, and Hunter. No matter where I end up, we agree, I'll come home every week for Shabbos. I've heard the freshman-year workload is brutal, so I'm looking forward to having a quiet place to do homework, anyway.

From inside my shoulder bag, I hear the muffled sound of my cell phone ringing and immediately panic. Rose is eight and a half months pregnant with baby number two, and we've all been on eggshells lately hoping she doesn't go into another preterm labor. I dig through my bag and get to my phone just before it goes to voice mail. I can see from the screen that it's my mother.

"Hello?" I say, punching at the call button and bracing myself.

"Devorah!" my mother cries, pots banging in the background. "I'm so glad I caught you before you left."

"Is it Rose?" I ask. Shoshana grabs my arm, raising her eyebrows and making a gesture that crudely approximates a baby shooting out from between her legs.

"Rose?" My mother sounds confused. "No, she's fine. Better than fine, actually. As of today she's thirty-seven weeks—full term!" Relief floods through me.

"Is she staying off her feet?" I ask.

"Yes," she assures me. "Jacob is waiting on her hand and foot." Ever since Jacob got dishonorably booted from the Shomrim for targeting Jaxon, he's been spending more time with the family, which has turned out to be a good thing. I suspect that my big sister has been doing some coaching on my behalf, because for the past six months or so, Jacob has actually been surprisingly tolerant of me. He's even stopped referring to my college plans as "the first exit on the road to hell." It's sweet, really.

"Good!" I say to my mother. "So then, what did you need to tell me?"

"There's a storm that's supposed to hit this afternoon while you're in the city," she says. "Make sure to stop by the store and get an umbrella from your father before you go."

I look up at the still, blue-gray sky and roll my eyes playfully at Shoshana. "It looks pretty clear right now, Mom. I think I'll survive."

"I just want you to be prepared," she trills in the singsong voice she uses when she wants to make a stern warning sound cute.

"I'll be *fine*," I promise.

"Hey, don't make fun of her," Shosh says once I hang up. "I'd worry, too. You don't have a great track record with weather disturbances. Watch, this time you'll probably get stuck underground in the subway with a handsome Latino." We fall back into step, and I throw my arm around her shoulders.

"From your lips to God's ears," I joke.

The 3 train is pretty empty for the time of day, and I take a seat in the corner where I can settle in and read. I'm in the middle of *On the Road* by Jack Kerouac, which is not my normal taste at all but which I found on a list of Ten Books Every High School Student Should Read Before College on Forbes.com (slowly but surely, I've been wearing my parents down on the house policy on Internet usage, and they're usually permissive as long as it's for school).

The train stops at Nevins Street, and I'm parsing out another of Kerouac's interminable sentences when I see a flash of red out of the corner of my eye and look up to see a tall boy with dark skin and broad shoulders in a crimson T-shirt lean against the center pole with his back to me. I get a heady flash of déjà vu and feel my stomach drop, but just as I'm allowing myself to believe that it's finally happening (*don't kid yourself, Devorah, you've been waiting to run into him; you know it will happen someday, it's just a question of when*) he turns in profile and I see that it's not Jaxon. Still, my heart is racing, so I close my book and hold it against my chest, grinning stupidly at nothing at all.

I still think about him sometimes. Last fall, when my parents and I were still working out the terms of our new rule system, and things got bad—a few screaming fights with my father come to mind—I thought about calling him. Once I even went so far as to take the CD out of its hiding place, tucked inside the cover of *Little Women*, and punch his number into my phone, but I could never go through with it. I miss Jax, and meeting him changed my life in a lot of ways, but I know it's not his job to rescue me every time I falter. And besides, one night this spring I let curiosity get the best of me and I looked up his Facebook page again, and he had posted a photo of himself with his arms wrapped around an Indian girl with a beautiful smile and black-framed glasses. He looked really happy, and although I'd be lying if I said I didn't feel a momentary pang of jealousy, I'm sincerely glad for him. He deserves to be happy. We both do. We just couldn't do it together.

I go back to my book but get only a few pages before the train stops at Clark Street and the conductor comes on the intercom to announce that there's a sick passenger and that the train is going out of service. I check my phone—it's nearly four; I still have plenty of time—and decide to go above ground and switch over to the C at High Street instead of waiting on the steaming platform with the rest of the disgruntled crowd. But then I step out into the fresh air, start walking toward the trees of Cadman Plaza, and remember that I'm right at the foot of the Brooklyn Bridge. And even though (or maybe because) the old Devorah would *never* go out of her way just for the hell of it on a warm afternoon when she was expected someplace in forty-five minutes, I decide to walk across into Manhattan.

The winds are picking up as I step onto the weathered gray planks of the wide walkway, which is bisected by a yellow line that demarcates the footpath from the bike lane. It's an odd hour on a Tuesday, but the bridge is bustling with commuters and tourists, so much so that I'm forced to walk slowly, swerving around people posing for photos against the backdrop of the Statue of Liberty or the Empire State Building, and jumping out of the way when a bike bell rings behind me. As I weave through the crowd, looking out at the river through the thick braids of cable, I realize that my mother was right: The sky is getting ominously dark, and I start to wonder if trapping myself on an elevated, unsheltered outdoor surface for a mile—the better to get struck by lightning!—is really the best idea. I consider running back to the subway, but the billowing charcoal clouds are too beautiful to turn away from, and seeing them from this vantage point feels rare and wonderful—the kind of chance that might only happen once.

I'm almost at the first tower when thunder booms overhead, sending umbrellas popping up all around me, a field of polyester blossoms. I pick up my pace, but sure enough, within minutes a light rain starts to fall, and the wind whips my hair onto my face faster than I can brush it off. *Great*, I think. *My first time on a college campus, and I'm going to look like I ran through a car wash.* But I can't deny that it feels thrilling, too, taking this entirely self-designed, totally spontaneous detour. And I might get to NYU soaking wet, but the important thing is that I get there. The important thing is that I'm on my way. I pause and grab on to the railing at the precise moment that the sky opens up.

Everyone else is running for cover, ducking under jackets and being brought to heel by runaway umbrellas blowing violently inside out, but for some reason I don't want to move from my spot, even though I'm more than a little scared. Maybe it's my view, the elegant chaos of the New York skyline stretched out before me, buildings stacked on top of one another, holding millions of stories, any one of which could soon be mine. Maybe it's the way the driving rain feels on my skin, cool and strong, commanding the attention of all my senses and making me feel hyper-alive. Or maybe it's the winds that lift my hair off my shoulders and stream it behind me like a flock of blackbirds, rushing in my ears and filling my lungs with an energy that seems unstoppable. All I know is that I'm standing in the middle of the Brooklyn Bridge, a lone girl in a long skirt watching a storm roll in with her eyes fully open for the very first time. And I'm not sure if it's G-d, or fate, or just air masses colliding over water, but I will say this: It feels, finally, like flying.

Acknowledgments

This book could not have existed without the inspiration, encouragement, and support of my amazing editor, Caroline Donofrio; Razorbill president and publisher Ben Schrank; and the entire Razorbill team. (I hope you guys aren't weirded out by how much I hug you when we have meetings—please understand that I spend most of my time alone on my couch and/or chasing a toddler around in literal circles until we get dizzy and fall down, so professional grown-up time makes me kind of emotional.)

I dove into *Like No Other* knowing that the book would be doomed if I couldn't give Devorah a real, vibrant inner voice, family life, and community, and I am forever indebted to the women who told me their stories so that I could tell hers. Thank you to Sara, Chaya, Esther, Yiscah, Miriam, and everyone else who helped me with my research. (Special thanks to Professor Kerry for correcting my usage of Yiddish and Hebrew.)

Anyone who knows me in real life knows that I'm a mess when working on a book, so thank you to my family and friends for putting up with me from February 2013 to present.

Finally, forever, unconditional love and thanks are due to Jeff and Sam Zorabedian for keeping me humble, happy, and sane, and to Hostess frosted donettes for sustaining my body—just barely—throughout the writing process.